Praise for *The Argentine Triangle*

"Allan Topol is back with another captivating and fascinating Craig Page thriller. Politics, history, international settings, great characters—*The Argentine Triangle* has it all. Be forewarned, this one will keep you turning pages late into the night."

—M.J. Rose
International best-selling author of *The Book of Lost Fragrances*,
What To Do Before Your Book Launch, and *Seduction*
Founder Authorbuzz.com

"*The Argentine Triangle* has everything I love in an espionage novel: a compelling, resourceful hero, an exotic locale, worthy villains, and a meticulously researched plot. Highly recommended."

—Mark Sullivan
New York Times best-selling author of *Outlaw*

"*The Argentine Triangle* is a dynamic blend of old-school nail-biter and modern thriller. Devious, lightning quick, and thoroughly entertaining."

—Jonathan Maberry,
New York Times best-selling author of *Code Zero* and *Extinction Machine*

"I read Allan Topol's *The Argentine Triangle* while riding the overnight train from Venice to Paris. It couldn't have been a more appropriate setting for reading an international thriller that takes its cue from the likes of the late great Tom Clancy. I didn't sleep much that night, but that wasn't because of a train that bucked and rocked as it sped its way through the Alps. It was because Topol's prose is locked and loaded with all the tension, plot twists, and romantic foreign locales you might expect of a bestselling espionage author writing at the top of his game."

—Vincent Zandri
Best-selling author of *The Remains* and *The Innocent*

"From a DC insider, Allan Topol is in the top tier of today's thriller writers! *The Argentine Triangle* is a thrill ride from beginning to end. It's a keep-you-up-all-night story of well-drawn characters, clever plot twists, and a blockbuster conclusion. This novel is a terrific blend of political intrigue and riveting suspense —a winner!"

—Karna Small Bodman,
Former Senior Director, White House National Security Council and
Best-selling author of *Castle Bravo*

A beautifully plotted nail-biter and a breathless romp across three continents. Don't start the last fifty pages unless you have time to read to the end.

—Maria Hudgins,
author of *Death of a Second Wife*

Other Masterful Thrillers
from the Mind of Allan Topol

China Gambit

"*The China Gambit* is a choice pick for those who love high end military plots, very much recommended."

Midwest Book Review

Spy Dance

"It's a smooth and exciting ride. You'll want to see these characters take on another problem or two. Yep, I was sorry the story stopped."

Carnegie Mellon Magazine

"The story takes off at warp speed."

Washingtonian Magazine

"*Spy Dance* is a must-read for fans of espionage thrillers, and deserves a place on the bookshelf alongside the works of Tom Clancy, Robert Ludlum, and even John LeCarre."

Hadassah Magazine

"This is a superb first novel . . ."

Newt Gingrich

Enemy of My Enemy

"Topol's turf is the old-fashioned novel of international intrigue. His scene shifts constantly from trendy clubs in Moscow to three-star restaurants in Paris to strip joints in Montreal to Cabinet-level confrontations in the Oval Office."

The Washington Post

"Topol is up there with such masters of the Labyrinthine as Robert Ludlum and Tom Clancy."

Washintgon Post

Dark Ambition

"Topol might be the most riveting spy-adventure writer in America today . . . I found myself solidly immersed in Topol's multi-faceted conspiracy and am eagerly anticipating his next work."

Newt Gingrich

"Unlike most other members of the lawyer-novelist fraternity, Topol turns out good old-fashioned spy stories that leave the corridors of big law firm business far behind in favor of the broader stage of foreign affairs, political intrigue, and the murky recesses of human desire."

"In this tightly written novel, Topol captures well the quiet neighborhoods of Washington, D.C., and the occasional ruthlessness of its people."

Legal Times

"John Grisham and Richard North Patterson may have a new successor in Topol . . ."

Publishers Weekly

Conspiracy

"Seethes with political intrigue, a cast of shady characters, and enough deception, smart dialogue, and behind-closed-doors deals to keep readers hooked until the final."

Publishers Weekly

"An entertaining and suspenseful thriller with a well-crafted plot . . ."
Stephen Frey, *New York Times* best-selling
author of *Silent Partner*

"*Conspiracy* is a perfectly executed combination of the best elements of legal and political thrillers. With a lightning-fast pace, a compelling story, and an insider look at Washington, Topol takes his readers on a memorable thrill ride. Find a comfortable chair and plan to stay up late. Highly recommended."

Sheldon Siegel, *New York Times* best-selling author of *Final Verdict*

"[Topol has] managed to weave a convincing conspiracy theory into near worldwide conflict. And it's done with the extreme finesse that keeps us guessing all the way, also hankering for more of Topol's penetrating portrayal of inside-the-Beltway deceptions."

The Sanford Herald

"A paranoia-inducing thriller . . . The action scenes and telling details linger long after you have finished the book."

Legal Times

"This Washington, D.C.-set thriller from Topol (*Dark Ambition*) seethes with political intrigue, a cast of shady characters and enough deception, smart dialogue and behind-closed-doors deals to keep readers hooked until the final scene."

Publishers Weekly

A Woman of Valor
"Few novels have kept me as involved as this one."

South Bend Tribune

"Topol has written an evenly paced story, introducing his characters slowly so that each has a chance to come alive before the plot takes off on a convoluting and deftly interwoven path leading to the climax."

The Free Lance-Star

The Fourth of July War
"The book is remarkably reflective of contemporary affairs."

Chicago Tribune

"Topol creates believable characters with real problems and emotions; he constructs a tight, suspenseful plot that has us flipping pages as fast as we can find out what happens while we root 100% for a hero we don't altogether like."

The Los Angeles Times

"Topol's scenario for this fast-paced, gripping novel has the ring of inevitability . . . Should be a best seller."

Houston Chronicle

"It's a screamer of a novel . . . So real it makes you believe it could happen."

Natchez Democrat

The Russian Endgame

"*The Russian Endgame* is a satisfying conclusion to the trilogy, and reading it is like a rush of adrenaline in your veins. The characters are three-dimensional and believable, and it's a book you won't want to put down."

Douglas Cobb
Guardian Liberty Voice
guardianlv.com

"Allan's novel, *The Russian Endgame*, brings to light what happens when two powerful countries and their leaders decide to team up against the United States! *Just Reviews* is honored to award this year's Author of the Year for Historical Fiction and Writing to best-selling author Allan Topol."

Presented by Fran Lewis and *Just Reviews*
November 20, 2013

THE
ARGENTINE
TRIANGLE

THE ARGENTINE TRIANGLE

ALLAN TOPOL

To Natalia
Best Wish
All Topol

SelectBooks, Inc.
New York

This edition is published by SelectBooks, Inc.
For information address SelectBooks, Inc., New York, New York.

First Edition

ISBN 978-1-59079-141-7

Library of Congress Cataloging-in-Publication Data

Topol, Allan.
  The Argentine triangle / Allan Topol. – First edition.
      pages cm
  Summary: "Undercover in the glamorous circles of Buenos Aires' wealthy elite, former CIA director Craig Page uses all the skills in his arsenal to avert cataclysmic events threatening the future of the United States and South America"– Provided by publisher.
  ISBN 978-1-59079-141-7 (pbk. : alk. paper)
  1. United States–Foreign relations–South America–Fiction.
  2. South America–Foreign relations–United States–Fiction.
  I. Title.
  PS3570.O64A89 2014
  813'.54–dc23
                  2013035457

Manufactured in the United States

10 9 8 7 6 5 4 3 2 1

*Dedicated to my wife, Barbara, my partner
in this literary venture*

Acknowledgments

I wish to thank my agent, Pam Ahearn, who helped me develop the Craig Page series. We are now on our fourth book. It has been a pleasure working with the people at SelectBooks. I very much appreciate Kenzi Sugihara's enthusiasm for the novel from the first reading.

Nancy Sugihara and Molly Stern did an outstanding job of editing, and I'd like to thank Kenichi Sugihara for his work as the marketing director.

Thanks to my wife, Barbara, for her enormous assistance. She read each draft and offered valuable suggestions for keeping Craig in character in Argentina. We had great fun visiting Buenos Aires, Bariloche, and Iguazu.

PROLOGUE

Washington

The morning after Craig Page's return to Washington from Moscow, he arrived at the office at 8 a.m. Since he had been in his job as director of the CIA for only three weeks, and was traveling most of this period, Craig hadn't had time to select his own secretary. He refused to inherit Jane, who had worked for the predecessor he despised, so he counted on his deputy Betty Richards to find someone more suitable.

He met her choice. Monica Donnelly was a tall, angular blonde with a runner's legs in her forties who had worked with the agency for twenty years. "She'll keep you out of trouble," Betty had told him. "If that's possible."

Knowing Craig had lived in Paris, Monica had installed an espresso machine in the outer office. For Craig, fighting jet lag and a couple of sleepless nights, the double espresso she placed on his desk was like manna from heaven.

"Welcome back Mr. Page," she said.

"Thank you. It's good to be in Washington."

"Miss Richards called and asked if she could see you as soon as you arrived."

Betty had beaten Craig to the punch. He was planning to talk with her first thing this morning.

"Have Betty come up," he told Monica. "And please fix her an espresso."

Minutes later, Betty arrived, dressed in a snug navy suit, strands of black hair streaked with gray falling haphazardly around her face. She was wearing black frame glasses with thick lenses, the kind that people refer to as looking like old Coca-Cola bottles.

Cup in hand, Craig led the way to the conference table where Betty's espresso was waiting.

Once they were seated, she said, "I want a briefing on what occurred in that airplane hangar in Moscow."

He sighed. "It was an unmitigated disaster. Nothing went as I had planned."

"I realized that when I heard that President Zhou was dead. What happened?"

"Well, my great plan to have the Spanish Special Ops kidnap Zhou and fly him back to Madrid to stand trial for the murder of scores of Spanish citizens never got off the ground. Orlov killed Zhou."

"Avenging the death of his sister?"

"Yeah. After that everything spun out of control. Zhou's aide killed Orlov and one of the Spanish troops shot Zhou's aide. I felt as if I were in a shooting gallery."

Betty pushed back her glasses. "That's not such a bad result. Even if the Spanish had gotten Zhou to Madrid, they might not have been willing to hang tough about putting the president of China on trial. They might have folded and coughed him up. At least this way the world is rid of a man who was on his way to rivaling Mao. And you have some form of revenge for Zhou arranging the heinous murder of your daughter."

"All of that's true, but I didn't want it to end that way."

"Have you briefed President Treadwell?"

"As soon as the plane landed at Andrews yesterday I went straight to the White House."

"What'd Treadwell say?"

"He was pleased. He realizes that Mei Ling, the new Chinese president, is someone he'll be able to work with. He already sent her congratulations and invited her to Washington for an early visit."

"So it sounds as if everybody came out a winner."

"Except Zhou. But as you said, the world's a better place without him."

He paused to take a sip of coffee before continuing, "Now that this operation is over, I'll really have to take on the job of being CIA director. No more shunting all the work off on you."

"That's true. You can't duck it any longer. How about if I schedule a meeting at three this afternoon for you with senior staff. Let them finally meet the boss."

"Sounds like a good idea."

His office phone rang. A moment later, Monica buzzed on the intercom. "It's the White House. President Treadwell wants to see you ASAP."

Puzzled, Craig replied, "Did they give you a reason?"

"Nothing. Just that it was urgent."

"Tell them I'm on my way." What else could you tell the president of the United States?

He looked at Betty. "What do you think? A new crisis?"

"I don't have a good feeling about this."

"That doesn't help me."

"Just a gut instinct. Washington is the city of sharp knives."

*   *   *

When Craig entered the Oval Office, he saw that Edward Bryce was there along with President Treadwell. Craig had met Bryce once before in another Oval Office meeting, when Craig had gotten Treadwell's approval for the Moscow operation that resulted in Zhou's death. At that meeting it had been the president, Craig, Elizabeth Crowder, and Bryce, whom Treadwell had introduced as "a close friend, a powerful Washington lawyer, and my informal advisor on certain sensitive issues."

Bryce was about sixty, Craig thought. Dignified and patrician was how Craig would have described him. He had a full head of gray hair and was dressed in a starched white shirt with diamond studded French cuffs and a red silk Hermes tie, loosened at the neck. No jacket.

Treadwell, looking grim, was seated behind his red leather-topped desk and made no effort to come forward and greet Craig. Bryce was standing next to one of the two chairs in front of the desk. Treadwell motioned to the other chair and Craig sat down.

"We have a problem," Treadwell began.

"What's that?" Craig asked.

"I received a call from Mei Ling. She and the Chinese leadership are publicly sticking with the story that President Zhou had a heart attack. No one was permitted to see Zhou's body. It was kept in a sealed coffin. Armed guards enforced that order. He was buried quickly."

Craig held his breath, waiting for what came next.

"Are you familiar with President Zhou's brother, Zhou Yun?" Treadwell asked.

"Very. He's one of the wealthiest and most powerful businessmen in China. He's every bit as evil and ruthless as his brother. Zhou Yun arranged the assassination of President Zhou's predecessor, President Li."

"Well at any rate, Zhou Yun met with Mei Ling. He told her that he had confirmed that the official reason given for his brother's death from a heart attack was untrue. He discovered that the president had died from a shot in the chest. Mei Ling thinks that somehow, either by bribing some of the president's guards or by paying off a good friend of Russian President Kuznov, Zhou Yun got the whole story of what happened in the airplane hangar on that Russian Air Force base.

"He learned that his brother was killed by Orlov, the former KGB agent the president was conspiring with to steal cutting-edge American military technology for an alliance between China and Russia to defeat the United States. He knows now that Orlov murdered the president to avenge the death of Orlov's gorgeous sister, Androshka, who died as a result of her entanglement with President Zhou."

Bryce interjected. "That's what really happened. Isn't it, Craig?"

"Yes."

Treadwell continued. "Even though Orlov fired the gun, Zhou Yun is blaming you for arranging his brother's death in Moscow on behalf of the American government."

"That's absurd. My plan, which you approved, was to let the Spaniards fly Zhou to Madrid to stand trial. I had no way of knowing that Orlov would kill President Zhou."

Bryce sprang to his feet. The trial lawyer was ready to cross-examine a hostile witness. He was staring at Craig and pointing a bony finger at him.

"You arranged this little gathering in the Moscow airplane hangar. Didn't you?"

"Correct."

"And you knew that Zhou killed Androshka, Orlov's sister. Didn't you?"

"Of course I knew that."

"But you didn't search Orlov for weapons. Did you?"

Craig didn't reply.

"So in a sense," Bryce was raising his voice, "you were to blame for Zhou's death."

Craig was forming an intense dislike for Bryce. He clutched the arms of his chair tightly. "Look here, Bryce. My plan was to assist the Spanish government in flying Zhou to Madrid to stand trial for crimes he committed against the Spanish people on Spanish soil."

"You couldn't possibly have thought you would succeed in having the president of China tried in a Spanish court."

Craig glared at Treadwell, but the president had no intention of interrupting his friend Bryce.

"I did. Zhou was responsible for the death of hundreds of Spanish people." Craig decided to go on the offensive. "When I presented my plan here in the Oval Office, neither President Treadwell nor you raised any objection."

Bryce was ready for that. "At the time, neither President Treadwell nor I had detailed knowledge of the situation. We had to rely on your judgment. Wouldn't you agree with that?"

Before Craig had a chance to respond, Bryce continued. "The truth is that you were intent on gaining your own personal revenge against Zhou for the death of your daughter, Francesca. Were you not?"

"Zhou was not only responsible for the death of hundreds of Spanish people, but also for the assassination of your predecessor, President Dalton," he said, looking at Treadwell.

Bryce glared at Craig. He was obviously not used to being challenged.

"So you did want President Zhou to be murdered?"

Bryce sat down. The cross-examination was over.

Treadwell picked it up. "Zhou Yun has powerful friends in China. His brother had support among top military people. Zhou Yun is threatening to have Mei Ling ousted from the presidency and to launch a trade war against the United States. Obviously this would be very detrimental to us. We can't let that happen."

While staring at Craig, Treadwell paused and tapped his fingers on the desk. "There's only one way to solve this problem." The president turned toward Bryce. "Edward, you tell Craig what we have to do. It was your idea."

Betty's words flashed through Craig's mind: "I don't have a good feeling about this."

Bryce was on his feet again, pacing and looking at Craig while he spoke. "We have to take the position that Moscow was a rogue operation that you conceived and implemented on your own to avenge your daughter's death. Neither president Treadwell nor anyone else in the American government had advance knowledge."

Craig was flabbergasted. "But you authorized it, Mr. President. Right here in this room. And Bryce, you were at the meeting."

Treadwell looked away from Craig. "Unfortunately, we don't have a choice."

"So you want to throw me under the bus, Mr. President."

"I wouldn't put it that way."

"Then how would you put it?"

Still on his feet, Bryce responded, "The president won't be charging you with a crime. He'll merely accept your resignation as director of the CIA."

Craig realized that Bryce probably would like to charge him to give their story credibility, but at trial they'd never be able to stop him from disclosing Treadwell's approval. He also realized that further opposition was pointless. Treadwell was being completely dominated by Bryce.

"Even for Washington," Craig said caustically, "three weeks in a job must be a record."

"Look. I feel bad about this," Treadwell said.

"It's only politics," Bryce added.

Craig stood up, wheeled around to face the president's advisor, and calmly said, "Go fuck yourself."

*   *   *

"You really told Bryce that in the Oval Office?" Betty said after Craig related the events of the meeting. They were in Craig's office.

"Damn right."

"Good for you. I can't believe them."

"C'mon, you were the one who told me Washington is the city of sharp knives."

"I know, but I never thought . . ."

She reached into her bag and removed a cigarette that she fiddled with, knowing she couldn't light it inside of the building.

Craig said, "And the world's record for the shortest tenure in a top Washington job goes to . . ."

"I'm out of here, too. We'll leave together."

"No," he said emphatically. "You have to stay. You'll be acting director. Maybe they'll even give you the job."

Betty shook her head. "It'll never happen. First, I'm a woman."

"Treadwell said he wants to appoint more women to top jobs."

"Second, you appointed me to be your deputy."

"But they have no idea how close we are. When they ask you about me, say 'Craig who?'"

She laughed.

"I haven't heard you laugh in a long time."

"That's true. I stopped laughing when Zhou murdered Francesca. I loved your daughter as if she were my own. You know that."

Craig nodded, saying "Yes, I understand and appreciate this. But the United States needs you. No one else has your wealth of information about the CIA. I don't want you to leave. Whatever I think of Treadwell and Bryce, I still love this country."

Craig decided not to say to Betty that the CIA had been her whole life. An orphan, she never married and never had children. She had nothing else. Although his wife and only child had died, he still had Elizabeth.

"What will you do?" she asked.

"Does that mean you'll stay?"

"Until the assholes across the river become too much for me to bear. Now tell me what you'll do."

"I'll have to sit down with Elizabeth and talk. Maybe we'll travel for a while if she can get time off from the paper. Perhaps we'll resume a vacation we were having in Corsica when we learned President Li had been assassinated. We'll have to sort it out together."

When Betty left, Craig remembered that he had turned off his cell phone when he entered the Oval Office and forgot to turn it back on. When he did, he saw that he had a voice mail from Elizabeth.

"I have news. We have to talk. I'm working on a story now. How about meeting me at Tosca for dinner at eight."

He wondered what news she had. Was she pregnant?

That would be something. He'd want to get married. Stay in Washington. Maybe open a private security firm here.

Buoyed by the possibility of being a father again, Craig was looking forward to hearing what Elizabeth had to say.

*   *   *

When he arrived at Tosca, Massimo, in his white chef's uniform, came out of the kitchen to greet him. He noticed that Elizabeth was already at the table, halfway back, next to the railing, far enough from other tables that they could easily talk. As he headed toward the table, he saw that she had a cosmo and was sipping it. He asked the waiter to bring him a glass of white wine, "And please open that Barolo from Bruno Giacosa that I had the last time."

"Absolutely, Mr. Page."

At the table, Craig leaned over and kissed her. Then he sat down across from her. While he was anxious to tell her what happened at the White House, he wanted to hear her news before he announced, "I've been fired!"

She definitely wasn't pregnant, he decided. If she were, she'd be drinking champagne or more likely just sparkling water.

"What's your news?" he asked.

"Henrie Morey called me from Paris."

"The publisher of your paper?"

"Yeah. That one."

She sounded nervous, he thought.

"And?"

"Rob decided to retire as foreign news editor and Henrie offered me the job."

"Great. Congratulations."

"There's a kicker, though."

"What's that?"

The waiter arrived with Craig's glass of wine. She waited until he left to respond to Craig's question.

"I have to live in Paris."

"What'd you tell him?"

"I'd take it." Sounding sheepish, she continued, "It's my dream job."

Craig was pissed. He couldn't believe that she didn't ask Henrie for twenty-four hours to think about it, so they could discuss what it meant for their lives. Of course they weren't married, but they had a life together, or so he had thought.

As if reading his mind, Elizabeth added, "We'll commute back and forth between Paris and Washington. Lots of couples do that."

It was clear to Craig that her job meant more to her than her relationship with him. He thought back to when they were living together in Paris and he had been offered the CIA director's job. He had discussed it with her before he took the job.

"You're upset," she said.

"I'm having one shitty day."

"What happened?"

The waiter returned with plates of ravioli stuffed with lobster. "Compliments of the chef." Craig thanked him and then told her about his meeting in the Oval Office.

"Oh Craig, that's outrageous. What a couple of crumbs. I was there when you laid out your Russian endgame. Neither Treadwell nor Bryce raised a single objection. Now you can move back to Paris with me."

"And do what?"

"Take back your old job as EU head of counterterrorism."

"I couldn't do that to Giuseppe. He was my deputy and my friend. I put him into the job."

Suddenly it struck Craig that he had another problem. "I have to worry about Zhou Yun."

"What do you mean?"

"You know Zhou Yun and how close he was with his brother. If he's blaming me for his brother's murder, he'll be coming after me with his thugs, and I won't have the protection of any government." He paused and thought about what that meant.

"I'll have to go somewhere, and damn soon, to arrange plastic surgery to change my face. Probably in Switzerland."

"When you're finished there, you can come live with me in Paris."

Craig shook his head. "Too dangerous. Some things can't be changed even with plastic surgery. Like how a person walks. Zhou Yun will be able locate you easily through your newspaper. When I drop out of sight, the first thing he'll do is have someone watch your apartment in Paris."

"I better get a gun myself."

"That's smart. I'll give you one of mine in the house."

"So how will we see each other?" she asked. "Separately sneak off to some place like Corsica and meet there?"

Craig had learned long ago that if he wanted to stay alive, he had to think the way his pursuers did. "That's exactly what Zhou Yun will be expecting."

"So what do we do?"

"We separate for a year or two. When I think it's clear, I'll contact you."

The waiter dropped menus on the table. Elizabeth looked miserable. "Don't you think you're being a little extreme?"

"Zhou Yun can't be underestimated. We're talking about a man who arranged the death of the Chinese president on an operating table during surgery. And he has unlimited money."

"I guess you're right," she said glumly.

From her face, he saw that even though Elizabeth had wanted the job first, she had wanted him, too. Now she was only getting the job. She never imagined that she would have to give him up, but there was no other way. With his life on the line, Craig had no emotions. He was hard, cold, and pragmatic. In his business, there was no other way to stay alive.

After dinner, they went home. Their lovemaking had none of its usual passion. They went through the motions, but the reality was that a chapter of their lives was closing, and they were moving on to the next.

In the morning while it was still dark, after a quick coffee together, Elizabeth left in a cab for the airport. She was flying to New York to meet her book editor. From there, she'd fly to Paris.

When they kissed at the door, her closing words to Craig were, "Be careful."

Craig took his cup out onto the verandah in the back, where he watched the sun rise.

He felt very much alone. His wife and only child were dead. Elizabeth was gone.

He felt as if he was starting a new life. What would he do with it after having the facial surgery?

"Something I always wanted to do," he said aloud. "Something just for me."

One Year Later

Bariloche, Argentina

"The goddamned market," Ted Dunn cursed as he looked in the mirror of his room at Hosteria La Balsas. He touched the strawberry mark on the side of his face and pulled a black ski cap over what was left of his thinning brown hair. It was all because of the stock market that he was down here in this mess.

After twenty-five years with the CIA, Dunn had retired last year. Despite being apart for so much of the time, he and his wife Alice still had a great marriage. The plan was to buy a place in Sarasota, then sell the McLean house outside of Washington and move to Florida. At long last, he was looking forward to spending time with Alice, playing golf together and walking on the beach. He didn't want to take a security job in private industry as so many of his colleagues had done. Even with the allowances for living abroad, his CIA salary had been meager by industry standards, but he figured he had enough from his pension and savings to live out the rest of his life without working.

Everything was on schedule. With a bridge loan, they bought a great three-bedroom along the beach on Longboat Key, with the extra room for Marion, her husband, and their grandchildren to use when they came. He was getting ready to sell the McLean house when—bam! The market took a nose dive. Dunn lost half his savings in three months. Unable to sell the house, he couldn't cover the bridge loan. He was facing financial ruin.

That was when Betty Richards, like a shark moving in on a bleeding seaman, called him in for a meeting. In her director's office on the seventh floor of the Langley headquarters, she told him, "One small contract job in Argentina. Off the books. $500K. You operate on your own. No contacts with agency or embassy personnel."

"Why not use Bill, who replaced me in Santiago, or one of the other agency people in Buenos Aires?" he had asked.

"I can't tell you. Are you in or out?"

Good old Betty. Always mysterious. Plays everything close to the chest. "You know I need the money, don't you?"

"We're in the intelligence business. Never forget that."

3

"What's the job?"

"Spend a week or two in Argentina. Pretend to be a tourist. Find out what General Estrada is up to."

Dunn knew Betty wanted the information badly because he bargained her up to $750K plus expenses.

"Reports are for my eyes only," she had told him.

That was ten days ago. Now he placed a .38 caliber pistol in a holster strapped around his shirt, zipped up his jacket, and stuffed a Beretta in the right side pocket. At ten thirty in the evening he left his second floor room and headed downstairs toward the entrance to the inn.

He hadn't heard from Pascual all day, which was good. Dunn had told the young driver, "Don't call or text me unless it's an emergency." Dunn was from the old school. He communicated only when essential. He didn't trust technology. With electronic equipment you could never be certain if someone was eavesdropping.

Since Dunn's arrival in Argentina, he had collected a significant amount of information about Estrada, and this had been relayed to Betty via a special diplomatic courier she had arranged. He expected Pascual to supply the most critical information about General Estrada tonight. Once Dunn received Pascual's report, he planned to wrap it up and go home. Betty would have gotten her money's worth. The weather was nice in Florida. It was time to get on the golf course with Alice.

Before leaving the inn through the back door, Dunn glanced around carefully. Everything looked normal. It was bitter cold in the October night air, the sky filled with clouds. Dunn guessed another spring snowstorm was coming over the Andes from Chile. Cautiously, he walked across the parking lot toward his rented gray Honda. He had left it at a remote spot and installed a motion sensor that would have alerted him in his room if anyone had approached the car. The sensor hadn't beeped.

He climbed into the car, kicked it into gear, and set off down the dirt road, wanting to be in place a little before Pascual arrived, but not so long as to raise suspicions if someone passed along the rarely used road.

At the rendezvous point Dunn checked his watch. Ten minutes to eleven. Ten minutes to the meet. Precisely when he wanted to be here. He pulled over to the side of the road and turned off his lights. The clouds were blocking the moon. Small farms lined both sides of the road. Dunn wondered how the farmers eked out a living in the depressed economy where so many had so little money for food.

Dunn was staring straight ahead through the front windshield, the Beretta on the car seat close by if he had to go for it. His jacket unzipped. He could grab the .38 in an instant.

At ten fifty-nine, a car turned off the main road, Route 21, and headed toward him. Pascual was right on time. Dunn kept looking straight ahead to see if anyone was following Pascual. Nobody else was on the road. So far, so good.

Suddenly, the car coming toward him flashed its lights. "Dammit," Dunn muttered. That was the warning signal he had told Pascual to use.

Gun in hand, he scrambled out of the Honda. He had developed an escape plan this afternoon. He would cut through the farm on the right side of the dirt road. That would take him to the main highway, a distance of about two miles. He had parked another rental car there that he could pick up and drive out of town before they had a chance to set roadblocks.

The approaching car now had its high beams on. Dunn moved fast to duck into the bushes before he was caught in the headlights. He just made it. Then, with his body low and close to the ground, he ran.

Up ahead was a large tree. Dunn stopped and hid behind it, looking back for an instant to see what was happening. Four armed soldiers sprang out of the Lincoln Town Car that he guessed was Pascual's and approached his Honda. He heard one of them shout, "Remember, don't kill him. The colonel wants the American alive."

Another soldier opened the front door on the driver's side. "He's gone," the soldier shouted.

They were standing around, puzzled as to what to do. One man took a cell phone from his pocket. Dunn didn't stick around to hear what he said. He resumed running. The earth was wet and muddy. It was slow going.

One of the soldiers had a powerful wide-beamed flashlight. He sent its rays flying out in a 360-degree arc. Dunn kept his body low and stayed in tall weeds and heavy brush. He didn't think they saw him. By the time he had covered about half a mile, he was panting. He was out of shape. Too much time on the golf course and not enough on the treadmill. He vowed to change that if he made it out of here alive.

Then he heard the dogs racing toward him from the farmhouse. He hated dogs. His shirt was soaked despite the cold.

Terrified and trembling, he put his head down and willed his body to keep going.

Sardinia

Coming out of the tight serpentine turn, Craig Page, calling himself Enrico Marino, gripped the steering wheel hard and slammed down his foot on the accelerator. The powerful V-12, XJS, light blue Jaguar with 510 horsepower responded instantly. The speed rose fast. They were roaring along the coast of Sardinia at sea level. The azure, sparkling Mediterranean was on the right.

"How long until the next curve?" Craig called to Luigi, his navigator from Rome, who was studying the map as if his life depended on it, which it did. They were communicating through microphones and headsets hooked up to their racing helmets that permitted them to hear over the drone of the engine.

"Another 4.2 kilometers."

"We'll make up the time we lost on the last curve. I was too timid."

"Good. Go for it."

Perspiration dotted the back of Craig's hands. Following the completion of his plastic surgery at a clinic outside of Zurich a year ago, Craig had changed his name to Enrico Marino. Using the proceeds from the sale of his house in the inflated Washington market, he had hired Paolo Fittipaldi, one of the best retired race car drivers, based in Torino, to give him a private tutorial. As Paolo told Craig, the zenzation—or in better English, the sensation—of speed is intoxicating. After four tough months of education and training, Paolo found wealthy sponsors for Craig, and he began driving in rally races, like this one in Sardinia. Cars raced against the clock on rural and town roads that had been blocked off from normal traffic. The drivers used modified standard cars, rather than Formula One or Indy cars. The fastest time wins.

Craig and Luigi were on the final segment of the Sardinia rally, a grueling one thousand kilometer three-day race, much of it over treacherous, twisting, mountainous terrain as they made a large loop from Porto Cervo and back. It was a difficult and dangerous course, demanding and unforgiving, with switchback turns, blind corners, and vertical drops.

Craig glanced to the left. With his usual thoroughness, he had spent enough time poring over weather data to know that sudden changes were typical for the northern Mediterranean island sandwiched between France and Italy. So it didn't surprise him when dark clouds appeared from nowhere in the western sky. Craig cursed. The blinding sun an hour ago had been hard enough. The last thing he wanted now was rain. He had started this final segment fifteen seconds behind Carlucci, an experienced driver from Milan who had run dozens of these rally races around the world. Craig was the new kid on the block. This was only his third world-class race. In Paris and Barcelona he had failed to crack the top ten. Today with Luigi, the experienced navigator Palo had persuaded to join Craig, he had a good chance of pulling a stunning upset. But if the roads became slick, Carlucci's experience would give him an added advantage.

Craig had no intention of finishing second. He was pressing hard, pushing to the edge, that optimum point where the driver is at the limit of his skill and the car at the boundary of what it can do. Under good conditions, there is no room for error. With rain the course would be downright diabolical.

They were nearing the end of a straight stretch. "What now?" Craig asked.

"The road snakes along the shore for two kilometers. Then we start up a hill."

On the left, the Jaguar passed a latticework of vineyards. They began a gradual climb along a twisting hill road. The terrain on both sides was filled with large, dangerous boulders.

Without any warning, the heavens opened and a pelting rain fell in sheets. Craig kept up his speed. On the right side, the road dropped off sharply. Rock-covered terrain fell down toward the sea.

"Hairpin turn to the right at the crest," Luigi barked, "coming up in seconds."

Blasting into the turn, Craig clutched the wheel with white knuckles. His body was soaked with perspiration. Luigi grabbed the support on the front dash. The windshield wipers were operating at full tilt, fighting a losing battle with the falling water. Visibility was poor. The road was treacherous.

He felt the rear wheels spin on the slippery pavement. The Jag was dangerously close to the vertical drop. "Always turn into the spin," Paolo constantly shouted. The command had been etched into Craig's brain.

I hear you, Paolo, he thought, as he eased up for an instant on the accelerator. The car bucked, then responded. It straightened out.

"Damn good driving," Luigi said. "You've got the reflexes of a twenty year old."

"What's next?"

"We head down. Sharp turn on the left coming up. Prepare to cut speed."

"Roger that."

Craig leaned forward, straining his eyes to see through the foggy windshield. There it was, almost an L in the road. On the left was the cliff and the sea below.

Luigi was right. He needed a little brake to take this turn. Just a gentle tap. But after three long days of driving, his body was weary. His control not as sharp. He was going into the curve too fast. He hit the brake too hard, cutting the corner too sharply.

Immediately, he knew he was losing traction on the wet asphalt. The car spun out of control and headed toward the precipice. He smashed his foot down on the brake, but this time he had pushed too far and was beyond the limit. On the slick tarmac, the Jaguar couldn't respond. It spun off the road at the edge of the drop, down toward the sea.

The car rolled over once. Craig was sure they would keep rolling over and over until they either reached the sea or the car hit a sharp rock and exploded. Either way, he had lost the race. He and Luigi were dead.

The car was on its roof on the first rollover. It began turning upright. Then it crashed into the trunk of an olive tree.

Craig's head snapped forward against the dash. "I'm sorry, Luigi," he mumbled. Then he blacked out.

*   *   *

Gradually Craig's vision cleared and his senses returned. In front of him he saw a beautiful, nubile young woman sitting on a chair. She was dressed in a pure white uniform, which accentuated her attractive, voluptuous figure. Her chestnut brown hair was tied up in a bun.

My God, I died and went to heaven.

She removed a gray instrument from the bag resting on his bed, cuffing one side around his arm and hooking up a stethoscope to her ears. Intent on her work, she didn't notice that he was watching her. He felt the pressure in his arm as the cuff inflated. As if he weren't there, she stared silently at the meter, then recorded some numbers on a clipboard chart and removed the device.

"So how am I?" he asked.

She was startled. "Oh, you're awake." She stared at him. "We didn't know when you'd come around."

"How long was I unconscious?"

"It's Sunday morning. Eight thirty. What's your name?"

He smiled. "That's a hard one."

"Well?"

"Enrico Marino."

"You were in an auto race yesterday, Mr. Marino. Do you remember that?"

His vision was cloudy. He blinked his eyes repeatedly until the room came into focus. "All too well. I lost."

That comment evoked a stern look. "You're fortunate to be alive."

"What happened to Luigi, my navigator?"

"Lucky. Alive, but with a broken arm. And some cuts and bruises. We kept him overnight for observation. Later this morning, he'll fly back to Rome."

Craig glanced at the name tag on her white uniform. "Adriana," he said. "What about me? How bad was the damage?"

"I'm just a nurse. You'll have to talk to the doctor."

"Oh, c'mon. At least give me a preview." He gave her that smile of his that usually worked with women.

"Cuts and bruises on your face and much of your body. Concussion, but no brain damage. Vital signs are all okay."

"Now tell me something important. I feel great. When can I get out of here?"

Actually he was still woozy, but he hated hospitals. They evoked memories of sitting in the hospital room with his wife, Carolyn, in Dubai, while her body spiraled toward death with bacterial meningitis. He had damn near gone crazy with guilt for moving Carolyn and their daughter Francesca from the comfort of the Washington area to the Middle East—ostensibly to give his CIA cover greater authenticity, but in fact because selfishly he didn't want to be without them.

"For that, you'll have to talk to the doctor. He'll be here in a few minutes. Just remember we've given you heavy doses of medication for pain, which is why you aren't feeling anything at present."

As if on cue, the gray-haired doctor, who looked as ancient as one of the forts along the northern coast of the island, walked in. He examined Craig, instructing him to "Call me Professor." His medical judgment was that Craig should spend another twenty-four hours in the hospital for further observation. No doubt the professor was accustomed to having everyone follow his edicts. Craig's flat refusal to obey set off a heated argument.

In the end, the doctor shook his head in resignation. "We can't keep you here against your will, Mr. Marino. At least rest for a couple more hours."

"Fair enough. I'll stay until noon."

That didn't ameliorate the professor's anger. He stormed out and slammed the door.

An hour later, Luigi, his arm in a cast, barged into the room.

"We almost won, Ricci," Luigi said.

"Sorry I couldn't hold the road."

"Nobody could in those conditions. We'll team up for Paris in April, okay?"

"That's a deal."

"We'll win in Paris, no problem. Ciao, Ricci." Luigi turned and waved a hand over his head as he left the room.

Craig thought about Adriana. She was really quite beautiful. Focusing on her made him think about his sexual life during the last year since he and Elizabeth had split. They had no contact. Meanwhile, he had no interest in developing a serious relationship with another woman. On the other hand, he was still alive and had strong desires. He was able to satisfy those to some degree with a widow in Milan whom he saw for a couple of days each month, going out to dinner with her and spending time at her house. She was a contemporary of Craig's with grown children, and like Craig had no interest in emotional involvement.

What didn't appeal to Craig were the racing groupies, as he called them, the young women who hung around the tracks and with the drivers, ready to grab any opportunity with them, any time, any place. My God, they were all at least ten years younger than Francesca would have been.

Everyone assumed Craig was Italian, as his father was, and he certainly spoke the language well enough. As a result his buddies were the Italian drivers, a hard-drinking crowd. It was amazing some of them were sober enough to get behind the wheel the next day. "Ricci," the other drivers called him. Nobody knew that he was twenty years older than most of them. Nor would they have cared. All that counted was how you drove.

He heard a knock on the door. Probably the doctor coming back for another round. Or maybe he had sent the beautiful Adriana to reason with his disobedient patient.

"Who's there?" he called through the closed door.

"May I come in?"

It was a woman's voice, one he recognized immediately.

The door opened slowly, and Betty Richards entered, clutching a thin burgundy briefcase he had given her for her fortieth birthday, ten years ago. She closed the door behind her. "Hi Enrico," she said and smiled. "Or should I call you Ricci?"

"What are you doing here?"

"I happened to be in the neighborhood so I watched some of the race yesterday. Sorry about the accident. I was rooting for you. We have to talk, but not here."

She handed him a piece of paper. "It has the name of my hotel. The nurse said the doctor will release you tomorrow. Come to my hotel. We'll have lunch in my suite and talk."

"The nurse was wrong. I'm getting out of here in about an hour. This is a hospital. Not a prison. I decide when to leave."

"Happy to see a brush with death hasn't changed the Enrico Marino I know," she said smiling. "Then come to lunch today."

"Only if you'll have good wine."

"For you, nothing but the best. Lunch will be ready at two." She turned and left the room.

Craig rang for the nurse. When Adriana came, he said. "Could you help me pack and get me a cab?"

"Your clothes are ruined. Would you like me to buy you some in the store across the street?"

"Thanks. I'd appreciate that."

Waiting for her to return, Craig climbed out of bed, clutching the bedpost for a few seconds to steady himself, then walked around the room. Everything seemed to work.

Looking into the mirror on the back of the closet door, he winced. The deep black eyes, curly black hair, and reconfigured nose, all the result of his plastic surgery, stood out on a face full of cuts and bruises. Fortunately, he healed quickly.

He walked over to the window and stared off at the sea in the distance. He should tell Betty no. Regardless of what she was planning to ask him to do. Thanks, but no thanks. The powers in Washington had shafted him—not once, but twice. He wouldn't let her suck him into the Washington morass again.

Still, he was curious to know why Betty had come all this way to talk to him. And he had to listen to her because of their long friendship.

Porto Cervo, Sardinia

Craig had never been to Cala di Volpe. He had heard about it from Paolo, his high-living driving coach. "A luxurious small hotel on Sardinia's Esmeralda Coast. One of the poshest watering holes in the world. The newest summer hangout for Europe's rich and famous."

The taxi pulled up to the front entrance of a three-story building constructed of stone and wood in a Moorish style. Walking into the lobby with its heavily polished stone floor, Craig felt as if he had entered an elegant oasis. Classy, not ostentatious.

As Craig expected for out of season October, the hotel was quiet. Going up to the reception desk, he found a dignified looking man who identified himself as Michele, the front office manager.

"I'm Enrico Marino, Betty Richards is expecting me."

Through the corner of his eye Craig saw a man lounging against a rounded white stone column, a wire hooked to his ear. Part of Betty's security detail. It always amazed Craig why they, like the president's Secret Service, were often so easily identified.

"I'll take you up," Michele said.

In the elevator Michele, exuding experience and self-confidence, told Craig in an Italian-accented English that he should come back during the summer when the weather was glorious and the hotel booming.

The presidential suite was tucked away in a tower with a private pool overlooking the sea. Exiting the elevator, Craig immediately spotted two more American security agents guarding the entrance to Betty's suite. As he walked alongside Michele, Craig's whole body ached. The painkillers were wearing off.

"Miraculously, no bones were broken," Adriana had told him, when she helped him dress in the hospital room. "You'll be very sore for a few days."

"And, I look like hell," he had told her.

"I've seen worse," she had said in a nurse's professional voice.

Betty was waiting for Craig inside the living room of the suite, decorated in pastel colors and furnished with dark wooden tables and large plush chairs. When Michele had gone, she said, "We can talk freely here. I've gotten rid of the waiters. I had one of our people sweep the suite for bugs. As you saw, there are two of my agents outside the door and another on the ground below."

"I couldn't miss them."

"I have to tell you, your surgeon did a hell of a good job. You look ten years younger. I would have never recognized you."

"They should have with what I paid them."

"It must be weird for Elizabeth."

"I haven't seen her since. It's a long story."

"Meaning I shouldn't go there?"

"Some other time, perhaps."

Betty led the way to an orange tiled patio. Three floors below, perfectly manicured grass grounds surrounding a huge swimming pool extended to the sea where three yachts were moored. In the pool a couple splashed each other, The woman was blond, topless, and strikingly attractive. Her companion was an Italian movie star Craig recognized.

The table was set with English bone china and Christofle silver. Craig saw Betty watching him wince as he tenderly eased down into a chair at the table.

"I have a bottle of Percocet in my suitcase," she said. "You want a couple?"

He pointed to the bottle of 1997 Turriga, an extraordinary red wine from Sardinia resting in a metal holder on the table. "That'll do the job much better and more enjoyably."

"When I look at you, I wonder if you should?"

"I survived yesterday. Somebody up there must be looking out for me."

She poured them both glasses of wine, which he sipped slowly. It was wonderful.

Then she removed the silver dome from the top of the serving bowl, scooped out cold seafood salad with chunks of calamari, mussels, and scallops, distributing them between the two plates. She picked up the basket of rolls and held it out. Craig took one and dipped it into the excellent extra-virgin olive oil. He didn't think he'd have an appetite, but it was coming back fast.

After they both took a couple of forkfuls of seafood salad, he said, "How in the world did you find me?"

"When I was appointed CIA director eleven months ago, a mysterious postcard arrived in the mail. The picture on the front was an auto racing track near Torino. On the back was a handwritten note that said 'Congratulations,' signed by Enrico Marino.

"It was partly because of your daughter. One time when I took Francesca to the movies when she was a child she told me, 'One day my dad's going to be a famous race car driver.' Besides, I recognized the handwriting and compared it with other notes you sent me over the years. The Internet is marvelous. So when I wanted to find you, all I had to do was Google Enrico Marino. I saw an item that said you were racing in Sardinia this weekend. I was impressed with the other things

I read about your new career. You've compiled quite a good record for yourself in a short period."

"Yeah, but I've only won small races. None of the biggies. I was hoping Sardinia would be my breakthrough."

"I've learned that from now until spring is an off-season for racing so I want to give you something else to do."

"You're my best friend in the whole world, Betty, and I owe you big time for so many things, but no way will I do anything for you or with you as long as Treadwell is president and that asshole Edward Bryce is telling him what to do. Sorry you came so far for nothing."

She smiled and said, "I'm going to tell you something that may change your mind."

"Nothing will change my mind."

"I'm here because Ted Dunn's gone missing. He was doing a job for me. Alice is desperate. She asked me to get you to help. We want you to find him."

She had blurted out her words as if dropping a live grenade on the table.

Craig's head snapped back. Ted Dunn was an old friend of his. A relationship that began when Ted had recruited Craig, then a senior at Carnegie Mellon, for the CIA. Ted had been Craig's mentor in training at the Farm in Southern Virginia. Craig had remained friends with Ted and Alice for more than three decades.

Craig recalled the last time he had seen Ted and Alice. He had learned they would be vacationing in Paris when he was director of the EU Counterterrorism Agency and took them to dinner at Apicius.

Ted and Alice had told Craig how happy they were that Ted had retired. They had their health and enjoyed being together after spending so much time apart during Ted's CIA days in Latin America. He remembered Alice saying, "It may sound trite, but this is our time."

Craig sighed deeply. Well, it may have been their time, but it had gotten fucked up. He wondered what in the world induced his friend to get back on the merry-go-round.

When he had first seen her, Craig thought there was nothing Betty could possibly say that would make him even think about working for her. Now he was willing to listen, but not necessarily do any more than that. And that was only for Dunn's sake.

"What the hell was Ted doing for you?"

"I asked him to do a job in Argentina off the books."

"So you want me to go to Argentina and find out what happened to him."

"For openers, yes."

Craig drank his wine while thinking about what Betty had said. Finally, he shook his head. "My God, Betty. I'm not the right person for that job. Unlike Ted, who knew the territory, I've never even been to Argentina . . . or South America, for that matter."

"That's precisely why you're right for it."

"I hate to turn you down, but you really should get somebody else."

"Let me give you an incentive to reconsider."

"What's that?"

"In doing this operation, you may have a chance for revenge on Edward Bryce."

Craig sprang to attention. "What's *he* have to do with it?"

"It's a complicated story. Now are you ready to listen?"

Craig drank some more wine. Then he said, "Before I do that, I have to tell you how Bryce behaved toward me in the Oval Office the day Treadwell fired me. I don't think I ever told you in detail."

"That's right. You didn't."

"Well anyhow, he put me through a cross-examination. The great trial lawyer jumped to his feet and pointed a finger at me. Let me show you."

Craig sprang out of the chair. As he moved toward the middle of the patio, the room became bleary. He felt queasy and reached for the edge of the table to steady himself. He missed and knocked over a glass of wine, collapsing into a heap next to his chair on the stone patio.

*   *   *

The nightmare woke him. He and Elizabeth were tied to stakes in a dusty field in the mountains of Morocco. Ahmed, the terrorist, and one of his henchmen were on horses at the end of the field. Spears in hand, they were ready to charge Craig and Elizabeth. "No," he cried. "Don't die. No."

He shot to a sitting position, his body in a cold sweat, his teeth chattering. He was in a strange bed. The sheets were soaked with perspiration. A woman came running into the room. It was Adriana in her nurse's uniform, who felt his pulse, then his forehead. She clamped a cuff over his arm and took his blood pressure. "Swallow this," she said and shoved a pill into his mouth. She held up a glass of water and forced him to drink a little.

"Where am I?" he asked.

"In a bedroom in a hotel suite."

Then she put his head back down on the pillow and placed a cool, damp cloth against his forehead. He fell asleep.

Buenos Aires

"I'm worried," Colonel Schiller said to General Alfredo Estrada, as he sat across the desk with his shaved head and wire-framed glasses.

The two of them were alone in Estrada's large corner office in the Argentine Defense Center.

"You shouldn't be," Estrada said calmly. "Our operation is on schedule. The meeting with the Brazilian generals went well. They're on board. Young men are flocking to join the army. Thanks to Gina and Edward Bryce, the arms are flowing from the United States."

"You're leaving out the American who was meeting with Pascual in Bariloche. I now have information on Pascual."

"Tell me," Estrada snapped.

Schiller pulled a thin file from the briefcase at his feet and began reading. "Pascual Frigero. Thirty-nine years old. A native of Bariloche, he spent two years at the university in Buenos Aires majoring in literature, then dropped out and returned home. Now a part-time limo driver, he played the guitar and sang in nightclubs in his hometown frequented by a drug-using crowd. He belonged to a gay and lesbian group and wrote left-leaning poetry. His sister, Antonia, lives in Bariloche. She's married to a bookkeeper. Has two children ages five and seven, both girls. Pascual's parents had been Communists. Both were killed in

1982 when their espionage had been uncovered. The details are available in an army report I can give to you."

General Estrada waved his hand. "I don't need that." He pushed back from his desk, stood up, and paced around the office. Dressed in a freshly-pressed brown army uniform, he was an imposing figure. He was a tall and broad-chested man with a thin mustache and coal-black hair parted in the middle. He had a scar above his right eyebrow. There were two versions of how he had gotten it. Supporters claimed he had received a knife wound in a battle with Communist insurgents in 1979, when the military junta ruled the country. Alone on the street at night, he had been ambushed by a gang of six and had fought his way out—killing all of them.

His opponents contended that the wound had been inflicted with a sword by a fellow officer whose wife he had seduced. The jealous man had attacked Estrada when the general was screwing his wife. Naked, she had watched in horror the battle that left her a widow.

Estrada encouraged both accounts.

"You worry too much," Estrada said.

"I'm your director of security. It's my job to be concerned about threats to our operation."

Estrada didn't like being challenged. He whirled around and stared hard at Schiller, who glanced away.

"Because of Bryce, I have control over President Treadwell's Argentine policy."

"It's possible someone in the American government may be acting on their own. Making an end run around Treadwell and Bryce."

"That's your job to find out."

Estrada cut across the room to a table that held a map of South America. Without saying a word, he focused his attention on the map, signaling Schiller that their meeting was over.

Estrada heard Schiller leave the office and close the door.

He ran his finger along the northeastern boundary of Argentina, along its border with Brazil. It was amazing, Estrada thought, that Argentina, which he loved so dearly—a country rich in land and natural resources, a nation of artisans and talented people, with more than half ethnically Italian like his own ancestors who came from Sicily—could have been for centuries such a chronic underachiever economically and militarily. And then it became the butt of jokes throughout the world after the war for trying to take back from Great Britain the Falklands, to which his country was fully entitled.

Well, all of that was about to change. Under his leadership, Argentina would be elevated to its rightful position as the preeminent military and economic power in South America. At the same time, he intended to raise the standard of living for the people. They wouldn't merely have pride in their country's accomplishments; they would be better off financially. They would revere him for what he did for them.

Estrada had developed a blueprint for seizing power in Argentina and had prepared the first step in his larger plan. He was ready to move. The next month was critical. No one would stop him.

Porto Cervo, Sardinia

With his head still on the pillow, Craig opened his eyes. Looking through the window of one of the bedrooms in Betty's suite he saw a gorgeous fireball of a sun rising straight ahead over the Gulf of Olbia. His whole body ached. His mind was fuzzy. He remembered fainting at lunch on the balcony, and he was embarrassed. He dressed quietly, then slipped out of the suite for a walk along the beach. He had to focus his thinking before he met with Betty again.

He took the path through the trees that followed the shoreline and lead to the beach. The emerald green waters were gently lapping against the sand.

At the edge of the water, clearer than he had ever seen in the Mediterranean, he reached down and scooped up a handful of pebbles. After rolling up his pants legs he waded in and began skipping them.

In the cool light of the morning, he had to decide if he wanted to take Betty's assignment.

Trying to help Ted Dunn was a powerful factor. The possibility of settling his score with Edward Bryce was even more compelling.

And weighed against those was how shabbily he'd been treated twice by the powers in Washington. Regardless of what she said, he'd be dealing with more than Betty. Was he willing to endure all that political crap again?

Yes, dammit. It will be worthwhile if I can destroy Edward Bryce.

Still, he knew there was something else that made him agree—his feelings toward the United States. His father, who owed his life to the US Army, having been rescued as a small boy from Nazi carnage on a farm in Northern Italy, had instilled that love for the United States into Craig.

"Never forget," his father had told Craig, in a hospital room hours before he died, "This is a great country."

He had learned long ago that working for the United States in espionage meant accepting all the political stuff that went with any organization. It meant working with people like Betty, who were good, but often restricted in what they could do by those above them. It also meant dealing with some despicable people like Edward Bryce. And there were others like him. Craig would have to remind himself constantly that he'd be serving the American people.

With determination, Craig turned and headed back toward the hotel.

As he entered the suite he saw Betty sitting on the patio sipping coffee and staring out to sea. He poured himself a cup from the silver thermos on the table and sat down next to her.

This was awkward. "I'm sorry about yesterday . . . I don't know what happened. I . . ."

She stared at him sympathetically. "You don't have to apologize. I had your nurse and doctor from the hospital come out here to examine you."

"What'd the old geezer say?"

She cracked a smile. "That you had been a damn fool not to follow his advice and rest longer at the hospital. The nurse was sure the wine did you in. Then when you stood up abruptly, your blood pressure dropped precipitously."

"And you didn't tell them it was really the memories of my encounter with Edward Bryce."

She laughed. "What I'm sitting here wondering," she said, "is whether I'm being fair asking you to do to this. It involves going to Argentina to find out what happened to Ted and to complete the job

I sent him to do. You've never even been to Argentina. And you have already done so much for our country."

"Yeah, I know that. I took a walk along the beach this morning. I sorted some things out for myself."

"And?" she asked expectantly.

"I'm prepared to do it."

"Are you certain?"

"Absolutely. Now, tell me what I'll need to know."

"Breakfast is inside. We'll eat while we talk."

He followed her to the suite's dining room. While Craig, starving, devoured pieces of an incredibly sweet green melon, she began talking.

"This all began about six months ago. I received a report from our station chief in Beijing that General Alfredo Estrada, head of the Argentine Armed Forces, had made a secret trip to Beijing, where he met with the top Chinese civilian and military leadership. Estrada didn't meet with President Mei Ling, but we're seeing increasing signs that she can't control her top military people. Perhaps not even the top civilians.

"Anyhow, there weren't any press announcements of Estrada's visit. Nothing public. As you might imagine, it rang alarms for me. As it would have for you."

Craig nodded.

Betty continued, "The Chinese already have a foothold in South America . . . in Venezuela. That continent is too close to the United States to risk it falling under Chinese influence. We're not talking some remote place like Afghanistan. This is our own backyard. Besides, the place is rich in natural resources, which we need."

Craig stopped chewing and interjected, "There's plenty of oil under the Atlantic off the coast of Argentina and Brazil."

"Exactly. And on top of all that, we can't afford instability in Argentina because it will lead to instability elsewhere in Latin America. That in turn will inevitably produce new waves of immigrants heading north and creating a major problem for us. So in a morning briefing with President Treadwell, I told him what our station chief had reported from Beijing about Estrada's visit, and that I planned to set up a special task force in the agency to find out what Estrada had in mind."

Craig put his fork down. He was listening intently. "And?"

"Treadwell told me, 'Lay off Argentina. Edward Bryce has the point for that.' Those were his exact words. I was so stunned I nearly fell off my chair."

"You're kidding."

"I wish I were."

"I did some investigations of Bryce. As you know, he's a powerful Washington lawyer and close friend and confidant of Treadwell. What I learned is that they've been close since they were roommates at Yale. Bryce started his own Washington law firm. It grew into a mega international organization with offices around the world. He began as a successful trial lawyer. Now he's a power broker and an influence peddler. Apparently Treadwell has blinders on when it comes to Bryce."

"I'll testify to that."

"I did a little more quiet checking and found, again to my surprise, that we were supplying arms to Argentina. Large quantities and sophisticated stuff, including advanced fighter jets, surface-to-air missiles, and tanks. I learned from a source in DOD that Treadwell told them to ship whatever Bryce put on a shopping list."

"You think Estrada's planning a military coup to take over the government? That could lead to coups in other countries in South America and would destabilize the continent? Or is he planning to attack a neighboring country?"

"You hit on the key point. I don't know what Estrada's planning to do, but I want to find out. The man's evil. As a young officer, he was part of the military group that ruled the country during the Dirty War. They arrested, tortured, and murdered thousands who were enemies of the regime, claiming they were Communists. We can't let him take over the country. He and his cohorts are likely to behave the same way."

"What's Bryce's game? You think Estrada's paying him?"

"So far, I haven't seen any evidence of that, but let me show you something."

She reached into her briefcase resting on the floor and extracted a color photograph depicting a couple sitting at a table against a wall in a restaurant. The picture must have been a candid shot. The man was Bryce. He was smiling, looking like a cat who had just swallowed a canary. And it was easy to see why.

In one hand, he held a drink, dark with ice cubes. Scotch or bourbon, Craig guessed. His other hand was extended across the table and clasped around a young woman's arm.

She looked to be in her mid-twenties. He was undoubtedly screwing her, which explained the look on his face. Hers was something different. She had a lovely face, without makeup. She had naturally beautiful features with perfectly sculpted lines. Her dark hair, parted in the middle, framed her face. Her sensuous dark eyes revealed a hint of sadness. Clearly she wasn't enjoying herself like the man was. She had a smile that looked forced. Her expression told Craig she was uncomfortable being with Bryce and maybe felt awkward in this particular situation. Below her enticingly long neck hung a small gold cross, resting against the dark material of her blouse that rose to the bottom of her neck.

"Who's the woman with Bryce?" Craig asked.

"Gina Galindo, a reporter for *La Nación*, a Buenos Aires daily. The picture was taken surreptitiously three days ago at the Grill Room, a fashionable restaurant in Washington."

Craig continued to study the picture. "Who said: get control of their dicks and their minds will follow?"

"That pretty well describes it."

"Is there a Mrs. Bryce?"

"Claire is her name. She left him about a year ago. Before he met this Gina."

"He must have been lonely."

Betty ignored his comment and pressed on. "At any rate, Claire went to Florence to live and study art."

"Do you know whether Gina is working for Estrada?"

Betty held out her hands. "I don't have any proof. If not, it's damn coincidental."

"Have you bugged her?"

Betty smiled. "Obviously, you've forgotten. We have an agreement with the FBI. We don't do domestic surveillance."

He shot back: "Amazing how quickly these things fly out of my mind."

Betty picked up a basket of rolls, selected one, and spread it thickly with orange marmalade. Craig refilled their coffee cups. After they ate in silence for a few moments, Betty resumed talking.

"I wasn't about to walk away from this, so I hired Ted Dunn off the books to go down to Argentina and find out everything he could about Estrada and what the good general is planning."

She pulled a blue folder from her briefcase and slid it across the table. "Inside is a compilation of the info I received from Ted about Estrada as well as materials our research department assembled. You'll see that Estrada's been quietly expanding the army and developing a power base with right-wing business interests."

"How strong is Estrada's organization?"

"Several other generals are close with him. Colonel Kurt Schiller, head of military intelligence, does his dirty work. He's the grandson of Carl Schiller, the high level Gestapo official who escaped with Adolph Eichmann to Argentina after the war and eluded capture. He died about ten years ago. No doubt it was after he had a chance to tutor young Kurt."

She paused to take a breath. "In Ted's last message, he said he was getting close to the answer of what Estrada was planning. He had a critical meeting scheduled that evening. Then he went silent. Complete blackout."

"What was his cover?"

"Tourist."

"Couldn't you do better than that?"

She reddened, opened her mouth to reply, and closed it.

"One advantage of you going is that between your recent complete change in appearance and your having never been there, no one will recognize you. I'll e-mail you some background info on Argentina. The country's 50 percent ethnically Italian. They came in waves. Many were from Sicily and Calabria. Almost all the rest are Spanish or of other European descent. The Spaniards who came first systematically killed off the natives who inhabited the place when they arrived. So unlike Peru or Venezuela, you feel as if you're in Europe. The language is an Italianized Spanish, but most of the top people, including Estrada, speak English well."

"With my Italian, I'm sure I'll be able to get by."

"I agree. You also should know that the Argentine economy goes up and down like a bungee jumper. This explains in part why military takeovers alternate with democratic rule like clockwork in Argentina."

Craig stood up and stretched his arms. Betty looked alarmed. "You're not planning to pass out on me again?"

He laughed. "Not a chance. Just stiff from sitting." He did a couple of knee bends and sat back down. "This will only work if I can find a way to get close to Estrada."

She gave a long, low whistle. "You want to play a high-stakes game?"

"It's the only way."

"And how do you intend to get close to Estrada?"

"He must need money for whatever he's planning."

She nodded.

"And he doesn't yet control the government so he can't tap international credit markets."

"Agreed. Where are you going with this?"

"Suppose I were to go into Argentina pretending to be the head of a private equity firm in the United States. I have ten billion dollars to invest—money raised from wealthy investors looking for a huge return. I would consider investing some or all of it in Argentina if I thought it was justified. That should gain me access to Estrada."

She was smiling. "I like it."

"From now on, I'm Barry Gorman. President and CEO of the Philoctetes Group."

"Philoctetes?"

"The name of the celebrated hero of the Trojan War who was memorialized in one of Sophocles' seven extant plays. Don't think engineers aren't educated. Carnegie Mellon has a great English department. And the best drama school in the country."

"So do I call you Craig, Enrico, Ricci, or Barry?"

"Craig will be fine for now."

"What can I do to help you protect that cover?"

"Create a website for the Philoctetes Group with Barry Gorman as president and CEO. Base it in San Francisco. Give Gorman his own phone line with a 415 area code. Calls to that number should automatically be routed to a special operator at CIA headquarters without the caller having any idea this happened. While the caller's telephone number is recorded, the caller should be told: 'Mr. Gorman is out of the country on business. I can take a message and transmit it to him.' In the shadowy and secretive world of private equity firms, none of this will stand out. But I need an emergency contact in Buenos Aires."

"If you're in trouble or have to get inside our embassy to reach me on a secure phone, call B. J. Walker, the cultural attaché. Tell him that Jimmy Carr wants to go home. B. J. will know what to do."

"He's one of yours?"

"Uh-huh. And I assume you haven't forgotten my cell phone number."

"Indelibly etched on my brain."

"Call me anytime, twenty-four hours a day. But I'm sure you would have done that if I hadn't said it."

He raised his eyebrows. "You're doing this yourself."

"It's too sensitive with the president and Bryce involved, and . . ." she hesitated, then completed her thought, "some of the top people in the agency didn't like the idea of a woman being placed in the director's chair."

"Big surprise."

"So I'm not exactly sure who I can trust."

"Any locals who would be useful?"

Betty sighed. "As always, you're impatient. I was getting to that."

"Sorry."

"A woman by the name of Nicole who operates a shoe boutique in La Recoleta, a fashionable area in Buenos Aires, or BA, as it is often called by residents, at Number 14 Avenue Quintana."

Craig committed the information to memory.

Betty continued. "Nicole is well connected socially on both sides of the political spectrum. She has excellent relationships with right-wing business and military types, while her sympathies are with the prodemocracy groups. Dunn paid her plenty, which she claimed to be funneling to anti-Estrada forces. In return, she gave him lots of help."

Maybe Nicole got a better offer from Estrada's people and sold Dunn out, Craig thought. He decided not to share that with Betty.

"As long as we're talking about money," she added, "we have to address the matter of your compensation for this job. I was thinking . . ."

"I'm doing this for free. You're giving me a chance to destroy Bryce. I would be willing to pay you."

"Really?"

"Yeah, but I'll want you to cover my expenses."

"I know you like to live well. How much?"

"With the cover I'll be using and the need to pay for information, I better take a million dollars to Argentina with me. All hundreds. Old bills. Not consecutively numbered. Pack them in a duffel, as small as possible. I'll need a Barry Gorman passport, California driver's license, a couple of credit cards with no limits, and business cards."

Craig saw her blench at the amount and squeeze her lips together. "C'mon Betty. Even in the three weeks I was in the job, I learned about the huge discretionary fund the director has. It can be spent without accountability and I loved tapping into it. For trips to Pakistan and Prague. Stuff like that."

"Okay. Okay. Stop in Washington before you go to BA. I'll have it all for you, as well as a couple of handguns. I'll arrange with American Airlines to let your stuff go through without a fuss."

He sat up in his chair. "Sorry, the head of a ten billion dollar fund doesn't fly commercial. Once I hit Washington, I'll hire a private jet with one of your credit cards to take me to Argentina."

He watched her squirming. "And when will that be?"

"In two days. I have to stop in Milan and buy a whole new wardrobe. My current stuff's a little casual. After that, I'll spend a day or two in Washington before going down to BA."

She looked anxious. "We have to move up on this. Dunn's life may be hanging in the balance."

"Let's be realistic. Enough time has gone by that if Estrada wanted to kill Ted, he'd be dead. If Ted's still alive, chances are Estrada wants to use him as a bargaining chip. If this is the case, a few more days won't matter."

"I guess you're right."

"Don't worry. I won't be wasting time in Washington. I'll move as quickly as I can. But if I don't do it the right way, you'll have two dead agents."

Washington

"Do you have time for another set?" President Treadwell called to Bryce across the tennis net.

They had just finished their first set in the basement of the White House. Bryce won 6-1 while barely breaking a sweat. Treadwell, on the other hand, was perspiring profusely.

Bryce was surprised he had won so easily. Generally, their matches were very close. They'd been playing singles for forty-two years, ever since they had been thrown together as roommates by the Yale freshman dorm lottery. That chance event and the relationship it fostered proved more important to both men then any course they took in their four years at Yale.

In the early days Treadwell, who had been on the junior team at a posh country club in Westchester County, New York, almost always defeated the scrappy Bryce, who learned the sport on the public courts on the west side of Chicago without lessons.

But after he became a successful Washington lawyer and joined the prestigious Kenwood Country Club, Bryce took lessons with Chris, the top pro, who perfected his game. Gradually he had drawn closer to Treadwell, winning some in close sets, but nothing like today. Must be the enormous tension and stress the president was facing.

"I've got time," Bryce shouted back.

"Good. Let's get some water and switch sides."

They went to the side of the court where Treadwell gulped water. Bryce thought the president's face was flushed.

"You okay?" Bryce asked.

"Sure. Just a little humiliated from losing so badly. But I'll turn the tables on you."

Bryce glanced up into the gallery above the court. Dr. Andrews, the president's physician, a urologist from Westchester and Treadwell's longtime golfing buddy called "Andy" by the president, was preoccupied with his Blackberry and apparently unconcerned. Next to Andrews sat the ubiquitous military aide with his briefcase. A secret service man was on each end of the court.

In the second set Bryce decided to take a little off his game, but he'd have to be careful. If the competitive Treadwell sensed it, he'd rip into Bryce.

During the first game, with Treadwell serving, Bryce returned one ball a little long and another just a tad wide. Bryce won the next two points. Then Treadwell prevailed in the next two after long rallies. Game for Treadwell.

Bryce was picking up balls, getting ready to serve when he noticed a commotion in the gallery. Dr. Andrews was leaving and being replaced by Dr. Deborah Lee, his thirty-one-year-old assistant who had done a fellowship in cardiology at Johns Hopkins.

On the first two points, Bryce eased up on his serve. Treadwell returned them deep, setting up baseline rallies, which they split. At 15-15, Bryce decided he'd better hit his normal serve to avoid suspicion. He blasted it, nicking the service line. Treadwell could only manage a weak return to Bryce's forehand. Bryce moved up on the ball and smashed a hard shot down the line. Treadwell was racing toward the ball. Bryce moved to the net, ready to catch the return in the air and put it away—if Treadwell managed one.

Before Treadwell reached the ball, he suddenly stopped, the racket slipping out of his hand. He collapsed to his knees and sat down on the court.

Bryce raced around the net to see what was wrong.

The president looked pale. He was gasping for breath.

"I better get the doctor," Bryce shouted.

"No. No," Treadwell protested. "Just get me something to drink. Some Gatorade."

"You sure?"

"Yeah. Do it now."

Bryce ran toward the cooler on the side of the court. Through the corner of his eye, Bryce saw Dr. Lee charging across the court, black doctor's bag in hand. Thank God for that.

Bryce returned with Gatorade as Dr. Lee was pulling a stethoscope out of her bag. Treadwell waved the doctor away. "No need for all that gear," he said. "I'm fine. Just gimme the Gatorade."

Bryce handed him the bottle and Treadwell chugged it down.

"With all due respect, Mr. President," Dr. Lee said, "I think that . . ."

Treadwell cut her off. "I'm alright. Andy tells me I get electrolyte depletion. I have to remember to drink more of this stuff."

Bryce saw Dr. Lee looking at him for assistance, but he turned away. When Treadwell sounded this firm, Bryce had learned long ago that challenging him could be risky. Even for a close friend.

"Let's call it a day," Treadwell said. "I want to shower. I have the treasury secretary coming over in an hour for a meeting about the budget."

With that, Treadwell turned and trudged toward the locker room. Bryce was at his side.

Dr. Lee followed two steps behind.

By the time he was dressed, the president's color had returned and he was walking normally.

Treadwell and Bryce split at the door to the Oval Office, with Bryce planning to head back to his office at the law firm, four blocks away.

The instant the president disappeared behind the door Bryce heard Dr. Lee's voice. "May I talk to you for a minute, Mr. Bryce?"

Bryce led her into a small, deserted conference room. "I know what you're going to say. The president needs to get his heart examined."

Dr. Lee nodded.

"How long until his next regular physical?" Bryce asked.

"Six months."

"Shit. He can't wait that long."

"You have to convince him to go out to Bethesda Naval for a cardio workup. I'll make the arrangements."

"I know him. It won't be easy. He's stubborn."

Dr. Lee shook her head. "We see that all the time. Many people are reluctant to do it. They're afraid of what they'll learn. They figure what they don't know won't hurt them. This is precisely the opposite of the truth. If there is something wrong with his heart, it can likely be fixed. If not, he will continue to deteriorate."

Bryce liked this young woman. "We have another problem here. The president's up for reelection next November. The country has major economic problems. The last thing he wants in the next thirteen months is a medical issue."

"He can't possibly wait a year to be tested. You know that. He could be dead before then if he doesn't get evaluated and treated."

Bryce nodded grimly. "Yeah, you're right. Let me work on it. It may take a while."

"You can't take too long or he'll have a heart attack."

"I understand. I'll come up with a way to get it done. I'll tell him that you'll keep the results quiet. I assume that's acceptable to you."

"I never disclose any patient's medical information."

"Even the president of the United States?"

"For me, the rules are the same."

Dr. Lee extracted a card from her pocket and handed it to Bryce. "My cell phone number. At the very least, please tell him to take an aspirin a day if he isn't already doing that."

"Okay, I will."

"And tell him to ease up on the physical activity."

"I'll do my best."

"One other thing. I'd appreciate it if you kept our conversation to yourself. Though my field is cardiology, Dr. Andrews is in charge of the president's health. He would think I'm overstepping my bounds."

Bryce smiled. "Which you are."

As the Washington lawyer left the White House, the skies were gloomy and gray. Bryce rejected the waiting White House limousine in favor of walking back to his office at Eighth and Pennsylvania, confident that the rain would hold off for a man as important as he was.

When Bryce had entered the White House a couple of hours previously to meet the president for their tennis match, it had been a gorgeous fall day and this seemed quite appropriate for Bryce—a man in the beautiful autumn of his life. But like the weather, life was in flux and surprises kept flying at him from left field. "Zingers" was what his Uncle Charlie called those unanticipated events that suddenly appear and turn one's life in a different direction. Plot points, they call them in Hollywood.

Bryce exited the White House grounds and turned eastward, walking at a slow, contemplative pace—not his usual long, purposeful strides. A year ago when Treadwell had been elected president, Bryce felt like he was on top of the world.

After Yale their professional paths had diverged, with Bryce going to Harvard Law, then coming to Washington for a clerkship on the Supreme Court before joining a prestigious Washington law firm; and

Treadwell getting an MBA at Harvard before making a bundle on Wall Street, which he used to catapult himself into the national political sphere. They had remained close friends with Bryce playing the role of consigliore as well as tennis partner to the rising Treadwell. Bryce could have had any position he wanted in the Treadwell administration, but he declined an official post, preferring to stay at his law firm and cash in on his relationship with Treadwell, who had built the court in the White House basement so he could play with Bryce.

It was well known that Bryce was the closest advisor to the most powerful man in the world. Treadwell needed him. Bryce, always top of the class, was much smarter and quicker than Treadwell, who had been a mediocre student.

Bryce was benefitting enormously from his relationship with the president. So many clients flocked to Bryce's law firm that he had to hire fifty additional lawyers. He was working sixteen-hour days shuttling between the White House and the law firm, loving every minute of it, particularly his personal profiles in the *New York Times* and *Washington Post* describing how much Treadwell relied on him.

About six months ago, zinger number one hit. Claire, his wife of thirty-five years and mother of his two children, announced on her sixtieth birthday that this wasn't what she had bargained for at this point in her life—a husband who was never home. It was late in the game, but not too late to do something she wanted to do. So she had set off to Florence to study art and to paint. "And there's nothing you can say to stop me," she snapped at him in a tone he had often heard from judges who wanted to make it clear to a lawyer that the argument was over.

Six months later, zinger number two flew in when a young reporter for *La Nación* in Buenos Aires showed up in the reception area at his law firm without an appointment and camped out until he would give her an interview. Bryce had planned to tell the reporter he was too busy, until he saw her sitting patiently with pen and notebook in hand, a beautiful, demure, virginal-looking, sensuous woman in a smartly tailored gray suit. Perhaps it was the fact that since Claire's departure he had little time or occasion to be with women other than in meetings, or perhaps he was just tired of working and wanted a change. Who knows why he said to Gina Galindo, "C'mon. I'll take you out to lunch. We can do the interview there."

He never expected they would hit it off so well. Bryce had no doubt that she liked him as much as he did her. By the fourth date they were sleeping together. With her, he was young again, aroused in ways he had thought were finished. Initially, Gina had been reluctant, but he had chalked this up to her inexperience. Now he was seriously thinking of asking her to marry him. That would set old Claire back a step or two. And he was confident Gina would agree. Why wouldn't she want to be married to the second most powerful man in the world? Well, Claire obviously didn't, but she didn't count. He was concerned that acquaintances would think she had married him for his position. That bothered him a little, but after they met Gina they would realize she and Bryce were in love.

Bryce crossed Pennsylvania Avenue without waiting for the light to change. A driver honked and swerved, narrowly missing Bryce, obviously unaware that Bryce was too important to stop for red lights. As he entered his office building he remembered that Uncle Charlie had also said, "Zingers show up in threes." He hoped to hell that a serious heart attack for Treadwell wasn't the final one in his little trilogy. If that happened, he'd lose his meal ticket. He'd no longer find his name in the newspapers on an almost daily basis. He'd have to lay off those fifty lawyers. But he was confident that Gina would stick with him because she really did love him.

Still, he couldn't let any of that happen. He had to persuade Treadwell to schedule that cardio workup.

*   *   *

By the time Craig's plane touched down at Dulles at ten in the morning, he had read and reread all of the materials Betty had left with him or e-mailed. He had developed in his mind a bio for Barry Gorman, even the courses and professors he had taken en route to a Stanford degree in economics and an MBA. He had mastered many of the nuances of the shadowy and secretive world of private equity funds. He felt that he knew General Alfredo Estrada as well as it was possible to know someone from written materials without a personal meeting.

One thing was clear: Estrada would be a tough nut to crack. The general was revered by his troops for the way in which he had rebuilt the army, taking poor and embittered men and women from the streets and giving them a reason to live, a source of pride. His accomplishment was all the more impressive because he had done it quietly. Many Argentineans continued to believe that the army, after the disasters of the Dirty War and the Falklands' battle with England, was no longer a factor in the political life of the country.

Others, more perceptive, saw what was happening. The editor of one BA daily, *La Opinion*, had described Estrada as "part visionary, part megalomaniac, and part thug."

Somewhere, Estrada had a wife and two children who were never mentioned in the media. Nor seen with him. He loved high living. Gambling and good-looking women. He made periodic trips to casinos in Europe and Vegas. Craig wondered whether Gina had been or was still sleeping with him when she was in Argentina.

As he stepped off the plane, his cell rang. He picked it up.

"Did you have a good flight, Barry Gorman?" He recognized Betty's voice.

"Very good. Thanks."

"Waiting for you upstairs in front of the terminal, at the curb, last door on the right, is a black Lincoln Town Car, Virginia plates, CCK220. The driver will take you to the Four Seasons in Georgetown. A duffel with everything you wanted is in the trunk."

"Thanks. I appreciate that."

"The car will leave you at the Four Seasons. You'll be on your own from there."

*　　*　　*

After checking into the Four Seasons, Craig called Tim Fuller to arrange a meeting. He and Tim had met when they were both trainees at the Farm. They had seen each other from time to time over the years. Fuller began in the economic espionage section, working at Langley. Later, he was stationed in Shanghai. Appalled at the Chinese wholesale theft of American technology, he repeatedly railed for Washington to take countermeasures. When his pleas fell on deaf ears, Tim quit the agency and ten years ago started a private security firm based in Washington.

Craig hadn't seen Tim in eight years, since the time he was in Washington for a conference about Middle Eastern terrorism.

One night over cheeseburgers and beers at Clyde's in Georgetown, Tim had told him, "My country didn't appreciate my talents so I decided to make a killing from people who do."

Tim's offices were on the top floor of one of the nondescript glass and steel eight-floor boxes that line K Street, known as Gucci gulch, because it houses the offices of many of Washington's highest paid lobbyists.

Once Craig stepped inside the reception area he knew that Tim was doing well. This was a far cry from the office of J. J. Gittes. Heavily polished dark wood floors were lined with oriental carpets. An antique grandfather clock stood in the corner. Sitting at a Queen Ann desk was a young receptionist smartly dressed in a tailored navy woolen suit. Ansel Adams photographs dotted the walls.

"I'll take you back to Mr. Fuller's office," the receptionist said.

Craig watched the receptionist swaying her shapely rear as if it were a pendulum as he followed her. Walking behind her, he swung his black leather briefcase, purchased on Via Monte Napoleone in Milan, keeping in rhythm with her.

As soon as he saw Craig, Tim, suntanned and dressed in a starched white shirt and Hermes tie, hung up on a call. The surprise was visible on his face. This wasn't the Craig Page he knew.

"Hello Tim," Craig said.

Tim told the receptionist to leave and close the door behind her.

"What the hell did you do to yourself, pal?"

"I went for a nip and tuck. My plastic surgeon got carried away."

"Seriously."

"Some people want to kill Craig Page, and I figured . . ."

"Smart move. But I see the scratches on your face. Did they get to you anyhow?"

"I was doing a little car racing."

"A dangerous sport."

"Now you tell me."

Tim laughed. "When I heard you were CIA director a year ago, I was plenty pissed that you didn't call me. Then I read you'd been sacked. So I relented. You weren't in the job long enough to call anyone."

"Ouch. That stung."

"What the hell happened?"

"Some people at 1600 decided to throw me under a bus."

Tim laughed again.

As they sat at a table in the corner, Craig glanced at Tim. His old friend's appearance, Craig thought, was at variance with his clothes and the office. He had the aura of a street fighter and was short and pudgy. His nose had been broken playing football in a coal town in West Virginia where he had won a scholarship to Dartmouth. And his thick brown crew cut was so flat on top that he could walk with a cup of coffee in a saucer on his head without spilling it.

"You've got nice digs," Craig said. "The security business must be good."

"It is, pal. Every company in America is worried about their records being stolen by terrorists or a desperate competitor in this economy. Those who do business abroad are scared shitless that one of their execs will be kidnapped and held for ransom. It's a tough world to do business in. One man's nightmare is another man's dream. Clients are flying in through the door."

Tim pulled back and studied Craig, dressed suavely in a double-breasted charcoal Brioni suit with a muted stripe he had bought in Milan. "Look who's talking. The new Craig Page, whoever that is . . ."

"Barry Gorman."

"Okay. Barry Gorman is obviously doing well."

Craig smiled, pleased that he had taken on the aura of a wealthy businessman.

"I need your help," Craig said.

"Anything for you."

"Betty Richards sucked me back in for a special assignment. I'm on my way to Argentina."

Tim's eyes sparkled with intensity. "Trying to penetrate Estrada's organization."

Craig pulled back in surprise. "How'd you get there so fast?"

"I do work for a multinational pharma company with a large plant outside of Buenos Aires. They're afraid they might be nationalized if Estrada takes over the government."

"Does that pose a conflict for you? Working with me."

Tim shrugged. "I doubt it. Ms. Richards has to be against Estrada as well. Too much instability if he takes over the government. Besides, we build Chinese walls all the time. No other client will ever know what I learn for you."

Craig was satisfied. "I want you for a limited assignment. For now. It may grow later."

"Tell me about it, pal."

Craig reached into his briefcase, pulled out the picture of Gina and Bryce at the restaurant that Betty had given him and put it on the table.

"Who's the beauty with Edward Bryce?"

"Gina Galindo. A journalist with *La Nación*, a BA daily. I want you to find out where she lives. Then plant a bug on her phone and in the bedroom. Tape every word that both bugs yield. Do transcripts. I'll let you know where and when to deliver them to me."

"Is this all business, pal? Or are you trying to make the broad?"

"Whatever gave you that idea?"

"Come on. Give me a break. When we were at the Farm, women threw themselves at you. Other trainees, waitresses, even an instructor—what the hell was her name?—it didn't matter. Every night my biggest goal in life was to get laid. Yours was to get a good night's sleep and rest your dick."

Craig laughed. "So how are you doing now?"

"I got married last year. I'm still trying to figure out how to get laid every night. Although I have to admit that having money sure helps with women in this town."

"Can we be serious?"

"I was. Painfully so."

"Do you want the job I'm offering?"

Tim pulled back and fiddled with a diamond-studded cufflink. Deep furrows appeared on his forehead as he pondered the request. Craig knew what he was thinking. Tim was probably at the point now where he made a good living operating within the law. Why jeopardize it?

Craig reached into his briefcase and pulled out a brown envelope. "A hundred K in cash. All hundreds. Old bills. Serial numbers are all over the place. They can't be traced."

Craig pushed the envelope across the table. Tim didn't reach for it, but tapped his fingers on the marble top. Craig's guess was that Tim would never pay taxes on the money. He'd plunk it down on a second home or a boat he'd been eyeing. In Washington, everyone had his price.

"How long do you want me to do this?" Tim asked.

"Two weeks max. Probably less."

"If I get caught, will Madame CIA Director step in and tell the FBI or local police to back off?"

"Don't get caught."

"I'm not planning to, but that's not the question."

Craig sighed deeply. This was a tough one. He didn't dare tell Betty what he was doing. She'd have a cow in view of her deal with the FBI not to do domestic surveillance. "I'll do my best to get her help after the fact. That's the most I can promise."

"That's not very much. If Bryce finds out somebody's been listening to him banging his girlfriend and the pillow talk afterwards, he'll throw a shit fit. Probably mobilize the president to make sure DOJ tosses the book at me."

Craig held out his hands, palms up. "Sorry. That's the best I can do."

"I'll have to think about it, pal."

Craig decided to ratchet up the pressure. "We don't have time for that. You're my first choice, but I have three other names on my list."

It was a total bluff. Craig had no other choices if Tim turned him down.

Craig glanced at the sweep second hand on his Franck Mueller watch. When thirty seconds had passed and Tim was still squirming in his chair, trying to decide, Craig changed the deal in order to sway him.

"We'll cut back your role. You get me the bugs, and I'll plant them. You'll still have to do the rest. And you arrange a car and driver for me for the next couple of days in Washington."

That was enough to do the trick.

"I'm in," Tim said. He walked over to his desk and picked up a business card he handed to Craig. Then he made arrangements for the car and driver. "Vince will be here in half an hour. Here are all my numbers. How do I get to you?"

Craig reached into his jacket pocket and extracted a Barry Gorman business card. He added another phone number with a 415 area code.

"It's my cell phone," he said, handing it to Tim. "I'll keep it on twenty-four hours a day."

Tim studied the card. "Barry Gorman, The Philoctetes Group, San Fran. Sounds like a money man."

"That's what I am. I manage a ten billion dollar private equity fund. We're investing in Argentina. We're open to investors with $100K minimum." Craig smiled and reached across for the envelope. "You want to make a killing? I can give you one share for what you've got there."

Tim broke into a laugh. "Keep your fuckin' hands off my money. I might need it for bail by the time I finish your job."

*   *   *

Craig was alone in the back seat of the dark blue Cadillac sedan. Tim's driver, Vince, was behind the wheel, heading north on Connecticut Avenue past small, trendy restaurants and cafés. The Argentine Embassy was on New Hampshire Avenue, one block east of DuPont circle. A light rain had begun to fall.

As they drove around the circle, Craig looked out of the car window and admired the memorial fountain in the center created by Daniel Chester French, the sculptor of the Lincoln Memorial, and commemorated to Admiral DuPont, a union Naval officer in the Civil War. Even on a grim day this is a beautiful city, he thought, laid out with a real plan and chock-full of statues, parks, and memorials.

Craig waited until Vince came around to open the back door with an umbrella in hand before climbing out. He had to behave like a powerful financial figure. He glanced up at the stately, tan, four-story brick building with the Argentine flag flying above the entrance, with its blue and white stripes and a gold sun in the center.

As he approached the black wrought-iron gate in front, a member of the US diplomatic protection force stopped him to see ID. "I have an appointment with Jorge Suarez, the economic attaché," Craig said. That and a California driver's license were enough to get Craig up the stairs and through the heavy wood and glass door where he repeated his words to the receptionist sitting behind a bulletproof glass window just inside the front door. Two armed soldiers standing in the reception area eyed him suspiciously.

"Your name?" the receptionist said into a microphone.

"Barry Gorman."

He slid a passport and one of his business cards through the opening beneath the heavy plate glass.

After perusing the items, she picked up the phone. Craig couldn't hear what she was saying. When she hung up, she activated the microphone. "Mr. Suarez is expecting you."

A smartly dressed young woman with a noticeably lovely figure identified herself as Suarez's assistant and escorted him via an elevator to the top floor where the economic attaché, a tall, thin, gaunt, gray-haired man, was waiting in his office. Craig had pulled up his bio on the Internet. Suarez wasn't a career diplomat. This was his first post abroad. He was here because of his contacts. Suarez's father was a large landowner, winemaker, and cattle baron. Jorge himself was a prominent figure in banking. Craig's guess was that he was well connected with the top business interests in the country and that he was closely tied in to Estrada. That's what he was hoping. Craig wanted Suarez to file a report on their visit—one that would find its way back to BA and perhaps even to General Estrada.

Preferring the element of surprise, Craig had provided very little information about what he wanted when he had called Suarez's assistant to arrange the meeting. All he had said was, "My private equity fund is considering a substantial investment in Argentina." That was enough for her to return to the phone and to offer Craig any time today he wanted.

Admitted to the inner sanctum, Craig sat down across a round wooden table from Suarez and waited for the secretary to deposit two cups of espresso, then depart.

He slipped another business card out of his pocket, handed it to Suarez, and watched his host do the same.

"I'm sure you've heard of the Philoctetes Group," Craig said.

Craig knew he couldn't possibly because the Group didn't exist. Suarez nodded eagerly. The economic attaché wouldn't want to display his ignorance.

Craig glanced at his watch anxiously. His message was subtle but clear: I'm an important man. My time is limited.

"Let me get right to the point, Mr. Suarez . . ."

"Please, you can call me Jorge."

"Jorge . . . I currently have a fund of ten billion dollars raised from wealthy individuals and companies around the world. These are people seeking a good return on their money. I'm focusing on Latin America because I see that as a relatively untapped market."

Suarez sat up ramrod straight in his chair. Craig had his attention.

Speaking rapidly, Craig continued, "One of my research people thinks Argentina merits a careful look. Frankly, I laughed at her when she said it, but she's never been wrong yet. So I decided to schedule a trip to Buenos Aires and have a look for myself. Before going down, I figured I'd stop in Washington and talk to you. Maybe you can give me a name or two I can start with in BA."

Suarez was bubbling over with enthusiasm. "That's an excellent idea. Emilio Miranda is the man you should talk to. He's the head of the National Business Alliance. My assistant will give you his phone number before you leave. I'll e-mail him and let him know you're coming."

"Don't raise his expectations too high. From everything I've read in the last couple of days, your economic recovery is stalled. Chile may be a much better place for me to invest."

Suarez frowned. "The economic numbers coming out of Santiago are phony. Made up out of whole cloth. I'm sure an intelligent man like you will realize that when you have an opportunity to study them carefully."

"In Argentina, your political system is killing the economy. Let's face it. Menem was corrupt and a playboy. But at least when he was president in the nineties, the country was booming. His privatization program stimulated the economy. Garcia is one more in a series of disasters you've had in that office."

"We have an election in January. That could . . ."

Craig scowled. "Another political hack with promises of pie in the sky won't make a difference. Unless the Argentine government is run in a radically different manner, you'll never achieve your economic potential. It's as simple as that. You need someone like General Estrada to take charge. Somebody who can get things done. Bring stability. Stop catering to the unions. Make the trains run on time . . . so to speak."

Suarez leaned back and studied Craig's face. Be careful, Craig cautioned himself. Don't overplay your hand.

"We have a democratic government with civilian rule," Suarez said defensively. "The military coup is a thing of the past."

Yeah right, Craig thought. You've had one every thirty or so years since becoming independent. Craig had no intention of being more candid than Suarez was being.

"I wasn't suggesting otherwise. Perhaps Estrada can become a candidate. We've elected generals in the United States as president. From Washington to Eisenhower."

"Perhaps . . ." Suarez said weakly. His lack of conviction confirmed what Craig had deduced: bitter recollections of the Dirty War in the last rule of the generals from 1976 to 1983 were still too vivid. Argentines would be reluctant to vote for a military man.

Having planted his seed about Estrada and his interest in the general, Craig decided to move on. "One other thing I want to do in Washington before I leave for Buenos Aires is to meet with an Argentine journalist."

Suarez looked puzzled. "For what reason?"

"It'll give me another perspective. Also . . ." Craig paused. "No offense intended, but journalists have independence from the government that you don't. Do you know which BA newspapers have someone stationed in Washington?"

"There are two of them. Gina Galindo from *La Nación* and Juan Leonardo from *La Opinion*."

"You have contact info for them?"

"They both have offices in the National Press Building. My secretary will give you their contact information on your way out."

Craig rose. "I have another appointment across town."

"When will you be flying to Buenos Aires? I can have someone meet you."

"That won't be necessary. I have a private plane on standby. My pilot will arrange ground transportation from the air."

Northern Argentina

General Estrada was with Colonel Schiller at a base in the northern part of the country inspecting troop readiness when his cell phone rang.

He saw it was Jorge Suarez in Washington. With the phone at his ear, Estrada moved away from the officers to an open area in the field. "Yes, Jorge," he said.

"Something occurred today that I thought you would want to know about."

"What's that?"

"I hate to bother you, but you said to err on the side of calling if anything . . ."

"For God's sake, Jorge, tell me already," Estrada said irritably. "I'm a busy man."

"I know. That's why I hesitated."

"Dammit, tell me now."

"I've just had a visit from an American, Barry Gorman, who runs a private equity fund. The Philoctetes Group. A big outfit based in San Francisco. He has ten billion dollars to invest and he wants to look at Argentina."

"You think he's legit?"

"Absolutely. Before I called you, I checked out his organization. It is authentic."

Estrada felt a surge of excitement. He thought about his recent meeting with Dr. Barker from England and the diamond discovery the British expert had made, not far from where Estrada was standing now. From Barker's report, Estrada realized that he needed money, lots of money, to get his hands on those diamonds. Barry Gorman could be the answer to Estrada's prayers.

"I hope you told him to come down here and see things for himself."

"Absolutely. I gave him Emilio Miranda's contact info, and I'll e-mail Emilio as soon as I get off the call with you."

"When will Gorman be in Argentina?"

"I don't know exactly, but soon."

"Good. Stay in contact with him. Anything else?"

Jorge coughed and cleared his throat. Estrada sensed there was something else. That Jorge was hesitating. "Tell me," Estrada demanded.

"Gorman said he was concerned about the political situation in the country. He wants to talk with a journalist in Washington to gain an independent perspective before he flies down."

"What did you tell him?"

"I gave him names and contact info for Gina Galindo and Juan Leonardo. I hope that was okay."

Estrada scowled. Jorge should only have given him Gina's name. Juan Leonardo wasn't one of Estrada's supporters. Jorge should have realized that. "Did he say who he'll call?"

"Barry Gorman's a healthy looking man in his forties." Jorge gave a short laugh. "I know who I'd call."

Estrada hung up with Suarez and called Gina. "You may be getting a call from an American financier by the name of Barry Gorman. He has a significant amount of money to invest in Argentina. I need you to be nice to him and give him positive information about Argentina."

"Of course. Don't worry."

He was confident in Gina. She loved her country, and she always did what he told her. "Oh, and if you talk to him, call and tell me what he said."

"I'll do that."

Estrada pulled Colonel Schiller away from a group of officers. "We may have caught a break," Estrada said in an excited voice. "The solution to our money problem."

Estrada relayed to Schiller what Suarez had told him. To Estrada's surprise, Schiller didn't share his enthusiasm. In fact, quite the opposite. As Estrada spoke, he noticed a cloud of suspicion and doubt descending over Schiller's face.

"What's bothering you?" Estrada said.

"We don't know anything about Barry Gorman or the Philoctetes Group."

"Jorge said they're legit."

"Jorge is naive and can be a fool."

Estrada was taken aback. "What do you mean?"

"First, the American in Bariloche. Now this."

"Why do you believe they're related?"

"If red comes up twenty straight times on a roulette wheel, would you say coincidence or a crooked wheel?"

"For twenty you would be right. Certainly not two."

Schiller was frowning. "We can't let the money blind us."

"Don't worry, I'm not."

"When this Barry Gorman comes to Argentina, I'll be waiting for him. I'll find out whether he's what he says he is."

Estrada was tired of Schiller's constant negative thinking. The colonel had even argued against Dr. Barker's diamond discovery. Estrada had enough of it. He raised his right arm. "Don't do anything to jeopardize my shot at that ten billion dollars . . ."

Washington

Craig waited until four in the afternoon to call Gina. When she said, "Hello, Mr. Gorman," she sounded as if she knew who he was and had been expecting the call. Suarez must have tipped her off, he decided. Or maybe Suarez called Estrada, who gave Gina the heads-up.

"Jorge Suarez gave me your name," Craig said. "I assume he called to tell you that."

There was an awkward pause. Gina coughed.

"I'd like to meet with you this evening. Any chance we can talk over dinner?"

"I have other plans for this evening. Perhaps tomorrow morning."

"That's too bad. My schedule's tight. This evening's the only opening I have."

Another awkward pause. "Then I'll be happy to rearrange my appointments."

He hoped she would be breaking a date with Bryce. "Good. I'll reserve a table for two at Marcel's on Pennsylvania at eight. I'll send a car and driver around to get you. Tell me when and where."

"My apartment at the Watergate East, 2500 Virginia Avenue, at seven forty-five."

"He'll be there. I'll meet you at the restaurant."

Craig smiled. Amazing what you can do with a ten billion dollar checkbook.

*   *   *

Craig was seated at a corner table in Marcel's facing the front with a side view of Chef Robert Wiedmaier in the open kitchen. He spotted Gina, following the tuxedo-clad maître d'. She was wearing a simple high-necked black sheath. Over her shoulders, she had a print Hermes scarf. A small gold cross dangled from a chain and stopped inches below her full bosom, which the sheath failed to hide. Its simplicity was a stark contrast to the heavy ruby and diamond bracelet on her wrist and her square cut emerald ring. In high stiletto heels, she was about five foot ten.

Her hair was black, worn the same as he had seen in the picture, parted in the middle. None of that surprised Craig. What did astonish him when she approached the table was her face and expression.

He saw a sweet young woman with an aura of class. She carried herself with dignity. What struck him most was the innocence and naïveté he saw in those sparkling dark brown eyes and the fresh-faced school-girl expression that marked her features with sincerity.

Craig cautioned himself to proceed carefully. Appearances could be deceptive.

When she introduced herself, she shook hands with him firmly, as if someone had told her that's what a reporter did when she was out on a business dinner, rather than having the man kiss the woman's cheeks.

After she was seated across from him, Craig pointed to a bottle of Krug he had ordered resting in an ice bucket. "Champagne to start?" he asked.

She nodded "Yes. Thank you."

He signaled to a waiter who came over and poured for both of them. Then he raised his glass and said, "To making new friends." She took a tiny sip and smiled warmly. "This is very good."

"What did Jorge tell you?"

"That you have a lot of money to invest. Perhaps in Argentina. That you want to learn something about what's happening in our country now."

"That pretty well sums it up. To be more precise, I have control of ten billion dollars."

She looked shocked. "That much?"

He nodded. "Before I go to Argentina, I want to pick your brain a little."

"Why mine?" There was a suspicious edge in her voice.

She may be smart, he thought. Don't underestimate her. "Well, I figure that journalists know everything. Jorge gave me the names of two Argentine reporters. Yours and . . ."

"Juan Leonardo."

"Yeah. And that was no choice."

"What do you mean?"

"I'd rather have dinner with a woman any day of the week. I never dreamt she'd be so beautiful."

Gina blushed. She pointed to his face. "Were you in an accident?"

"The motorcycle didn't turn the way I wanted it to."

"I never rode on one of those."

"Would you like to?"

"Sure. I like to try new things."

They both sipped the champagne.

A waiter approached with two menus. "Let's order first," Craig said. "Then we can talk."

She closed her menu and looked across the table at him. "You've obviously traveled and eaten at great restaurants, but I haven't. You order for me."

Was she for real, or was this all an act, he wondered. Gee, I'm just a simple girl from a third world country. Regardless, he'd play along. "Do you like fish or meat?"

"Meat please. I'm from Argentina," she smiled.

He ordered them both seared foie gras followed by roast venison and a bottle of 2005 Echezeaux from Mongeard Mugneret.

"Before we talk about Argentina," he said, "tell me a little about yourself. How'd you end up being a journalist in Washington?"

Her eyes looked sad. "There's not much to tell. My parents both died when I was young. My grandparents, who have a cattle ranch, sent me to a Catholic girls' boarding school in the countryside outside of Mendoza. After I graduated from university in Buenos Aires, I wanted to come to the United States and get a job, but my grandparents insisted that I go back to the girls' school in Mendoza to teach history. It's a wonderful, beautiful place. Peaceful and tranquil." She took a deep breath. "My father had been a famous general in the army."

Her whole face lit up with pride when she mentioned her father. "He was a great man. A hero of the Republic. A young officer who had served under my father and had revered him took an interest in me like a surrogate father. One day he told me that he had arranged a job at *La Nación* in Buenos Aires. He convinced my grandparents to let me take it."

Craig was dying to ask if the officer was Estrada, but he decided to take it slowly, not wanting to arouse her suspicions.

"So I worked for the newspaper in Buenos Aires for about three months. In June they transferred me up here."

And was that Estrada's doing as well? he wondered. "Do you like Washington?"

She fiddled with her hands. Her nails had been freshly manicured. "It's a totally different world from the school in Mendoza. And not at all like Buenos Aires. I do a lot of exciting things here. Things I never imagined."

He was tempted to ask, "With Edward Bryce?" but he bit his lip and kept his silence.

"I view it as an adventure," she added. "As long as it lasts, I'll enjoy it."

She smoothed down the tablecloth with her hand. The sommelier arrived with the wine. Their first courses followed a moment later.

After Craig tasted the Burgundy, he told her to try it.

"This is really lovely," she said with exuberance. "Is it French also?"

He nodded, waiting for her to taste the foie gras.

"Fabulous," she said.

Now, beginning to believe that her enthusiasm might be genuine, he smiled.

"I've never been to Argentina. Tell me about it."

His request launched her into a description of how beautiful and exciting Buenos Aires was. She spoke for several minutes with passion about her wonderful country and its capital city. As she spoke, she took generous sips of the wine. He could tell she was enjoying herself.

"Buenos Aires sounds like Milan," he said. "The wide boulevards and all that."

"You're right. That's what all the books say. I've never been to Europe, but I've always wanted to go. And the Andes mountains in the west are magnificent. We have beaches in the east and the greatest waterfall in the world at Iguazu in the north on the Brazilian border."

"Better than Niagara and Victoria Falls?"

Earnestly, she nodded. "I've never seen those, but from what I've read, it's not even close. When you go to Argentina, you have to travel to Iguazu and decide for yourself."

He laughed. She was a refreshing change from the hardboiled cynics he was used to dealing with.

"When exactly are you going to Argentina?" she asked.

He shrugged. "Next couple of days."

"I find that American Airlines via Miami is the best way to go."

Craig smiled. "I have a private plane on standby."

His words made her start. Perhaps she couldn't imagine having enough money to do that.

By now their venison had arrived. As the waiter placed it on the table, a cell phone rang in her purse. "Darn. I always forget to turn that thing off."

Other patrons were staring at her. "Oh I'm so sorry," she said, fumbling to pull it out and stop the noise. "I'll tell them I'll call back. I won't talk."

He watched her as she held the phone up to her ear. She listened for a minute, then whispered, "No, Edward, I can't see you tonight. I'm sorry . . . I told you I'm working on a story."

She hung up and turned off the phone. "It's gone for the rest of the night."

That had to be Bryce, Craig decided. "Hope I didn't keep you from your boyfriend."

Her face reddened. "No, no. Just an acquaintance. I'm not married, and I don't have a boyfriend."

Alright, Craig thought. That's a clear signal she likes me. A green light if there ever was one.

But a green light for what?

Craig had made up his mind that he couldn't possibly sleep with Gina. It wasn't merely her age and immaturity, but the fact that he was deceiving her. He had to achieve his objective of planting those bugs in her apartment without ending up in bed with her.

"What about you?" she asked.

"Me for what?"

"Are you married?

He recalled the fictitious Barry Gorman bio. Barry had been married once and divorced. Had to stick with the cover.

"I was married for a couple of years," he said. "It didn't work out."

"Any children?"

"Happily not."

She smiled at him. That genuine smile. "Jorge said you live in California."

"The San Francisco area."

"I've never been to California. I'd like to go."

Craig brought the subject back to Argentina. For the rest of dinner, he let her rattle on about how great the country was and how it made sense for him to invest. All of this chatter made him wonder whether she was following a script given to her by Suarez or Estrada.

With dessert, Craig ordered a half bottle of Sauterne. She put up a mild protest. "Oh my. I'm not sure I can drink more wine. I'm not used to drinking so much."

"Wait until you taste this Chateau d'Yquem," he told her. "It's called the nectar of the Gods. There's nothing like it in the world."

By the time she had sipped a little, she was agreeing with him completely.

While Craig signed the check, she finished the golden liquid in her glass.

"My driver's waiting outside," he said. "I'll give you a ride home."

"That would be great."

As they left the dining room, she was wobbling and reached out for his arm for support. "Oh my, I've had a lot to drink," she said.

"You'll be fine when you hit the air."

Ten minutes later, the blue Cadillac ground to a stop in front of the Watergate building. She said, "This has been the best business dinner I've ever had. The best evening."

He rested his hand on her shoulder. "It doesn't have to be over quite yet. I'd love to see the view from your apartment. I'll bet you face the river."

"I do," she said. "I'm on the top floor. And I have a balcony. You want to come up?"

He smiled. "If you're not too tired."

In the glow of the streetlights, she nodded her head. "I'm from Argentina. We're night people."

*   *   *

Her apartment was a huge two-bedroom. Craig knew that she didn't get this on a journalist's salary, and newspapers didn't fund expenses lavishly. That meant somebody was bankrolling her. He doubted it was grandma and grandpa. A more likely guess was Bryce or Estrada. Was she really the sweet innocent she seemed to be? Or was this all a great snow job on her part?

"The apartment is a sublease," Gina said, as she took off her bracelet, "so don't think this type of furniture is my taste."

Looking around, he saw why she made the comment. The furnishings were starkly modern. All done in whites. White carpet. White sofa and chairs. Glass topped coffee table.

"I like Italian provincial furniture," she said.

As she opened the sliding glass doors that led to the balcony, she said, "Fabulous view from up here." Craig followed her outside. The clouds from earlier in the day had passed. It was crystal clear with a sky full of stars shining over the Potomac River. He pointed his hand to the right. "Georgetown."

Shivering from the cold, she moved up close to him, putting an arm around his shoulder.

Craig pulled away and said, "I've got a great idea."

"Whatever it is, I hope we can do it inside."

"Of course."

Back in the living room he told her, "I love to tango. Do you have any music?"

"Of course. I may have been stuck in that girls' school all those years, but I still picked up something of sin."

"I didn't know tango was sinful."

"It depends on how you do it," she said laughing. "Although I don't think the sisters would have approved of any style."

While she put on the music, Craig removed his jacket. He began hesitantly, uncertain how good she was. Once he felt her responding intuitively to his face and his body, not his feet, he realized that he had a facile partner.

Gracefully, he followed the rhythm, leading her through the erotic, undulating thrusts and motions of the tango, and as he pulled her in tight against him, their bodies fused at the hips and torso and their legs dovetailed. The tango was in her blood. She was a natural for it, full-busted and well-proportioned in her hips and rear, and knew perfectly well how to move her body in time with the music.

To Craig the tango, the most sensuous of all dances, was like making love on your feet. "Vertical expression of a horizontal desire," he remembered Angela Rippon had described it. "Sensual coupling, forged by raw emotion. Sexy and synchronized. Salacious and sultry. The dance of desire. The dance of lust."

Around and around the white-carpeted floor they glided, their bodies colliding, molding together as one, then pushing apart. She was anticipating his every move, sliding her body against his, then moving with him.

Perspiration dotted their foreheads, but still they danced, until finally she stopped, pulled away, and stood still, her face flushed.

"I'm a little tipsy . . . not used to drinking so much," she mumbled. "The whole room's spinning. I better lie down for a minute. To get a second wind."

He led her into the bedroom and helped her onto the bed. Fully dressed, she was on her back. He removed her shoes and looked at her face. Her eyes were closed. She was sound asleep.

Moving quietly, he went back into the living room and put on his jacket. From the pocket, he removed the two bugs Tim had given him. His guess was that of the three phones in the apartment, she probably used the one in the bedroom the most. He could see well enough with the light shining in from the living room to unscrew the hearing portion of the handset on the pink phone next to the bed and install the bug. The other one could go anywhere in the apartment, but if Bryce was doing her here, then the bedroom was the place for it. He surveyed the room in the dim light and settled on a white wooden night table next to the bed. A lamp sat on top. He pulled the sticky strip off the listening device and slipped it under the top shelf of the table. He fastened it to the center of the wood, where it wouldn't be spotted.

Then he took one of the Barry Gorman business cards out of his pocket. On the front, he added his cell phone number. On the back he scribbled, "Had a great time tonight. Can't wait to see you again. I'll call on the way back from Argentina."

He left the card in the center of the desk in the bedroom.

Before leaving the apartment, he took one more glance at her. He was now convinced that her innocence was genuine. Gina was out of her league, playing a dangerous game with Bryce and General Estrada.

*   *   *

Early the next morning, Craig called Alice Dunn from the hotel. She was expecting him.

As he walked through the door of the McLean two-floor colonial, the woman who greeted him was a shell of the woman he had last seen in Paris. Her eyes were bloodshot. Her long brown hair was scraggly. She had lost twenty pounds, he guessed, and she had only been about 120 to start.

She hugged him and began crying. His insides were ripping apart with sympathy.

She pulled away. "Thanks for coming, Craig. You want something to drink?"

He saw several half empty coffee cups scattered around the living room. Half a dozen ashtrays filled with cigarette butts. She had quit ten years ago.

"Just some water. Thanks."

She brought him a glass from the kitchen. He sat down across a coffee table filled with cups and ashtrays.

"What'd Betty tell you about Teddy?" she asked.

"How she recruited him. How . . ."

"She's a parasite. A bloodsucker. They all are in Langley. He gave so much to those people for so long and they wouldn't let him enjoy the years of peace that he deserved. She refused to tell me where she sent him."

He had to give Alice the truth. "Argentina."

"Thanks for telling me. He never worked there. Only in Chile and Colombia"

"That's why she picked him."

"What did she tell you about his situation down there?"

"That he sent back valuable information. That he was almost finished. Then she stopped hearing from him. A complete blackout. He's 'gone missing' Betty told me."

"You think she's telling the truth?"

Craig nodded. "I do. What do you think?"

"That somebody kidnapped him. They're demanding a ransom and she's refusing to pay."

"Has anyone contacted you?"

She shook her head.

"I don't think it's that," Craig said. "Rather, somebody is holding him as a bargaining chip to play later. Or he's . . ."

"Dead," she completed the sentence for Craig, closed her eyes, and ran her hand roughly through her hair.

"I'm going to Argentina to find out what happened to him. And hopefully bring him back."

"I asked her to give you that job. Did she tell you that?"

He nodded.

"Do you hate me for doing that?"

"Of course not. You and Ted have been my friends for so many years. I'd do anything for the two of you."

She rolled her small hands into fists. "Thank you, Craig."

"In the meantime, is there anything I can do to help you? Financial or anything else?"

"With the money Betty paid Ted, I'm fine. All I care about is getting him back."

He finished his water and stood up.

She walked him to the door. As she opened it, she spoke in a hoarse whisper. "Please, Craig. Don't leave him in some hellhole to die. Find him and bring him home."

Her words cut through Craig like a machete. "Please . . . I'm begging you . . ."

*　　*　　*

From the Dunn's house, Craig told Vince to drive him back to Tim Fuller's office on K Street.

Tim was waiting for Craig in the reception area. "State of the art technology's incredible," Tim told Craig. "Let me show you."

Craig followed Tim to a room marked "Sound Lab" in Tim's suite of offices. A technician, wearing a set of earphones, was watching wheels turn behind glass on a console resting on a large table. A printer was spitting out a transcript.

"We have a voice recognition system," Tim said. "Everything the bugs pick up is fed to a computer that prepares a written transcript. If anything critical is ever garbled in the typing, we can go back to the oral."

Craig glanced at the white clock with the black hands on the wall. It was five minutes after two in the afternoon, almost fifteen hours since he had planted the bugs and left Gina. "Any useful information yet?"

Tim grinned broadly, showing teeth stained with nicotine from cigars.

"Depends on what you consider useful," Tim said with a lascivious grin.

"What the hell's that supposed to mean?"

"Same old Craig. When our subject woke up at 9:24 this morning, the first words out of her mouth were, 'Oh, I can't believe I did that with him.'"

Craig blushed. "Who'd she say that to?"

"Herself, I think. Nobody responded. What exactly did she do with you?"

Craig dismissed the question with a wave of his hand. "Tell me what else you picked up."

Tim handed him three bound volumes of transcripts and pointed to an empty office. "Go read them for yourself, pal."

As Craig sat down at the desk and opened the first volume, he hoped there wouldn't be a call from Gina to Estrada. She was immature, little more than a schoolgirl in some ways. But he liked her. He didn't want her to be the general's pawn in Washington. The first transcript came from the telephone bug and was made at 9:50 a.m., less than half an hour after she woke up. An outgoing call from Gina to Rosie.

As he read, he realized Rosie was a good friend of hers back in Argentina.

Gina described Craig as suave and debonair. She then told Rosie in detail everything she and Craig had done. At the end, Rosie said, "I can't believe you fell asleep. He would have been great in bed."

"I'm not worried. I'll see him again."

"Well, you better be careful, Gina. These are much older men you're involved with."

The second transcript was a call Bryce had made to Gina. As he suspected, she had canceled her date with Bryce last evening to go out with him and Bryce was furious about that, forcing her to apologize repeatedly. Craig learned from the transcript that Bryce would be taking her to the White House that evening to a party with the president and then to see a movie. Bryce was turning 1600 Pennsylvania Avenue into a bordello. She had to be doing this for Estrada. He bristled thinking about her in bed with Bryce. She couldn't possibly like that old fart.

These two transcripts were interesting, but no smoking guns. Then he picked up the third one. Bull's-eye. General Estrada calling her at 11:02 that morning.

Estrada: Did Barry Gorman call you?

Gina: Yes. Yesterday afternoon.

Estrada: Why didn't you call me. I told you to call me.

[A pause.]

Gina: Well, nothing much happened.

Estrada: What did he say?

Gina: That he was planning a trip to Argentina to consider making some investments. He wanted to know whether this was a good time.

Estrada: What did you say?

Gina: It's an excellent time. Our economy is starting to rebound.

Estrada: What else?

Gina: That was pretty much it.

Estrada: Didn't he want to see you?

Gina: No. he sounded very busy getting ready for his trip to Argentina.

Estrada: Okay. Now what about the surface-to-air missiles and rocket grenade launchers Bryce promised they would ship? When will we receive them?

Gina: I don't know.

Estrada: Well, ask Bryce. I need them.

Gina: I'll do that. I promise.

Estrada: And call me with the answer soon. This is important. Do you understand?

Gina: As soon as I can.

Craig nearly felt ill when he finished the transcript. Estrada had used Gina to put her in this position with Bryce. Estrada was despicable.

Why hadn't she told Estrada she had been with him last evening? Shame for what they had done and how she behaved?

Was she afraid it took away from Estrada's primary mission for her—the one of sleeping with Bryce to receive the weapons he needed?

She could have told Estrada they had dinner. Maybe she wasn't a good enough liar and afraid Estrada would have forced the rest out of her.

Craig closed up the transcript and thought about calling or seeing Betty to give her a report of what he had learned so far before he left for Buenos Aires. Quickly, he rejected the idea. The money and guns he needed from her were already locked in the vault at the Four Seasons. He didn't want to risk blowing his cover.

Time to go to Buenos Aires, he decided. He placed a call to Wilmington, North Carolina, where a private charter company maintained a fleet of jets. "We'll meet you at Dulles Airport in two hours," the dispatcher said.

*   *   *

Craig finished packing and was about to leave his room at the Four Seasons when the phone rang. It was Jorge Suarez.

"When are you flying to Buenos Aires?"

"In a couple of hours."

"Excellent." Suarez coughed and cleared his throat. "There's one suggestion I forgot to make yesterday."

"What's that?"

"Occasionally, but not often, Americans have been robbed or kidnapped for ransom. We're a peaceful nation, but in these difficult economic times some people do crazy things."

"I'm well aware of that. But thanks for reminding me."

"What I wanted to suggest is that you have an armed bodyguard with you at all times. I can arrange that. At the government's expense, of course. After all, you are a valued visitor. We'd hate to have anything happen to you."

And lose my ten billion dollars, Craig thought. He smiled to himself. Suarez was smart. Or Estrada. Whoever thought of this. What a great way for them to keep track of him.

"The offer's appreciated," Craig replied politely. "I've been in some pretty rough places in the world. I find that bodyguards draw attention to a man and increase the risk. I can take care of myself."

As Craig put down the phone, he was glad Suarez had called. Now he knew that Estrada would find another way to keep tabs on him. He had to watch his six o'clock from the minute he stepped off the plane in Buenos Aires.

Buenos Aires

An hour out of BA, Craig asked the pilot to call Ezeiza Airport and arrange a car and driver to take him to the Alvear Hotel. Waiting for him when he cleared customs was a tall, well-conditioned man, standing erect like a military officer in a civilian suit with a light brown crew cut.

"Mr. Gorman, I'm Peppone, your driver," the man said.

Craig resisted the urge to salute as Peppone turned and headed toward his Mercedes sedan parked at the curb. Though it was seven in the morning, Craig was rested and energized. The private jet had a bed and he had slept well.

On the way into the city, Peppone asked, "Is this your first visit to Argentina?"

"Sure is, and I've been looking forward to it."

"Perhaps I can remain with you as your driver for your stay. Take you for sightseeing. Deliver you to meetings. Whatever you need."

Craig had learned long ago that attaching a driver to a foreign visitor was a good way to keep track of the visitor. Suarez had offered Craig an armed bodyguard but he had refused. It was possible that Estrada or one of his people had learned about Craig's request for a car and driver and inserted their man, Peppone. Craig would have to be careful with the driver, but he might be able to use him as an advantage.

"That's a nice offer. I like sightseeing alone on foot with a guidebook, but I may need a driver to go to meetings. Give me your cell phone number."

Peppone passed him a card.

"I'll give you as much notice as possible. Don't worry if you're busy."

Peppone laughed. "These days, I'm never busy. Until the weather gets warmer, we don't have many tourists."

"Do you drive for a company, or is this your own business?"

"The company I worked for went bankrupt last year. I'm on my own now. I have a wife and three kids to feed."

The driver's words pleased Craig. At the right point, for enough money, he might be able to turn Peppone.

Determined to play tour guide, Peppone continued, "There are almost forty million people in Argentina, but more than a third live in Buenos Aires, where the residents are called porteños because of the port in this city. We have over three hundred theatres in Buenos Aires, more than a hundred art galleries, at least seventy museums, and hundreds of bookstores. How many other cities in the world can say that?" he added with pride. "And the city never sleeps." He began discussing all-night movie theaters and restaurants.

Craig tuned him out. He already knew the basic facts about the city from guidebooks. With his photographic memory, he now had a street map in his mind.

The Alvear Palace, the most luxurious hotel in Argentina and all of Latin America, was located in La Recoleta, an elegant residential and shopping district near the center of town. As the Mercedes approached the hotel, Craig looked out of the window at the fashionable boutiques, cafés, and handsome old apartments. They were only a few blocks from Nicole's shoe boutique.

The Mercedes turned into the circular driveway of the stately eight-story building. An armed guard stood on each side of the driveway. The economic depression had brought with it increased crime, Craig had read. Anyone with enough money to stay at the Alvear could be a target.

The hotel manager, a burly, heavyset man with thick lenses in black frame glasses, was waiting for Craig on the other side of the revolving front door in the marble-floored lobby, ready to pounce. A team of four bellmen rushed out to the car. Craig told them to take his suitcases, but he clutched the duffel and briefcase tightly in his hand.

After greeting Craig, the manager, Mario Fernandez, introduced himself and led Craig to a heavily polished wooden desk where he signed the registration card.

"How long will you be staying, Mr. Gorman?" the manager asked.

"Indefinitely. I'm considering some investments."

Fernandez nodded. "Very good, sir. The economic ministry has advised me that they will be taking care of all charges. You'll be staying in the presidential suite. I believe you'll be quite comfortable."

That was one of the great understatements of all time, Craig realized, as the manager led him up to a door marked 801 on the top floor of the hotel. Inside, the suite had a reception hall, a spacious living room with a Steinway baby grand piano, a wood-paneled dining room, a private study, and two bedrooms and baths, both with a Jacuzzi and sauna. All were tastefully decorated. Original paintings and objects d'art were scattered throughout. A butler offered to unpack for Craig. He declined, but gave the man his suits to press. This life as a money man with ten billion to invest had lots of perks.

"Anything we can do to make your stay more comfortable," the manager said, "call me personally. Extension 2500."

First stop for Craig was the room that held safe deposit boxes off the lobby. He placed into a vault box all of the cash except $100K and one of the two guns. The $100K and the Beretta he stashed in the briefcase he was clutching.

In the lobby the manger was waiting with a piece of paper in his hand. "You received a call from Mr. Miranda," he said, pronouncing the man's name with awe. Craig reached for the paper with Miranda's telephone number. Suarez and Estrada were anxious. He'd play hard to get. Besides, he had other things to do right now.

"Would you like me to get Mr. Miranda on the phone?" the manager said.

"No thank you. Today is for sightseeing."

"Can I offer you a car and driver along with a guide?"

"I like being on foot."

Fernandez had a pained expression on his face and in his eyes behind those thick glasses. His assignment must have been to get Craig to Miranda, or at least to keep track of him. The poor man was failing.

The morning sunlight was bright. The day would be unseasonably warm. Craig was dressed in khaki slacks and a light, powder-blue cotton shirt. He wanted to blend in on the street. In one hand he gripped his briefcase tightly. He held his guidebook in the other.

Exiting the hotel, he turned left along Avenue Alvear passing jewelry stores and fashionable boutiques. He was headed for Teatro Colon, the world famous opera house south of the hotel, about a thirty minute walk. It was long enough for Craig to stop from time to time, pretending to window shop, to see whether anyone was following him. After fifteen minutes, he understood the surveillance. He saw two men, not very good at the job. On foot, was a powerfully-built man with black curly hair in a suit and tie. In a gray Ford sedan, trailing behind, was a man wearing sun glasses.

Craig entered the Colon Theater through the door on Tucuman as any tourist might do. Then he headed for the gilt and red velvet auditorium. He raised his eyes skyward to the huge chandelier in the center with a twenty-foot diameter, and the six balconies that went around the perimeter, reminding him of La Scala in Milan. As he expected, the black curly head didn't enter the hall, but peeked through the main front door, prepared to run if Craig raced toward a side door, but he had no intention of doing that. It would have been too easy for them to follow him.

Craig lingered in the lobby for a few minutes to look at pictures of famous performers who had appeared in this hall, including Maria Callas, Arturo Toscanini, and Lucinano Pavarotti. Then he walked out of the front door, raised his hand, and signaled for a cab.

"The intersection of Calle Florida and Avenue Corrientes," he told the driver.

Midmorning traffic on Avenue Corrientes, lined with movie theaters, restaurants, and bookstores, was heavy. Craig exited the cab, turned the corner and began walking down Calle Florida, a pedestrian thoroughfare jammed with shops selling clothes, shoes, leather goods, electronics, toys—every retail item that anyone might want to buy. The street was mobbed with throngs of people.

Craig threw himself into the crowd. Over his shoulder, he glimpsed the man with curly black hair jumping out of the Ford and following. The driver remained in the car. First there were two. Now only one.

Craig walked quickly, making it difficult for his pursuer to keep up in the crowd. Then he went into a men's shop. The curly head remained on the street. Inside, Craig bought a navy blue shirt, sunglasses, and a dark blue baseball cap, which he shoved into his briefcase. When he was back on the street he was carrying an empty plastic bag from the shop.

Black curly hair picked up Craig again and resumed following on the sidewalk. In the next block Craig saw what he was looking for: a good sized café. He entered, sat down at a table where he could be seen from the outside and ordered a cappuccino and a croissant while black curly head remained on the street. Craig put the guidebook on the table, pretending to read it as he studied the layout of the café through the corner of his eye. The toilets were in the rear. He heard a lot of commotion coming from that direction. A beer truck was being unloaded and cases carried into the café.

As soon as the waiter put down the cappuccino and pastry, Craig handed the man some money and asked, "Where is the bathroom?"

The waiter gestured with his hand. Craig left the guidebook and the empty bag from the men's shop on the table and slowly walked toward the bathrooms, briefcase in hand. Anyone watching would be certain he was returning. Once he turned the corner and was out of sight of the front door, he broke into a run toward the rear entrance.

He nearly crashed into a man carrying a case of beer. "Hey, you can't use that door," the man shouted, but Craig was past him. The shop backed up to an alley running between Calle Florida and Maipu. Craig darted among trucks making deliveries to other shops until he found the rear entrance of a tea room, which fronted on Maipu. It was unlocked. He ducked inside. A quick look told him the back was deserted. In an instant, Craig changed shirts, donned the sunglasses and cap and headed toward the front entrance. A gray-haired woman in a pale green waitress uniform was arranging pastries in a glass enclosed case. Startled by Craig, she jumped from fright. "What are you doing in here?"

"I came in from the back."

"We're not open now. I should call the police."

"I didn't realize that," he said politely. "When do you open?"

"Eleven o'clock."

Craig saw that the front door was locked. He couldn't risk her calling the police. "If you'll let me out, I promise to come back at eleven."

Outside, Craig pressed his back against the door of the shop. No sign of black curly hair or the gray Ford. He saw an endless stream of empty black cabs on the street. Craig raised his hand and one ground to a halt. He raced to the curb and jumped in. "Plaza San Martin," he told the driver.

As the cab moved, Craig slipped down on the seat, keeping his eyes just above the rear window line, but he didn't see the gray Ford.

At the Plaza he cut across the grassy park toward the bronze statue in the center. General Jose de San Martin on horseback. Pretending to be a tourist inspecting the statue of the Argentine military leader who commanded the colonial forces in the war against Spain for independence, Craig was in the perfect vantage point to see if he was still being followed. After several minutes he was satisfied that he had gotten rid of his tail.

He left the park and walked around for fifteen minutes, climbing a steep riverbank, up to Avenue Quintana, a distance of eight blocks. Several times he stopped to look into windows and glance over his shoulder. Nobody was following.

From a block away, he saw the sign across the street that read, "Nicole's Shoe Boutique." As he crossed, he looked in the window. Judging from the merchandise and the prices, this was a high-end shop for women. Even in the current economy, some people had money.

Without hesitating, he entered the shop.

"Can I help you?" a woman of an indeterminate age with short brown hair, dressed in a short black skirt and a sheer lavender pullover, asked in a throaty voice. Her eyes were locked on the stranger's face.

He took off the cap and studied her. She was well built with powerful legs that testified to exercise. Her face was good looking, but she had a bit of a tough edge. Her head was cocked as she gave him a wary glance.

"I'm looking for Nicole."

She studied him with deep brown eyes like lasers. "I'm Nicole. Who are you?"

Craig discerned apprehension in her voice, even fear.

He took a deep breath. Betty's information had better be right. If not, he would be blowing his cover before he even began. "Barry Gorman," he said. "And . . ."

He was wavering.

"Well," she said, nervously glancing past him at the door.

"I'm a friend of Ted Dunn's."

Swiftly, she walked over to a staircase and shouted down. "Vicki, come up and handle the store. I have to go downstairs."

Waiting for Vicki to appear, Craig took another look outside. He didn't see the man with black curly hair.

He followed Nicole down a creaky wooden staircase, leading to a storeroom. Rows and rows of wooden shelves were filled with shoeboxes. Two chairs were next to a small table covered with shipping documents and sales slips.

She eyed him nervously. "Who sent you?"

"The same people who sent Dunn. He was supposed to come back and never did. He hasn't even called in. He was my friend. I want to know what happened to him."

She sighed deeply and pointed to a chair. When they were seated across from each other, she said, "I never heard from Dunn again after he went to Bariloche. I assumed he obtained the information he wanted and left the country."

Craig couldn't decide whether to believe this woman. "Why did he go to Bariloche?"

"He had learned that General Estrada was having an important meeting. Some foreign visitors were flying in. Dunn wanted to know who they were."

"How do you know so much about it? What did you have to do with it?" he asked in an accusatory tone that made her head snap back.

She picked up a pack of cigarettes from the table and offered him one. When he declined, she lit up and blew smoke into the air. "Your friend, Dunn, needed a contact in Bariloche. Someone who could help him. I gave him a name."

"Whose?" he pressed.

"You don't know me," she said in a feisty tone. "Why do you imply that I had something to do with Dunn's disappearance?"

"It's precisely because I don't know you that I'm not sure what to believe."

"Then listen. Don't interrogate and accuse."

He pulled back. "Fair enough."

"I gave him the name of Pascual Frigero who lives in Bariloche. He drives for the biggest limo company in the area, but he's also a poet and a musician. He hangs out with a crowd that's opposed to Estrada and the military people."

"Who were the foreign visitors coming to meet Estrada?"

"You're so busy trying to intimidate me that you're not listening. I already told you Dunn didn't know. That was the point of his trip to Bariloche."

Craig had to run out the string with Nicole. At this point, it was all he had. "I'll have to go to Bariloche and find this Pascual. Tell me about him. How old is he?"

Nicole took another puff and inhaled deeply before responding. "Mid-thirties, I think."

"Married?"

"No. Lives with his sister."

"I need a name and address."

Nicole hesitated.

"I'll pay you for it. How much was Dunn paying you?"

She laughed. "You Americans always think money is the only reason people do things."

"For something like this, I've found it usually is."

"Well this time it's not."

Craig was surprised. "By helping Dunn and me, you've put your life on the line. I've read enough about Estrada and his henchman, Colonel Schiller, to know that. If not for money, then why?"

Her face was tight and drawn. She paused to light another cigarette. "You're a smart man, Barry Gorman. My father owns a shoe manufacturing plant, which makes high-end shoes. Even in this economy, a minority live well. We belong to all the best clubs. This shop is a hobby for me."

"Then why are you putting your life on the line?" Craig repeated.

"Do you have any idea what happened in my country in the late seventies and early eighties? The last time the generals ruled?"

"I've read about the Dirty War if that's what you mean?"

Her eyes were blazing with emotion. "You have no idea. You were a schoolboy then. Safe in your cocoon in the United States where nobody gave a damn. Here, it was state-sponsored terrorism. The generals claimed that they were attacking the country's economic problems by eradicating leftist guerillas who were instigators. In fact, they arrested, tortured, or killed thousands and thousands."

She paused and puffed deeply on the cigarette, blowing out the smoke in circles. "Military patrols roamed the country. Day and night they snatched people from their homes and jobs. Not just leftists. Anyone who dared to disagree with them. Union leaders. Women. Especially women. A third of the ones they grabbed were women from all social classes without any link to the guerillas, just so they could get them into prisons and have their way with them." She was talking fast now, her voice choked with emotion. "They even took teenagers who campaigned for better school facilities.

"Los desparecidos, we called the ones they took and we never heard from again. They disappeared. This was total repression. Due process of law was cast aside. Nobody knows how many were taken altogether. The best estimate is that twenty thousand were killed. Most were buried in mass shallow graves." She shrugged. "Many more were tortured. All went without trials."

"I had no idea the repression and deaths were so widespread."

"Of course not," she said bitterly. "Your government did its best to hide the facts. Our generals were an ally in your wars against the leftists in Central America."

She had a glazed look in her eyes as if she was remembering a specific incident. "The military acted arbitrarily and indiscriminately, making the events all the more terrifying. No one knew when they would hear a knock at the door and find a group of soldiers who came to take a family member away. All normal life ceased. Some who could went abroad. Very few had that option for financial and other reasons. So we lived and we suffered.

"A few dared to speak out. Every Thursday evening a group called Mothers of the Plaza de Mayo defied government threats and intimidation by holding weekly silent protest meetings. Each mother stood with a candle, whispering the names of their children who had disappeared."

"After civilian rule was reestablished in the early eighties, how many were tried and punished?" Craig asked.

She sighed and shook her head. "Only a handful were brought to justice. There never was a full accounting. It's disgraceful."

"So that's why you put your life at risk to help Dunn. You don't want the generals to return to power."

"It's much more than that," she said, her face now a mask of hatred. "Estrada is a monster. Even in a group of thugs, he was particularly venal. During the Dirty War, he did things . . ."

"What kind of things?"

She screwed up her face in a terrible grimace. "I don't want to talk about it. The point is that Estrada's not fit to rule my country. And now he's rebuilt the army. He's taking poor boys from destitute families and molding them into a tough, fighting machine. I have a friend in the Ministry of Defense who told me that thanks to the weapons you Americans have shipped here in the last few months, the Argentine military is a match for anybody in South America. They're on a par with Chile, Brazil, and Paraguay, something that seemed inconceivable two years ago. The trouble is that a man like Estrada shouldn't be armed in this way. Am I making myself clear?"

He nodded. Craig found her compelling. He was persuaded by the sincerity of her words. Though he was anxious to hear what Estrada had done in the past, he didn't press her.

She continued in a sharp tone. "It's a formula for disaster for all of us. If I can stop the train wreck from happening, I will."

"What's Estrada want to do? Take over the government?"

"To be sure. But he doesn't merely want to rule Argentina, he wants this to be a country that's an economic power as well. As a result, most business people support him."

"Your father, too?"

She shook her head. "Never. Not after what Estrada did in the past, but Papa has to play along. Otherwise, they'll burn his plant to the ground, the way they've done with some other opposition businessmen."

"Don't the business leaders who support Estrada know about these terrible things the general did. The ones you won't talk about."

She shrugged. "Some do. Most don't care. They want to forget the past with a collective amnesia and have the country's economy expand. It's a Faustian bargain."

"Get the trains running on time?"

She nodded. "Something like that."

"In the materials I read Estrada refers to himself as a Peronist. For the life of me, I can't understand what that means."

She laughed. "Welcome to the crowd. You obviously know all about Peron and Eva."

He nodded.

"As a young officer, in the thirties, Peron was sent to Italy for training. There he found something more valuable: a hero to emulate. Mussolini. Since then almost every Argentine politician says he wants to help the poor so he pins the Peron label on himself, hoping he'll gain labor and popular support. For Estrada, it might fit. Like Peron himself, Estrada is a general bigger than life and equally fraudulent. But I'm outspoken on the issue of our monumental Peron. If you're committed to doing something to stop Estrada, tell me what I can do to help. And if you're not," she pointed to the staircase, "You can go to Bariloche and find out about Dunn on your own."

He had no doubt that she meant it. This tough-talking, no-nonsense woman had suffered or seen others suffer at Estrada's hand. He respected her convictions. She would be a valuable ally.

"We have the same objective," he said forcefully.

"Good," she replied softly.

"I'm supposed to meet Emilio Miranda. Where does he fit into this?"

"Miranda owns a large oil and gas company based in Patagonia in the south as well as a huge estancia, a cattle ranch, you call it. Also, a winery in Mendoza. He was one of Estrada's earliest supporters, and he has the general's ear. Miranda's a man without principle for whom profit is the only driver. You have people like that in the United States. I'm sure."

"Every country has them."

Though he was convinced he could trust her, that she hadn't set up Dunn, he thought perhaps Pascual had. "Let's go back to the driver—the poet and musician in Bariloche. I need an address for him, where he lived with his sister."

Nicole hesitated. "You can't bother her."

"Why not?"

"As a young girl, she suffered."

"And if we don't stop Estrada, she'll suffer again. You know that better than I do. Everybody in this country will suffer."

Nicole rifled through a shoe box filled with papers until she found what she was looking for. He watched her take a blank piece of paper and write down the name Antonia along with an address and telephone number.

"Your filing system is impressive," he said, trying to add some levity.

When she handed him the piece of paper, her expression was grim. He read it, committed it to memory, and set it on fire with a match in her ashtray.

She looked surprised.

"I've memorized it," he said. "I won't create problems for her."

Nicole snarled: "You may not be able to avoid it. Are you finished with me now?"

He shook his head. "I need something else."

She eyed him with trepidation. "What's that?"

"Dunn learned that Estrada has a secret headquarters in the north somewhere. Dunn never found where it was and why Estrada needed it. But he thought it was important. You obviously have good sources of information. Will you try and find out for me?"

While she pondered the question, Craig reached into his briefcase and pulled out ten thousand dollars. He placed it on the table as if he were paying for a pair of shoes. "I know you won't take money for yourself, but you might have to persuade people to give you information."

She got up, pulled an empty shoe box off the shelf, stuffed the money inside and put it back. "If I manage to get the information, how will I find you to pass it on?"

"I'm at the Alvear. Leave a message that Fiona called to say she has the briefcase I wanted. We'll meet inside the Metropolitan Cathedral at ten that evening. If one of us doesn't show, we repeat it at ten the next morning and every twelve hours after that."

"No. The Metropolitan Cathedral is too dangerous. I have a better place."

"Go ahead."

"Take highway twelve north from Buenos Aires. You'll wind up in the hills. Pass the intersection with highway eight and continue on twelve. About two kilometers after the intersection, you'll pass a restaurant and gas station on the right. Immediately following, there's a scenic overlook at the crest of the road. Pull into the overlook and park. That's where we'll meet."

Craig was impressed with Nicole. He closed up his briefcase, preparing to leave when she reached her hand across the table and put it on his arm. "I like you so I'll give you some advice."

He wondered what was coming next. "Yeah?"

"Stay here in Buenos Aires and talk to Miranda. Schiller is vicious and sadistic. If he finds out you're snooping around in Bariloche, he'll kill you."

He was moved by her entreaty. The concern was genuine. "I have to know what happened to Ted Dunn. The answer is in Bariloche."

She squeezed down tightly on his arm with her nails digging into his flesh. "You'd be better not to go."

Pulling away, he said, "I have to know. Dunn has a wife. She's my friend, too."

Nicole sighed in resignation. She added one more bit of advice. "With Estrada, you have to be strong. Tough as nails. He destroys weak people."

He thought about his dealings with Chinese General Zhou who had planned to wreck the American economy. He had stood his ground with Zhou, refused to be intimidated, even in Beijing when Zhou was trying to kill him and Elizabeth. "I don't know how to behave any other way."

"Good." Now she smiled and reached into a pile of papers and extracted an airline schedule. After studying it for a few seconds, she said, "A plane leaves in two hours from the domestic airport, Jorge Newbery. You have plenty of time."

"I have a gun," he said. "Will I be able to take it?"

"I'll give you a small suitcase. Check it through. They'll never x-ray it. We're erratic on security down here."

She pulled a small black wheelie out of a closet and handed it to him. "I appreciate your help, Nicole."

She locked eyes with him. "I'm just glad some people in your American government are smart enough to know they have to block Estrada before he comes to power."

Craig watched her yank a plastic shopping bag from a box. "When you walk out of here," she said, "I want you to look like you've been shopping for shoes." She disappeared among the rows of shoe boxes. "What size does your wife or girlfriend wear?" She called to him.

He thought about Gina. She would no doubt love a pair of those beautiful shoes. That wasn't an option. It would link him to Nicole. "I'm between girlfriends," he called back.

"I'll give you one thirty-six and one thirty-eight. Try to find a woman to match," she said, as she reappeared with the bag.

"Can I pay you for them?"

She smiled. "My shoes are expensive, but ten thousand should cover two pairs. Be careful. I want to see you again someday. Alive. Not in the morgue."

Bariloche

In the plane Craig took copies of *La Nación* and *La Opinion* from a flight attendant and sat down on the aisle in the last row of the business class cabin for the flight to Bariloche. The window seat was empty.

Once the cabin door closed, he scanned the front page of *La Nación* and stopped on the upper right hand corner. An article under Gina's byline reported on a meeting that the Brazilian president had with President Treadwell at the White House. According to the article, Luiz Dumont, the Brazilian president, was complaining about the huge shipments of American arms that had been made to Argentina in the past few months, and which according to Dumont, threatened "to destabilize the region."

Gina had interviewed the Brazilian president after the meeting and obtained a quote; "I told President Treadwell there was no reason for Argentina to be so heavily armed, that the United States should cease sending arms to Argentina and begin arming Brazil to the same degree. If the United States continues on this path, Brazil will have no alternative but to seek arms from another supplier, such as China." So on top of everything else, Estrada was destabilizing the region. But to what end? Border issues among the various South American countries were always flaring up. Estrada must have some reason for putting the Brazilians on edge. Right now Craig couldn't figure out what it was. Estrada was playing a dangerous game.

As Craig ate lunch on the plane, he continued reading *La Nación*, which was filled with gloomy economic news. The Argentine stock market had fallen sharply in the last week. Health officials were warning about child malnutrition in rural areas. In Buenos Aires hordes of porteños, as residents of the capital were called, came out of the barrios at night to scavenge garbage cans for food and search for paper and other objects they could sell for recycling.

He put down *La Nación* and picked up a copy of *La Opinion*. To his surprise, on the front page, he saw an editorial with a black box around it. Craig began reading.

Some have told us that we are foolish and subjecting our families and employees to great risk by speaking out. However our obligation to the noble profession of journalism and to the wonderful country of Argentina compels us to break our silence. There is a cancer in our land, pernicious and growing. That is the movement of Alfredo Estrada and his fellow generals. Many of us remember all too well and painfully the horror of the last rule of the generals from 1976 to 1983. Those who value and cherish freedom cannot permit this to reoccur. Already, honest citizens are being murdered for speaking their minds. We, the editors of this paper, are aware of the risks we are taking in making this plea. Our names are well known. Should we die suddenly, do not mourn us. Do everything possible to eradicate this cancer and defeat Estrada.

—The Editors

The editorial rocked Craig. He had spent his CIA career in the Middle East where Americans had fought and died trying to create a semblance of democracy for people far from the United States in places such as Iraq and Afghanistan. Now, Estrada was planning to curtail freedom in one of the most important countries in the United States' backyard—in South America. The rights of the Argentine people deserved as much protection as the Afghans and Iraqis.

No, even more, Craig thought. The United States always had a special relationship with South America, dating back to the Monroe Doctrine in 1823. Moreover, a military dictatorship in Argentina was likely to spill over to other South American countries. Freedom was always tenuous on that continent. And as freedom was snuffed out, waves of immigrants would try to get into the United States.

Craig recalled Betty telling him about Estrada's trip to Beijing. Estrada's regime might expand its relationship with China, trading oil and other natural resources the United States needed in return for arms. And once armed, Estrada could make a move, with Chinese support, on one or more neighboring countries—Chile, Brazil, or Paraguay—to seize their oil and other resources. This would destabilize the continent, creating a devastating problem for the United States. So while the editors of *La Opinion* were terrified of what would happen to the Argentine people if Estrada seized power, Craig saw a whole set of additional adverse consequences for the United States.

As Craig put the paper down, he thought about Nicole's warning to him. She, much more than he, knew how dangerous the situation was and the risk he was taking. There was no turning back.

"We're on our final approach to Bariloche," the flight attendant announced. Craig looked out of the window at the pristine blue waters of the lake below. Snow was on the ground in the hills above the lake, but it wasn't fresh. The roads looked clear.

*   *   *

Once he hit the frigid mountain air, Craig realized that spring hadn't yet come to Bariloche. In the small terminal he bought a blue ski jacket with thick, fluffy material in the lining.

On his way to the Avis counter, he spotted, standing near an exit, a heavyset man with a red, beefy, pockmarked face who was watching him. The man wasn't making any effort to leave the small terminal.

He's planning to follow me, Craig decided.

Craig rented a bulky SUV with four-wheel drive. He climbed into the vehicle, studied his map, and then set off.

The sign at the end of the access road pointed toward the left for the city of Bariloche. This was where Antonia, the sister of the driver, Pascual, lived. After what Nicole had told him about Antonia, he couldn't risk endangering her. If he was being followed, he had to lose his tail before he approached her house. Craig turned to the right. In a matter of minutes, he was on the main road circling the lake, which was on his left. Traffic was light. A maroon sedan was behind him, hanging back, making no effort to close the gap or to pass, even when Craig slowed to a crawl. That had to be the red-faced man.

In an effort to lose him Craig sped up as he reached a curve in the road. He saw a tree lined driveway and turned in. Confident he couldn't be seen from the road, he waited ten minutes, then pulled back out and drove in the opposite direction. The maroon sedan was parked along the side of the road. As soon as Craig passed it, the driver of the maroon sedan executed a U-turn and resumed following Craig.

He must have worked with the Avis people to plant a tracking device on my SUV, Craig decided.

Craig decided not to stop to locate the tracking device and destroy it. That could come later. For now, he continued following the lakefront road until he saw a cutoff on the left that climbed into the hills. He turned off and began a gradual ascent in a deserted area. There were no houses or other buildings that he could see.

Through the rearview mirror, he watched the maroon sedan trailing. Suddenly, he got a queasy feeling in his stomach. He may have outsmarted himself by isolating the two of them this way with the red-faced man behind him. Unwittingly, he had given his adversary the superior position, reversing their relationship, so that red-faced man was now the hunter and Craig the hunted.

Maps were useless on these mountainous back roads. Craig was determined to get back in control. Using his best driving skills, he revved up his speed in the bulky SUV and shot forward, picking his turnoffs from one muddy dirt road to another by instinct while trying to avoid taking curves so fast that the SUV would roll over. No matter how fast he went, the maroon sedan kept pace. The man was a good driver. Craig figured his car must have four-wheel drive.

A few kilometers ahead, at the crest of the mountain, Craig spotted a building that looked like a cabin or a hunting lodge. There were no cars in sight. His guess was that it was deserted.

Hunched forward and gripping the steering wheel, he floored the accelerator, kicking mud from the rear tires. He wanted to get to the cabin quickly, as much ahead of his pursuer as he could.

On the last turn, he narrowly missed slipping off the road. Holy shit, he thought, it was a helluva long way down. He had no intention of duplicating his crash in Sardinia. He straightened out, then blasted through a small decrepit wooden gate and into the parking area on the side of the cabin. In an instant, he was out of the car, racing toward the front door of the cabin, Beretta in his jacket pocket. He grabbed the rusty doorknob and twisted. The door was locked, but it was old. When he smashed his shoulder against the rotting wood, it easily gave way.

Inside, he took stock of the cabin. It had a living room, kitchen, two bedrooms, and a bath. No clothes or other signs of occupancy. The kitchen led to a wooden patio in the back, surrounded on the side, away from the house, by a wooden fence about three feet high. Crossing the patio, he saw beyond the fence a sheer drop, several kilometers straight down to a mountain stream.

He ran back into the cabin, leaving the door open to the patio in the back and ducking into one of the bedrooms, where he hid behind a heavy wooden chest. Through the bedroom window, he had a clear view of the patio. As he expected, the red-faced man thought he had gone out through the door in the kitchen to the patio.

Craig watched him pull a gun from his pocket and walk slowly across the patio toward the fence. When he reached the edge of the wooden deck, he stopped and peered over the fence, gun in hand, looking for Craig.

That was Craig's signal to move. He ran back into the kitchen and out onto the patio.

From a distance of ten yards, Craig shouted, "I have a gun aimed at your back. Raise your hands and don't turn around."

The man followed the command.

"Toss your gun down the hill. Then raise your hands again."

Once he complied, Craig ran up behind the man, looped his left arm around his neck and pressed the Beretta against his right temple.

"Now you're going to answer some questions," Craig barked.

"Anything. I don't want to die." The man was trembling.

"Tell the truth, and you'll live. Otherwise you're a dead man."

Sweat was flowing down the man's red, pockmarked face. "What do you want to know?"

"Why did you follow me up here?"

"I didn't," the man responded in a halting voice.

Craig jammed the gun so tightly against his flesh that the end of the barrel made an indentation. "You're lying. Now tell me, or I shoot."

The man hesitated.

Craig pressed the gun hard. "Tell me now."

"Colonel Schiller sent me," he stammered. "To keep tabs on you."

"Why'd you pull out your gun?"

"I can't get caught, or the colonel . . ."

Craig saw fear in the man's eyes. "You have a cell phone. Don't you?" Craig asked.

The man nodded. "In my pocket."

"I want you to take it out slowly. Then call Colonel Schiller and tell him you lost the man you were following. That's all. You got that?"

"I got it."

If he made the call, Craig planned to take his cell phone, knock him out, and tie him up, making sure there were no other phones in the cabin. Then he would disable his car. That should give Craig enough time to meet Antonia and get out of Bariloche.

"Okay. Put one hand in your pocket. Nice and easy. If you say one other word, I'll blow your head off."

The man placed his right hand in his jacket pocket. As he began to lift it out, everything happened so quickly that Craig thought he was in a video that someone had turned to fast-forward. First the man's right hand, gripping a shiny metal object, shot out of his pocket. With a jerking motion he brought it up and smashed the metal object against Craig's wrist, knocking the Beretta from his hand. Helplessly, Craig watched it slide across the patio.

To his horror, he saw that the metal object wasn't a cell phone, but a switchblade knife.

The man pressed a button and out snapped a long blade, glistening in the sun. He had fast movements for a large man. With the knife, he lunged for Craig's chest, but Craig darted away. All he struck was the heavily padded sleeve of Craig's ski jacket. The knife was embedded in the lining, and the man had trouble getting it out.

That was the break Craig needed. Ignoring the pain in his wrist, he raised his right arm and swung it in a powerful backhand motion with all the force he could muster, going for his assailant's face. As he did, the man lifted his leg and aimed a powerful kick for Craig's groin. Craig felt a jolt of searing pain just as the back of his hand struck the man's face. It was a direct hit on his cheek and the side of his nose. Craig heard the crunching sound of bones breaking, but that wasn't all. The man was off balance when the blow came. It was so powerful that it propelled him toward the fence.

From the ground where Craig was clutching his genitalia and writhing in pain, he watched the heavy, bulky man crash through the rotten wood of the fence. From the force of Craig's blow, his assailant was now on the precipice of the cliff, leaning down the hill, trying desperately to straighten up and move back toward the cabin. Craig wanted to pull himself up to help the man. But he was barely conscious himself. That coupled with the pain prevented his body from responding. He watched the man pitch over the cliff, screaming, "Help," and roll like a boulder side over side all the way down to the creek in the gully below.

A few seconds later, Craig's mind cleared. The pain eased. He staggered down the hill, grabbing onto rocks and small bushes to keep his footing in the slippery mud. Once he reached the bottom, he realized he had come for nothing. The man had hit his head on a rock that had cracked his skull. He was dead, his face covered in blood.

Craig made no effort to move the body. Climbing back up was even more difficult. Several times he thought he would black out, but finally he made it.

On the patio, bruised and weary, he staggered toward the house. In the mist, in front of the Andes, the sun was dropping fast, but there was still a little more daylight. When he reached the door, he remembered his Beretta, which had skidded into a corner of the patio. He backtracked, picked up the gun, stuffed it into his pocket, and dragged himself outside to the SUV. He found the tracking device attached to the vehicle's rear bumper. When he got back on the road, he would toss it into the lake.

Washington

Gina couldn't believe that she was at a black-tie state dinner at the White House for the president of Brazil. She wasn't there as a reporter, but as Edward Bryce's date. Though she found Bryce increasingly repulsive after her evening with Barry Gorman, she was still awed by her surroundings.

The State Dining Room, its walls freshly painted a light blue, contained seven round tables of eight people each. Gina, dressed in the low-cut silk magenta Valentino Bryce said made her look ravishing, was seated between Bryce and Justice Thompson of the Supreme Court. President Treadwell and his wife, Polly, were at an adjacent table with the Brazilian president and his wife.

The only other person Gina knew was Amy, the president's speech writer, seated across the table from her.

Amy was the president's mistress, Gina had learned last evening when she and Bryce went to the White House to watch Hitchcock's *Vertigo* and Polly was out of town. Amy was there supposedly to work on a speech, but midway through the movie the two of them had disappeared into a bedroom. When they emerged, half an hour later, her face was flushed and the president's clothes were disheveled, his hair uncombed.

Gina was thinking she had to find a way to persuade Edward to arrange the delivery of the arms Estrada wanted. He must be planning to use them. He was sounding increasingly anxious.

A waiter in a white jacket with white gloves served the first course of warm Gulf shrimp over arugula and radicchio with a red pepper coulis.

"Where are you from, Miss Galindo?" Justice Thompson asked as he turned his mostly bald head surrounded by a ring of gray toward her.

"Argentina. Have you ever been there?"

"Once for a conference on human rights issues a year ago. We traveled around. It's a wonderful country. What I really liked was . . ."

As he was speaking, she noticed that through his glasses he was looking down her dress, which had slipped a little, exposing the tops of her breasts.

She glanced across the table at Amy who must have sized up the situation because she was winking at Gina and smiling.

Before Gina came to Washington, she would have been embarrassed and humiliated by this situation.

But no longer. Anything was now possible. Her life had taken a bizarre turn. She had been content teaching history at the girls' school. She never thought about being a journalist. That had been Estrada's idea. He had arranged a job for her at *La Nación* in Buenos Aires. After a couple of months, she wasn't enjoying being a reporter—all the sitting around for a story and then meeting deadlines. She decided she should stick with it for a year, because of what Estrada had done for her. Then one day he told her, "Good news. I've arranged with the publisher of the newspaper to transfer you to Washington."

That sounded like fun. She had always wanted to go to the United States to visit. The foreign editor briefed her on her assignment. It didn't seem that difficult because the White House and State Department regularly issued press releases. All she would have to do was repackage those into articles.

Two days before she left, Estrada had taken her to dinner. In a soft voice, just above a whisper, he explained that he had an important assignment for her in Washington, in addition to being a reporter. He told her about Edward Bryce and how critical he was for Argentina. Then Estrada told her, "I want you to find a way to become close with Edward Bryce. This would be valuable for Argentina. And your father would be proud of you for doing it."

She had asked Estrada how she could get close to Bryce, but as soon as the words tumbled out of her mouth, she blushed, realizing how naive and stupid she sounded.

Estrada had placed his hand on hers, and said, "In the way that women always get close to men. And after you do, I'll want you to pass along messages to Bryce."

Gina may have been inexperienced in many things, but she had studied enough history to realize Estrada wanted her to be a spy. She had left that dinner with Estrada feeling excited. She would be serving her country, as her father had.

Shortly after she began sleeping with Bryce, her enthusiasm collapsed like a balloon that was punctured on a spike. The sex wasn't fun. She felt dirty after she went to bed with him.

The jewelry he was giving her and the Watergate apartment he had rented made her feel like a whore. The reality sunk in that Estrada had plucked her from teaching as a way of getting to Bryce.

She would have preferred abandoning Washington and returning to teaching in Argentina. But she couldn't let Estrada, the Republic, and her father's memory down. She had been depressed about her situation. Then Barry Gorman came along.

Justice Thompson touched her arm. "Don't you think so?"

"Oh absolutely," she replied without having the vaguest idea what he was talking about. I better pay attention, she decided.

"As I was saying," he continued, "your country is democratic now, but it wasn't that long ago during the Dirty War that babies were kidnapped and pregnant women arrested, their babies taken from them at birth, and then they were executed.

"At the conference we heard from an organization, called the Abuelas de Plaza de Mayo. It was trying to find those children who had been given to supporters of the regime for adoption and restore them to what remained of their biological families."

"What happened to those babies was terrible," Gina said, "but don't judge our whole country by the actions of a few evil people."

*   *   *

Bryce turned to his right and was pleased that Gina was engaged in an intense conversation with Justice Thompson. Gina was young; still she had intellectual sophistication. If he married her, he wouldn't have to worry about her gaining the respect of his contemporaries or others in Washington power positions.

A waiter returned with the main course, a rack of lamb with an assortment of vegetables. Another poured wine. Bryce looked at the bottle: Silver Oak cab, a very fine California wine. He was reminded of what President Nixon did at some White House dinners. He had waiters pour American wine for all the guests and Chateau Margaux for himself from an unmarked bottle.

Before eating the lamb, he glanced at the next table and at Treadwell. The president looked well, Bryce thought. Still, Dr. Lee had told Bryce not to be deceived by that. He was happy he had persuaded Treadwell to go to Bethesda Naval for a cardio workup. He prayed it would come out alright. That was about all Bryce had succeeded in convincing Treadwell to do. His entreaties to end the affair with Amy had been summarily rejected by the president, who laughed and said, "Sex with her does my heart good. Keeps my blood moving. You know what it's like with a younger woman."

"Yes, but I'm considering marrying Gina," Bryce had told Treadwell.

"Then do it," the president had said.

"I'm worried people will think she's marrying me for my money and position, even though we're in love."

"Do it," Treadwell had repeated.

Bryce decided he would. He had to wait for the right time to ask her.

Thirty minutes later, after dessert was cleared, Bryce watched Treadwell stride to the podium. Speaking without a note, he delivered a five-minute speech extolling the long friendship and ties binding the United States and Brazil. He then moved on to praise the great progress the Brazilians were making in strengthening their economy. He closed by looking forward to close cooperation on many issues in the future.

Treadwell had told Bryce that was what he called his standard one-two-three foreign visitor speech. The format could be adapted for the visiting head of any country. Treadwell was a good enough speaker that he didn't have to memorize the words written for him. He always got the essence right. What Treadwell totally ignored this evening, was the acrimonious discussion he had had with the president of Brazil that afternoon, with Bryce in attendance, on the issue of United States arms supplies to Argentina.

Treadwell sat down. When the Brazilian President Dumont stood up, Treadwell leaned back in his chair and relaxed, expecting a similar couple of minutes of meaningless platitudes. Then he heard the Brazilian president say, in halting English, "Many of you in this group are our friends, and there are certain times that blunt talk is necessary among friends."

Bryce sat up in his chair. He looked at Treadwell who was now ramrod straight in his own chair, the president's eyes focused on the speaker. Protocol was being breached. State dinners were never for serious talk. That only came in the meetings before and after dinner. A deathly silence fell over the room.

"For several months," Dumont continued, "we have watched with increasing dismay and alarm the huge quantities of American arms flowing to our neighbor Argentina. I mean planes, tanks, grenade launchers, and all of the other weapons for a state-of-the-art army. You should not delude yourself. Those weapons have no defensive purpose. They can only be used by General Estrada in some new aggressive military adventure.

"Let's not forget that Brazil and Argentina fought a number of wars over the years, primarily in connection with border issues. We had thought all of those issues were resolved, but perhaps our neighbors believe otherwise.

"Let's also not forget that Argentina is the nation that attacked Britain in the Falklands. If they dare to move against Brazil, they will be humiliated as thoroughly as they were in the Falklands. For we have our own sources of arms, a much larger population, and a more powerful army.

"I strongly suggest that you halt these arms shipments and reign in General Estrada. If not, Washington will suffer the consequences of these actions."

The Brazilian president sat down to a stony silence and a horrified audience.

All eyes turned to President Treadwell. Bryce wondered whether he would accept the challenge and respond in kind, telling the Brazilian that Argentina had reports and satellite photos confirming significant Brazilian troop movements near the Argentine border. Estrada had forwarded the reports to Bryce through Gina, and he had given them to the president.

Treadwell stood up to the deathly silence. He said, "We will move into the Green Room for a concert by the Tokyo String Quartet."

Bariloche

Craig drove forty-five minutes from the cabin where he had struggled with the red-faced man to Antonia's house. He decided not to call first, rather to show up and hope she was home. If she had time to think about it, she might not want to talk to him.

Taking a cautious approach, he turned the corner onto Avenue Santa Fe and drove by the house, a simple wooden structure in a neighborhood jammed with other similar houses, without stopping. Everything looked normal. He didn't dare park the new SUV in front of Antonia's for fear of bringing attention from a policeman who happened to be passing. He continued driving for two more blocks until he reached the parking lot for a soccer field. He parked there and hobbled back to number fifteen. As he did, he kept looking around, making certain he wasn't being followed.

Before he had a chance to knock the front door opened. Someone had been watching him approach the house. A frail man in his forties with a professorial appearance, metal frame glasses, and thin brown hair was staring at Craig.

"What do you want?" he said.

"I'm looking for Antonia."

"Who are you?"

"A friend of Pascual's." At the mention of the name, a look of terror gripped the man. "She's not here," he said softly, turning his eyes away from Craig.

"I can wait."

"She's not coming back."

Craig was certain the man was lying. "Then where can I find her? I want to help her."

"Give me a number. I'll pass it on."

Neighbors were now staring at Craig from nearby houses. He felt very uncomfortable. "Can I come inside?"

Before the man could respond, a woman hiding behind the doorway said, "Let him in Pierro."

When the man moved away from the door, Craig followed him inside. As Pierro closed the door the woman stepped out of the shadows. She was tall and willowy with short black hair and dark skin from time in the sun. She was dressed simply in a white blouse and navy blue skirt.

"I'm Antonia," she said, and pointed to the man at the door. "Pierro's my husband. Who are you?" She spoke in a husky voice that showed none of the fear Pierro demonstrated.

He heard girls giggling nervously and looked across the room. Two sets of eyes, young girls, maybe six and eight, were watching from behind the edge of a curtain.

"Back to your room, you two," Antonia called. "Do your school work."

The girls disappeared into the back of the house. "What do you want?" she asked Craig.

"To know what happened to an American who met your brother Pascual a week or so ago. I'm a friend of his."

Before Antonia could respond, Pierro said, "Don't talk to this American. He'll get all of us killed."

"That's not true," Craig said.

Antonia turned toward Pierro. "I've been searching for someone to tell. Someone who could avenge Pascual."

"Leave it alone," Pierro said, his voice trembling with fear. "Tell him to go now before it's too late."

Craig was watching Antonia. From her face he knew she disagreed with her husband. Would she defy him?

"Give us a few minutes to talk," she told Craig. Then she led Pierro into another room. For several minutes, Craig heard whispers, angry ones, coming from Pierro. Finally, the voices stopped. Antonia returned alone.

"Let's go into the kitchen," she said to Craig.

She turned on the light and closed the blinds. "I have nosy neighbors. We don't have to advertise that I have a foreign visitor. Want something to drink?

"I could use a glass of brandy."

She poured one for him and water for herself. He took a large gulp. It made him feel better.

"You're walking badly. An injury?"

"One of Colonel Schiller's thugs attacked me."

She looked alarmed.

"Don't worry, it was thirty kilometers from here. I made sure no one followed me."

As Craig sat down at the table, he winced.

"You want me to take a look at it?" she asked.

"Are you a nurse?"

"No, but I'm a ski instructor and lifeguard. I'm trained to give first aid."

"I'll be okay."

"I hope you gave as good as you got. For my brother's sake."

He realized she had decided to take a chance with him, putting her life and her family's at risk by talking with him. He could do no less. "I killed the man."

She closed her hand into a fist. "Good for you." Then she sat down across from him. "You'll have to forgive my husband, Pierro. He's a good man, but timid by nature. He just wants to protect us. And now is a tough time for him. He's a bookkeeper. He's been out of work for more than a year since the factory closed."

"Tell me what happened to your brother and the American he met."

She sighed and closed her eyes.

"If it's too painful or you're afraid of putting your family at risk, you don't have to talk to me."

When she opened them, she stared straight at Craig. "No," she said. "Quite the opposite. I'm glad you came. As I told Pierro, I made an effort to learn the truth. I've wanted to tell someone what happened, but I was afraid of taking it to the wrong person."

"You can trust me."

"I'm willing to take a chance."

She took a deep breath and began. "Pascual met an American with a strawberry mark on his face . . ."

"He was my friend," Craig said interrupting her.

"Pascual met the American . . ."

Craig couldn't bear to hear Dunn being referred to as a nameless American. "Please call him Dunn. That was his name."

"Alright, Pascual met Dunn at the café where he was singing in the evenings. Maybe it was a chance meeting, or maybe Dunn knew Pascual was a driver for the biggest limo company in town and targeted him." She shrugged. "I don't know that part. The first I heard about it was the night before it all happened. He told me that an American CIA agent wanted his help. He had told Dunn he had to think about it. He wasn't only afraid for himself. He was worried about the danger to me and the girls. I convinced him to do it . . . Because of what happened to our parents, he had to help.

We have to stop the generals." She shook her head and bit down on her lower lip.

Craig deduced she was sorry now that she had convinced Pascual to help Dunn, leading to her brother's death.

"What exactly did Dunn want from Pascual?"

"To arrange to be the driver meeting some foreign visitors arriving by private jet the next afternoon at one for a meeting with Estrada at a villa on the lake."

"And then?"

"To find out who the visitors were. Listen to what they said in the car. He was to meet Dunn that night and report."

"Where were the visitors coming from?"

"Your friend Dunn didn't know. That was one piece of critical information he wanted."

"Did Pascual pick up the visitors?'

She shrugged. "I don't know. I never spoke to my brother after he called Dunn that morning and said he would help. That greasy swine, Jose Lopez, who runs the limo company wouldn't say a word to me."

"What were you able to find out?"

She rolled her hands into fists and gripped the chair hard. Her whole body was shaking. The words tumbled out of her mouth. "The day after the airport pick up, the police pulled the Lincoln Town Car Pascual was driving out of the lake. My dead brother was in the driver's seat with his seatbelt on. The official police explanation was that Pascual was drunk and drove into the lake by mistake. They had the results of a blood-alcohol test to back it up, but I didn't believe it for a minute."

"Why not?"

"The police said Pascual had a bottle of scotch in his pocket. But he never drank scotch."

"That's not much to go on."

"I talked to an old friend of my father's, an auto mechanic. For me, he went down to the garage where they were trying to salvage the car for Lopez. What he learned was that the brake line had been cut. He saw indentations on the rear bumper. He had no doubt that someone had cut the brake line then pushed the car from the back into the water."

She looked at Craig with huge, round eyes, pleading with him to help her comprehend. "How could they have done this to Pascual? He was kind and gentle. He wasn't Dunn. What could he do to them?"

Craig looked at her sympathetically. "There are some evil people in the world. There always have been."

That didn't satisfy her. She shook her head pensively.

"What about my friend, Dunn? What happened to him?" Craig asked.

"Soldiers ambushed him at the deserted spot where he was supposed to meet my brother that night. They were shooting at him. He tried to escape by running across a farmer's field to reach a getaway car he had parked on the main road. Unfortunately for him, the farmer had two German Shepherds. The dogs took him for an intruder. They chased and attacked him in a muddy field."

Craig gulped hard, visualizing the terror Dunn was facing—soldiers firing bullets at him, dogs howling and flying through the air to pounce on the heavyset former agent. He held his breath, waiting to hear what happened next.

Antonia continued in a quavering voice. "He was able to kill one of the dogs. But the other one drove him to the ground and was mauling him when Estrada's soldiers reached him. They were yelling at him, 'Who sent you? Who sent you? Tell us and we'll shoot the dog.' He screamed out, 'Betty Richards.' They let the dog kill him, then they shot and killed the dog."

Craig was horrified. "No," he cried out. "No. Are you sure that's what happened?"

"This whole area is a small community. People talk. I found the farmer, who was cursing Estrada's men. He was sickened by what they had done. When this was all happening, he had come out of his house and run toward the scene. He reached your friend when the soldiers did. Afterwards, he heard them say they would cut up the American and bury him in the woods. The farmer wanted them to pay for his dogs. They threatened to kill him if he didn't bury his dogs, then go back into the house and keep his mouth shut."

"You blame Estrada for all of this?"

Her face hardened with conviction. "He had to be responsible. The visitors were coming to meet the general. These troops the farmer encountered must have been working for him. And . . ." She was hesitating. Craig knew there was something else.

"Please tell me," he said.

"The evening after my brother's funeral, two soldiers came here to the house. They vowed to kill me and my children if I ever tried to challenge the police report about what they called 'Pascual's accident.'"

For Craig, horror at what had happened to Dunn gave way to rage that permeated his entire body. He rolled his hands into fists. One day, he would kill Estrada and whoever else ordered Dunn's death—if it was the last thing he ever did.

Antonia's eyes filled up with tears. Some rolled down her cheeks. She wiped her face with a paper napkin. "I'm sorry. My brother was an innocent. Come. I'll show you."

She led the way. Craig followed into what had obviously been Pascual's room. It looked as if he still lived there. Two guitars rested against a wall. Several piles of music were on a desk. Next to them was a woman's picture and an unfinished poem with the title *Love Not Guns*. A tennis racket and a couple of cans of balls stood in the corner.

Craig pointed to the woman's picture. "His girlfriend?"

"A woman in town he was seeing. Her husband died last year. She has three small children. They were planning to get married next year."

"I'm sorry."

"Pascual had so much to live for. He was a dreamer. I have to live with the guilt. I encouraged him to help your American friend. I couldn't let Estrada and the generals come to power again. Not after what happened to our parents. These people have to be stopped before they create the nightmare all over again."

She had alluded to that earlier, and Craig had let it pass. But not now. It was a critical part of the story. "Tell me about it."

"Pascual and I were always close. We were children the last time the generals ruled. They said my parents were Communists, but they weren't. So in March of 1981 they came to our house. There were five officers with machine guns. It was this house." Her face turned pale and sad. Craig thought she would cry. Then her grim determination took hold.

"This is a great country," she said. "With many wonderful people. But sometimes a few rotten ones take control, and one night, the army was on a sweep through the Bariloche area searching for Communists. An informer had given their commander the address of our house.

"My father was an auto mechanic. He was also a brave man and believed in freedom. Though he had rejected the appeals of the Communists to join their party, he had been vocal in speaking out against the rule of the generals. He had also armed a bomb that blew up a military transport killing ten soldiers.

"When he heard a knock on the door, he shouted to my mother, 'Take the children into the bedroom and hide under the bed.'

"I was peeking out through a crack in the door. I saw my father run into the kitchen and grab a heavy knife he used for carving beef. He put on a light jacket, and concealed the knife underneath it, gripping it tightly in one hand. The commander didn't bother to knock. He kicked open the door with a powerful boot.

"With a machine gun at his side, the commander moved up close to my father, who held his ground in the center of the room, refusing to cower before this Fascist and his four armed soldiers.

" 'Eduard Frigero,' the commander announced, as if he was preparing to announce a death sentence.

" 'I am Eduardo,' my father responded proudly.

" 'You're coming with us. You and your whole family.'

"Before the commander had a chance to raise his gun and anyone had a chance to fire, my father yanked his arm out from behind the jacket. He took two steps forward and plunged the knife into the commander's chest.

"As he did, all four soldiers opened fire. Machine gun bullets riddled my father's body."

Antonia began to cry again with loud sobs, her body shaking with emotion. Her story was ripping Craig apart with anguish. He sensed there was more to it, but he didn't want to prolong her agony. "You don't have to continue."

"I want to. You have to know it all."

She cleared her throat and continued, "My mother grabbed Pascual and me and pulled us under the bed with her. 'Be still,' she whispered. 'Maybe they won't find us.'

"My mother's hopes were futile. Minutes later, I heard powerful boots pounding on the wooden floor of the bedroom. Those same boots kicked the bed across the room, exposing my terrified mother, Pascual, and me. We were all screaming. It didn't do any good."

The pain was written on Antonia's face. She turned away from Craig.

"They had their way with my mother, one after another, while they forced me and Pascual to watch."

She spat on the floor. "Pigs."

Craig's heart went out to her. He didn't want to interrupt her until she was finished.

"When the last one was done, he strangled my mother with his bare hands while he was still on top of her.

"They were laughing when they left the house. As soon as they were gone, Pascual and I ran to our aunt's house.

"I can still hear their laughter. They were young officers. Like Estrada at the time. Now I imagine they're cronies of his. No doubt some of them are also generals, who will be in power if he takes over the country. That's why I encouraged Pascual to work with Dunn. You Americans are our only hope to prevent Estrada from coming to power. If you stand by and acquiesce, the way you did the last time the generals seized control, then we are all lost."

Craig couldn't speak after hearing her story. He squeezed her hand empathetically.

Then he reached into his briefcase and pulled out several piles of hundreds of dollars. "There's ten thousand altogether."

She threw the money at him. It bounced off his chest and fell on the floor.

"You think money is a substitute for my brother's life?"

He shook his head. "Believe me, I'm not suggesting that ten thousand dollars is the value of Pascual's life. But it's something. It's small compensation from the American government for your brother's death. He was helping us at the time."

"I won't take your money."

He put it back into the briefcase. "I'm sorry."

Her eyes were blazing with hatred. "If you want to do something for me and Pierro and my two daughters, then stop Estrada and his generals from taking over my country and recreating the nightmare."

That was precisely what Craig was trying to accomplish. He locked eyes with her. "I'll do my best. I promise you."

He stood up and paced the room, thinking about what she had told him. The visitors who flew into Bariloche that day were the key. Estrada was so intent on concealing their identity and the purpose of the meeting that he was willing to have two people killed for it and threaten three others. All that Antonia knew was that they had arrived by private jet at Bariloche Airport at one o'clock in the afternoon.

"What was the date that Pascual did this job for my friend?"

"October the twelfth," she said, without hesitation.

"You sure?"

"I'll never forget that date."

Antonia let Craig out through the back door. It was dark outside with heavy cloud cover blocking out the moonlight. Cautiously, he walked toward his SUV, wondering what he'd find. It looked exactly as he had left it. That didn't mean one of the red-faced man's friends hadn't planted a bomb. He checked the wheels and tires. He climbed under the car and opened the hood, but found nothing.

He held his breath and started the engine. Everything sounded normal. He eased back on the road and drove toward the airport. Hopefully, he'd find some answers there, the information that Dunn had paid for with his life.

*   *   *

Two soldiers armed with Uzis were on duty outside the airport terminal in Bariloche, talking and smoking cigarettes. They didn't seem interested in Craig as he headed toward the Avis counter, key in hand. After paying for the car, he asked the car rental agent for the office of the airport manager. A stubby finger pointed to a frosted glass door with black letters that read: "Operations."

Craig didn't know what to expect behind that door. It was evening and not a busy time for the airport. There was only one man in the office. Señor Ferraro was what the badge said on his navy shirt. He was tall and dapper with a thin, perfectly trimmed mustache and coal-black hair. The instant Craig saw Señor Ferraro, he liked him. What he most liked was that the man was wearing a Rolex watch and a gold ring with a diamond in the center—items Señor Ferraro could hardly afford on his income from the Airport Authority.

"I want to hire a private plane to fly back to Buenos Aires," Craig said to Ferraro.

"The charter company is out front to the left. They have planes ready to go twenty-four hours a day."

Craig shifted his feet, coughed, and feigned embarrassment. "It's a little complicated. I've been up here seeing a woman. There could be a messy divorce. I was hoping that if I chartered a plane you might be willing to omit it from the daily log of flights in and out of here. I can't afford to leave evidence behind."

Ferraro winked and smiled. He undoubtedly fooled around himself. "The conspiracy of men. I know what that's like. But the Airport Authority has rules." For emphasis he repeated the last word. "Rules."

"I was hoping you could bend them a little."

As Ferraro studied him, Craig knew that Ferraro realized where this was going. Craig would have to make the first move.

"Suppose I were to make a contribution to the Airport Authority?"

Ferraro was watching his visitor carefully. If Craig was right that the man had been on the take, then he had to be worried about a possible sting. Since he wanted the money, he'd be willing to rationalize that they'd never use a foreigner, certainly not an American, for a task like this.

"How much of a contribution are we talking about?" Ferraro asked.

The fish had bit down hard on the bloodworm. "Five thousand US."

Ferraro's face lit up. "In cash."

"Uh-huh."

"You have it here?"

Craig patted his briefcase.

"I think I can arrange what you want," Ferraro said.

Craig reached into his briefcase and pulled out a bundle of hundreds. Five thousand dollars in a rubber band.

Ferraro snatched the money and quickly put it in his desk drawer.

"There is one other thing," Craig said.

He was met with a cold, blank stare. "Yeah, what's that?"

"When I flew in here, I was promised there wouldn't be a record of that flight. I'd like to get a look at the log and make sure that was done."

Ferraro eyed him suspiciously. Craig's guess was that Ferraro had figured that the story about the divorce had been fiction. That what Craig really wanted was a look at the log. "I know that you have rules, but I was hoping that . . ."

Ferraro cut him off. "What date are you interested in?"

Craig swallowed hard. Ferraro might be a cheat, but he was no dummy. Once he mentioned the date, Ferraro would realize this was aimed at Estrada. Too much had happened on that day. He had to assume that Ferraro would make the connection. Craig was now exposed. He had to gamble that Ferraro wanted the money enough that he was willing to cross Estrada and his henchmen.

"October the twelfth," Craig said. "This year."

Ferraro's upper lip twitched. He fidgeted in his seat, confirming that he knew. Craig didn't want him to agonize over the decision for fear the answer would be no. He extracted another five thousand from his briefcase and placed it on the desk. Ferraro stared at it without saying a word. Craig realized he had Ferraro in a bind. It was no longer merely the man's desire for the money. If he blew the whistle on Craig now, how would he explain the five thousand he had already taken?

Finally, Ferraro reached across the desk, snatched the money, and placed it in his desk drawer and locked it. He got up, walked over to a bookshelf and removed one of several heavy, dark green leather volumes. With reluctance, he put it down on the desk. "The log is arranged chronologically," he said. "The date you want is in here . . . Now you'll have to excuse me. I have to go to the bathroom."

Before Craig could respond, Ferraro turned and walked smartly from the room. Was he going to get one of the soldiers, Craig wondered, or trying to create an excuse for himself so he could later say, "The American must have gotten the log down and looked at it when I left the office for a minute to pee."

Craig didn't waste any time considering that question. The minute Ferraro closed the frosted glass door, he opened the log and turned pages until he reached October twelfth. Antonia had told him that her brother was supposed to meet a private jet arriving at 1:00 p.m. He ran his eyes down the rows of handwritten entries for arrivals on that day until he found the one he was looking for. The entry read:

Time	Aircraft	Embarkation	Passengers
1300	Private	Porto Alegre, Brazil	Not Specified

Craig turned more pages until he located departures for that date. A private jet left Bariloche at five-fifty that evening. The destination was Porto Alegre. The passengers weren't specified.

Craig closed the log and swiftly returned it to its place on the bookshelf. Once he did, he mulled over the words "Porto Alegre." He had no idea where in Brazil that was. Craig spotted a map of South America taped to the wall. He crossed the room and began searching. Finally he found Porto Alegre in heavy black letters. It was the capital of the state of Rio Grande do Sul in southeast Brazil, the state in Brazil that has a western border with northeast Argentina.

For a full minute, he stood facing the wall, trying to decide what was so important about Estrada's meeting with people who came from Porto Alegre that Estrada killed Dunn and Pascual to preserve its secrecy. Forget it for now, he told himself. You have more urgent things to worry about. Like getting out of this place alive.

Behind him was the frosted glass door. In a few seconds Ferraro would return, perhaps accompanied by soldiers. Craig grabbed his briefcase with the Beretta. Moving quickly, he positioned himself behind Ferraro's high-backed leather chair. He now had some cover as well as the element of surprise if he had to shoot his way out. He had blasted his way out of a similar situation in Iran.

But how the hell would he get out of Bariloche? Coercing the pilot of a private plane to fly him over the Andes into Chile was the best scenario he could develop. And then what? He'd worry about that later. One step at a time.

Gripping the gun hard, Craig held his breath when the frosted glass door opened. It was Ferraro. If he brought the troops, I'll kill that bastard, Craig vowed.

Sheepishly, Ferraro slipped into the room and closed the door behind him. There were no soldiers. The man was alone.

Craig let his breath out as he slipped the Beretta back into his brief-case and stepped away from the chair.

"I arranged a plane for you," Ferraro said curtly. "Gate 2. You can pay the pilot once you're on board. Go now and hurry."

Craig opened his mouth. Ferraro cut him off. "Don't thank me. Just go before you get both of us killed."

Buenos Aires

It was almost midnight when Craig stuffed the blue ski jacket into a trash bin at Jorge Newberry airport in Buenos Aires and climbed into a taxi outside of the terminal. At this hour, any city in the United States would be silent and deserted. Buenos Aires was alive.

He realized that he hadn't eaten much all day, and was suddenly starving. He decided to go to Lola's, about four blocks from the Alvear. It was one of the more fashionable restaurants in town, frequented by the rich and powerful as well as movie and television people. He knew he would stand out the way he was dressed, but that was what he wanted. He would say that he was topping off a great day by seeing the sights of Buenos Aires.

The radio in the cab was blasting a tango. He thought about his evening with Gina, closed his eyes imagining her in his mind, and smiled. Then he heard the words, "We'll interrupt for another update on the hour's top story."

He leaned forward in the seat, not wanting to miss a word.

To his horror, he heard the newscaster say, "Police have now con-firmed that twenty people have died in the explosion and fire that hit the headquarters of the newspaper *La Opinion* this evening. Police have attributed the cause of the accident to a gas leak in the boiler room. The fire is still raging out of control. No one knows how long it will be until the paper is up and running again. Among the dead are Carlos Cantina, the editor-in-chief."

That's terrible, Craig thought. Estrada didn't wait long to get even for this morning's editorial. He was sending a frightening message to the rest of the country.

The maître d' at Lola's insisted that Craig wear a navy blue sport jacket from the restaurant's cloak room so he didn't look totally out of place in the dining room that was still only half full. "The steak here is incredible," the tuxedo-clad waiter told Craig with pride. "We permit our cattle to graze on grass. Not like in the US where you feed them chemicals."

Craig had no idea whether that was true, and he didn't care to discuss it. He felt like Alice in Wonderland with everything swirling around him. His mind was focused on the danger confronting him, and what to do about it. Instead of the loud conversation he would have expected at this hour as patrons were lubricated with free-flowing wine, he heard a low murmur. In people's voices he detected concern as they spoke about what happened at *La Opinion*. Perhaps Estrada and Schiller had gone too far. At some point, fear creates opposition, but most people are cowed.

His own situation was devoid of choices. I'm not going to cut and run. I'll have to tough it out. He knew that he had to tell Betty and Alice what had happened to Dunn as soon as possible, but he couldn't risk using a phone, even one of the company's cells in case his conversation was picked up. He didn't want to risk going to the American Embassy to make the call in the event he was being followed.

After dinner, walking along the pedestrian mall that led to the Alvear, he was approached by a woman with a heavily made-up face, framed by long blond hair and wearing a short skirt. "You want some company?" she asked, smiling, and showing crooked teeth.

Craig smiled back. "I'm too tired to be any good tonight."

"We could try," she said hopefully.

Desperation and despair were written on her face. Craig reached into his pocket and handed her two one-hundred-dollar bills.

"God bless you," she said.

"Thanks. I need all the help I can get," he mumbled back.

Crossing the wide boulevard to his hotel, Craig saw Peppone standing on the sidewalk next to his Mercedes, smoking a cigarette. He felt relief when Peppone gave him a broad smile. To Craig it said, "You managed to outsmart my masters. Good for you."

Fernandez, the manager of the Alvear, wasn't smiling when Craig sauntered through the revolving glass door into the lobby. He looked distraught and harried. Contrary to instructions, he had lost track of his guest for an entire day and evening.

"You certainly put in a long day," Craig quipped.

"Mr. Gorman, I was worried about you," the manager said as he stared at Craig, demanding some explanation.

"You have a great city. I had a fabulous day seeing many of the sites."

"But you were gone so long. We were afraid you were kidnapped."

Craig was tempted to ask who the "we" was, but he overcame that and joyfully slapped Fernandez on the back. "You worry too much, my friend."

Fernandez retorted, "I worry about all of my guests. Is there anything I can do now?"

"You bet. Make sure nobody disturbs me until ten. I'm exhausted. And call Señor Miranda in the morning. See if he'll meet me for lunch."

"I'll be happy to."

"One other thing . . ."

"Anything."

"Arrange for Peppone, who's outside now, to drive me tomorrow."

Once he was in his suite, Craig checked the papers he had brought with him to Argentina—all copies of public materials about the Argentine economy. Before leaving the hotel that morning, he had arranged them in a very precise manner in the center desk drawer. They had been moved. Bastards must have searched the room, he decided. He had expected it. He hadn't left anything behind that undercut his cover. He had to assume that the room and phones were bugged, and there were probably hidden cameras placed strategically. He made no effort to find and disarm them. Barry Gorman wouldn't do that. Barry Gorman would take a long hot bath, soaking his weary body, and then collapse into bed. That's precisely what Craig did.

*　　　*　　　*

At 6:00 a.m. Estrada was pedaling furiously on the stationary bike he had in a gym he had installed off his office. He had loved jogging every morning rain or shine for decades, but that ended a couple of years ago when his knees cried out, "No more!"

One advantage of the bike was that he could read. His eyes were focused on Dr. Jeremy Barker's report about the diamonds. Perspiration was dripping from his forehead onto the pages.

Through the corner of his eye, he saw Colonel Schiller burst into the room, "I was right about Barry Gorman," he said in an excited voice. "The CIA sent Gorman to find out what happened to Dunn."

"How do you know that?" Estrada asked while he continued pedaling.

"Yesterday in Buenos Aires he eluded the two men I had following him as only a professional could have done."

"Your men must have been incompetent."

"Then he flew to Bariloche yesterday afternoon."

"So what? Plenty of people go there the first time they visit Argentina."

"In Bariloche he did something to the man I had following him. I can't reach him and he was very experienced."

Estrada stopped pedaling and put his head into his hands thinking.

Schiller continued talking, "Suppose Gorman doesn't have $10 billion to invest. Suppose it's all a cover for a CIA agent."

"Jorge Suarez checked him out and said he was legitimate. I'm accepting that."

"But is it wise?"

Estrada could barely contain his anger. He didn't like being challenged. And Schiller was being disrespectful. If he kept at this, Estrada might replace Schiller with someone who would follow his orders. "That's the way I intend to play it. As long as there's a chance of getting the $10 billion, I don't want to lose it."

"But . . ."

"Don't you interrupt me."

"Yes sir."

"Did Gorman come back to BA yet?"

"Very late last night. Peppone, the driver I hired for Gorman, saw him going into the Alvear."

"Good. You can keep track of him with Peppone. But don't do anything to harm Gorman."

After Schiller left, Estrada resumed peddling. He resented the insulting way Schiller had spoken to him and that might have caused his reaction to dig in and dismiss what Schiller had said. With Schiller gone, Estrada was thinking more clearly. Schiller was savvy about security matters. If he smelled a rat, his fears had to be taken seriously.

Estrada couldn't let the possibility of $10 billion blind him. Estrada believed he was a good judge of character. If he got close enough to Barry Gorman, spending time one-on-one, he'd test Gorman, cutting to the core of the man to determine whether he was genuine or a fraud.

But he didn't have much time to do that.

He had the London trip coming up. That was critical and couldn't be postponed.

London. Of course. That was it. London presented a unique opportunity for Estrada to deal with Gorman. It was not only an opportunity to get to know the man, but if he was convinced he was genuine, he would then have a chance to separate him from some of that $10 billion. In London he'd find out whether Gorman was really a wealthy money man or just a spy like Dunn, which was what Schiller thought. And if he concluded Schiller was right, then the man calling himself Barry Gorman would drop out of an airplane over the Atlantic without a parachute.

*   *   *

"Morning, Peppone," Craig said to the driver as he approached the Mercedes in front of the Alvear.

"Morning, Mr. Gorman, Where are we going?"

"The Buenos Aires Racket Club. The hotel manager told me that I should be there at 1400 for a luncheon with Mr. Miranda."

Peppone drove in a northerly direction through San Isidro and the other wealthy residential suburbs with large houses and estates. Craig asked the question of any first time visitor. "What do the people do who live here?"

Peppone provided the stock answer: "Business executives, bankers, and professionals."

Miranda was waiting for Craig in the entrance hall of the posh club. Aristocratic was the adjective that came to Craig's mind when he saw the man. Miranda was in his mid-sixties, tall, and well-conditioned. His complexion was ruddy, no doubt from lots of time on the tennis courts. His brown hair was graying at the temples. He had soft gray eyes. Beneath his double-breasted navy blue blazer, he wore a powder-blue shirt and a tie with tennis rackets and the crest of the club.

He came forward and shook Craig's hand, then led his visitor across the thickly carpeted corridor to the dining room where a large picture window faced perfectly maintained red clay courts—twelve that Craig could see from his vantage point.

The dining room was only half full, but practically everyone nodded to Miranda and stared at his visitor as they made their way to a table along the window. Miranda stopped to shake a couple of hands. He introduced Craig as an American investment banker.

"You're obviously well known here," Craig said, when they sat down.

"I've been a member a long time. They talked me into taking the club presidency a couple of times, and I won the singles and doubles championship for seniors last year. Are you a tennis player?"

Craig remembered from the bio that tennis wasn't Barry Gorman's sport. "I tried it for a few years, but developed a rotator cuff problem. I decided the sport didn't like me."

"A pity. I've had my share of injuries over the years. My wife says I'm not fit to live with when I can't play." He laughed. "I guess that means I am fit to live with the rest of the time."

A waiter came over with two menus. "What do you recommend?" Craig asked.

"A mixed salad. Then the grilled sirloin. Cooked rare."

"Sounds good."

After Miranda placed the order, Craig asked, "Does anyone here worry about their cholesterol?"

His host laughed. "We have a solution." He signaled to the sommelier. "We'll have a bottle of my 1990 malbec." He turned back to Craig. "You Americans are ridiculous. You should realize that with enough olive oil and red wine you can eat whatever you want."

"I understand from Jorge Suarez that you're a business leader. What sectors are you involved in?"

"My winery is in Mendoza. I have a cattle ranch not far from that city. And I have an oil and gas business in Patagonia and other businesses as well. Fortunately, I have good managers for all of them. I don't have to spend much of my time in the operation."

The sommelier brought over a bottle of wine. As he showed it to Miranda, Craig noticed a man's picture on the front bearing a striking resemblance to his host.

"You?" Craig asked, pointing to the bottle, when they each had a glass.

"My father. He started the winery. Now it's mine."

Craig tasted the wine and said, "This is superb."

Miranda smiled. "In Argentina the malbec grapes do best, and it's what we're known for. Our cabs are underrated. Some of them are excellent. For all of these wines, order the 1990 or 1995 if you can find them."

"Do you produce pinot as well?"

Miranda made a face. "God bless the Burgundians. They're the only ones in the world who can make good pinot."

"Lots of people in Oregon and Napa Valley would dispute that."

"Just a bunch of chauvinistic Americans. I know all about them. I did my paper on the wine business when I studied for an MBA at your school," Miranda said.

Craig was about to ask Miranda when he had been at Carnegie Mellon, the only school he had graduated from, but he caught himself. Barry Gorman had a Stanford BA and MBA.

So Miranda, or someone, had done their homework, looking up Barry Gorman on the Internet. "When were you there?"

Miranda laughed. "Probably before you were born. Let's change the subject. This one depresses me."

That suited Craig. He had never been to Stanford and would have difficulty talking about it.

The salads arrived. Craig asked Miranda how his family had come to Argentina.

"My grandfather came from southern Italy almost a hundred years ago. He was eighteen. He arrived with about ten lira and the clothes on his back. He worked hard and he bought land down south with every cent he could save. He had no idea there was oil underneath."

"Sounds like a smart man as well as a lucky one."

"Very. Smart's good. Lucky's even better. He built the family fortune." Miranda smiled. "And I'm trying not to lose it . . . You've heard the old joke. How do you get $10 million?"

"No, how?"

"Inherit twenty."

Craig laughed, then let Miranda talk some more about his family until the waiter brought their steaks. "I assume that Jorge Suarez told you why I'm here."

Miranda took a taste of the meat, sipped some wine, then wiped his mouth with the linen napkin. "He said you have money to invest for a private equity fund and you're considering Argentina."

"Precisely. I have $10 billion."

The sum didn't seem to faze Miranda. "What industries are you focusing on?"

Craig lowered his voice. "I haven't gotten that far in my thinking. I'm worried about your economy as a whole. In a macro sense."

Craig paused and locked eyes with Miranda. "Can I be real blunt? One business man to another."

"Sure."

"From everything I read and what I hear on the street, your economy is stagnating at best. There's no real growth."

Miranda nodded.

Craig continued. "President Garcia and his advisors seem to be clueless about what to do. If that's true, I would be pouring my money down a shithole—to be very crude—and I know that's not how a Stanford MBA is supposed to talk, but it happens to be true. Also, remember it's not my money. The Philoctetes Group raised it from investors. I have an obligation to them. So there we are."

Miranda rubbed his fingers together, thinking about how to respond. "There is a light at the end of the tunnel," he finally said.

"The last time somebody told me that it was a train bearing down on us."

Miranda scowled and brushed aside the comment. Though they were too far from the nearest table to be overheard, he was whispering. "Garcia is a fool. He'll be out as president by the end of the year."

"Then what?"

"General Estrada will take over the government, and our economic misery will be over. The military has saved this country before. It must happen again now, or we're all doomed."

Craig was whispering as well. "You're talking about a coup?"

Miranda shook his head. "I'm expecting a special election. Estrada will be swept into power by the voters."

That wasn't the answer Craig had been expecting. "I didn't think Estrada had that much popular support."

"Not yet, but wait a couple of months. Then people will realize that only Alfredo Estrada has the key to what's needed to get us back on our feet economically."

Craig wrinkled up his face and pulled back, pretending to be stunned by what he had just heard. "How about your friends? The other business leaders. What do they think?"

"We're all supporting Estrada. We've been encouraging him to take charge. There are constant strikes. Our labor unions are out of control. Workers don't work. They want more money for doing nothing. Discipline is needed to straighten out our economy. Only Estrada can provide it."

That's what the generals always say in these situations, Craig thought. General Videla had used the same rationale for the military seizing power in 1976. He pretended to be thinking out loud. "If what you're telling me will happen, then this would be the perfect time to invest in Argentina."

"That's precisely what I'm doing with all of my cash," Miranda said.

"There's a big difference between us, however."

"What's that?"

"I presume you know Estrada reasonably well."

"Correct. He has charisma, as well as being smart and tough. That's important. The psychology of the people is critical to turning the country around."

Craig pretended to be evaluating Miranda's words.

"The trouble is it all depends on the general, and I know very little about the man." Craig screwed up his face in doubt. "How can I commit to an investment of this magnitude without having my own personal sense of the man?"

Craig stopped talking. He leaned back calmly in his chair and waited. He had tossed out the bait. The question was whether Miranda would bite. It took only a couple of seconds for Miranda to say precisely what Craig had hoped to hear.

"Then I'd like for you to have a chance to meet the general. Once you do and you get to know him, you'll realize what a difference he can make when he's in charge of this country."

"Maybe so," Craig said Craig said, not trying to sound too eager. He wanted all of the pushing to come from Miranda.

"I'll arrange a meeting for you," Miranda quickly followed up. "I'll ask the general to spend some time with you."

"He's a busy man. Can you really do that?" Careful, Craig warned himself. Don't overplay your hand.

Miranda laughed. "I'm sure even in the United States $10 billion gets you an introduction."

Craig laughed easily with him. "Well, as long as you put it that way."

Miranda stood up. "Phones aren't permitted in the dining room. I'll go outside and call the general. Why don't you stay here and order coffee?"

When his host had departed, Craig turned his eyes toward the red clay tennis courts on the other side of the window. Two women, very good players, were pounding the ball back and forth. One of them reminded him of Gina—her shape, her moves, even a similar looking face. The tango with her had been incredible.

Miranda returned carrying two cigars. He handed one to Craig. "Cubans."

They both lit up. "I can't understand how business interests in your country tolerate that stupid Cuban embargo," Miranda said.

Craig nodded in agreement, though at this moment he could care less about Cuba. He wanted to know about his meeting with Estrada. Miranda must have sensed this and was making Craig wait.

Miranda took a puff, blew smoke into the air, and said, "You're all set. Today, Estrada is up in the north at a military base."

That must be the base Dunn had focused on, the one Nicole had agreed to check out for him. Something important must be going on up there.

Miranda continued, "The general flies back tonight. I arranged a meeting for you tomorrow morning at ten, at his office in the Ministry of Defense in the Government complex."

"Excellent."

"And one final thing," Miranda added. "When he persuades you that the time is right and you consider what to do with your $10 billion, I hope that you will talk to me. Our oil and gas business is poised for expansion. With new investment, we could begin exporting massive quantities to the United States. Our untapped reserves are immense. We would be a much more reliable source of supply than Saudi Arabia and your other so-called friends in the Middle East."

"Anybody would be better than they are."

Miranda took a pen and piece of paper out of his pocket. He scribbled down the address of the Defense Ministry and handed it to Craig. "Estrada is looking forward to meeting you."

I'll bet he is, Craig thought. After hearing about me from Suarez, Gina, and Miranda.

Bethesda, Maryland

Bryce accompanied President Treadwell to Bethesda Naval Hospital, a large US government medical complex on Wisconsin Avenue in the suburb of Bethesda, Maryland. No one in the press had taken any notice when this morning's handout for President Treadwell's "schedule for the day" showed a visit by the president to the National Institute of Health to discuss the latest research developments in women's heart problems, followed by a stop at Bethesda Naval Hospital to visit a wounded pilot whose plane had been shot down over Afghanistan and who had been flown to Bethesda Naval for treatment.

As they were leaving the White House, Bryce heard one reporter describe the day as "a yawner." That was precisely what Bryce had intended when he persuaded Treadwell to let him make the arrangements, which he had done with Dr. Lee. Bryce and the doctor were the only ones who knew what was actually planned at Bethesda Naval.

Dr. Lee and Bryce were at the president's side when he visited the Navy pilot. Reporters had been restricted to the press room off the ground floor lobby. "This is a working hospital," the director had told them. From that room, Lee led the way down an inside staircase with one secret service agent behind, then Treadwell and Bryce, followed by two more agents, one of whom was carrying a duffel bag.

When they reached the cardiac floor below, Treadwell snatched the duffle bag and said to the three agents, "You guys wait outside."

They didn't look pleased, but they kept silent.

"Edward, you're coming with me," Treadwell continued. "This was your idea."

The two of them and Dr. Lee disappeared behind the door of the testing room.

Bryce sat down in a corner trying to be unobtrusive.

"Change into your exercise clothes, Mr. President," Dr. Lee said. "We'll start with an echo stress test."

Bryce was impressed that Dr. Lee could work the equipment without a technician.

An hour later, the tests were over, and the president was dressed again. "Well, what's the verdict?" he asked anxiously.

Bryce leaned forward, listening carefully to what the doctor said.

"I'd like to schedule you for a cardiac catheterization, Mr. President."

"You doctors always want more tests. Do you know what I had to go through to have these done without the press being all over us?"

"I understand, sir. I only mean that . . ."

"Why don't you tell me what you found today?" Treadwell asked.

Bryce didn't have to wait for the words to come out of Dr. Lee's mouth. The grim expression on the doctor's face told him this wouldn't be good news.

"Your stress test was abnormal. You have coronary artery disease. If we do a cardiac catheterization, we will have a better idea of the condition of the blood vessels to your heart. We might be able to do an angioplasty and avoid a long hospital stay, but if your disease is severe, you will need surgery."

"Suppose I were to put it off a year or so?"

"I don't think that's a good idea. You are likely to have a serious heart attack. You could die."

Bryce was cringing. He hoped that Treadwell would follow the doctor's advice. But the president fired back, "You don't know for sure that something bad will happen if I don't have the procedure. Do you?"

"No. I can't say for absolute certainty. If it were me or someone I care about, I'd have the procedure and any intervention necessary done right away."

"But you're not facing a difficult election in a little over a year. Are you?"

"A presidential campaign is a demanding stress test. You might not survive this one."

Dr. Lee's words were met with a hard, cold stare and a rigidly set jaw.

She continued. "I'm sorry, Mr. President. All I can provide you with is my best medical advice. You're free to consult another cardiologist. You may want another opinion."

Bryce considered interjecting, but decided to hold his support for Dr. Lee until he was alone with Treadwell.

"I appreciate you giving me your best judgment," the president said. "But at the end of the day, the decision is mine. Isn't it?"

"It's always up to the patient, Mr. President," she responded respectfully.

"Is there anything you can prescribe to help me get through the year? To minimize the symptoms and all that."

She pulled out a prescription pad and began writing. "Sublingual nitroglycerin will help. When you get chest pain, place a tablet under your tongue. It will tingle. Your blood pressure is elevated. It's 160 over 98. I am also prescribing Prinivil to control your blood pressure. Your cholesterol is 260. You'll need to take Atorvastatin to lower it. Avoid all strenuous physical activity. And be sure you remember to take an aspirin every day. Let me know if your chest pain gets worse or happens more frequently."

"Good. I trust you won't discuss this with anyone else. No one. If they ask, I want you to tell them it would violate your ethical standards, which I think it would."

"I had planned to talk only to Dr. Anderson."

"Don't do that. Andy sometimes flaps his mouth when he's had too much to drink. He might talk to my wife."

Treadwell looked up at Bryce. "C'mon, Edward. Let's get out of here."

As they headed for the door, Treadwell suddenly wheeled around and said, "I want you to destroy all the records from this exam today, Dr. Lee." He pointed to one of the machines Dr. Lee had used. "All of the charts from that gadget. Everything."

Looking troubled, Dr. Lee tore the charts from the machine and handed them to Treadwell. "These records are your property, Mr. President."

Treadwell snarled, "Humph," and shoved them into his pocket.

Treadwell and Bryce didn't say a word until they were alone in the back of the presidential limousine with a soundproof barrier separating them from the driver. Then Treadwell said, "Do you think I'm being a fool? By not having the procedure she recommended?"

"You have to decide that for yourself."

"Dammit, Edward." Treadwell sounded exasperated. "I want your honest opinion. That's why I brought you out here."

Bryce hesitated, then said, "Truthfully, I think you should do the procedure."

"Thank you for being honest."

"We never bullshit each other."

"I may end up doing it, but I need a little time to mull it over. I'm not quite there yet."

Bryce was now optimistic that Treadwell would make the sensible choice. He just hoped the president wouldn't take too long to come around.

Buenos Aires

The Army officer, with a shaved head and wire framed glasses, who came to meet Craig in the reception area of the Defense Ministry, looked openly hostile and suspicious. "I'm Colonel Schiller," he said coldly, making no effort to shake Craig's hand.

"Barry Gorman."

"Well, well. At last we get to meet the famous Mr. Gorman. We've heard so much about you."

And I get to meet the infamous Colonel Schiller, Craig thought.

"All good things, I hope."

"But of course. You're not suggesting there's another side to you we don't know about?"

Craig forced a laugh. "I'm afraid what you see is what you get."

"That's good to know because I've spent twenty years in military intelligence. I don't like receiving surprises about people."

Schiller managed to make his position clear, Craig thought. The colonel had obviously checked out the Philoctetes Group and found out it was on the up and up and Barry Gorman a principal. He cautioned himself against getting too cocky. On the other hand, he wanted Schiller to know he wasn't frightened. "I have a ten o'clock meeting with General Estrada," he said curtly.

"That's where you're going."

After they exited the elevator on the sixth floor, Schiller led Craig down a long, dimly lit marble corridor. As they walked, Schiller said, "I hope you've had a chance to see some of the sights in the city."

"Absolutely. Two days ago I did major touring in Buenos Aires. The opera house, museums, parks. As much as I could cram into a day."

Looking at the rage on Schiller's face, his firmly set jaw and clenched mouth, Craig sensed that Schiller was ready to explode. The colonel knew that Craig was toying with him. Only Estrada and the prospect of $10 billion had to be holding him back.

Schiller knocked twice on a heavily polished wooden door, waited for a booming voice to call out from the other side, "Enter," then pushed it open.

The man in a military uniform, heavily decorated with medals, who rose behind the desk, took the measure of Craig with piercing, mocha brown eyes. The general had a commanding presence. His lips parted beneath a thin mustache into a friendly smile. Intimidation gave way to charm and charisma as Estrada moved across the large office to greet his visitor. The light from the ceiling reflected from his shiny coal-black hair parted in the middle. The clearly visible scar above his right eyebrow cautioned Craig that, notwithstanding what he saw, here was a man accustomed to violence.

Estrada reached out and shook Craig's hand firmly. "You made a wonderful impression upon Emilio Miranda," Estrada said. "And Emilio is a good judge of character."

"In that case, I'm flattered."

Estrada pointed to a rectangular conference table in a corner of the office. As Craig moved toward a chair on one side, Schiller followed him. To Craig's delight, Estrada cut off his aide. "I won't need you for this meeting."

Schiller left the room visibly pissed.

Estrada sat at the head of the table, as Craig expected. "Welcome to Argentina, Mr. Gorman."

"Please, it's Barry."

"Is this a first visit?"

"It is, and I'm very impressed with Buenos Aires."

"It's a fabulous city," Estrada said with enthusiasm. "I was born here. A porteño, as we say. It easily rivals Milan and Rome as one of the great cities of the world. And we'll have to get you out into the countryside. This is a huge and beautiful country. With wonderful people. Enormous energy and drive."

"That's all true, but your economy has been a consistent underachiever."

Estrada dismissed the comment with a wave of his hand. "Economic ups and downs repeatedly occur in all great nations. We're on our way now to our destiny."

"And what is that?"

"Are you a student of history?"

"I've read some."

"Then you're aware that we were the first country in South America to assert our independence from Spain. Once we did, we took the lead with our General José de San Martín out front in freeing other parts of the continent from Spanish rule. Chile, Peru, and Venezuela followed. Now we have a new opportunity for leadership in our region."

"To do what?"

The general smiled. "To lead all of South America in putting together an economic and trading bloc to take its place alongside North America and the EU." He said it with so much confidence that Craig was convinced he believed it.

"An ambitious undertaking, isn't it?"

"Visionaries are always doubted."

"I didn't mean to express doubt."

Estrada shrugged. "That's alright, my friend. We have to move in stages. The first step is to strengthen our own economy. Powerful economic incentives will be put in place right after the first of the year."

This fit with the schedule Miranda had described yesterday, Craig recalled. Estrada would take power early next year.

Estrada looked squarely at Craig. "Emilio told me why you've come to Argentina. Your timing to invest here couldn't be better. I would expect you easily to quadruple your investment in the next year."

Craig gave a long, low whistle. "At home, people would kill for a 400 percent return per annum."

Craig had been watching Estrada as he said those words, trying to see if the general flinched at the word kill. He showed no visible reaction. Instead, the general returned the focus to the money. "Emilio also said that you want to get to know me before committing your money."

"Precisely. I've learned enough to know that you are the future of Argentina."

Obviously pleased with the comment, Estrada's chest expanded. "Nothing I do is for myself. Only for my Argentina."

"But of course. That's what I understand."

"I'd like to have you out to my country house for a weekend," Estrada said.

Craig held his breath. That would be a perfect way to make inroads on penetrating Estrada's organization. To get close enough to Estrada to pick up hints of what he was planning.

"But I'm afraid it won't work this weekend. It's already Friday. Tomorrow morning I have meetings. Then tomorrow evening, I'm flying to London for a couple of days. Do you have business in London?"

Take it slow, Craig thought. Maybe Estrada would invite him to come along. "I have a major investor in London who has been wanting me to come over and meet with him."

"Why not do it now? You can fly with me."

Craig didn't want to appear too anxious. He leaned back in the high wooden chair pretending to mull over Estrada's proposal.

"My plan," Estrada added, "is to rest Sunday in London and relax in the evening. I have a Monday morning meeting. After that I intend to return."

"Sounds perfect. I'll make mine a breakfast meeting on Monday." Craig remembered what Betty's bio said of Estrada's interest in women and gambling. "Also, I have friends who can get us access to one of the best upscale dinner and gambling clubs. Lots of interesting people, including some top models, hang out there . . . if that sort of thing appeals to you."

Estrada laughed.

Craig could read his mind. A night on the town in London with another savvy man would be a pleasant interlude from the pressures of his life in Buenos Aires.

"You could twist my arm."

"Good. I always stay at the St. James Club. If you'd like, I could arrange a suite for you there."

"Excellent. I'll have them cancel my reservation at the Dorchester."

Craig was pleased. This was better than he had hoped. "How many in your party?"

"Just myself."

Craig concealed his surprise. This had to be a secret trip.

"Actually, I was planning to take Colonel Schiller." Estrada laughed. "But I'm sure you'll be more fun."

Now Schiller will really be out to get me, Craig thought. A deadly enemy had become even more dangerous.

"I'm going over in an Air Force plane. Be at San Martin Air Force Base tomorrow evening at seven."

"I'll be there."

Estrada hit the intercom and this brought Schiller marching into the office.

"Cancel the London plans you made," Estrada barked to Schiller. "I'm going with my new friend, Barry. You'll stay here and watch the office."

Craig could see that Schiller was engaged in a massive effort at self-control to keep his anger in check. "But . . ." he stammered.

Estrada cut him off. "It's already decided. Now walk Barry down to reception."

So now we're on a first name basis, Craig thought.

"Yes, sir," Schiller replied.

As Schiller led Craig along the corridor, he suddenly stopped at the top of a staircase. Without any warning, he grabbed Craig tightly by the arm. For an instant Craig thought Schiller planned to push him down the stairs. "I'll find out what you're game is," he whispered, "if it's the last thing I ever do."

Craig leaned his face in close to Schiller. "The general wouldn't like to hear that you're threatening me."

Schiller pulled back. "But you'll never tell him because he might take that as a sign that you have something to hide."

Schiller was right of course. Craig made a pass at softening. "I'm here to invest in Argentina. You and I are on the same side."

"Take your lies and get out," Schiller hissed with saliva bursting out of his mouth. "Before I kill you."

"You wouldn't dare do that," Craig responded coldly. "General Estrada would never forgive you if you cost him my $10 billion."

Schiller locked eyes with Craig. "Accidents happen. If I were you, I'd be careful." He tightened his mouth into a sadistic sneer. "Real careful."

Craig wanted to throw the events of two days ago in Bariloche in Schiller's face, but he decided that wasn't wise. He bit his lip and kept silent.

He took a taxi to Puerto Modero, a trendy area along the river that had once been warehouses and was now filled with restaurants and boutiques. He had read about a good steakhouse called Lilas Cabanos. It had a deck that looked out over the river, perfect for lunch on what had turned out to be a warm, sunny day.

Craig didn't care whether he had been followed or not. He was sitting far enough away from the next table that he couldn't be overheard if he talked softly on his cell phone. Even if Estrada had the technology to monitor his calls from the air, Estrada wouldn't learn anything harmful to Craig.

When Craig had left the clinic in Switzerland after plastic surgery, he had not only paid his bill but made a generous contribution to the clinic, which as he explained to Hans Wilhelm, the business manager, was to ensure absolute confidentiality. "But of course," Hans had told Craig. "And if I can ever do anything for you in Europe, Mr. Maura, please let me know."

Craig called Hans in Geneva to arrange plans for the London trip. The St. James Club for rooms, the Blue Giraffe for dinner and gambling, and the models, using the name Barry Gorman for everything. Hans understood why a man would want to use a different name for a trip like that.

Then Craig dialed Tim Fuller's cell phone with a Washington area code. "Tim," Craig said. "It's Barry Gorman." Tim didn't miss a beat. "How are you doing with the Philoctetes Group these days?"

"Still making money."

"That's not easy in this economy."

"You can say that again."

"What's up, pal?"

"I have to be in London on Sunday, and I remember you telling me you'd be there as well."

There was a slight pause.

Craig had no doubt that Tim knew what he wanted. Tim must be glancing at his calendar to see if he could shake loose to make the trip.

"You have a memory like a steel trap," Tim said.

"Good. Can you give me a call at the St. James Club Sunday afternoon? I'll buy you a drink or two that evening."

"You've got a deal."

Craig put the phone away and looked at the menu resting on the table. A waiter came by. "I'll have the sirloin, cooked rare." He said. "And a bottle of Miranda's cab, 1990 or 1995."

"We have the '95."

"Great."

Craig settled back and looked over the river. The Rio del Plata was alive. Boats of all types were passing before his eyes, large cargo ships, oil tankers, even small pleasure crafts. He tried to assess where he was, what had happened in his meeting with Estrada.

What didn't make sense was why Estrada had agreed so readily to go off to London with a man he had just met. Chances were the $10 billion had been the driver. He wanted to learn the general's plans and to penetrate his organization at the same time that Estrada was courting him. The cover he was using was brilliant. The models and the gambling had been a further enticement. Craig put his head in his hands and thought about it some more. Estrada had been so eager, even anxious to take Craig to London. Estrada must have an agenda of his own that involved Craig. He could never forget that beneath the cordiality, was a hard, cruel, military mind. Craig would have to be careful in London. He couldn't drop his guard.

Middleburg, Virginia

"I'm glad you could come out to Chesterfield to spend the night with me," Bryce said to Gina.

They were sipping champagne and eating caviar in the living room of the manor house of Bryce's country estate in the Virginia hunt country, just beyond the ever-expanding Washington suburbs. A crackling fire sent flames shooting up in the stone fireplace. Gina's eyes scanned the room, focusing on the costly antiques and original paintings. There were no pictures of Bryce with his wife or his two daughters, both of whom Gina knew were older than she was. She guessed that Bryce had asked one of the servants to remove them.

"I hope you don't mind if we eat in," he said. "My chef, Jean Pierre, is better than anyone in this part of the world. The rest are country bumpkins."

She smiled. "What's a bumpkin? I never heard that word before."

He shrugged and smiled back. "It's slang for I'm not sure what. It sounds like it fit."

Over dinner, a rich country pâté followed by grilled quail, Gina asked Bryce about the house. "Have you had it long?"

"I bought it about five years ago when it looked like my good friend, Edward, would become president. I wanted a place to entertain important visitors and to provide a refuge for him where he could escape from the pressure of the job in a way that he couldn't at Camp David. I even put a billiard table downstairs because he and I like to play."

She paused to eat some of the pâté. It was wonderful. "What's billiards?" she asked.

He smiled. "It's like pool, but much more of a gentlemen's game. Later I'll show you . . . unless of course we're busy with other things."

He smiled at her and she looked away. Every other time they had been alone together after a dinner, it had been for an hour or so at most. She was sorry she had agreed to spend the whole night with him.

It seemed so much more intimate. But she had to do it. Estrada was anxious to know about the surface-to-air missiles and rocket grenade launchers.

"A place like this must have cost a lot of money," she said, wide-eyed.

"It did, but the law practice has been good to me. Other things have held surprises. I expected Claire to be sharing this house with me on weekends. She's gone. Life sometimes throws you a curve," he said bitterly. "But then you came along." His entire face brightened. "If things continue to work so wonderfully between us, maybe you'll be sharing it with me."

She cringed. How could he think she'd ever agree to marry him. She felt as if she were sinking deeper into quicksand. She'd have to persuade Alfredo to let her end this assignment and come home.

Anxious to change the subject, she said, "Tell me about the horses you have here."

For the next half hour they talked about horses, a subject she knew something about. Her grandfather raised them on his farm.

"I never would have guessed that you knew so much about horses," she said. "You're not only wise, but so worldly as well."

He responded with a large smile as she fed his ego.

She waited until dessert, an orange tart, to raise the subject Estrada had been pressing her about.

"I know you're busy, Edward, and you have so much on your mind. Also, you've been wonderful to me and my people. So I hate to bother you."

"You're never a bother," Bryce said as he sipped wine.

"Last night you said you would find out about the shipment of surface-to-air missiles and rocket grenade launchers. What their status is. I wondered if . . ."

"I checked first thing this morning."

"And?" she held her breath.

"They'll be arriving in Buenos Aires in the next twenty-four hours. I had to pull some strings at the Pentagon, but it'll be done."

"We're so fortunate to have you because there are very few people like you who understand the complexity and importance of my country."

"You sound worried."

"I am. The Brazilians have given us lots of threats in the last few days. I've been so anxious about my friends and family that I haven't been able to sleep. At least this way, we'll be able to defend ourselves if they attack."

Bryce reached over and put a reassuring hand on her arm. "They're not going to attack. President Treadwell told the Brazilian president that we wouldn't tolerate that."

"And what did he say?"

"He denied that they had any offensive plans. He said the threats were coming from Argentina."

She winced. "Ah, they're such liars. Those Brazilians. But you, you're the best."

She got up, walked around the table and kissed him on the lips. "Thank you so much for helping us with the arms."

He reached for her, to pull her down on his lap, but she slipped away. She picked up a bottle of cognac on a cabinet and poured them each a large glass. She had no intention of taking any more than a tiny taste. It was nothing like the delicious sauterne Craig had ordered after their dinner in Washington. She was hoping Bryce would finish it all. So he wouldn't bother her later.

When he had drunk half of it, he said, "C'mon. I'll teach you to play billiards."

She was delighted to follow him downstairs. Anything to avoid going to bed with him.

"Hey, there are no pockets in this table," Gina said. "I thought that in pool, you shoot the balls into pockets."

Bryce laughed. "Pool is a game for lowlifes. Gentlemen play billiards."

Gina struggled to suppress a laugh. From the profiles of Bryce she had read in newspapers and magazines, she had learned that he had grown up in very modest surroundings. His father had been a truck driver in Chicago, and here he was trying to act like an aristocrat.

"But what's there to do without pockets in the table?" she asked.

"It's quite simple, my dear. You use a stick or cue like a pool cue. There are two white balls and a red ball. One of the white balls has a dot, and one player uses it as his cue."

"But what do you do with these three balls?" Gina asked, genuinely bewildered. "Since you're not shooting them into pockets."

Bryce was ready for her. "You try to score points, and you score a point each time your cue ball hits one of the other balls and three or more cushions on the table before it hits the third ball."

Gina thought about it for a minute. "Okay, that's a little confusing, but I think I have it. I still don't know why anyone would rather play this game than pool."

"Ah, my dear," Bryce said. "This is a game of endless sophistication, elegance, and subtlety. I'm sure you'll get the hang of it,"

She watched Bryce begin playing. When it was her turn, she held the cue in an odd way and leaned well over the table. Just a beginner, she didn't play very well, but she had the spark of a competitor in her eyes.

Fifteen minutes into the game, when Gina had the cue in her hand and was leaning over the table, Bryce came up behind her. He was supposedly helping her to aim, but she knew he had something else in mind when she felt his erection poking her in the rear. He was breathing on the back of her neck as he leaned over her. Then he reached his hands around her body and grabbed her breasts as if they were a couple of melons. "Ouch," she said pulling away. "I'm just learning the game."

"But I know of another game you're already good at. Let's go upstairs."

She decided to accede. After all, he had done what she had asked with the arms. When they reached the bedroom, he rushed her to take off her clothes. It was as if he was worried he would lose his desire. He became angry at her when she insisted on folding up her clothes. She took off her cross. Then she pulled a condom out of her purse and slipped it on him.

"Do we really need that?" he protested.

"Absolutely."

She wasn't worried about pregnancy. She was on the pill. She simply didn't want his fluid inside of her. He was on top of her in an instant, sliding himself back and forth. Feeling nothing, she wondered if this was how prostitutes did it time after time.

She began moaning. "Oh, Edward . . . oh Edward . . . That feels so good. Really good."

To speed him up, she reached down and grabbed the upper part of his penis that wasn't inside of her.

That worked.

He cried out. "Oh God yes." She felt his body shudder and he was done.

She reached down, pulled him out, then slipped off the condom and tossed it on the floor.

"Thank you so much," he said.

In a few minutes he was sleeping. But not Gina. She had something else to do tonight.

She checked the clock next to the bed. It was eleven forty. She decided to wait an hour to make certain he was truly asleep.

At twelve forty she took one final look at the snoring Bryce, eased herself out of bed and over to her purse resting on a chair. She grabbed her cell phone, then put on her cross and her white silk panties. Cell phone in hand, she tiptoed down the stairs to the living room.

The first floor of the house was deserted. All of the help was asleep in a separate, smaller building twenty yards from the manor house.

Enough light was coming in the windows that she didn't need to turn on a lamp. She sat down on a sofa. From memory, she punched in the number for Estrada's cell phone. He answered immediately, "Yes," in his normal curt voice.

"Alfredo, it's Gina."

"Do you have news for me, dear?"

"Very good news. Bryce told me that the surface-to-air missiles and rocket grenade launchers will arrive tomorrow in Buenos Aires."

"That is good. Very well done."

"Now can I stop seeing Bryce?"

In a sharp tone that displayed his irritation, Estrada snapped, "I'll tell you when, and stop asking me."

Suddenly a light came on above the staircase leading down from the bedroom. Through the corner of her eye, she spotted Bryce, dressed in a blue velvet robe, at the top of the stairs watching her on the sofa. The cell phone was tight against her ear; her arms bunched in close against her naked breasts. She was terrified. My God, did he hear my conversation?

"Can't talk any more now," she whispered to Estrada and hung up the phone.

With Bryce, she decided to take the offensive. "What's wrong, Edward? Why are you up?"

Moving down the stairs, he brushed her words aside. "Who were you calling?" he demanded to know.

Then it struck her. He didn't understand Spanish or Italian. The relief she felt quickly evaporated. She had spoken the words, "surface-to-air missiles and rocket-grenade launchers" in English. She hoped he hadn't heard them.

Looking sad, she shook her head. "I was calling my grandmother in Mendoza. She hasn't been well."

Bryce looked at her skeptically. "Argentina's practically on the same time as we are. It's the middle of the night."

"Since she got cancer, she can't sleep. She was happy to hear from me."

"I'm sorry. What kind of cancer is it?"

"Lymphoma. It's spreading." Please God, she thought. Forgive me for lying.

"Come to bed. I'll comfort you."

"You're a nice man, Edward, but go back to sleep. Leave me alone with my pain. Later I'll come upstairs."

"Okay. But wake me if there's anything I can do."

When he disappeared up the stairs, she began crying. She wept for what she was doing, for what she had become. They were both using her. Alfredo, for his political reasons. Bryce, for sex and to fill a void in his life left by the flight of his wife. She thought about her evening with Barry Gorman. He was someone who wanted her for herself. With him, she could be a regular person. She closed her eyes and smiled, thinking of the evening with Barry Gorman.

London

At eight Sunday evening, a black Rolls Royce, the house car from the Blue Giraffe, was waiting on Park Place in front of the St. James Club. Craig had to admit that Estrada's appearance in his army uniform exuded power as the general bounded down the five stone stairs and into the car.

Everything was in place at the Blue Giraffe when they arrived, just as Craig had wanted. Jane and Lucy, both blond, busty, and dressed in tight black sweaters and short black miniskirts—matching bookends—were waiting in the bar next to the dining room at a table. A bottle of Dom Perignon was chilling in a nearby ice bucket. Downstairs, the casino was still quiet. It was early.

Let the games begin, he thought as he led General Estrada across the bar to Jane and Lucy.

A tuxedo-clad waiter rushed over with a large dish of Beluga caviar. "The manager would like you to be his guest for dinner. Please order anything you'd like."

Craig could tell that Estrada was impressed.

Three hours later, Craig was pleased at the good time Estrada was having. Despite Craig's effort to minimize his own alcoholic consumption, the four of them consumed two bottles of Dom Perignon, a bottle of Corton Charlemagne, a bottle of Chateau Margaux, and four glasses of Remy Martin along with a superb meal. Even Estrada had to concede that the Scottish beef was in a class with the finest Argentine.

Jane and Lucy were educated women who could talk. They both had day jobs in the financial sector. The escort business was a way to pick up some extra cash because share prices were tumbling and action was slow in the city. During dinner they maintained a constant banter with Estrada and Craig about world political and economic affairs, life in Argentina, as well as about their careers as models, which were mostly in the past.

When they were finished eating, Craig led the other three to the lift that took them downstairs to the casino. It was now going full blast with the main room crowded with an international polyglot of Arabs, Russians, Americans, and Chinese predominating. "Let's get some chips," Craig said to Estrada.

At the cash window, Estrada reached into the leather case he was carrying, took out a hundred thousand dollars and converted it into chips.

You don't get that on a military salary, Craig thought. Big surprise. Estrada has his hand in the public till. "What do you like to play?" Craig asked the general as he cashed $100K of his own into chips.

"Craps. The fastest game. You can win the most in the shortest time. I have a system for winning."

Craig suppressed a smile. Every gambler thought he had a system, but the odds of any of them winning were still less than 50 percent. "What is it?" he asked.

"The key to winning big is to wait for one of those streaks that sometimes occurs when the dice get hot. Then you have to ride it hard, betting more and more on each roll, while siphoning off some of the winnings from each bet. The other key is to make bets that bring the odds as close to fifty-fifty as possible."

"So what so you do?"

"I bet the pass line. Over here, they call it the win line. I'm betting that the shooter will make his point. I also add come bets to increase my possible winnings."

Craig had to admit that Estrada's "system" was well thought out mathematically and increased the chances of winning to the max—just a fraction below 50 percent

"I like it," Craig said. "I'll bet with you."

"Good, but don't get impatient. Like much of life, patience is often rewarded. I keep betting small amounts until someone gets a hot hand and a streak begins, then I make my move. If it never happens, we move on to other forms of amusement." He smiled. "I mean the two women who are waiting for us in the other room."

"Got it."

"And I'm not greedy. I try to quit before the streak ends."

Without saying a word, Craig led Estrada through the hoi polloi into a private back room where five men, two of whom were accompanied by heavily jeweled women, stood around a craps table.

Jane and Lucy had their marching orders. One of them was on each arm of the general.

With his military uniform garnering respect and Jane and Lucy turning heads, Estrada moved up to the edge of the table. Craig went to the other side, chips in hand, prepared to mimic the general's bets.

For the first hour, Estrada showed great restraint. The dice were cold regardless of who threw them. He bet only small amounts. At that point, he and Craig were each down a couple of thousand. Then a Chinese man picked up the dice. He scored the point on each of his first two rolls. Estrada was ready. He bet ten thousand on the next point. When that won, he put aside five and let the rest ride. Each time he won, Jane and Lucy were cheering. For the next point, he put aside fifteen and let fifty-five ride. Craig was doing the same. After the Chinese made his point three more times, Estrada wasn't willing to push his luck any further. Ready to quit, the general signaled to Craig and began gathering up his chips. Craig did the same.

Craig estimated each of their winnings at a little over $300,000. That should help Betty's budget.

Estrada was thrilled as they cashed in their winnings. Smiling broadly, he nodded to Craig and headed toward the men's room. Craig followed him inside.

When they were standing at adjacent urinals relieving themselves, Estrada said, "I assume we're going back to the hotel now."

"You got it."

"What's the arrangement with Jane and Lucy?"

"They're ours until the sun comes up tomorrow."

"Well, you were so good to set this all up, I'll give you first choice."

Craig zipped up his pants and smiled. "Listen, Alfredo, you take them both up to your suite. I have a little piece of my own. Sally. Lives nearby. She's waiting for me to call."

"You hiding her on me?"

"You'll meet her the next time we come to London. So have a good time with Jane and Lucy, but there's only one thing."

"What's that?"

"Don't pay them a cent. Please. I've made sure they're well taken care of."

Estrada washed his hands and reached into his bag. "I should pay you back for the girls."

Craig shook his head. "Put your money away. What are friends for?"

Estrada nodded, giving Craig the impression that he had expected that response. The offer had been a formality. The general was whistling with joy as they approached the front door of the Blue Giraffe where Jane and Lucy were waiting. The black Rolls Royce was out in front.

At the St. James Club, the four of them exited and climbed the stairs. Inside the reception area, Craig said, "Here's where we split. So I'll say good night."

Estrada refused to shake hands. He insisted on a giant hug. Craig kissed each of the women on the cheek, then watched them disappear into the small elevator for their ride to the sixth floor and room 603, "The Palace Suite." Craig's own suite was one floor below, 503. Craig was pleased that he had solidly ingratiated himself with the general.

He went into the small bar off the lobby and turned the corner of the L-shaped room. As he had arranged, Tim Fuller was sitting at the bar, a drink in front of him.

"Did you see us come in?" Craig asked.

"How could I miss you, pal. Mother of God, those two . . ."

"The objective was for you to get a good view of the general. I wanted you to see what he looks like."

"Man the headlights on those two."

"Did you see the general?" Craig said irritably. It was late. He was in no mood for Tim's humor.

"Yeah, yeah. I saw him. Why's he got both of them?"

"It's good for business. You really think I'd prefer to be down here with you instead of up there with one of them?"

"That's for sure."

"Let's go up to my suite. So we can talk."

Tim picked up his briefcase and followed Craig into the elevator. "Jesus, the scent of those broads is still in here. When you're finished with me, I think I'll camp out in the lobby. I should be able to pick up one of them when he's done with her."

"Don't be disgusting. Besides, you need sleep. I have big plans for you tomorrow morning."

"Okay, pal."

Craig let them into suite 503, took off his jacket and kicked off his shoes. "Do you have anything for me?" he asked.

Tim reached into his briefcase and extracted two volumes of transcript. "These are the only worthwhile discussions to come off the tapes."

"With whom?"

"One with Bryce. Live in Gina's bedroom. Yesterday. The other with your gambling buddy, Estrada, later the same evening. She must have reached him when he was on the plane with you."

That was certainly possible, Craig thought. Estrada had been in his own cabin in the rear of the plane for much of the flight.

Craig raised his eyebrows. "How'd you get them already? Weren't you flying yourself?"

"Transmitted to me electronically. I travel with my own printer. The advantages of modern technology."

"I assume I can destroy these when I've read them."

"I wish you would. Generally, I don't like to leave around evidence of a felony I've committed."

"You still worried about that?"

"I don't think I'd enjoy jail. Now tell me what nefarious things you want me to do tomorrow."

Before Craig had a chance to answer, he heard a loud pounding on the ceiling.

"Jesus. What's that?" Tim asked.

Craig raised his hand and pointed upward. "The general's suite."

"One of the three of them must have fallen out of bed."

"Something like that."

Tim started toward the door. "Don't you think I should go up and make sure they're okay? Maybe apply some mouth-to-mouth."

"You don't quit. We have a job to do and a narrow window in which to do it. So sit down and listen."

Tim did as he was told. "Okay pal, what about tomorrow?"

"I want you to stake out the St. James Club from the crack of dawn. At some point in the morning, General Estrada will leave for a meeting. I have no idea when, or where he's going. I want you to follow him. Find out everything you can about his destination. Call me periodically with reports. This could be the break I need."

*   *   *

At eight the next morning, Craig was seated at the desk in his suite. After a continental breakfast with two double espressos, he was ready for the transcripts. The first one was Bryce and Gina in her bedroom.

Gina: *Oh Edward. You're a wonderful lover, but you're really heavy now. Could you get off me?*

Bryce: *Sure. Whatever you want.*

[Pause.]

[Snoring sounds.]

Gina: *I'm going to the bathroom now. As if you'd know . . . you're asleep . . . pig.*

Craig broke into a broad smile. You're quite a lover, Bryce.

The telephone rang. Craig grabbed it from the cradle. It was Tim Fuller.

"Subject is on the move."

"Where is he?"

"Just came out of the St. James Club. Dressed in a dark suit and tie. No military uniform or insignia. I'm around the corner on St. James. He's walking in my direction."

"Don't let him see you."

Tim laughed. "Don't worry, pal. I'm good at what I do."

"Well? What now?"

"Patience. Patience . . . Subject raised his hand and hailed a cab. Hold on. I gotta jump in the car. I'll tell my driver to follow him."

Craig could guess why Estrada had eschewed a private car in favor of a cab. Fewer records. More anonymity.

Wherever he was going, he didn't want anyone to know about it.

"We're crossing Piccadilly and moving north through Mayfair. I'll let you know when I have a destination."

Craig turned back to the transcript.

Gina: *C'mon, Edward, wake up. You have to go home.*

Bryce: *I'm so tired. Can't I stay the night?*

Gina: *You have to leave. Tomorrow morning I have to be up early to cover a story.*

Bryce: *Skip it. The paper will survive.*

Gina: *Don't talk to me that way. I'm not your property.*

Bryce: *Hey. What's wrong with you?*

Gina: *Nothing's wrong.*

Bryce: *You've been acting differently the last several days. Since you broke the date with me last Monday. Not like my angel. Did you meet someone else?*

Craig remembered that Monday was the evening he had taken Gina to dinner.

Gina: *No, of course not.*

Bryce: *Well what is it?*

Gina: *I'm worried about my friends and my family back home. I talk to them all of the time. They're terrified.*

Bryce: *Nothing will happen, honey. They'll be safe. You don't have to worry.*

Gina: *It's easy for you to say. You don't know those Brazilians. They're illiterate animals, those people, and they hate us. They're moving troops up to our border. The only thing that will stop them is if they know we have enough arms to destroy them if they attack us.*

Bryce: *They're not going to attack. You don't have to worry.*

Gina: *Then why are they moving troops up to our border?*

Jesus, what the hell's going on? Craig thought. He reread the last lines several lines to make sure he had it right.

Bryce: *Because of you, Gina, and our relationship, the Pentagon has already sent so many arms to Argentina. I was told that the surface to air missiles and rocket grenade launchers you wanted so badly arrived today in Buenos Aires. Don't worry. Your people will be safe.*

Gina: *You have to tell the president how worried we are that Brazil will attack.*

[A pause.]

Bryce: *I'll tell the president. He likes you. He wants us to come back again for another movie night with him and Amy at the White House. Like last Tuesday.*

Gina: *I see his wife on television all the time. Does she know about Amy?*

Bryce: *I don't think so.*

Gina: *You're not divorced yet? Does your wife know about me?*

Bryce: *I don't care. Can we talk about something else?*

Gina: *The president. You have to talk to him.*

Bryce: *I'll do it. I promise, honey. Now I better get dressed and go home.*

The transcript ended. Craig stared at the last page with a sick feeling in the pit of his stomach. The innocent girl he had danced the tango with was a very effective agent for her government. Originally, Craig had planned to burn the transcripts in the fireplace of the suite when he finished reading them, but this one was critical. He had to get it into Betty's hands as soon as possible. With the reference to Amy, if anyone in the press or rival politicians got hold of it, the political storm would make Watergate seem like a fairy tale. Before deciding how to forward it to Betty without anyone else reading it, he picked up the other volume of transcript. He might want to send that to the spy master as well. As he opened it, the telephone rang again.

"You're not going to believe this, pal." Tim sounded excited.

Craig was gripping the phone hard. "Yeah, what?"

"Your friend's taxi drove east past the law courts."

"And?" he asked anxiously.

"They turned onto Charterhouse Street and he went into number seventeen."

"Well?"

"Don't you know what's there?"

Craig was nonplussed. "Obviously I don't. It's not like you said Ten Downing Street."

"Okay, pal, don't get pissed. It's the international headquarters of DeBeers."

"The outfit that controls the world's diamond market?"

"Precisely."

"How long's he been in there?"

"About ten minutes."

Craig was thinking. "Can you find out who he's meeting with?"

"You've got to be kidding. This place is like Fort Knox. The building reminds me of a prison—gray and somber. Narrow, sealed windows on all six floors. Armed guards in front."

"You used to be a pretty resourceful guy."

"Save that con job for somebody else. I'll tell them I'm writing a book on how they market diamonds from West Africa, being sold by terrorists to support their networks. The DeBeers people always hate to hear that. They might be willing to try and co-opt me."

"Do it."

"I'll let you know."

Craig turned back to the second volume of transcript, the record of Gina's phone call with Estrada.

Gina: *Alfredo, it's Gina.*

Estrada: *How are you, my dear?*

Gina: *Bryce told me that the surface-to-air missiles and rocket grenade launchers arrived in Argentina today.*

Estrada: *And he's right. You're doing so much for Argentina. Your father would be proud of you.*

Gina: *Now can I stop seeing Bryce? I've persuaded him to do everything you wanted. These weapons were the last thing you asked for.*

Estrada: *For now. There will be more in the future.*

[Pause.]

Gina: *I hate spending time with Bryce . . . that way. I've told you that. Can't I stop? Please, Alfredo.*

Estrada: *It's critical for our country, dear. You know that. Your father was a hero. He gave his life for our country. This is what Argentina needs from you. If there was any other way, I wouldn't ask you to do it. You know that.*

Gina: *But Bryce's so . . .*

Estrada: *It's only for a little while longer. That's all.*

[Pause.]

Gina: *Have you met Barry Gorman, the banker? I think he's a wonderful man.*

Estrada: *Humph. I don't care about him personally. I'm interested in his money.*

Gina: *Well he has $10 billion to invest. I tried to persuade him to invest it in Argentina.*

Estrada: *And you did a good job, dear.*

Gina: *If Barry Gorman comes back to Washington and calls me again, I want to see him.*

Estrada: *That's alright, but don't forget you have to keep up your relationship with Edward Bryce.*

Gina: *But Alfredo—*

Estrada: *There are no buts. Your father and your country require it of you.*

Craig stared at the transcript and shook his head in disgust. To do his bidding, that bastard Estrada was twisting and manipulating Gina in order to force her to climb into bed with Bryce. Appealing to her patriotism and her love for her father made him even more despicable. He felt sorry for Gina, who had no way to extricate herself from the horrible situation.

Craig glanced at his wristwatch. Even though it was only four thirty in the morning in Washington, he couldn't wait to call Betty.

She answered on the second ring. "Yes."

"I hope I didn't wake you."

"Ever since I took over this job, I haven't slept more than an hour or two solidly at night. So don't worry about that. Where are you?"

"London."

"Secure phone?"

"Negative."

"Get to the Embassy. Ask for Billy Boyle. He'll be expecting you."

"Done."

Craig hung up and dressed quickly. It didn't matter if Estrada returned before he did. He had told the general he had a morning meeting.

He had the cab drop him at Berkeley Square and walked the last several blocks on foot, making certain no one was following him.

At the guardhouse in front of the Embassy on Grosvener Square, he used Billy Boyle's name. That was all it took to gain admittance. No one asked him for an ID. A secretary, young and fresh looking with blond hair flowing over her eyes, who reminded Craig of a woman fresh from the Iowa cornfields he had dated at Carnegie Mellon, escorted him to a communications room in the basement, showed him how to operate the red phone, and departed.

Betty answered on the first ring.

"What are you doing in London?"

"Gambling with your money. You'll be pleased to know we won $300,000 last evening."

"That's a comfort. Now what are you really doing?"

"I'm here with Estrada. Just the two of us. He had some business and he invited me to come along."

"What have you found out about Dunn?" she asked impatiently.

Craig swallowed. His heart ached as he recalled what Antonia had told him about the way Dunn had died.

"He's dead. He was close to finding out about a meeting Estrada had with people who flew in from Porte Allegre, Brazil, when his cover was blown."

"Oh damn."

"A couple of Estrada's troops killed Ted in a farmer's field while he was getting mauled by a German Shepherd. They hacked up his body and buried it."

"Oh God."

"This is the first chance I've had to tell you. Will you let Alice know? And that Ted had been killed the night he broke communications with you. So there was nothing you or anyone could have done."

"Of course."

Craig was choked up. "I feel so bad for Alice. Please tell her that. Also, that I'm sorry I couldn't tell her in person."

"I'll go over to her house and explain it this morning."

"Thanks."

"Who blew Dunn's cover?"

"I don't know."

"Nicole?"

"Negative. She's a good woman."

"You sleeping with her as well as Gina?"

"What makes you think I'm sleeping with Gina?"

"I know precisely when you entered her Watergate apartment last Monday evening and when you left. I assume you weren't watching television or playing Monopoly."

"Negative for both women. Gina and I talked. That's all. My relationship with Nicole is still strictly professional."

"What's Estrada doing in London?"

"This morning he had a meeting at DeBeers."

"The diamond people?"

"Exactly. I don't know why, but it's obviously a top priority."

"What have you learned so far?"

"Estrada's objective is to take over the country in an election by the end of the year. The business interests in Argentina are backing him. And most important, I now have solid evidence that Estrada is using Gina to get what he wants from President Treadwell by having her sleep with Bryce."

"What's the evidence?" Her voice didn't show surprise.

Craig bit down on his lip before responding. He hoped that Betty wouldn't get pissed about his domestic surveillance. "Someone happened to deliver a couple of transcripts to me. One from a conversation in Gina's apartment. Pillow talk with Bryce. After sex. The other one from a phone call Gina made to Estrada."

"How convenient."

"She talks about troop movements on the Argentine-Brazilian border. I have no idea what that's about."

"We've picked those up as well. Units from both armies are on the move toward their border. Each one is blaming the other. The Brazilian president has called Treadwell twice to report that Argentina has fortified its border positions in the northeast. So Brazil's doing the same. It's an area that the two of them contested in the past, but not for some time. Garcia has called Treadwell from Buenos Aires claiming that Brazil initiated the activity. We're following it closely here."

"I want to get the two transcripts to you ASAP. One's very explosive for another reason."

"Spell it out."

Craig took a deep breath. "There are some extracurricular activities going on at night at 1600 Pennsylvania Avenue. Someone named Amy is involved."

"Oh Christ, he's still doing her," Betty sounded distressed.

"What would you like me to do with the transcripts?" Craig asked.

"Talk to Cynthia Nightingale. She's one of ours. Tell her you want a gray envelope. 'For the director's eyes only.' Put the transcripts in and seal it yourself. They'll deliver it to me with a military escort."

"Will do."

*   *   *

Craig returned to the St. James Club and called Tim. "What's the status?"

"Subject is still in the DeBeers building. I haven't been able to find out squat about what he's doing. I tried my brilliant writer's scam to get inside but the chap behind the bulletproof glass window wouldn't even let me in the reception area. He told me to call Carolyn in the Diamond Information Office. All I got is her voice mail and no call back. A great way to blow off the uninvited. Sorry about that, pal."

"Don't worry about it. Just the fact that you found out he went to DeBeers is significant. Keep me posted."

With nothing else to do while he waited to hear from Tim, Craig hooked up his laptop and went online, trying to learn as much as he could about DeBeers and the diamond business before Estrada returned.

Since the 1930s DeBeers had made a concerted effort to maintain a stranglehold over the world diamond business and to keep prices artificially high. In its building on Charterhouse Street, which looked on the computer screen like a six-story dark gray fortress with narrow windows suggesting secrecy, DeBeers controlled the world diamond industry. Within those walls, $500 million a month in rough-cut, gem-quality diamonds were sold to buyers DeBeers selected from a myriad of applicants to be its customers. By the time those stones were cut and made into jewelry, their retail value became many multiples of the $500 million a month.

Astonishingly, Craig learned that in the past decade, approximately 75 percent of those diamonds had been sold in the United States, but that was now changing. The DeBeers strategy, like any good monopolist, was to keep supply limited and under their control. Thus, whenever any new source of diamonds was discovered, DeBeers moved aggressively to tie up those stones and put them under the DeBeers umbrella.

Usually it worked, but not always. In the late 1990s, high quality diamonds were discovered in Northern Canada by a Canadian company independent of DeBeers. The Canadians invested huge quantities of cash to mine those diamonds and eventually defied DeBeers and went it alone on marketing. Their diamonds were currently 10 percent of the world market.

Craig flashed a map of the world on his computer screen, showing the location of diamond sources with estimates of the quantities available. As he expected, Africa dominated. South Africa, Botswana, Sierra Leone, and other locations on the dark continent had a major market share. In comparison, apart from Canada, there were only tiny "estimated resources" in other parts of the world including India, Russia, and South America.

The phone interrupted Craig. He pounced. It was Tim. "Subject left DeBeers. He's in a cab, heading in a westerly direction. I'm in a car following behind."

"Stay on the phone with me. Give me a running report where you're going."

Craig was trying to piece together what this all meant. He felt as if he now had a complex jigsaw puzzle on the table in front of him. Estrada. Gina. Arms. Money. Argentina. Brazil. Now diamonds. He pushed the pieces around in his mind.

"We're leaving Piccadilly Circus," Tim said. "Heading south on Regent Street."

"He's probably coming back to the St. James Club."

"That's what I figure."

"If he returns here and goes inside, you hang back at the corner and watch the entrance. When the two of us leave in a car and my window's rolled down, you'll know we're on our way back to the airport. Then you can close up shop and go home."

Twenty minutes later, Craig received a call from Estrada. "I'm ready to fly back whenever you are."

Over the Atlantic

Once the plane took off for Buenos Aires, Craig leaned back in his seat with copies of the morning *Financial Times* and *London Times*. He wondered if the general, now dressed in his military uniform, would say anything about his visit to DeBeers.

"I want to thank you for arranging a great evening last night," Estrada said. "Those two girls were a treat. I owe you for them."

Craig smiled. "Happy to help a friend."

"I like coming to London, Barry, although not many of my countrymen agree with me on that. And we're not exactly popular here."

"C'mon, Alfredo," Craig said laughing. "After the Falklands War, you can't blame them."

Estrada shrugged. "The Falklands have no economic, military, or strategic significance. The British can have them. I prefer to concentrate on more pragmatic objectives."

Finally, Craig felt as if he were getting somewhere. "Such as?"

The plane hit an air pocket and bounced. Estrada waited until they leveled off to answer. "Resuscitating our economy. Rebuilding the military."

"Where do you intend to use it?"

Estrada narrowed his eyes and stared hard at Craig, who met his gaze. He's a smart man, Craig thought. Better not push so hard that I arouse his suspicions.

"Our neighbors have powerful armies," Estrada said. "Who knows when they may wish to embark on an adventure. We have to be vigilant."

"Are you worried about Brazil, Paraguay, or Chile?"

Estrada ducked the question. "Besides, a powerful military is a source of pride for a country. A Japanese leader wrote a hundred years ago: 'Strong army, strong nation. Weak army. Weak nation.' Our young people have to realize that Argentina can be a great nation if we have the will to make it so. We have everything. Land. Resources. Wonderful people. We should be to South America what the United States is to the North. Yet, we have become a joke in the world community. It's time to restore our nation to its rightful place—as the aristocrat of South America. Once we believe we can succeed, then we will."

Estrada was speaking with conviction from the heart, his eyes burning with determination. To Craig, he seemed part visionary, part dreamer, and part lunatic. "We've been hurt for years by corrupt leaders and by a feeling of helplessness. We don't have millions of uneducated people like Brazil. General Peron understood this."

"Would you call yourself a Peronist?" Craig asked with curiosity.

Estrada nodded vigorously. "But of course. Like Peron, I believe it is critical to unite the military, the labor unions, and the industrialists. The entire society. We simply have to do more with what we have. With our talented people. With our magnificent resources. Our destiny is in our hands. As Shakespeare expressed it so well in *Julius Caesar*, 'The fault . . . is not in our stars, but in ourselves that we are underlings.'"

Craig had no doubt that Estrada meant what he was saying. "Before coming to Argentina, I stopped in Washington to obtain some background information about your country. There I met with Jorge Suarez, the economic attaché at the Argentine Embassy, and also with a reporter for *La Nación* by the name of Gina Galindo."

Estrada was watching Craig carefully, but not displaying any visible reaction. Craig continued, "Miss Galindo's statements about Argentina's potential were similar in substance to what you just said."

Estrada nodded. "I'm not surprised. I know the young woman. Her father was a great man. A military hero in the war against the Communists."

"Did you serve under him?"

Estrada shifted uncomfortably in his seat, then changed the subject away from Gina's father. "What did you think of her?"

Estrada's boldness surprised him. "She's extremely intelligent, and—"

Estrada cut him off. "Beautiful as well."

"I noticed that."

Estrada laughed and punched Craig playfully in the ribs. "From the look on your face and the sound of your voice, I think that you're not just interested in Gina for her great brain."

Craig pretended to blush, then hesitated, uncertain how to respond. He didn't want to put Gina into play in the dangerous game he was conducting with Estrada. Finally, he decided that she was already a participant so he said, "You're very perceptive."

Craig was trying to decide how to raise the subject of diamonds, when Estrada abruptly said, "I'm tired. I'm going in the back for a nap."

The plane was outfitted with four beds in the rear, but Craig was too wired to consider sleeping.

A couple of hours later, Estrada was awake, and they were seated across from each other at a table eating pasta with seafood that the crew had cooked. Craig decided to wade in slowly. "I hope your meeting was successful this morning. Worth the long trip."

Estrada nodded. Craig kept still, not pressing it.

After several minutes, Estrada said, "I've given thought to where you might invest some of your money."

Craig leaned forward in his chair. "You have my attention."

Estrada took a forkful of pasta and chewed while he studied Craig carefully. "Do you know anything about diamonds, my friend?"

Bingo, Craig thought. He masked his enthusiasm and replied deadpan. "A little bit. The Philoctetes Group was consulted a couple of years ago about a possible investment in a new Canadian field. Nothing came of it."

"You mean the diamond discovery didn't materialize?"

"No. A huge quantity of diamonds was found. We were unable to work out the terms for the deal. Why do you ask?"

"Well suppose . . ." Though the air force officers who made up the crew were out of sight, Estrada lowered his voice to a whisper. "Suppose we discovered a huge new source of diamonds, gem quality. Would you consider investing in that operation?"

Craig squeezed his hands together, looking very interested. "Where is the diamond field?"

Estrada waved his right hand and pointed to the ceiling of the plane. "Up in the north," he responded vaguely.

"That doesn't surprise me. From what I've read, Argentina is rich in minerals. You have oil and iron ore as well."

Estrada nodded.

Craig continued, "I'd have to satisfy myself that the diamonds are gem quality. You'll have to get me a report by a qualified geologist that I can forward back to California to our expert there."

Craig had no idea what he was talking about. He was totally winging it, so he was relieved to hear Estrada say, "That makes sense. But you should know for openers that my experts are predicting this field, when fully up and running, could be 15 percent of the world supply. They estimate a gross per year of $1 billion in rough cut at current market values."

Craig gave a long, low whistle. "That puts it on a par with the Canadian discovery. Perhaps a little more."

"Have you continued to follow developments in the diamond market?"

"Not since our Canadian deal fell through. What's happened?"

"Within the last year, diamonds have been rising sharply in price. Outpacing gold by a large percentage."

"What's causing it?"

"Sharply increased luxury spending in China, India, and the Middle East. And an expanding middle class throughout the world. Experts are predicting a 9 percent rise to $145 a carat next year and at least 5 percent a year after that. They forecast a global supply shortage of seven million carats."

"I had no idea."

Estrada reached into his bag and pulled out a spiral bound report. "Wait, there's more," he said while looking at the document. "The price of rough diamonds advanced by 24 percent in 2011. Buyer demand in China and India will be 40 percent of global demand by 2015. Up from 8 percent in 2005. Meanwhile, mature mines are being depleted. So while global demand is expected to grow by 6.4 percent to 247 million carats by 2020, the output that was 133 million carats last year, will be up to only 175 million carats. None of these numbers, of course, takes into account a new Argentine diamond field."

"So if you did have a new diamond field, you would have an incredible source of wealth."

"Exactly."

"Who prepared the report?"

"A consultant I hired."

"Can I read it?" Craig asked, hoping it disclosed the location of the diamond field.

Estrada shook his head. "Not now. Perhaps in the future."

"You have to remember it's not easy to get those shiny little suckers out of the ground. The material is extremely hard and the drilling tough work. It'll take big money to get them into commerce."

Estrada smiled. "That's where you come into it." He walked over to the briefcase, took out two Montecristos, and tossed one to Craig.

When they both lit up, Estrada said, "My proposal is that you invest a billion dollars in the project in return for 10 percent of the gross from the mine for the next thirty years. That means you can earn back your investment in ten years. After that it's pure profit for you."

Craig shook his head. "I like the idea of the investment, but the terms you propose are a terrible deal for me. There'll be a delay until diamonds are sold. Also, this projection, that you expect a gross of one billion a year, is little more than a guess. I know how these things are done."

Estrada leaned back in the chair and puffed on his cigar while he evaluated Craig's words. "Then what do you want?"

"A third of the gross, and I put my money in $100 million at a time as construction proceeds. The first installment would be due when you break ground."

Estrada looked incredulous. "A third? You're insane."

Craig didn't appear too anxious. "My money comes from other individuals. I have a duty to them."

"I'll give you 20 percent. That's the most. We expect to discover iron ore, petroleum, and other minerals in the area. If we decide to develop those, I'll offer you the same deal."

Craig nodded in approval. "That's worth taking back to my investors. I'll recommend it. They're likely to accept my recommendation."

He held out his hand and Estrada shook it.

The general seemed pleased. "When we get further down the road," Estrada said, "I'll have the attorney general's office draft the papers for the deal with you. We'll also need an agreement with DeBeers to purchase our output. They'll be the ones selling the stones on the world market."

So that explained Estrada's meeting this morning at DeBeers. Craig twisted up his face in a grimace. "Don't sign any agreements with DeBeers. We'll revisit their participation when our operation is up and running."

Estrada was puzzled. "What do you mean?"

"I'll bet they'll want a 50 percent cut, or some other ridiculously large percentage, for marketing your diamonds."

Estrada nodded.

"It's bullshit," Craig said. "We don't need them. Why give away half our profit. We'll do a lot better marketing the diamonds on our own the way the Canadians did, or even teaming up with the Canadians in an American cartel. The key to getting a high price is to carefully control supply. Alternatively, we may decide to play ball with DeBeers and threaten to dump large quantities on the world market unless they secretly take a very low cut. We'll have a number of options."

Estrada seemed impressed. He picked up a pad and pencil and wrote down a phone number. "It's my private phone. Very few people have it."

Craig responded by giving Estrada a card with his number in San Francisco at the Philoctetes Group and a cell number with a San Francisco area code. As he handed it to Estrada, one thought kept running through Craig's mind: I hope this man never finds out that I'm not Barry Gorman and I don't have $10 billion to invest.

For the last two hours of the flight, Estrada was in the back of the plane on the phone. Though Craig strained to eavesdrop, over the roar of the engines it was impossible to pick up more than an isolated word. He heard, "troops . . . arms . . . border," but he couldn't make sense out of it.

Ten minutes before touchdown when Estrada came to the front cabin, he seemed determined, but self-confident. "Is everything okay?" Craig asked.

"Couldn't be any better," Estrada replied. Then he changed the subject. "I've arranged to have a car meet you and take you to the Alvear."

Craig sensed that Estrada had erected a wall between them. His buddy from last evening was operating in his own world now with

Craig on the outside. The spontaneous confidences they had exchanged about diamonds a few hours ago were ended. But as Craig thought about it, he wondered if there had been anything at all spontaneous about their discussion. Estrada must have planned to present his proposal to Craig on the way back to Buenos Aires after the meeting at DeBeers. That was why he had jumped so quickly at the idea of taking Craig to London.

It was clear to Craig that Estrada was now preoccupied with other matters. Something big would be happening. Craig expected to find out what it was very soon after they arrived in Buenos Aires.

Buenos Aires

Craig spent the morning working out in the hotel gym and then visiting the National Museum of Fine Arts to view its collection of Impressionist paintings. For Craig, the most interesting rooms were those with Argentine art and particularly war scenes from the nineteenth century war with Paraguay painted by an Argentine soldier. He was aware that he was being watched and tailed the whole time. He made no effort to do anything about it.

As he exited the museum and crossed the wide Avenue de Libertador, he glanced over his shoulder. The surveillance was still there.

Back at the hotel, he hooked up his computer and went online, delving deeper into the diamond business. For their next discussion Estrada might include an expert on mining and marketing the gems. The superficial information Craig had learned in London wouldn't be enough.

When the telephone rang in the late afternoon, he grabbed it immediately. "This is Fiona. Your briefcase has arrived," a woman said. Though the voice was tense and strained, it was unmistakably Nicole's. That distinctive, throaty sound, giving him a coded message that she had obtained information about Estrada's activities in the north and she wanted to meet with him at the place she had designated.

"Thank you," he replied tersely.

She hung up.

He had no doubt that the people Schiller had following him now would be more experienced than the men he had given the slip on Calle Florida the day he arrived. Losing them this time wouldn't be easy. Craig studied a map of the Buenos Aires area and found the intersection of highways twelve and eight. He zeroed in on the location of the overlook that Nicole had fixed for their meeting place. It would be dark. Gradually, a plan formed in his mind. It meant trusting Peppone, which was risky, but his instincts told him it was the right thing to do. Besides, the alternative of driving himself was a nonstarter. He didn't know the roads.

He called Peppone's cell. "Can you pick me up at eight thirty this evening at the Alvear?"

"Sure. Where are we going?"

"I'll let you know that when I get into the car."

*   *   *

"The Metropolitan Cathedral," Craig told Peppone once he was seated in the back of the Mercedes.

"You want to pray?" the driver asked with a grin on his face.

"Something like that."

"You don't seem like the type."

As they drove, Craig's eyes were darting out of the car window. From the moment they left the Alvear, a midnight blue Ford had been following. It was a loose tail, but the Ford was always there.

About ten blocks from the Cathedral, they were driving on a wide boulevard with an inside service road where a car could park. "Pull into the right and stop the car," Craig said.

As Peppone followed the instruction, the blue Ford pulled over as well, about twenty yards back. In the bright lights of the boulevard, Craig saw two men in the front of the Ford and one in the back. None of them made a move to get out of the car.

Worried about a bug in Peppone's car, Craig said to the driver, "I heard a strange sound coming from the engine. Let's look under the hood."

"I didn't hear anything."

"I might be wrong, but to be safe, let's take a look."

With Craig standing beside him, Peppone lifted the hood and shielded them from the eyes of the men in the Ford.

"I have a proposal for you," he told Peppone.

The driver turned his head toward Craig.

"Keep your eyes on the engine," Craig snapped. "I'll give you $20,000 if you do what I tell you."

"What's that?"

"I have a plan to lose the people following me in the dark blue Ford."

Peppone began twitching. "I don't know about dangerous stuff like this."

Craig detected the fear in his voice. "Look here, I know they're working for Colonel Schiller, the same as you."

Peppone made a feeble effort to protest. "Who is Colonel Schiller?"

"I'll fix it so you'll be able to say I coerced you. Nobody will be able to prove otherwise."

"I'm not sure . . . I . . ."

"Stop stalling. There won't be any risk to you. Are you in or out?"

"Cash?"

"US currency. All hundreds."

"You have it all with you?"

"In the car."

The duffel he had brought contained cash, his two guns, and a liter of olive oil he had purchased at a market a couple of blocks from the Alvear after Nicole had called.

Peppone reached into the engine and fiddled with something. He's considering my offer, Craig decided. Finally, Peppone said, "I'm in."

"Good. Drive to the Metropolitan Cathedral and park in front. I'll go inside. You keep the engine running. Be ready to drive fast when I get back in. I'll have a gun aimed on you to give your story credibility."

"I have a wife and kids," Peppone stammered.

"That's why I want to do this in a way that you or they won't get hurt."

Peppone slammed the hood and they climbed back into the car.

*   *   *

The cathedral was in an area of government buildings, deserted at night, which was what Craig wanted. When Peppone stopped the car and turned off the lights, Craig got out with the duffel in his hand and walked toward the main front entrance. The Ford parked about twenty yards back under a large tree. They'll be convinced that he had come here to meet someone, Craig told himself. His guess was that two of the men would follow him inside and leave one in the car.

The interior of the cathedral was dimly lit with candles. Blinking his eyes, Craig saw only a couple of old women on their knees in front of the alter. From the doorway, which opened in the back of the cathedral, he raced for the right side and the marble mausoleum holding the remains of General Jose de San Martin. His vantage point behind the mausoleum enabled him to watch the entrance.

As he expected, two men burst through the door. Each one ran up one of the two long aisles searching the rows of pews.

He watched them carefully. When they were almost at the altar, he ran back toward the door. At the same time, he yanked the bottle of oil out of his duffel. In front of the door, he poured it on the stone floor. When they chased him, they would lose their footing. Opening the door, he heard a shout behind him, "Hey you. Stop." Then the sound of a gun firing. Bullets flew over his head. An old woman screamed. Craig slammed the door behind him.

Outside on the street, he grabbed his own gun from a shoulder holster. He took three steps toward the blue Ford and fired, blowing out one of the front tires.

Then he turned and jumped into the back seat of Peppone's Mercedes. He pressed the barrel of the gun against the driver's neck. "Step on it," he shouted. "Or I'll kill you."

Peppone floored the accelerator. The wheels spun on gravel as the car lurched forward.

"Get to Highway Twelve and drive north," Craig barked. "Toward the intersection with Highway Eight."

Once they were out of the city, traffic became light. Peppone drove fast. They were making good time.

Craig was constantly looking around. After several minutes, he was convinced they weren't being followed.

They were gradually rising into the hills. He saw signs for the approaching intersection of Highways Twelve and Eight. "Slow down and go straight."

Craig leaned forward, looking over Peppone's shoulder at the odometer. The road continued moving upward. Two kilometers later, he saw a small restaurant and gas station, exactly as Nicole had described it.

"There's an overlook just ahead on the right," he told the driver. "Pull in there."

When Peppone came to a stop in the parking area of the overlook, Craig rolled down the car window and scanned the area anxiously. It was deserted. He checked his watch. Twenty minutes until ten. Perfect. He wanted to be here when Nicole arrived to make certain no one was following her. "I'm getting out. I want you to go back to the restaurant with the gas station down the road and wait there. I'll come in about an hour."

"What about my money?"

"You'll get all of it then."

Before the driver had a chance to protest, Craig climbed out of the car. He watched Peppone drive slowly down the hill. In front of Craig was a magnificent view of Buenos Aires with millions of lights glowing in a clear sky.

No wall or other structure separated the overlook from the road. On the far side of the overlook, a small stone wall, waist high, ran along the perimeter. It was a barrier that would stop anyone who got too close to the precipice from slipping down the steep hill. In places, the wall was crumbling and in need of repair.

Using the light of passing cars and careful to maintain his footing, he climbed over the stone wall. He squatted down in order to have a clear view of the overlook, while not being seen.

Promptly at ten o'clock, a white BMW convertible with the top up pulled into the overlook. He watched Nicole get out and look around. She was wearing tight black leather pants that looked as if they were painted on and a matching jacket over a powder blue sweater. He waited a full minute to make sure she hadn't been followed before he rose and climbed over the wall.

Nicole was facing the road. The sudden movement from behind startled her. She reached into her purse, grabbed a .22 caliber pistol, and pivoted in his direction.

Once she recognized him, she put the gun away. "I wasn't expecting you to come from that direction."

A chilly wind blew through the hills. She shivered and said, "Can we go in my car and talk."

Craig shook his head. "We're too exposed that way. I pissed off some important people on the way here. Let's climb over the wall. We can sit behind it and talk. Assuming you can sit in those pants."

"Are you coming on to me?" she said, laughing to ease the tension.

"Right now the only thing on my mind is staying alive."

Craig positioned them so they were squatting on the ground, behind the wall, facing each other, while they still had a view of the overlook. The duffel with his guns was beside him.

"What information do you have for me?" Craig asked.

"Later in the day, after you left my shop, I went out of town. I . . ."

Before she finished her sentence, Craig saw a midnight blue Ford race into the overlook parking area. The car slammed to a halt. A side window in the back was rolled down and the barrel of an AK-47 shoved out. The man holding it raked the white car and the entire overlook area with automatic fire.

Craig pushed Nicole down flat on the ground and covered her body with his. He heard the sound of bullets ricocheting off the sides of stones, not far from his head.

The automatic fire stopped as abruptly as it had begun. Through a crack in the stones, Craig watched the gunman yank the pin out of a grenade and roll it under the BMW. As he did, the blue Ford roared away.

Craig sprang to his feet and pulled Nicole by the arm down the hill, wanting to get as far away as he could before the explosion. They stumbled in the dirt until he spotted a large tree with a thick trunk. He pulled them both behind it.

"Close your eyes and hold your ears," he shouted.

The explosion was deafening. Fire and shards of metal shot into the air. That bastard Peppone must have double-crossed me, Craig decided. He must have used his cell phone to tell the people in the Ford their location.

"Let's get out of here," he said.

With Craig in the lead and Nicole following, they ran through the dirt parallel to the road toward the restaurant and the gas station.

Hiding in a row of trees, he saw Peppone's Mercedes parked ten yards away. Strange that the driver had remained there after the double-cross, Craig thought. He had to settle the score with Peppone and, more important, commandeer the Mercedes to get out of the area.

"Wait here until I call you," he told Nicole. He grabbed the Beretta and dropped the duffel at her feet.

On tiptoe, he approached the front of the Mercedes from the passenger side. In the dim light coming from the restaurant, he looked through the front side window of the car and saw Peppone sitting up behind the steering wheel.

Craig opened the passenger side door and cried out, "You bastard!"

When Peppone didn't respond, Craig got into the car and pulled him by the arm. Peppone fell toward him. Craig tossed his gun on the floor of the car and felt for a pulse. There wasn't one. In the interior light of the car, he saw that the driver's neck was heavily bruised. Someone had strangled him.

He sat up and looked at the dash. The keys were still in the ignition. He began pulling Peppone's body out of the car when a man suddenly jumped up from the floor of the back seat. Before Craig had a chance to react, the man grabbed his neck with powerful hands in a vise-like grip. Craig lunged for his Beretta, but it was too far away.

He tried punching the man, but all of the strength was quickly ebbing from his body. His blows were nothing more than harmless taps. "Ah . . ." he cried gasping for breath. He barely had any air left in his lungs. He felt tightening in his chest. I'm done, he thought. A dead man.

Then he heard it: the most wonderful sound he could ever have imagined. The firing of a gun.

The vise opened. Craig was gulping in air.

"Are you okay?" Nicole called, the hot .22 in her hand. "Are you okay?"

"God, I'm glad you had the gun. Another couple of seconds and I was finished."

The assailant was prone on the back seat, bleeding from the head. He wasn't moving.

Craig felt his body returning to normal. "You scored a direct hit," he said. "Help me dump these two bodies in the trees. Then let's hit the road. The police will be here soon because of the explosion."

As they moved the bodies, he thought of Elizabeth. Fearless and gutsy like Nicole, Elizabeth had saved his life in Aspen.

Minutes later, they were in the Mercedes, with Craig driving, heading down the hill back toward the city. "Thank God that's over," Nicole blurted out.

Craig looked in the rearview mirror. A car was barreling down the hill too fast and too close. He pressed hard on the accelerator. "It's not over yet. Bastards must have had a homing device attached to the Mercedes. You navigate. Tell me where to turn. Get me out of town on steep hilly roads. I'll take it from here."

Nicole didn't miss a beat. "Turn right at the next intersection. I'll tell you what to do after that."

Fortunately, traffic was light in this remote area. Craig ignored the red light at an intersection and sped around the corner. The car squealed as he floored it.

Despite the cold in the hills, Craig's forehead was dotted with perspiration. He was gripping the steering wheel hard, tapping his left foot on the floor of the car trying to burn up nervous energy. "What color's the car following us?" he asked.

"Dark. Maybe blue."

"Probably the thugs who destroyed your BMW."

The road wound higher and higher into the hills with one hairpin turn after another. Craig heard gunfire from behind, but his assailants were too far away to get a good shot. The Ford was no match for Peppone's Mercedes, particularly with Craig, a trained rally racer, behind the wheel. The gap between the two cars was widening. A light rain began to fall. *Shit. That's what I don't need right now. A slick pavement.* It was if he were back in Sardinia in the rally race. *Except I'm not going to fuck up this time.*

"Grab my Beretta from the floor," Craig called to Nicole, "and hold on to it. Then tighten your seatbelt."

His eyes were riveted on the road. He was looking for a turn off, some private road, the entrance to a property. Up ahead on the left, he saw a dirt road. Just what he wanted. They were far enough in front of the Ford that with the bends in the road, their pursuers would never see where the Mercedes turned off.

"Hold on tight," he said.

He cut sharply to the left and onto the dirt road. Then he spun the car again hard left into a muddy area with a scattering of pine trees he narrowly avoided. He jammed on the brakes and cringed when he heard a loud squeal. But the car stopped dead parallel to the road.

"Give me the Beretta."

Once he had it in his hand, he jumped out of the car and hid behind the Mercedes on the passenger side. Nicole was next to him.

He heard the Ford coming up the highway before he saw it. They had no idea he had turned off. The perfect ambush.

As the Ford passed by, through the open car window, Craig saw the look of recognition on the driver's face. By then it was too late. Craig aimed and fired three shots at the driver. He only needed the first one. The bullet slammed into the side of the head of the driver, who lost control of the car. It spun off the road, flying down a steep embankment where it rolled over and over until it struck a rock, exploded, and burst into flames.

Craig doubted that anyone survived, but he had no intention of checking to find out. Examining the rear bumper of the Mercedes, he found a small, round metallic object affixed to the bottom. That had to be the transmitter of the homing device. He crushed it under the heel of his shoe. "Now let's get the hell out of here," he told her.

They climbed back into the Mercedes. At a speed of a hundred and twenty miles an hour, they raced down the hill with Nicole holding on to the front dash and gasping for breath.

Ten minutes later, Craig told her, "Nobody's following us. Take us back to the city, and find a quiet out of the way place where we can talk. We were rudely interrupted in the middle of a discussion. I want to finish it."

"We'll go to my house," she said without hesitation.

"I don't want to put you in danger."

She burst out laughing. "You're a little late for those sentiments. I've been shot at. My car blown up. I've been riding with a maniac behind the wheel. And you don't want to put me in danger."

"I meant any more danger."

"A few days ago you weren't sure you could trust me. Now suddenly you want to be my great male protector. I've had enough macho crap from the men in this country to last a life time. I don't have to take it from an American. And by the way, remember I saved your life."

She paused for an instant, then continued, "I doubt if anybody who works for Schiller and is still alive saw us together. I'll show you where you can ditch the Mercedes in the woods. Then we'll call somebody who works for me to pick us up."

*   *   *

Nicole lived in a large stone two-story house surrounded by a twelve-foot red brick wall. An armed guard was stationed in front of the metal gate and another on the other side. Two sleek black Dobermans snarled and sniffed Craig as he walked alongside Nicole on the path cutting through a perfectly manicured lawn into the house. "It's okay," she called to the dogs. "He's my friend." They backed away.

"Pretty impressive security," Craig said.

"A girl can't be too careful these days when she lives alone. Especially when she's made some powerful enemies like your friend Colonel Schiller."

"Aren't you worried he'll arrest you?"

"For now, they have to tolerate me. My father not only has a lot of money, but powerful friends in the business establishment. If they harm me, Estrada will lose the support of his friends. The general's not willing to do that—at least not at this point."

"You lived here long?"

"I grew up in this house. When my mother died three years ago, Papa turned it over to me and took an apartment in the city not far from the Alvear. I'm an only child, so he hoped I'd move in and fill up the house with little bambinos, the grandchildren he never had. Not much chance of that. I tried marriage once to somebody who I thought was a nice man. A university professor who taught the Greek classics. A year into the marriage, I showed up at his office as a surprise to take him out for his birthday. Timing is everything in life." Her tone was bitter.

"He had a female student on her back on his desk. Her skirt was up around her waist, her panties off, legs spread and high in the air. His own pants were down around his ankles. He was getting ready to plunge right in. Quite a graphic scene. The men in this country think it's their God-given right to fuck anything that moves. But not if they're married to me. So it was the end of the marriage. I won't accept screwing around with somebody else. Fortunately, we didn't have children."

She led the way through a formal living room with a baby grand piano into a book-lined den paneled in rich cherry wood.

"Grappa?" she asked.

"Precisely what I need."

"Me too."

After she poured two glasses, he raised his and said, "I didn't mean to sound macho. I know that if it weren't for you, I'd be a dead man." His neck was still sore from the thug's grip.

"Isn't there a Chinese proverb about that? I'm responsible for you from now on."

"Something like that. How'd you learn to shoot?"

"One night during the Dirty War a couple of soldiers stopped my car for supposedly a routine identity check. When they told me to get out of the car and one of them began running his hands over me, doing a body check, he said, I understood where this was going. I'd join the ranks of los desaparecidos. They'd put me into a jail cell and take turns raping me. When they'd had all the fun they could, they'd kill me and dump me into one of those mass graves. Fortunately for me, they got a call on their radio ordering them to go somewhere else. I vowed I would never again be defenseless so I bought a gun and took lessons. If I was going down, I'd take a couple of those thugs with me." She paused and gulped some of the potent liquid. "I have to admit, though, I never fired it for real before tonight."

For Craig, that made what Nicole had done ever more awesome.

She took another sip. "I'm damn glad to be alive."

He raised his glass. "I'll drink to that."

"I should feel some remorse for the ones we killed, but the way those people act, they don't deserve to live. All they do is cause innocent people to suffer."

Craig realized he had a valuable ally in Nicole. Together, they had to find out what Estrada was planning and stop him.

She pointed to a plush brown leather sofa and they settled down at each end.

"When we were so rudely interrupted, back at the overlook," Craig said, "you were explaining to me that you left your shop later in the day of my visit and went out of town."

She kicked off her shoes and paused to light a cigarette. He waited patiently for her to begin.

"First, I called some people in the north. One of them told me that our troops were massing on the Brazilian border. So I flew up to see what was happening."

Craig was leaning forward, facing her. "Yeah."

"I couldn't find out what they were up to. The area was sealed tight with security like you would not believe."

"Where's the border area you're talking about?"

Nicole walked over to the desk, reached into a drawer, and pulled out a map. With Craig standing next to her, she pointed to the area in northeastern Argentina on the Brazilian border.

"I learned something else you'd like to know," she said.

"What's that?"

"General Estrada is operating up there from an old castle near Iguazu. The building's in an area that's a virtual rain forest—lots of trees and thick vegetation. According to a sign on the entrance gate to the grounds, the building is identified "regional headquarters." She pointed it out on the map. "I did all the surveillance I could from the road without drawing attention to myself from the armed guards in the gatehouse."

Craig was studying the map.

"You ever been up to Iguazu and the Falls?" she asked him.

He shook his head.

"It's one of the few places in the world where three countries have a common border. You can stand at the top of a high bluff above the river and look across into Brazil on the right and Paraguay on the left. The waters flow at a ferocious rate most of the year, particularly now in the spring." He remembered Gina telling him about the Falls.

"How do I get up there?" Craig asked.

"There are direct flights from Buenos Aires to Iguazu. A fair number every day because it's a big tourist destination."

Craig's mind was churning. Everything Nicole had said was consistent with what Betty had told him about the troop movements. In the morning, he'd fly up to Iguazu and find out what was happening.

"If I had my way," Nicole added, "I'd put Estrada and Schiller in a boat without a paddle and send them over the Falls."

Craig laughed as he pictured it in his mind. "Let's talk about Estrada," he said. "When we were in your shop, you told me he had done something so bad twenty-five or so years ago that you didn't even want to talk about it."

"That's right."

"Tell me now."

She shook her head. "It's part of our history, I don't like to share with an outsider. An ugly event from the Dirty War. But after what you went through tonight, I figure that you're one of us." She hesitated. "Still, I won't tell you unless you open up to me. Tell me who you really are."

When he didn't respond, she said, "If you won't level with me, I won't tell you what I know about Estrada." Her voice was firm.

He looked insulted. "Even after what we went through tonight, you don't trust me."

She was staring at him hard. "It's not a question of trust. Either we're in this together or we're not."

He sighed deeply. He couldn't argue with her. "You're right. Barry Gorman is a cover. My name is Craig Page. I've spent my whole career either with the CIA, the EU Counter Terrorism Agency, or doing private security work in Europe."

"A year ago, you were CIA director for a short period."

He raised his eyebrows. "Very short. How do you know that?"

"You may be surprised to learn that we have the Internet even down here in Argentina, and I follow the news."

She sure had a sharp tongue. "I left the espionage game and was racing cars in Europe."

"Which explains your driving this evening."

"Well, anyhow, the director, Betty Richards, wanted me back for this project. Ted Dunn was my friend. That's why I agreed."

She pulled back and stared at him. "You don't look like the pictures of Craig Page I saw."

"I decided to have my face touched up a bit. I had made enemies with some nasty people. Now tell me what happened."

She lit another cigarette, then began in a soft, melancholy voice. "I was working in the office of my father's shoe factory in those days. The last rule of the generals. It was June of 1979. I had just finished at the university. A young woman worked in the payroll department. Maria was her name. Sweet girl. Smart. Good worker. Her husband worked for us too. He was a leather cutter. He was also a leader in the labor union. Not a troublemaker, but vocal. My father didn't mind him or the union, but it was a good way to make enemies."

"So what happened?"

Nicole swallowed hard. "One day, Maria came to me and asked if she could talk to my father. She needed his help, she pleaded with me. The woman was in tears. Her eyes were bloodshot. I had never seen her like this. So I took her in to see my father. I stayed and listened."

Nicole picked up a napkin and wiped her eyes. "Jesus, I'm going to start crying myself just thinking about it."

"What happened?" Craig repeated.

"Maria had three little kids, girls age five and three and a six-month-old boy named Benito. Her mother took care of them during the day when she and her husband worked. The night before, when her husband was out at a union meeting, General Estrada, who was then a captain, barged into her house with three soldiers. Her mother lived at her own house with Maria's father. So it was just Maria and the three children at home."

Craig thought about the rape and murder of Antonia's mother. The hackles rose on his neck. "What did they do to her?"

"To her, nothing. That would have been much kinder. Estrada ordered one of the soldiers to reach into the crib and take her son."

"Kidnap him?"

Nicole nodded. "Here, as in any society, we have people who can't have children or want another one without going through the discomfort of a pregnancy. So the military regime supplied babies to people who helped them or were in the government or the armed forces. When pregnant women were arrested, the military waited for the child to be born, then took the baby and killed the mother."

While Craig had read about kidnappings during the Dirty War, it was still chilling to hear the details about a specific incident.

Nicole continued in a somber voice. "Nobody knows how many babies like Benito were taken. Hundreds. Maybe thousands. Unlike the Nazis in Germany, our thugs didn't keep records of their crimes.

You may have noticed we're not a very methodical people. It's both our strength and our weakness. They tried to justify it by claiming they were taking babies from people who were Communists and enemies of the State. Whatever that meant. It certainly didn't fit Maria."

"You made a very serious charge against Estrada. Can you be sure he was directing the kidnapping of Maria's baby?"

"Maria told me that the leader of this gang had a scar above his right eyebrow. Also, the three of them got into an argument."

"About what?"

"One of the soldiers wasn't content just stealing Maria's baby. He wanted to take her in the bedroom and rape her. Estrada told him he couldn't do that. So the soldier shouted, 'What's wrong with you Captain Estrada? You can't feel sorry for these people.' Those were his exact words. I'll never forget them . . . I'll never forget anything Maria said that day."

"How did Estrada respond to the soldier?"

Nicole's voice rose to a shrill, high, angry pitch. "He slapped him in the face and said, 'We don't have time for your games. You were there with Gimo. You heard him say that we had to take six babies tonight. That means five more.'"

"Six." Craig was incredulous. "Six babies?"

"That's what he said."

"Good God. So Maria's son, Benito, wasn't the only baby Estrada and his goons stole for this Gimo."

She nodded. "I heard from reliable sources that lots of money was paid for these babies. No doubt much of it ended up in Estrada's pocket to finance his gambling and whoring. He was frequently seen in the casinos of the resorts in Punta del Este in those days and ever since. Now he wants to run our country."

He had Estrada pegged as militant, corrupt, responsible for Dunn's and Pascual's murders, and willing to do anything to get control of the country, but direct involvement in atrocities like this made the man even more evil.

Before he could respond, Nicole added, "And if Estrada does take over the presidency, he'd better have bodyguards around the clock because there are plenty of mothers like Maria who'd like to kill him."

"What did your father do when he heard Maria's story?"

"Papa was beside himself with anguish. Rumors about these kidnappings had been circulating, but it's another thing to hear about it firsthand. That it happened to somebody you know. He made calls as soon as Maria left his office. He went to see everybody he knew in the military regime. He realized he was one small man. He couldn't stop the practice in general. All he tried to do was to get back Benito for Maria."

"And?"

"He came up empty. Blank stares. No one ever heard anything about Benito again. A group was organized called Grandmothers of the Plaza de Mayo who vowed to track down and locate these kidnapped infants, but they got nowhere. As for me, I was so devastated that I left the country for the next couple of years. I went to London and New York. I spent time with the émigré communities there—others who had fled the country because they were being pursued or repulsed by what was happening. We spoke to anyone who would listen to us—government people, writers, journalists, anybody who could raise their voice to broadcast to the world what was happening. We wrote plays and articles. Some people listened, but the issue never moved the American people sufficiently to urge your government to act. Even worse, a couple of years ago, documents were released from the American archives which established that your government secretly supported the military regime. And they knew about their crimes."

"I won't try to defend what we did in the past," he said, "but now my government sent Dunn, and they sent me. Some people in Washington are trying to stop Estrada."

She paused and shook her head. Her expression showed anger and contempt. "I gave up after a couple of years and came home at Papa's urging. I went back to work at his company and remained passive politically. But now that Estrada and these hoodlums, like Schiller, want to take over again, I can't let that happen."

"What happened to Maria?"

"She never saw Benito again or heard about him. She never had another child. A part of her died that night. She became a woman in perpetual mourning, always in black, who aged prematurely. She keeps a picture of Benito on her desk and in every room of her house."

"Does she still work for your father's company?"

"Even now. In the office, her work's not good, but Papa pays her as if nothing were wrong."

Nicole's eyes were blazing with intensity as she continued. "History will repeat itself if we don't stop Estrada. I don't want that to happen."

She crossed the room and refilled her glass, then offered some more grappa to Craig, who declined. He could only handle one of those in an evening. He was impressed that she was still drinking.

She placed her glass down on a table and pointed a finger at him. "What were you doing in the United States when I was hearing Maria's story? Playing baseball with your friends and trying to get into girls' pants?"

He shifted awkwardly. "Yes. The accident of birth. But still, I've had my own sadness. I joined the CIA. It was to do some good, to make a difference in the world, not just for the game. Along the way, my wife died when she was living with me in the Middle East. My daughter, my only child, was killed by a venal rogue Chinese general who later became their president. So don't judge me on insufficient information," he said angrily.

"I hope you killed Zhou in Moscow to avenge your daughter's death."

"You must spend a lot of time in front of the computer."

"When you live in a place like Argentina, it's the only way to be informed. I want you to know that I never believed that heart attack story about Zhou in Moscow."

Before he could respond, the telephone rang. Why this late, Craig thought with trepidation. It had to be bad news. Perhaps they were about to be arrested, and it was a warning. He heard a staccato series of "Yes . . . yes . . . yes," from Nicole. Then she hung up the phone and turned on the television set.

They saw pictures of an angry crowd marching and shouting. Craig and Nicole moved close to the screen to see what was happening. A mob was burning Brazilian flags. Shouting people were attempting to storm the Brazilian Embassy in Buenos Aires and being repelled by soldiers. An announcer said, "If you just tuned in, I want to summarize for you what has happened this evening. Close to the town of Santo Tomé in northeastern Argentina, along the Brazilian boarder, a group of Brazilian soldiers—how many we don't know—armed with Chinese weapons entered Argentine territory for the purpose of seizing some of our land. All of the invaders were shot and killed on Argentine soil by our brave defenders."

Then Estrada's face was on the screen. Craig recognized the furniture. The general was seated in his office. He looked indignant, yet calm and in control.

"What is happening is totally despicable. In the nineteenth century we fought a number of wars with Brazil over border issues. In one, our heroic army, led by the great patriot, General Rosas, stopped Brazil's efforts at expansion and forced the creation of the independent nation of Uruguay.

"Our borders with Brazil were drawn in 1870 following a bitter war that ended Paraguay's attempts at military conquest. At that time, both of our nations took parts of Paraguay. Now the Brazilians are claiming that they were deceived in that settlement and they are seeking to seize some of our land. This is a total falsehood. If anyone was treated unfairly in that settlement, it was Argentina. If Brazil persists, we will defeat them and make a new resolution of the border issue more favorable to Argentina. They will pay dearly for this hostile adventure."

Estrada shifted to a reassuring voice. "There is no danger to any citizen of our Republic. The Brazilian soldiers who executed this criminal act have all paid with their lives. Those in Brazil who planned it will realize now that if they ever try anything like this again, those whom they send will meet a similar fate. I will personally make sure that happens."

He was painting himself as the defender of his nation, Craig realized. A people being attacked by a larger, more powerful enemy.

Craig tried to sort out what was happening. The scenario that came into his mind was that the Brazilian government had found out about the diamond discovery in northern Argentina Estrada had told Craig about. Using a past border dispute as a phony excuse, the Brazilians had tried to seize the territory where the diamonds were located before the discovery was announced publicly. Then later, in possession of the territory, they could claim to have made the discovery themselves. Perhaps Estrada had known a Brazilian attack like this was on the horizon. That could have been the reason he was so desperately seeking the arms Gina was obtaining from Bryce. The visitors from Porto Alegre that

Pascual picked up could have been Brazilians passing secret information to Estrada about the planned attack. With that information, the Argentine army was ready for them. That would explain why Estrada had been so intent on maintaining secrecy about the Brazilians' visit to Bariloche.

The television went back to the demonstrations. Craig led Nicole over to the map. "Show me where this occurred."

She pointed out the area. It was on the Argentine border with the Brazilian state of Rio Grande do Sul. The military people Pascual had picked up at Bariloche Airport were from there.

He didn't want to tell her about the diamonds and what Estrada had confided in him. "What do you make of all of this?" he asked her.

She grumbled. "It's damn convenient. Brazil attacking now. Going to war always creates popular support. It'll provide the perfect excuse for the military seizing power. It fits with the schedule Estrada had for taking over the country."

Craig weighed her words. This was another possibility that had nothing to do with the diamond discovery. "So you think that Estrada put the Brazilians up to it?"

"I don't know what to think. All we have is his version of what occurred. The man is a vicious liar. He's capable of anything."

"But why would the Brazilians go along with this?" Craig asked. "What do they have to gain?"

She waved her arms, dismissing his skepticism. "The military leaders in the different countries down here work together."

Her explanation made Craig stop and think. Her thesis was consistent with the trip to Bariloche by the Brazilians. But Craig wasn't convinced that she was right. He didn't know what to make of the attack.

What was clear to him, though, was that a war between Argentina and Brazil would have devastating consequences for the United States. It would be difficult for Washington to avoid being drawn into the conflict even if it was only those two. And if foreign governments—China or Russia—intervened on one side or the other, then the United States' military involvement would be a virtual certainty. South America was too close to the United States' southern border. Inaction would not be an option. And after Iraq and Afghanistan, the United States certainly didn't want another war.

"I better get back into the heart of the city," he said. "And see what's happening for myself."

She handed him a key. "Come and use my house any time you need to. Or any time you think I can help you. I'll alert the staff."

"And the Dobermans," he said smiling. "Them too."

She instructed one of her guards to drive him back to the Alvear.

*   *   *

About four blocks from the American embassy, they hit gridlock. Craig jumped out to cover the rest of the way on foot. It was slow going. Protestors, carrying signs and placards demanding American help, filled the streets. Milling in the crowd, he had no doubt that it was all carefully orchestrated. Estrada and his people had been ready for the Brazilian attack.

Craig tried to tread his way through the mob to get to the main front gate of the embassy, but people were packing the street and sidewalks. Without any warning, one of the demonstrators smashed a sign against the side of Craig's head. He would have fallen, and he might have been trampled, but a set of powerful arms grabbed him. The man who caught him had a friend who turned on Craig's assailant with the sign. "What's wrong with you," he shouted. "This is supposed to be peaceful." The assailant moved away taking refuge in the crowd. Must be another one of Schiller's goons, Craig decided.

His head ached, but he had recovered his footing. He felt a warm liquid oozing down his right cheek. He reached up, touched it, and saw the blood on his fingers. *Shit, they must have had a nail on the board.*

From a distance of twenty yards, he stared at the gate of the Embassy through the crowd. Half a dozen armed American soldiers stood in front, but the crowd stopped ten feet from them. Those who had organized this demonstration had done a good job.

Craig desperately wanted to get inside the embassy to call Betty on a secure phone, but it was too risky to go up to the gate. If one of Schiller's people spotted him, like the man who smashed the sign against his head, all of his credibility would be lost with Estrada. He'd have to find another way.

He turned around and walked swiftly away from the embassy. When he had walked for about thirty minutes, he was in a high-rent area, with luxury apartment buildings where the streets were deserted. The buildings were dark. The upper class was in bed asleep, or at least hiding in their homes with the lights off. He was certain no one had followed him.

He found a pay phone on the corner and dialed the American Embassy. "Please connect me with B. J. Walker," he said, following Betty's instructions.

"This is B. J.," a man announced a few seconds later, in a gruff sounding voice. "Who's calling?"

"It's Jimmy Carr. I want to come home."

"Where are you?"

Craig gave his location.

"I'll have a car there in ten minutes. Longer if we have difficulty getting out of the embassy. Look for a black Cadillac sedan. License 5147."

Craig checked his watch. Twelve minutes later, a car pulled up and stopped. A young man with a blond crew cut, powerfully built like a football lineman, jumped out on the passenger side. He opened the trunk. "Get in," he said tersely.

"Will I be able to breathe?"

"It's ventilated and bullet proof. Everything except a mini bar."

Craig disliked dark enclosed spaces. The last time he had been forced to hide in a car trunk was in Beijing with Elizabeth. He hated it then; he hated it now.

After they drove for several minutes, the Cadillac came to a stop. Craig heard pounding on the outside of the trunk. They must be in the demonstration area, he decided.

The car began to rock. It can't possibly be fireproof. He hoped he wouldn't have to find out.

They began moving again. Minutes later, the car stopped and the trunk opened.

They were inside the embassy garage. The blond crew cut helped Craig out. "I'm B. J. Walker," he said. "And you've got a nasty cut on your head. I'll get one of the nurses to clean it up."

The antiseptic stung like hell, but the nurse said it was no big deal. She put on a bandage and gave him a bottle of antibiotics in case it became infected. B. J. led Craig down to a basement communications room, then departed.

He glanced at his watch. This would be the second time in three nights he was calling Betty in the middle of the night.

"I'm sorry to call at this hour, but . . ."

"I was hoping you'd call. I'm at the office with two of my aides watching video feed from Buenos Aires about what's happening with Brazil. I assume you're on a secure phone."

"Yes. In the embassy."

"Good. I'll put you on the speaker. Tell us what the hell's going on."

First, he reported on his discussion about diamonds with Estrada on the plane. He described what he had heard on television from Estrada, and what the protests were like, spinning out the possible scenarios he and Nicole had articulated. Then he asked, "What are the Brazilians saying?"

"They refuse to talk to us," she responded. "They claim we're responsible for all of this because we've been funneling arms to Argentina and we didn't listen to what they told us. It's now a matter of machismo for them. They don't want or need help from Uncle Sam, the UN, the OAS, or anybody else. Once they've moved their troops into place, they'll 'destroy Estrada and his army,' was what the Brazilian Ambassador in Washington said on CNN before he left to fly home."

A man with Betty broke in. "Very diplomatic language."

"Did you get my transcripts?" Craig asked.

"Everything was as you represented. They're now in my office safe."

"What's your next move in Washington?" Craig asked anxiously.

One of the men with Betty said, "The choices are paralysis or confusion."

On Betty's end they all laughed.

"Sorry, Craig," she said. "Too much pizza out of a box and too little sleep is making us all crazy. We have a meeting of the national security team at the White House in about three hours. My proposal will be that Treadwell send down a high level delegation to visit the area and meet with Estrada and other Argentine leaders. I'd also like them to go to Brazil if the Brazilians will meet with us. As I envision it, the objective of the mission will not only be fact finding, but hopefully to quiet down emotions. What do you think?"

Craig rubbed his tired eyes while he evaluated Betty's proposal. "I like the idea," he said.

"Good. Before the meeting, I'll float it with the secretary of state and hope he likes it enough to pass it off as his own."

"You don't want to let Edward Bryce hijack the delegation. Even better, keep him off it altogether."

"Though we're not as smart as you are," Betty said, "I figured that out. The president will have the final word."

*　　*　　*

With breakfast in his suite at the Alvear, Craig was reading the morning issue of *La Nación*. The newspaper's story of the border incident was consistent with what Estrada had said on television. The Argentine stock market was expected to take a nosedive as a result of the war. In a few minutes, he planned to leave for Iguazu. Then the telephone rang. It was Estrada.

"Sorry to have split from you so abruptly at the airport on Monday," the general said.

"You don't have to apologize. When I heard the news last evening, I understood why you had to rush off."

"By the time we landed, our troops had confirmed the movement of a Brazilian unit toward the border. It was a question of making certain we were ready. Our men fought with courage. Though we killed all of them, there were casualties on our side."

Craig was wondering why Estrada had decided to call now. As if reading his mind, the general continued. "I'm well aware that investors shy away from unstable situations so I want to reassure you that we have the matter under complete control. If I were you, I would stick with your plan, remain in Buenos Aires, and stay the course. The opportunity we spoke about on the plane is still viable."

"Well, that's good to know," Craig replied. "I am concerned, but I'm not going anywhere. From my experience, those who panic almost always lose out."

"I couldn't agree more." Estrada was obviously pleased.

Craig decided that the call presented an opportunity. Following the old adage, when you throw rocks into the air, sometimes you get apples, he decided to pump Estrada for information.

"What prompted Brazil to attack?"

There was a long pause. Finally, Estrada responded, "Most of my advisers think it's an effort by the Brazilians to divert attention from their own economic problems. This argument that their land was improperly taken by us at the end of the Paraguayan war is total and utter bullshit."

"Is it also possible," Craig asked gingerly, "that the Brazilians found out about the diamonds we discussed on the plane, and they're trying to grab the land on which they are located?"

"That thought occurred to me, but security about the discovery has been super tight."

"In my experience, scientists always talk to other scientists."

"Perhaps," Estrada sounded troubled. "But regardless, if they attack again, we'll be ready for them. Thanks to the arms your country has sent us, those Brazilians won't get a kilometer of our territory."

"Please keep me informed?" Craig said, trying to sound like a concerned investor.

"Absolutely. I'm personally directing our military movements, and I view you as my business partner."

As Craig hung up the phone, an uneasy feeling settled into the pit of his stomach. For openers, he didn't like being a partner with this man. But more than that, something in Estrada's version of last evening's border confrontation and this phone call wasn't ringing true. He couldn't put his finger on it, but he was bothered.

One thing was certain. He had to adjust his plans and defer the trip to Iguazu. Estrada was the center of the action. Estrada was not only in Buenos Aires, but willing to talk to him.

After canceling his airplane reservation he changed into running clothes. While he jogged, his mind often unlocked complex puzzles. Perhaps he'd get some insight into what was really happening in Northern Argentina.

Washington

Bryce sat next to Treadwell on one side of the rectangular table in the White House Situation Room. Across the table were the Secretary of Defense, Hugh Tompkins and the Chairman of the Joint Chiefs, General Forbes. At one end sat Betty; at the other the Secretary of State, Kent McIntire, and the Assistant Secretary for Inter-American Affairs, Hal West.

The president looked in the direction of the duo from Foggy Bottom.

"Kent, where are we on this South American business?" Treadwell asked his secretary of state.

Kent nodded to West, sitting in front of a laptop.

The assistant secretary took that as his cue to rev up his PowerPoint presentation. He pushed a switch on the wall lowering the screen and another one closing the curtains.

Up on the screen flashed a map of the border area between Argentina and Brazil where the battle took place. Then a series of slides showing how the territory had changed hands in the last five hundred years.

Bryce was watching the president whose eyes looked glazed over, focused away from the screen, and whose mind seemed to be wandering in a distant place.

The next slide was entitled "Argentina's version of the events." Set forth in a series of bullets were the claims made by Estrada on the television last night, followed by a series of photographs, showing dead Brazilian soldiers armed with Chinese weapons lying next to a stone tower at a locale identified by markers as clearly being in Argentine territory.

The following slide entitled, "THE BRAZILIAN VERSION," contained the words "A PACK OF LIES."

"That," West said, "was what the Brazilian foreign minister told Kent in a telephone conversation about two hours ago."

Kent piped in. "And it was all he would say because he muttered an obscenity about the weapons we've shipped to Argentina and hung up the phone."

West flashed on his next slide:
"PROPOSED AMERICAN COURSE OF ACTION.
SEND HIGH LEVEL AMERICAN DELEGATION TO THE AREA."

West explained, "This is a proposal Kent and I jointly developed. We view the delegation as having a dual purpose. First, to gather facts for an understanding of what happened, and second to cool tensions between the two countries."

West left the recommendation on the screen, opened the curtains, and sat down.

All eyes turned toward Treadwell. The buck always stopped at the president. Before Treadwell had a chance to respond, Bryce spoke up. "With all due respect Kent, if the Brazilians won't talk to us, what's the point of sending a delegation to the area?"

"We believe that the Brazilians will change their minds if we come to South America. They won't let us leave hearing only one side of the story."

Bryce shook his head in disbelief. "That's wishful thinking."

Betty interjected, "We can't sit by and do nothing, Mr. President. This conflict isn't in the Middle East. It's in our own backyard."

When the secretary of defense and General Forbes weighed in on Betty and Kent's side, Bryce said, "At least, let's keep the delegation small and have minimal press coverage. Only take a couple of journalists we can work with. So we don't end up with egg on our face if this fails to accomplish anything."

The secretary of state looked at West, who nodded. "We can live with that," Kent replied.

Suddenly, Treadwell tuned back into the discussion. Facing Bryce, he said, "Edward, I want you to head up our delegation."

"Perhaps, Mr. President," Betty said, sounding tactful. "Our delegation might have more clout if Kent headed it."

"Kent's going to Paris to try and improve our relations with Europe," Treadwell replied. "I don't want to cancel that trip. Hal West knows the issue. He'll be part of Edward's delegation."

Bryce shot her a supercilious smile. Take that, bitch, he thought.

Buenos Aires

Estrada, in his office, hung up the phone with President Garcia who had told him about the American delegation headed by Edward

Bryce that would be visiting. "Since military issues are key," Garcia had said, "I want you, Alfredo, to take the lead in planning the agenda for our visitors."

Estrada was delighted. He already had Bryce in his pocket. He could use this delegation to his advantage. His mind was churning with ideas. Then his cell phone rang. It was Gina.

"Yes, dear," he said.

"Alfredo, I'm flying to Buenos Aires tonight with Edward Bryce's delegation. They're taking along two American journalists, and Bryce added me to cover the story for *La Nación*."

He leaned back in the high leather desk chair and told Gina, "I'm very pleased you're coming."

She coughed and cleared her throat. "There's something I have to ask you." The anxiety was apparent in her voice.

"Sure, dear, what is it?"

"Well, if that banker, Barry Gorman, is still in the country, could I see him?"

Estrada's initial reaction was to respond with a sharp rebuke, reminding her that she had better not do anything to upset her relationship with Bryce, because it was critical for Argentina at this time. Then he thought about it some more. Despite being cloistered with her grandparents and at a private girls' school, Gina was a young, hot-blooded, Argentine woman. He could tell from the sound of her voice that she had passion for Gorman. And he couldn't blame her, preferring the much younger macho Gorman to the old, tired Bryce. Estrada decided he could use her passion to his advantage.

In London and on the plane, Estrada had concluded from Gorman's behavior that he really was a wealthy money man. How he had handled a casino and women. How he had negotiated Estrada's diamond offer.

When Estrada had told all of this to Schiller upon his return, he knew the colonel still wasn't convinced. Now he had a further way of testing Gorman. See how he behaved around the Americans. Gorman's suite and hotel phones were bugged. All of the other Americans' would be as well. He'd find out if Gorman made contact with them. Gina had just given Estrada the perfect way to have Gorman around when the Americans were here. A perfect way to see how Gorman behaved.

"Of course, you'll be able to see him, my dear," Estrada said. "I'll include him in many of the events. I just want you to be happy."

*   *   *

Jorge Newbery Park was not far from the Alvear. Dressed in shorts and a tee shirt, Craig jogged along a deserted dirt trail, lined with tall trees. After the long days he had been keeping, his body felt stiff and lethargic, but he pushed himself hard to keep up the pace. Meantime, his mind kept coming back to Estrada's speech last night on television and the call this morning. Something big was definitely brewing, but he couldn't figure out what it was.

Up ahead, a small, rickety wooden bridge crossed a creek. On the other side lay a thick wooded area. Craig cut his speed and watched his footing to avoid stumbling on the bridge. Once he was on the other side, he ran faster. It had rained earlier that morning—a brief, strong spring shower. The ground was soft and muddy.

Two joggers, a man and a woman, passed him heading the other way. Bright sunlight glinted through the trees. He was approaching a sharp bend on the right. As he reached it, he saw a thick tree branch, too high to hurdle, blocking the path. He slowed down to slip around it. At that moment, two men jumped up in the underbrush. A powerful set of arms grabbed him from behind. Craig tried to fight back, but a sharp punch to the kidneys sapped his strength and left him gasping for air.

The two men, one tall and one short, pulled him deeper into the woods. After making certain no one could see them, they stood him up with his back against a tree and his arms at his sides. Around his midsection, they fastened a rope that rendered his hands useless and held him tight against the trunk. Bark was cutting into his back. A greasy gray cloth was tied over his mouth.

As he watched in horror, the tall man reached into a black canvas bag and extracted a pair of boxing gloves. "I hate to damage my hands," he said sadistically.

"What do you want?" Craig asked. "I'll give you money."

"Leave Argentina now," the short man said, "for good."

Craig spit on the ground. "Tell Colonel Schiller that's my answer."

The boxer went to work on Craig's upper body, his abdomen, and genitalia with blow after blow. Craig heard the smack . . . smack . . . smack . . . He felt the pain. First he threw up. Then he passed out.

When he regained consciousness, Craig found that the rope tying him to the tree was loose. He slipped out of it. His whole body aching, he staggered back to the Alvear.

"Are you alright?" the alarmed manager asked when he saw Craig pass through the revolving door and enter the lobby.

Since his clothes covered the bruises, he forced a smile. "Just a little winded from running in the park. I may have pushed myself too hard."

The portly manger smiled. "You'll never catch me running. It's not healthy."

When he reached his suite, he found a message on his voice mail. "Please call General Estrada."

Before returning the call, he went into the bathroom and peeled off his clothes. The front of his body was covered with welts and bruises. In a few hours, he'd be every possible shade of black and blue.

He was tempted to tell Estrada, but he decided that would be a bad move. He had no intention of leaving Argentina. If he told Estrada about the beating and remained in the country, Estrada would doubt that he was here as an investor.

A secretary put him right through to Estrada.

"I have an invitation for you," the general said.

"What's that?" Craig tried to squelch the pain and sound natural.

"Tomorrow morning, an American delegation, headed by Edward Bryce, one of President Treadwell's advisers, arrives in Buenos Aires on a fact finding mission about the Brazilian attack. During the day, I'm taking them up north to see the area. In the evening, there'll be a dinner at the Alvear. I'd like you to attend both."

This was quite an offer. Craig wondered what prompted it.

"I'd be delighted to be there. What do I have to know about the meetings?"

"Very little. My objective is to have the Americans understand what happened."

Craig would have liked to know himself. But he wished to hell Bryce wasn't coming.

"I'll let you know where and when to meet us. Oh, and something else you should be aware of."

"What's that?" Craig asked warily.

"I've been informed that your friend Gina Galindo will be with the press group covering the meetings. In fact, she asked me to include you."

Well, well, isn't that nice, Craig thought.

"So you might have time for a little fun," Estrada said and laughed. Then he hung up the phone.

Craig stared at it for several minutes trying to discern what Estrada had in mind for him and Gina. His guess was that Estrada wanted Gina to pick his brain. He'd be extra careful in what he told her.

He had to find a doctor, and he couldn't do that in the hotel or word would get back to Estrada. He had only one option.

Clumsily, he got dressed. Out in the corridor, he hid behind a doorway until the service elevator came. Then he took it to the basement. In the kitchen area he passed men loading a large industrial dishwasher. He looked around until he found what he wanted: a staircase leading to a delivery door in the rear of the hotel. Certain that he wasn't being watched, he slipped out.

In the bright sunlight he walked a few blocks down the hill, away from the entrance to the hotel. Then he ducked into an indoor shopping mall lined with luxury boutiques.

From an isolated corner, he called Nicole. Without identifying himself, he said, "I enjoyed seeing your house last evening. I may be prepared to give you an offer to buy it, but I'd like to take another look first. Can you go out there with me now?"

She didn't miss a beat. "Where are you?"

When he described his location, she said, "I'll be there in a few minutes, driving a dark green BMW sedan."

The instant she pulled up in front of the mall, he stumbled out and collapsed into the front seat of her car.

"Drive," he said as he ducked his head down.

"What's wrong? You look like hell."

He pulled up his shirt.

She grimaced. "Good God. Schiller's thugs?"

"Yeah. Thanks for picking me up. I need a doctor to look at me."

"I have a friend who'll come to the house. We can trust him."

*   *   *

Craig woke up in a strange bed. Fluttering in through an open window was a gentle breeze. Outside, it was dark.

He boosted himself to a sitting position, rubbed his eyes, and looked around. Nicole was sitting in a rocker, dressed in a white terry-cloth robe, gently moving back and forth and watching him.

Anticipating his question, she said, "You're in my house."

"How long did I sleep?"

"Well it's almost ten at night. The doctor gave you a powerful pain-killer that he expected would knock you out."

"What was his diagnosis?"

"Just bad bruises. No serious damage. He said you might try moving in a different crowd."

"Very funny."

"You feel like eating?"

"I'm starving. I haven't had a bite since breakfast, and I left that in the park."

"Good. Let me help you out of bed."

Before she reached him, he lowered himself onto the floor. The pajamas he was wearing were about two sizes too large.

"You obviously date a big guy," he said.

She shook her head and laughed. "Those are Papa's. He spends the night here sometimes."

"Thanks for taking care of me. I appreciate it."

He suddenly remembered the meeting tomorrow. "What happened to my cell phone?"

She pulled it out of his jacket pocket. "Did you sleep through a hot date tonight?"

"No, but I have to call for my messages. Estrada wants to meet me in the morning."

Craig called his hotel. From the answering machine in his room he found out what he needed. He was supposed to be at Estrada's office at nine in the morning.

She had sent the servants home, so the two of them settled down at the wooden butcher block kitchen table with cold, cooked steak, several different salads, and a loaf of homemade bread the cook had left.

"You want some wine?" she asked.

He started to say "yes," then remembered what happened to him with Betty in Sardinia and changed his mind. "Plain old water."

As they began eating, she asked, "What are you doing with Estrada tomorrow?"

"The American government is sending down a delegation headed by Edward Bryce to find out what happened up north with Brazil. Estrada wants me to tag along."

"You've certainly managed to become a player."

He laughed. "It's the money, honey. Ten billion would get you invited to the festivities as well."

She picked up a forkful of food. As he watched her eat, he thought Nicole had a very sensuous mouth. Her eyes were radiant in the light. She wasn't wearing any make up. Perhaps he had been too busy worrying about survival the other times he had been with her to notice, but she was a strikingly beautiful woman. Her robe was loose on top, and he could see some cleavage and the round sloping portion of her breasts.

"Does Bryce know anything about my country?"

"He's been getting an education in bed."

"You're kidding."

"Nope. Do you know a reporter from *La Nación* named Gina Galindo?"

"I read her articles in the newspaper. That's all."

"Well anyhow, she's an innocent kid who taught at a Catholic girls' school in Mendoza. Estrada, who knew her old man, an army buddy of his, now deceased, plucked her out of the convent and coerced her into sleeping with Bryce. He's willing to destroy her to get what he wants."

Nicole glowered. "Estrada's such a bastard. He'd do anything to advance himself." She paused, then added, "I guess that explains why American arms have been flowing down here like water."

"You've got it. Estrada told me that Gina's coming with the American delegation as part of the press entourage."

Craig decided he had better stop right there about Gina. She'd be upset if she later found out he'd been using Gina even though he hadn't slept with her.

He changed the subject. "In the morning, Estrada's taking us up north to the battle site. In the evening, there's a dinner at the Alvear. Since I'll be with Estrada, Schiller will have to keep his thugs under control."

When they finished eating, she said, "The doctor suggested you take a long soak in a warm bath. I've got a large Jacuzzi off my bedroom. I'll fill it up, dump in some bath salts, and let you do your thing for about half an hour. How does that sound?"

"Great."

* * *

The warm water with soapsuds felt good against his bruised body. He was sitting in the center of the tub so water from the jets wouldn't strike his body directly. Immersed to his shoulders, he closed his eyes and felt his strength returning.

He was convinced that Colonel Schiller had sent those men to beat him. Craig vowed to get even with Schiller. It might take time, but eventually he'd have Schiller pleading for mercy.

Behind him, he heard the door open and a rustling noise. "How are you doing?" Nicole called over his shoulder.

"Great," he said, without turning around. "Thanks so much."

With the jets running, he never heard her walk across the room. But he did hear her climb into the tub behind him. And he felt her arms around his chest ever so gently and her breasts pressing against his back.

She planted little kisses on the back of his neck. "I hope I'm not hurting you," she said.

"Never." He loved the feel of her body.

She reached her right hand down and wrapped it around his soft, flaccid member. "And I'm not hurting you now am I?"

He laughed. "That's pure pleasure, but they beat me a lot . . . I don't know."

He was stiffening in her hand.

"My, my," she said. "You underestimate your powers of recuperation."

"And obviously your powers of stimulation. Looks like the painkillers I took didn't have any debilitating effect."

"You don't have to worry about that. I asked the doctor to prescribe something that wouldn't be a problem that way."

"Sounds to me like you knew what you had in mind."

She laughed. "Actually, I wanted it last evening, but you had to leave quickly."

She reached her other hand around and played with his balls.

"Oh God, that feels so good."

"When I'm with a man I like, I become a sexual predator. How's that strike you?"

"I'm used to calling the shots."

"Then it'll be a first for you. Now, why don't you keep quiet, listen to me, and enjoy yourself."

After several minutes of kisses on his neck and gentle stroking, he thought his rock hard penis would explode, but she sensed that and knew how to squeeze tightly at the base to pull him back from the brink.

"Can we go to bed?" he murmured.

"You're not in charge. Remember."

She pulled away, and moved around him. Facing him, she lowered herself on to his rigid cock, careful not to press against his chest. The jets in the tub were going full blast.

She wrapped her hands around the back of his neck and kissed him hard, letting her tongue dart into his mouth. At the same time she began moving, sliding up and down on him, magnifying the pleasure for herself. Looking into his eyes, she must have sensed that he couldn't hold back any longer. She drove herself faster and faster until she came with him.

"Oh God!" he cried out.

She smiled warmly, slid off, turned off the jets and positioned them both with their backs against the wall of the tub side by side.

He was falling asleep. After a few minutes, she woke him, helped him out of the tub, dried him, and led him back to bed.

*   *   *

What woke Craig was Nicole's warm, wet mouth moving up and down his erect cock. At first, he thought he was having an erotic dream in which he was on his back and she was stretched over his body with her legs straddling his head and her feet against the headboard. But then she took him completely into her mouth while pressing her soft, moist, folds of skin against his face. It was the wonderful aroma of her that made him realize it was no dream.

Wild sensations were rippling through his body. He spread her open with his hands and used his tongue on her clitoris. She was moving herself up and down against his mouth, while driving him wild, pushing him further and further to the edge. Suddenly, she stopped.

Totally in control, she spun around and sat on him, sliding him inside of her. Once he reached up and cupped a breast in each hand, she arched her back and anchored her hands against the mattress. In that position she began thrusting herself up and down, slow at first and then faster and faster. Drops of perspiration fell from her forehead onto his chest. "Oh yes," she moaned with pleasure, "oh yes."

Through his own lust and passion, he looked at her face, contorted with joy. Her driving desire and animal-like emotions made her look even more beautiful than any other time. He watched her bite down hard on her lower lip, throw her head back and scream, "You too. Now. Oh God, now," loud enough to be heard back at the Alvear.

"Yes," he shouted back and exploded inside her.

When he softened, she rolled off and cuddled up next to him. The sun was streaming in through a crack in the white curtains of a window facing the garden in the back of the house.

She leaned over and kissed him on the lips. "You have a tough day coming up with Estrada. I wanted to get you off to a good start."

Craig thought about the time he would be spending with Gina today. Though he tried to resist it, comparisons came into his mind. Nicole was a mature adult, a savvy partner, not only in bed, but in his mission in Argentina. Nicole understood the stakes involved in Estrada's power grab. She was willing to take risks to stop him. In contrast, Gina was a naive schoolgirl, who had been manipulated by Estrada into Bryce's bed to advance Estrada's agenda.

He turned back to Nicole. "From this point, it'll be downhill the rest of the day."

Buenos Aires

Craig was standing close to Estrada when the American delegation arrived at an Air Force base outside of Buenos Aires. Introductions were made on the tarmac, while photographers snapped away and television cameras were running. The American delegation was small—Bryce, West, Major Thomas, an Air Force officer from the staff of General Forbes, the Assistant Secretary of Defense, and an Army captain assigned to the Pentagon for military intelligence matters. For the Argentines, it was Estrada, Schiller, and two military aides. Estrada introduced Barry Gorman as an American investor and an informal advisor of his for economic matters.

The three reporters who came with the delegation—Gina and two Americans—were joined by an Argentine television crew.

Craig wondered how Gina would greet him in this crowd. She had to know she was under Bryce's jealous and watchful eye. Craig was relieved that she gave him a perfunctory nod as if they were meeting for the first time.

During the introductions, Craig was worried that Bryce might recognize him. But the presidential advisor was focused on Gina. Though Craig breathed a sigh of relief, he realized that his fears were unjustified. The Swiss plastic surgeon had done such a good job. There was no way that Bryce could recognize him.

Estrada motioned to Colonel Schiller, who herded the group onto a military aircraft for the flight north. Once they were airborne, one of the colonel's aides distributed a kit of materials to everyone on the plane that included a set of pictures of the dead Brazilian soldiers and their Chinese weapons.

Then Schiller moved to the front of the cabin. Utilizing blow-ups of the photos on an easel, he presented the Argentine version of what occurred. It was a smooth and well-rehearsed presentation. "The facts are very simple. Under cover of darkness, a gray van driven by a Brazilian civilian with six Brazilian soldiers in the rear crossed the border into Argentina. They drove up to one of our army outposts where the six climbed out of the back. Without any warning, they opened fire on our position with automatic weapons and grenade launchers, all manufactured in China. The surprise attack left our side with three dead and four wounded before the six were finally neutralized. Five were killed immediately. One was wounded seriously. We tried to save him with emergency medical treatment, but he died."

Bryce broke in. "Did you have an opportunity to question the one who was wounded?"

"We did. He said that Argentina had stolen the territory from Brazil and that they were the vanguard of a larger force to retake what belonged to Brazil. We immediately moved more troops into the area. We are now prepared for a further attack."

"What happened to the bodies of the Brazilian soldiers?" West asked.

"All were returned to Brazil for humanitarian reasons. We kept their weapons. You will have a chance to inspect them. You will also have a chance to talk to some of our soldiers who fought against the Brazilians. And to inspect the damage they did to our outpost."

Listening to Schiller, Craig became convinced that the colonel's presentation was too slick, too pat to be a rendition of reality. Left out were some nagging issues such as precisely how the Brazilian unit slipped into Argentina with the state of readiness that existed along the border and the point of capturing a single Argentine outpost. He kept those concerns to himself, wondering if he'd find answers in the north.

Northern Argentina

As the plane came in for a landing, Craig looked out of the window. The area was characterized by thick vegetation that one would expect from the heavy rainfall. Even in October, temperatures were into the nineties with high humidity. Rain was falling lightly when they walked down the stairs to the tarmac of the military base.

Craig had no doubt they were in an area on the verge of becoming a war zone. At the military base where they landed, row after row of spanking new American-built fighter jets and bombers, F-18s and F-16s, sat poised and ready to go. Riding in the back of one of the air-conditioned vans with Bryce, West, Estrada, and Schiller, Craig saw scores of Argentine troops on foot on their way toward the border, and he also saw trucks carrying heavy guns and Abrams tanks. Uniforms were fresh. The men looked eager for battle. This was no ragtag army, but a well-oiled fighting machine.

They pulled up to a heavily fortified stone tower about eight stories high.

The vans stopped and everyone climbed out. Estrada pointed to the pockmarks in the stone structure. Pieces of concrete were missing at several points.

"The Brazilians snuck through the woods and tried to take this position," Estrada said. "Here's where the battle was fought."

"Can we climb up in the tower?" West asked.

"Yes." Estrada looked at the reporters. "There is no elevator."

None of them was concerned.

When they reached the platform at the top, sweating profusely and breathing hard, Craig took a pair of binoculars out of his pocket. From an opening in a gun position, he looked toward the east, through rain falling in sheets. The Brazilians had a large number of troops and armored units on their side of the border. Off in the distance he saw a Brazilian airbase with French planes close to the runway. Through the corner of his eye, he saw Schiller glaring at him.

He worked his way around the platform until he had a view of the Falls shrouded in the mist. He couldn't see clearly, but what was visible was breathtaking in its grandeur. Gina had been right. Niagara couldn't hold a candle to Iguazu. Not just in the size of the drop, but the breadth of the Falls. Miles, it seemed to him. He'd never seen anything like it.

Glancing across the platform, he watched Gina, looking very serious and professional with her hair tied back tightly in a bun and a pair of glasses halfway down her nose. In one hand she held a steno pad; in the other she had a pen for making notes. From time to time she looked in his direction.

Colonel Schiller turned to one of the soldiers manning a lookout post. "Were you on duty two nights ago, Lieutenant?" Schiller asked.

"Yes, sir. I was."

"Can you speak English?"

"A leetle bit."

"Tell our visitors in English what happened."

"They sneak across. So many Brazilian soldiers. When it's dark. Then they begin shooting. Some get into the tower. We shoot back."

"Why didn't they blow up the tower?" one of the American reporters asked.

Schiller responded. "The wounded man died before we had a chance to ask. Our guess is that they wanted to occupy the tower, which they would then fortify. Let's go back down. You can see the weapons we captured."

It had stopped raining by the time they reached the ground.

Schiller led the entourage to a shed about ten yards behind the tower. The doors were thrown open and two soldiers wheeled out a metal bin filled with weapons—pistols, rifles with bayonets, automatics, grenade launchers, hand grenades.

"These are the arms the Brazilians brought with them," Estrada said.

He reached into the bucket, pulled out an automatic weapon and held it up. "All made in China," he said. "You're welcome to inspect them."

Craig had to admit that everything they had seen today was consistent with the story Estrada had told on the television. It was a well-orchestrated presentation. Estrada had designated Schiller to be the conductor, and the colonel had handled the baton with incredible acumen. Too much for Craig's comprehension. He hoped his hatred for the colonel wasn't coloring his perception.

Buenos Aires

"To the friendship of our two great nations," President Garcia said as he raised a glass of sparkling Argentine wine.

Everyone else in the ornate first floor state room at the Alvear—all twenty-three of them—raised their glasses as well.

"To President Treadwell," Garcia added.

Once people had sipped, Bryce lifted his glass, "And to our host President Garcia and the other leaders of the Republic of Argentina."

"Hear, hear!" murmured the crowd.

Bryce touched his glass against Gina's, who was standing next to him looking exquisite in a white Gucci suit with a black knit blouse, a perfect backdrop for her mother's gold cross. Watching them, Craig could barely suppress a smile. Half an hour before the reception, while he was still in his suite, Gina had called him.

"Have you been enjoying Argentina?" she had asked.

"Immensely," he told her. "It's exactly the way you described it. I can't thank you enough."

"It was my pleasure. I enjoyed being with you in Washington." She gave a short girlish laugh. "I'm sorry we couldn't talk today, but it was awkward. I want to see you tonight."

Go slow, he cautioned himself. Let her take the lead. The only reason she was here was because of her closeness to Estrada, the general's efforts to manipulate Bryce, and perhaps because of Craig as well.

"I'll be at the dinner," Craig had told her on the phone.

"No. I mean alone. Later. This town has lots of good tango bars. Can you find one for us?"

"Of course," he said, knowing that the concierge could supply the info and for a generous tip would keep his mouth shut. "But will you be able to get away?"

"I have my own room. I can do anything I want," she said sounding suspicious. "Why did you ask that?"

He backpedaled fast to recover from his foolish comment. He wasn't supposed to know about her relationship with Bryce. "In my experience, press people tend to hang out in packs on trips like this."

"Oh that. You don't have to worry. I don't know the American reporters."

He had satisfied her. "I'm in room 614," she had said. "Later after the party breaks up, I'll come back up here. You call me."

*   *   *

Following the reception, they moved into the adjacent room for dinner. Three round tables of eight were set. Place cards were on the tables for each guest. Craig had no doubt that Estrada had arranged the tables. With a proper sense of political decorum, President Garcia and his wife were seated at table number one and joined there by West, the American ambassador to Argentina, and some top Argentine business leaders. Estrada was seated at table number two. On Estrada's right was Bryce. On his left, Gina, with Craig on the other side of Gina. Then came Miranda, an Argentine general, and an American military officer. On Bryce's other side was an attractive Argentine opera singer. Colonel

Schiller was seated at the third table along with a mixture of American and Argentine military and civilian officials.

Once dinner began, Craig leaned toward Gina and talked with her about Buenos Aires and the sights he had seen. As he did, he was trying to eavesdrop on Estrada's conversation with Bryce. What he heard Bryce say was, "Everything bears out your version of the facts."

"Because that's what happened," Estrada said. "But I'm happy to hear you say it. There is still one thing I would like from your government."

Gina was rattling on about the beauty of Iguazu Falls. "I know you couldn't see much from where we were today. But you must go back and visit. The Falls are 269 feet high over an area of two and a half miles. The flow this time of year is fast with runoff from the winter snow. The best ways to appreciate the incredible sight are from a helicopter over the Falls or in a boat. At the bottom of the Falls, you can move up so close in the boat that the spray from the water soaks you."

Craig strained to hear the discussion between Estrada and Bryce.

"Surely," Bryce said, "You can't want more arms or planes from us. After the surface-to-air missiles and rocket grenade launchers, your army should be loaded. We've even agreed to a reduced, deferred payment schedule with lots of aid to offset much of the bill."

Estrada nodded. "No. You've been very generous. I couldn't ask for any more in that sphere. What I want now is very easy for you to supply."

"What's that?" Bryce asked.

"And you also have to go to the far south," Gina said to Craig, "to Patagonia and . . ."

"If Brazil attacks again," Estrada was telling Bryce, "we intend to give them a powerful beating to deter their aggressive behavior once and for all. I'd like the commitment of your government to stay out of it and let us finish the job. That's what I want."

"That sounds reasonable," Bryce responded. "I'm sure President Treadwell will agree to it. I'll talk to him as soon as we get back."

"Good and when you go to Brazil, you can deliver the message that we are prepared to defend ourselves."

Craig heard Gina say, "Have you ever seen penguins?"

He shook his head.

"They're amazing animals. They . . ."

"I won't be going to Brazil," Bryce told Estrada. "They refuse to meet with our delegation. They claim we're too biased to be a mediator."

That comment elicited a wry smile from Estrada. "I think there's another explanation."

"What's that?" Bryce asked.

"They recognize how wise you are. That you'll cut through their deceit in a minute. For my part, I'd like to take advantage of that wisdom. We seem to understand each other. I hope that you and I can open up a direct line of communication between the two of us for the future. Perhaps you'll come and visit at my country house in January and provide some advice."

Bryce swallowed Estrada's blatant flattery. "I would be delighted to do that."

Estrada then directed the conversation and Bryce's attention to the singer on Bryce's other side. "Our Melina," he said, "has performed with opera companies all around the world."

Craig turned back to Gina, who was telling him, "You haven't touched your Argentine steak. It's superb."

A waiter came by and filled his wine glass. It was Miranda's excellent 1990 malbec, he noticed.

He sipped the wine and leaned toward Miranda to tell him how good it was. When he turned the other way, Gina was locked in a whispered conversation with Estrada, too low for him to overhear. Through the corner of his eye, he watched them and tried to understand the nature of their obviously close relationship. It wasn't romantic. More like a close father-daughter relationship, but with business components. A daughter working in a family business, where she did her father's bidding. It was odd. Everything about this situation was bizarre.

Several different wines, all from Miranda's winery, were freely poured during the multicourse dinner. As Gina drank more and more, she became demonstrably friendly toward Craig, not only giggling like a schoolgirl, but touching him from time to time. First, she placed her hand on his. He moved it away gracefully. But then she rested it on his arm. When he also moved that, she reached behind his chair and stroked the back of his neck.

"This is not smart," he wanted to tell her, but he kept still. The alcohol had broken down her inhibitions and eroded her discretion. Through the corner of his eye, he noticed Bryce watching what was happening. The American lawyer was shooting green poison dart looks at both Craig and Gina.

This was not what Craig needed right now.

He was happy when she told him, "I have to go the little girls' room to pee. You want to come and go to the little boys'?"

"I'm okay." The last thing he wanted right now was for Bryce to see him leave the room with Gina.

He took a deep breath when she spun off the chair, touched his cheek, and cut across the room toward the entrance, which was being guarded by three armed soldiers.

Craig's relief was short-lived. The minute Gina was gone, Bryce stood up, moved over, and sat down in her empty chair.

"We never really had a chance to talk today," Bryce said to Craig. "I gather from General Estrada that you're an investment banker from San Francisco down here looking for opportunities."

"That pretty well describes it," Craig said warily. He was altering his voice because Bryce had heard him speak as Craig Page in two meetings with Treadwell.

"Been here long?"

"Oh a week or so."

"Where are you staying?"

"Here at the Alvear. In fairly modest digs." He smiled, but Bryce, his face stone rigid, was in no mood for humor.

"I would think it's a tough economy to make money in." Bryce's voice had a suspicious edge.

"In my experience, that's the best time to invest. Find the opportunities before others do. When the storm is abating. Anybody can sail a boat in calm water."

"Are you married, Mr. Gorman?"

"Please, it's Barry." He guessed that the jealous Bryce wanted to point out to Gina that her new friend was married as a way of pulling her back, but Craig was ready for him. Sticking with the Barry Gorman bio, he said, "I tried it once. It didn't agree with me. What about you? I'll bet you're part of a forty year marriage. My parents had one of those."

Bryce reddened slightly. Before he had a chance to respond, Gina returned. "Listen, honey," Bryce told her, "go take my seat for a while. This is all guy talk. Business and boring stuff like that."

Craig could tell that she was clearly pissed, but she did what Bryce said.

"What firm are you with?" Bryce asked.

"The Philoctetes Group."

"I haven't heard of that one."

"It's a private equity fund based in San Francisco. I specialize in international investments."

"Really. How interesting. I've been looking for something like that for myself. I'm tired of having my own net worth repeatedly battered by the American stock market."

Staring at Bryce, Craig said sternly, "We have a $10 million minimum."

Bryce smiled. "I can handle that. Do you have a card?"

Play it natural, Craig cautioned himself. "Sure." He pulled out his wallet and handed Bryce a card, which the American lawyer studied.

A waiter passed cigars. Craig took one and lit it up. Bryce declined.

"Do you have a cell phone number?" Bryce asked.

"All of my business calls go into the San Francisco office. The number's on the card. They always find me."

With the card still in his hand, Bryce stood up and said to Gina, who was in a pout, "You can have your chair back." In a voice dripping with sarcasm, he added, "I'd say I warmed it up, but you're so hot tonight that I probably cooled it down."

She glared at him and moved over.

"What'd he want?" she asked Craig.

This is getting so dicey it's almost funny, he thought. Back to his own voice. But softly, "Bryce wants to talk to me about investing some of his money."

Any thought Craig had that the situation with Bryce was humorous dissipated rapidly. Through the corner of his eye, he watched Bryce, still with the Barry Gorman card in hand, walk over to Colonel Schiller, standing near the doorway puffing on a cigar and talking to one of the soldiers. Once he saw Bryce approach, Schiller moved forward to meet him.

Craig couldn't hear what Bryce and Schiller said, but he saw Bryce hand the card to Schiller, which the colonel glanced at and returned. They chatted for a couple of minutes. Then Schiller reached into his pocket, took out a card of his own and handed it to Bryce.

At that point, Craig made a decision. Tomorrow morning he would fly back to the United States. The focus had shifted to Washington. The key now was whether Bryce could convince Treadwell to do what Estrada wanted. Besides, he had pushed his luck with Schiller as far as he possibly could. If he didn't get out of the country damn fast, he'd end up like Dunn. He had no doubt that Schiller would make his death look like an accident in order to avoid Estrada's wrath.

A few minutes later, the dinner was breaking up. As Gina stood and Craig held the chair for her, she whispered in his ear. "Remember room 614. I'll be waiting for your call."

"Absolutely," he replied softly.

On her way to the door, Bryce cut her off. Pretending to say good night to Miranda, Craig moved close enough to hear Bryce say to her, "Let's go out on the town. You've always told me that Buenos Aires starts at midnight. That's ten minutes from now."

Gina yawned. "Oh William, not tonight. I'm so tired."

"But I thought you were a night person."

"On last night's flight I was in the press section of the plane. We didn't have beds like you people. I'll take a rain check."

"Just for a little while."

"Please. I'm too tired for anything."

Bryce was visibly annoyed, but there was nothing to do about it. She wasn't going.

* * *

El Bodegon was a grimy down-and-out tango joint in a seedy area of San Telmo, a fifteen-minute cab ride from the Alvear. While mentioning the name of the place to Craig, the concierge said, "I doubt whether any foreigners have ever been there. At any rate, with the increased crime that's an unfortunate consequence of our recession, I would not recommend it."

"Then I certainly won't go there," Craig had told him, in case any of Estrada's people asked.

Walking through the front door of El Bodegon, he and Gina looked like porteños. She was dressed in a bright blouse and short black skirt. Her shoes were black patent leather with a strap across the instep. She had left the cross in the hotel room. He was in a pair of khakis and muted plaid shirt.

Since neither of them wanted to be seen, he had told her to come to the eighth floor of the Alvear, to which she readily agreed. He had met her at the elevator, then took her down to the basement and outside through the service entrance he had used yesterday.

It was still early. El Bodegon was dimly lit and half empty. He led her to a booth in the corner and ordered a couple of margaritas with salt.

The accordion-like *bandonéon* was playing a hauntingly sad song. The words described a lonely man at a bar drinking to drown his troubles to forget the woman who had left him. On the dance floor, couples, quite adept at the tango, moved together, giving the appearance of one stalking the other. Two sweat-slicked bodies fused, simulating copulation. Wide-eyed, watching their overt sexuality, Gina said, "I've never been to a place like this before. I can't believe it took a gringo to get me here."

She had given him the opening he wanted. He took a sip of his drink, then moved right in. "Have you ever lived in Buenos Aires?"

"Only for a few months when I began at *La Nación*. I was born in Mendoza. My mother died when I was only two. With my father in the army, I grew up with his parents on their farm. They're wonderful people. The family has been in Argentina for more than two hundred years.

"Though I was only ten when my father died, he had spent lots of time with me—whenever he could. He was kind, warm, and caring. A marvelous human being. I loved him so much. Everybody did. He was a great man, a hero of the Republic. Very popular. My grandparents told me that people cried for days when they found out the Communists assassinated him. I was away at school at the time. It was horrible." She paused to wipe tears from her eyes.

"What was his name?"

"Miguel Galindo. General Miguel Galindo." Looking over at Craig with pride, she asked, "Have you heard of him?"

He hadn't, but he didn't want to admit that. So he said, "I saw his name in some of the articles I read before coming down here. They were all very complimentary."

She gulped down the rest of her drink. "I'm so thirsty."

The waitress was passing by. Gina told her, "I'll have another one."

The waitress looked at Craig. "You, too?"

"I'm good for now."

"How'd you get to know General Estrada?"

"What makes you think I do?" She sounded defensive.

"The way he was talking to you tonight. The fact that he selected you for his dinner partner."

She was beaming. "I guess that's right. Alfredo served under my father. After papa's death, Alfredo treated me like one of his own children. I spent many weekends at his country house. He'd send an army car to pick me up at the girls' school. He took me skiing with his family in the winter and to a mountain lake in the summer. Now that I'm grown up, he's helped my career at the newspaper." She paused to take another sip. "But I'm tired of talking about myself. I want to talk about you. How did you get into this investment business?"

She said it in such a forced way that he decided Estrada had told her to obtain information from him.

The waitress brought her drink. She sipped it and looked at him, waiting for an answer.

"I always liked money," he said, laughing easily.

She laughed with him. "Most people do."

"And I found that I'm good at it."

"Your office is in San Francisco?"

He nodded. "I'd love to show you around California some time. What do you think, Gina?"

"That would be great," she said with enthusiasm. "Also, I like that you call me by my name. Not honey or dear. You treat me like a real person."

She was slurring her words, blinking her eyes as if getting them to focus. She'd had too much to drink.

"And of course you are a wonderful person," he said. "If you give me your cell number, I'll call you when I can arrange it."

She took a pen out of her purse and sloppily wrote down a number on a paper napkin. "My cell," she handed it to him.

"I have to go back to San Francisco for a couple of days. To do some work on one of the investments I'm discussing with your friend Alfredo."

She smiled like a cat who had just swallowed a canary. In a soft voice, she began singing. "A kiss on the hand may be quite continental, but diamonds are a girl's best friend."

She picked up her left hand and waved her ring finger at him.

Startled, he responded, "How did you know that?"

"My friend Rosie has tons of CDs from Broadway musicals. That's from *Gentlemen Prefer Blondes.*"

"No. I mean how did you know that Alfredo and I were discussing diamonds?"

She held a finger up to her lips and gave him a coquettish look. "There's plenty that I know, but I'll never tell."

Just how tight with Estrada was she, he wondered. He decided that it was time to close up shop before arousing her suspicions. He had already gotten more from her than he had hoped. A new song was beginning. "We didn't come here to talk," he said. "We came to tango."

He led her out to the floor, where they joined half a dozen other couples.

*   *   *

Back at the Alvear, Bryce was calling Gina's room for the third time. As before, it rang and rang with no answer. In a white fury and in his stockinged feet and Alvear terrycloth robe, he charged down the hall from his suite in 601 to 614. He pounded on the door so loudly that a security guard came up an inside staircase and eyed him with apprehension, ready to go for his gun.

"I'm sorry," Bryce mumbled. "I must have made a mistake."

But he knew damn well he hadn't made a mistake. He was absolutely certain what had happened.

Going for total certainty to make himself as miserable as possible, Bryce went back to his own suite and asked the operator to connect him with Barry Gorman.

"It's quite late, Mr. Bryce," she said.

Bryce tried to sound polite. "I know that, but we're working on something very important. I'm the head of the American delegation. Don't you know that?"

"I'm sorry, sir. I'll connect you right away."

Again the phone rang and rang without any answer. That lying bitch had to be with Gorman. He'd find a way to get even with him.

*　　　*　　　*

The song was a tale of passion and unrequited love, its tones melancholy and bittersweet. "It's over between us / you said / in a goodbye of sugar and ice."

As they reached the dance floor, Craig took charge. She followed where he led, anticipating his movements, her hair swinging freely, her face a mask of sexual desire, her eyes focused on him. With a fervor they moved, their bodies slapping together recklessly, generating a sense of mutual desire. Her face flushed, she raised her right leg high, pressing it against his left side, their bodies entwined. Roughly, he clasped her ankle, held it for a couple of seconds, while her chest pressed against his and their faces were an inch apart. Then he released her and their bodies unraveled.

As she pulled away, no longer content to follow, she challenged him for the lead. They were in her country. Lust had given her a self-confidence she had never known before. She stalked him in their ritual of desire. At first surprised by her aggression, he quickly backed down, yielding to her as the predator. Other couples had stopped dancing and were watching in awe the strangers, gliding around the floor. The temperature in the room was high. That combined with their intense motion and the alcohol they had consumed through the evening made their skin glisten with perspiration.

When they came together now in the dancers' embrace, they were equals. Suddenly, she stopped dancing and squeezed him tight. "Oh Barry, I'm so happy. When I'm with you, I don't want anything else."

From deep down inside, a little voice whispered to him, "I hope you know what you're doing. Don't let her be destroyed."

The music overrode that voice as they resumed dancing. When the music stopped, without any warning, she leaned up and kissed him hard on his mouth. Pulling away, her face was flushed with desire. "Let's go back to the hotel," she whispered.

In the back of the cab, she leaned her body close to his. As soon as the wheels began turning, she fell sound asleep, snoring softly.

When they got out of the cab in front of the Alvear, she woke up. Cautiously, he led her through the revolving door into the lobby. She held his arm to steady herself.

Except for an armed guard and a tired looking clerk behind the desk, the lobby was deserted as he expected at three in the morning. No sign of Clay or Schiller.

Craig's suite was on the eighth floor. As he pushed six, her floor, Craig, who had quite a bit to drink himself, wasn't sure how this would play out.

When the elevator stopped on the sixth floor, she suddenly looked pale. Walking along the corridor, she handed him her room key.

"Open the door fast," she said.

As soon as they were in the room, she cried out, "Oh God, I'm going to be sick."

She ran to the bathroom. Standing near the door, he heard her throwing up.

White as sheet, she emerged from the bathroom minutes later.

"Can I get you anything?" he asked.

"Please go. I don't want you to see me like this. Just leave."

She ran back to the bathroom and threw up again.

Once she returned, she stretched out on the bed. "Please, Barry. Leave me. I'll be okay."

He left her room.

Back in his own suite, he showered and dressed, then packed everything he needed for a trip to the United States. He called American Airlines and booked first class to San Francisco via Miami on a morning flight. In the lobby, he stuffed several thousand dollars in a briefcase but left the rest of the cash and the guns in the vault box.

In a loud voice, he told the clerk on duty at the desk to let Mr. Fernandez, the hotel manager, know that he had to make a quick trip to San Francisco, he'd be back within the week, and please continue

to keep him registered in the suite because he left many of his posses-
sions behind. Then he shouted for the doorman to get him a cab to the
international airport. He wanted to leave behind lots of witnesses so
Schiller would think he had gotten what he wanted—Barry Gorman
leaving the country.

*   *   *

After a few hours of sleep, Bryce, cursing under his breath, was
ready to go on the offensive against Gina. After all he'd done for her.
Shit, he'd given her all that jewelry. Bought the Watergate apartment.
Arranged for the arms shipments to Argentina as she had asked.
He had a right to more than lies and deceit. He'd find a way to get
even with her and that investment banker, Barry Gorman. Colonel
Schiller didn't like the man and was suspicious of him. That goaded
Bryce, now convinced that the two of them were shacked up together
somewhere.

He picked up the phone in his room and called Barry Gorman's
suite. It rang and rang with no answer. He repeated the process with
Gina's room. Same result. That confirmed Bryce's suspicions.

His next call was to the hotel manager. "This is Edward Bryce.
The head of the American delegation," he said in a sharp intimidating
voice. "I'm trying to locate Barry Gorman. Can you help me? It's quite
important."

"Mr. Gorman left this morning for San Francisco."

That rocked Bryce back on his heels. "Are you certain of that?"

"Very. He left me a message. He'll be back within the week. I'm
keeping his suite. The doorman arranged a cab."

"Humph," Bryce snorted. "What about Gina Galindo?"

"I just saw her go into the breakfast room off the lobby. Shall I ring
her for you there?"

"No, I'll go see her myself," Bryce responded.

With the green face of jealousy, fire in his eyes, a man on a mission,
his gray hair messy, his shirt buttoned unevenly, Bryce took the elevator to the lobby. Outside of the glass enclosed patio dining room was
a magnificent buffet. Caviar on ice was surrounded by accouterments.
Ice buckets with bottles of champagne. Platters of exotic fruit—kiwis,

mangoes, raspberries, and papayas. Silver chafing dishes of quiche, sau-téed fish, eggs benedict, and baskets of fresh bread waiting to be sliced.

Bryce charged past the hostess at the desk and looked around, his eyes squinting in the bright sunlight pouring in from outside. He spotted Gina sitting alone at a table next to a wall, reading *La Nación* and the article she had filed yesterday after her visit to the border area in the north. In front of her was a cup of tea and some toast.

Snarling, he plopped down in the empty chair across from her at the table for two. "You weren't in your room last night." He hissed angrily. "I called several times. I even knocked on the door."

She waited several moments before responding in a soft voice. "You're right. I called my girlfriend Rosie to tell her I was in town. She said that she's having trouble at work with her boss. Some older guy who's always letching onto her. So I went over to her house to comfort her."

Bryce wasn't buying that. "You told me you were too tired to go out."

"Rosie's my closest friend. I had to help her. It was the Christian thing to do."

Bryce knew a bald-faced lie when he heard one, and he intended to expose it. "I'm no idiot," he said. "You were out with Barry Gorman. At least admit it. Then we'll be done with it."

She pulled her head back, a sad expression on her face, looking as if she might burst out into tears at any second. "How can you talk to me like that?"

"I'm not blind. I saw how you were with him last night at dinner."

Acting wronged, she reached into her bag and pulled out her cell phone. Placing it down on the table close to the astonished Bryce, she said, "Rosie's number is 3020-6742. Call her yourself and ask her where I was. She speaks good English."

Bryce started to reach for the phone, then realized he was about to make an ass out of himself. "I'm sorry," he said. "Please forgive me for being jealous. It's just that you mean so much to me."

She responded with a pout. "I don't like having my honor questioned."

"You're right," he said. "I'll make it up to you. Yesterday I passed by the jewelry store next door. In the window they had earrings. One large emerald surrounded by diamonds. If I buy them for you, can we forget about all of this?"

"I guess so."

"The earrings would look beautiful on you."

"If you insist," she said reluctantly.

"I do. I'll buy them for you before we leave for the airport." He glanced at his watch. "Let's go up to my room. We still have time for a quickie."

"I'm really sorry, Edward. I don't have time. I'd still be upstairs sleeping, but I have to be at the newspaper for a meeting with my editor. From there, I'm going to the airport."

"Cancel the meeting."

"You know I can't. I could lose my job."

He sighed. "Alright. I'll see you on the plane. We'll have a special date in Washington. I'll give you the emerald earrings then."

"Okay."

He left her at breakfast and returned to his hotel room where he took Barry Gorman's card out of his pocket and called the number at the Philoctetes Group in San Francisco. He heard a recorded message. "You have reached the office of Barry Gorman at the Philoctetes Group. Mr. Gorman is out of the office on business. Please leave a message and someone will return your call."

Bryce hung up without saying a word.

Perhaps he had been wrong. He wanted to believe that everything was as it had seemed. Barry Gorman was an American investment banker in Argentina in search of opportunities. He and Gina had merely been making conversation at the dinner. She did go out to meet her friend Rosie. If Gorman were interested in Gina, he would never have rushed off to San Francisco early this morning. She was still his Gina; and she was in love with him. The rest was the jealous paranoia of a man his age, worried he would lose a beautiful young woman.

To be sure, Colonel Schiller had said he was suspicious of Gorman, but Schiller had nothing specific he could point to. He and Schiller had exchanged phone numbers. "We should stay in touch," the colonel had said. "And notify the other if we learn anything about Barry Gorman's deception."

San Francisco

Once the plane from Buenos Aires touched down in Miami, Craig would have liked nothing better than to hop on the next plane to Washington and meet with Betty there, but he decided that Schiller or Bryce, with his White House access, might determine that he had changed his ticket. Out of an abundance of caution, he completed the ticketed itinerary.

Five hours later, the instant he stepped into the terminal in San Francisco, he called Betty on his cell phone. "We have to talk," he said tersely.

"Where are you?"

"San Francisco Airport."

"You want to get to a secure phone?"

He had been flying for almost twenty hours after a sleepless night. The last thing he wanted to do right now was get on another plane, but he didn't have a choice.

"We better do this in person. I can get into Dulles about four this afternoon."

"Good. Come right to my office."

His next call was to Tim Fuller. In a weary voice, he said, "How about meeting me when I arrive on UAL 844 from San Fran at four this afternoon. Then drive me to one of the Virginia suburbs to meet a friend. Bring along any reading material you have for me."

"I'll be there, pal."

Ready to collapse with exhaustion, he boarded the plane and fell fast asleep.

Washington

Feeling refreshed after sleeping for four and a half hours on the plane and dousing his face with cold water, Craig bounded out of the terminal at Dulles Airport and into the back of a Cadillac with Vince behind the wheel.

My God, he thought, *has it only been seven days since I left Washington for Buenos Aires?* It felt like an eternity.

Tim Fuller was in the back seat with a pile of papers on his lap. "CIA headquarters, I presume?" he asked Craig, who nodded. Fuller barked their destination to Vince then hit the button raising the thick, soundproof glass and giving them privacy in the back.

Tim pointed to the transcript on top of the pile. "You've been busy, pal."

Craig was in no mood for jokes. "What do you have for me?" he said sharply.

"When Gina returned from Buenos Aires to the Watergate, she immediately called her friend Rosie in Buenos Aires."

Fuller handed him what looked like a twenty page transcript. He glanced at his watch, then out of the car window. In one of the strangest traffic situations anywhere, they were speeding along a US government road, leading to and from Dulles Airport, while ordinary commuters, prohibited from using it, were in rush hour gridlock on a parallel State of Virginia highway. The fun would end for them in a few minutes when they were on a local road leading to the Agency's Langley head-quarters. Even with that, they should be at Langley in twenty minutes. "Did you read it?" Craig asked.

"Every word."

"Good. Summarize it for me. We don't have much time."

"Better yet. Read pages four and five. They have all that matters for you. The rest is schoolgirl gossip."

Craig flipped through the transcript to page four and began reading.

Gina: *I had to give Edward Bryce your phone number. Did he ever call you?*

Rosie: *Never heard from him.*

Gina: *Good. I figured that'd get him to stop pestering me. Thanks for covering for me.*

Rosie: *You don't have to thank me. You'd do the same for me if I was fortunate enough to be seeing two men.*

Gina: *You make me sound like a loose woman.*

Rosie: *That's not what I meant. I'm just a little envious.*

Gina: *The only reason I ever dated Bryce was because it was important for Argentina. I'm almost finished with all that, which is good because I think I'm in love with Barry Gorman.*

Rosie: *He's the rich American investment banker?*

Gina: *Uh-huh. Ah, I can't stand Bryce. He thinks if he gives me more jewelry, I'll love him.*

Rosie: *That doesn't sound so bad.*

Gina: *The next time I see you, I'll give you a pair of emerald and diamond earrings.*

Rosie: *You're kidding.*

Gina: *Absolutely not. Bryce bought them at the shop next to the Alvear. He's planning to give them to me in Washington.*

Rosie: *That's not right. To give them to me. They're yours. You earned them.*

Gina: *That's the whole point. I don't want anything to remind me of that old man.*

Craig closed up the transcript. "No smart aleck comments. What else do you have?"

"Estrada called her about an hour after she finished talking with Rosie. He was pressing her to stay close to Bryce. He's anxious to find out whether Treadwell will agree not to intervene if Brazil attacks Argentina again and Estrada's army gives them a pounding."

"Did she agree to do it?"

"With reluctance and after a lot of coaxing. He really leaned on her with a lot of shit about her great father and all that. He promised her that in another week, she'll be able to tell Bryce to fuck off."

Something big was happening in the next week, Craig decided.

"Oh and one other thing," Fuller said, breaking out in a broad grin. "Once he lets her break off with Bryce, he's given her permission to do anything she wants with you. Even marry you. He'll walk her down the aisle and give away the blushing bride."

"You're kidding. He said that?"

Fuller nodded. "You think I'm creative enough to make that up? Would you like me to be your best man?"

"Go fuck yourself."

Fuller patted the transcript. "You can read it for yourself."

They were pulling up to the Gate House at CIA headquarters.

"I'll take your word for it," Craig said.

"It gives new meaning to the term shotgun wedding. If I were you, I'd be careful when I returned to Argentina."

Craig grabbed both volumes of transcript and exited the car.

*   *   *

"What brought you back to the United States?" Betty asked Craig as he walked into her corner office on the seventh floor and plunked down on her desk the two volumes of transcript Tim had given him.

"The action has shifted to Washington. Bryce's taking Estrada's request for the US to stay out of the fray back to Treadwell. Meantime, I thought my health could use a change from beautiful, sunny Buenos Aires."

"You mind explaining that? It was a little too elliptical for me."

"Sure. One picture is worth a thousand words." He unbuttoned his shirt. The bruises were now black. He wondered what color was coming next.

"Good God," she blurted out. "Schiller?"

"His people."

"You should get a doctor downstairs to take a look."

He thought about his afternoon and evening with Nicole after the beating. "I already had somebody check me out in Buenos Aires. No serious damage. I'm a lot luckier than Dunn. But I'm not here simply to run away from Schiller." He paused thinking about the colonel and his goons. "Although it's nice not to be watching my six o'clock all the time. Anyhow, I figured it was time to come back here, meet with you, and reassess where we are."

"Good timing. I was trying to decide how to get in touch with you."

He rebuttoned his shirt. "What happened?"

"Barry Gorman received a phone call at the Philoctetes office in San Francisco."

He held his breath. "And?"

"The call immediately rolled over to our telecommunications unit downstairs. The caller listened to the recording, 'This is the office of Barry Gorman,' and so forth, didn't leave a message, and hung up. We traced it. The call came from the Alvear yesterday morning. With a little help from B. J. Walker at the Embassy in Buenos Aires, we established that the call came from Edward Bryce's room. So you have to assume he's suspicious of your cover."

Stiff from flying, Craig stood up and paced around the office, trying to decide how much Bryce knew about his activities with Gina. He had to assume the worst: that she had told Bryce, or Bryce had seen them together when they returned from the tango joint. Either way, Bryce would conclude that his honey pot had been invaded. If Bryce thought he was at risk of losing Gina, he'd fight hard; and he had plenty of resources at his disposal in the United States.

"I guess we'll find out how good the cover is," Craig said. "Meantime, has Bryce gotten Treadwell to make any decisions on the Argentine issue?"

She glanced at her watch. "I'm on standby for a meeting with the president and some of the others about the South American crisis. That's where Treadwell will decide what to do next. The White House will call me as soon as the president finishes a meeting with congressional leaders about the economy."

Craig pounced. "I'll eliminate the suspense for you. Bryce will be trying to persuade Treadwell to agree that we do nothing if Brazil attacks again and Argentina pounds the hell out of them."

When she didn't respond, Craig added, "Makes good sense if you assume Brazil already attacked once. That's the story Estrada is pushing, but it's total bullshit. The trip by Bryce and West wasn't a fact-finding mission. They went along with whatever Estrada and Schiller said, and as for West," Craig was raising his voice, "that bozo was totally duped by Estrada and Schiller with their slick presentation. Or maybe he was cowed by Bryce and his relationship to Treadwell."

Betty looked grim. "You have good instincts." She stood up, walked over to her desk, and picked up a book.

"Read pages 120 and121," she said as she handed it to him.

He glanced at the cover. *Inside the Gestapo*, by Jonathan Martin.

He took it with him back to the table and began reading.

"It was Kurt Schiller, head of special operations for the Gestapo, who fabricated an attack by Polish army units to justify Germany's attack on Poland."

He recalled what Betty had told him in Sardinia. Kurt was Karl Schiller's grandfather, a high level Gestapo official who escaped with Adolph Eichmann to Argentina after the war. He resumed reading.

"The operation is described in testimony at the Nuremberg trials. On the 25th of August, 1939, Schiller ordered ten German prisoners who had lived near the Polish border and had been arrested for crimes against the State to dress up in Polish army uniforms. The ten were transported to a German lookout tower close to the Polish border. There, they were shot and killed. Their bodies were placed on the ground as if they had been attacking the tower. Polish weapons were placed near the bodies. Guns were fired at the tower, chipping away some of the concrete. Then foreign reporters were taken to the scene, shown the bodies as well as other evidence and told 'Poland has attacked us. We should not have to tolerate this aggression.' Six days later, Germany invaded Poland."

Craig tossed the book down on the table. "One's a carbon copy of the other. Grandpa Kurt told his grandson, Karl, about some of his wonderful accomplishments for the Fatherland. How'd you dig this up?"

"I recalled reading about it a long time ago. So I had somebody here do a little research. In testimony, several Nuremberg witnesses confirmed the facts of this faked border incident."

"This is just what we need," Craig said, now excited. "You can take this into your meeting at the White House and blow Bryce out of the water." He began speaking faster, his voice rising. "When Bryce starts talking about how Brazil attacked Argentina, you can stuff this book down his throat. Now we know for sure that Estrada's planning a major attack on Brazil." He was talking loud, the words pouring out with gusto. "The so-called incident that occurred was fabricated in order to justify the attack that Estrada has planned and to persuade the United States not to intervene. If Treadwell makes it clear that we're not buying Estrada's lies, and we'll come to Brazil's aid, there won't be an attack. Estrada will back down. I'd give anything to be at the meeting and see the look on Bryce's face when you spring it on him."

Carried away with his own enthusiasm, Craig hadn't been watching his audience. When he finished talking, he stared across the table at the somber, stone-faced Betty.

"I have to disagree with you, Craig. Something I've almost never done in the many years we've known each other."

He was incredulous. "What do you mean?"

"Unfortunately, while you were off racing cars, I've gotten to know Bryce and Treadwell. Trying to surprise Bryce won't accomplish a thing. The smooth double-talking barrister is too nimble on his feet. He'll insist that this doesn't prove a thing. He'll say that he's a lawyer, and this isn't real evidence of anything. We'll have a big argument. In the end, Treadwell will side with his good buddy, Bryce. All I will have done is tip my hand that I don't believe Estrada. Word of what happened in the White House meeting will reach the general via Gina. From now on, Estrada will be super careful to make sure you and I never get the evidence we need. So I have no intention of mentioning this Gestapo incident at any White House meeting."

Furious, Craig shot to his feet. "I can't believe I'm hearing this." His voice was loud and surly.

Betty stood up and stared at him. "Look, Craig, I can understand why you're emotional about this. You want to destroy Bryce for what he did to you. And you've taken a pounding from Schiller, but . . ."

Red in the face, he shook his head, making no effort to lower his voice. "It's the dumbest thing I've ever heard. It makes no sense at all."

Betty let him rant on.

"I'm not prepared to believe," he shouted, "that Treadwell will follow Bryce with what we have here." He charged over to the table, picked up the book about the Gestapo and waved it at her. "It's so stupid."

"That's the hand we've been dealt with Treadwell in the Oval Office and Bryce in his lap."

"Then let me go with you to the meeting at the White House," he pleaded. "I'll convince them."

"No way. I sympathize with you. Really I do. And I'm your friend. Not the enemy. I know you're right, but if I take you to the White House, they'll end up hauling you out of there in handcuffs."

"It's all so damn frustrating," he cried out. For emphasis, he slammed the book to the floor.

As she opened her mouth to respond, the phone rang. Then the intercom. It was Betty's secretary. "They want you at the White House for the meeting."

She turned to Craig. "You want to wait here until I return? I'll give you a report."

"I'm so angry I want to go down to the exercise room and run on the treadmill so fast that I either break the machine or have a heart attack."

"After that, you can stick your head under a cold shower. Then we'll be able to deal with this rationally."

*   *   *

Bryce entered the Situation Room two steps behind President Treadwell and looked around. In addition to the usual suspects seated around the table, Kent, West, the Secretary of Defense, and General Forbes, he saw Vice President Doug Worth.

The president had told Bryce on his return from Buenos Aires that he wanted to involve Worth in more of his day-to-day activities without any explanation.

Bryce deduced that Treadwell was now worried about his health. Treadwell must have realized he was playing a game of Russian Roulette with his heart condition. If he lost, he didn't want to leave the country in too much of a mess.

When they were seated, the president turned to Bryce. "It's your show, Edward."

Bryce had assigned the factual report on the South American mission to West, who was ready with another PowerPoint presentation, giving a summary of what they saw, which was precisely what Estrada and Schiller had told them. At the end of that, Bryce took over and said, "Our recommendation is that if the Brazilians attack again, the United States should stay out of it."

"Suppose the Argentines ask for our help?" General Forbes asked.

"They won't," Bryce said emphatically. "Estrada and Garcia both emphasized to us that the situation can only be stabilized if they're free to exercise their own deterrence."

"But isn't there a risk of this conflict between Argentina and Brazil developing into a broader war?" Betty asked.

"I don't see how," Bryce responded. "Chile and Paraguay are the other two countries in the region with powerful armies. We've seen no indication that either of them would become involved."

Glancing at the president, Bryce observed how wan and pale, almost ashen, he looked, a sheen of sweat across his brow. He is not a well man, Bryce decided. Treadwell winced and sat up straight in his seat, as if he had experienced a sudden pain. Irritably, he said, "I've had a long day. Let's wrap this up. I like Edward's recommendation. That's what we'll do."

Bryce was convinced that all Treadwell wanted was to get out of this damn meeting to take a nitroglycerine tablet.

*   *   *

Craig was sitting in the outer office of Betty's suite where Monica was typing away, waiting for the director of the CIA to return from the White House. As soon as he saw her, he stood up. "Sorry, I got a little carried away."

"Don't worry about it. You have strong convictions. That's one of the things I like about you."

Betty led him into her office and kicked the door shut. "Let's talk about where we go from here."

"Somewhere in the middle of a forty-five minute run on the tread-mill, I came up with a game plan to beat Estrada."

"You want to tell me about it?"

"Sure. But first, can I assume that Bryce got what he wanted for Estrada at your White House meeting."

"That's right. Treadwell agreed not to intervene."

"So we now need hard evidence that Estrada fabricated the initial, so-called Brazilian attack like Schiller's grandfather. We also have to find out precisely when Estrada is planning to mount his major attack. That's what it will take to turn Treadwell around."

She nodded. "Agreed. But how can we obtain that information?"

"I have a plan." His self-confidence had returned and he was sounding rational. "But you have to supply a key component."

"What's that?"

"Have your people in research dig back through the archives of our documents from the years of the Dirty War. There must be cables and reports from CIA agents in Argentina as well as original Argentine documents. I want them to put together a complete dossier on Estrada with particular emphasis on his involvement in kidnapping babies. And . . ." he hesitated. Hell, there was no other way. "Have them prepare a second dossier. This one on Gina's father, General Miguel Galindo. Call me on my cell phone the minute you have the information."

He didn't know what he'd find in the file about Gina's father, but his instincts, coupled with what he had learned about Estrada and the general's behavior during the Dirty War, persuaded him that Miguel Galindo could not have been the white knight Gina thought her father was.

Craig needed every possible weapon to turn Gina away from Estrada and to convince her to help him.

*   *   *

"That was a wonderful dinner," Bryce said to Gina as they returned to her apartment from dinner at the Capital Grille on Pennsylvania Avenue where people had repeatedly stopped by to say hello to Bryce.

Successful was how Gina thought of the evening so far. As Bryce was finishing his large sirloin and the last of the Chateau Haut Brion, following two glasses of scotch before dinner, he had told her what she wanted to know. They had a meeting that afternoon at the White House and President Treadwell had agreed to what Estrada was seeking: a commitment by the United States not to intervene if warfare erupted between Argentina and Brazil. She couldn't wait for Bryce to leave so she could call Estrada and give him the news he was so anxious to hear.

"The emerald earrings are exquisite on you," Bryce said.

She was sure Rosie would like them. "They are special. Thank you."

Bryce would be pressing her now for sex, but she had no intention of submitting tonight. Never again. She was in love with Barry.

"Would you like a Remy Martin?" she asked.

Bryce smiled lasciviously. "Perhaps later. Now I have something else in mind." He took off his tie and jacket; and began unbuttoning his shirt.

"I can't tonight," she said awkwardly.

He scowled. "Why not?"

"It's that time of the month. You know. I'm really sorry." She tried to sound sincere so he wouldn't suspect she had told him a complete lie.

"That doesn't bother me."

"Well it does me," she said with a tone of finality. "You'll just have to wait a couple of days."

He persisted. "We could do other things."

"Please, Edward. Just the cognac."

He sighed in resignation. "Okay. A Remy Martin then."

As they sipped the cognac, he said, "Listen, honey, have you ever been to an American football game?"

She shook her head.

"One of my clients has a box for the Redskins. He invited me to attend tomorrow afternoon, provided that I bring you. What do you think?"

Since Estrada wanted her to string Bryce along for a little while longer, she was pleased to do something that didn't involve sex. "I'd love to," she said, faking an enthusiasm she didn't feel.

"Good. Even though it's Sunday, I have to be at the office for a while in the morning. Catching up from being away in Argentina. I'll send a car around to pick you up at noon. Now let me tell you a little about the game. It's much different than your football. To start with, the ball isn't round, it's . . ."

She interrupted. "How can a ball not be round? Balls are always round. That's what a ball is."

He laughed. "Well, I guess that's right, but . . ."

He was interrupted by her cell phone that was ringing where it rested on an end table. She had constantly left it on and close at hand since returning from Buenos Aires, where she had given Barry the number.

"Don't answer," Bryce said.

She glanced at the screen on the phone. The caller's number wasn't one she recognized. "I have to," she responded. "My friend,

Rosie, could be in trouble. Don't worry. I'll talk fast and call her back later."

"Hello," she said.

"This is Barry."

"Hold on for a minute," she said into the phone. Then she dashed with it into her bedroom and closed the door.

"Is this a good time for you to talk?" Craig asked.

"When you call, it's always a good time."

"I have to be in Southern California. How would you like to fly out tomorrow and spend a couple of days with me? You can bring a bathing suit. We'll have a good time."

"Really. I'd love it," she said impulsively, without thinking about Bryce and how she'd justify it to him.

"That's great. American Airlines has a three o'clock plane from Dulles Airport to Los Angeles. I'll arrange for your ticket. All you have to do is show some ID at the ticket counter. When you arrive, I'll be waiting in the baggage claim area. We'll have a fabulous time."

"I'll be there."

"Ciao."

After he hung up, she stared blankly at the phone. What had she done? She had to find some way to handle this with Bryce. Otherwise, Estrada would be furious. Still, she rationalized, he liked Barry. So by seeing Barry, she was advancing Estrada's agenda. Not certain whether Estrada would see it that way, she decided not to tell him when she called later that night.

As for Bryce, right now, she wouldn't say a word to him. She put a grim look on her face.

"It's horrible," she said when she returned to the living room.

Bryce had been leaning back in a comfortable leather chair, his eyes closed. "What's horrible?"

"You know I told you that Rosie's boss has been coming on to her, and she's been trying to avoid him and not lose her job."

"Uh-huh," Bryce said, sounding bored. She was convinced he didn't have the least bit of interest in Rosie's travail.

"Well, anyhow, when she was in the supply room he snuck up behind her and stuck his hand up under her skirt." Gina was getting carried away with the story she was creating. "I mean like before she had a chance to react, he was inside her pants with one hand and grabbing her breast with the other. He stuck two fingers inside of her . . . yuck . . . then she managed to slip away and run out of the supply room."

"That is horrible."

"I told her you were here, and I'd call her back when you went home."

"But what can you do about it in Washington?"

That stopped her for a minute. "Well, I can listen and maybe give her some ideas. That's what friends are for."

"She's lucky to have you for a friend," he said, as he gathered up his jacket and tie.

When Bryce left, she was feeling quite pleased with herself. That was a good story and fun making it up. Maybe she should try her hand at writing a romance novel when this was over. If Rosie wasn't involved, Gina could have made up a much juicier ending. "And then her boss forced her back against the boxes of copying paper. As they tumbled to the floor, she felt his hard member jutting out . . ."

What's happening to me, she wondered. She had sex on her brain all the time. Barry. It must be Barry. She couldn't wait for California.

Northern Argentina

General Estrada's northern headquarters, from which he was directing the Brazilian operation, was in an old castle built by the Spanish overlooking the Falls at Iguazu. The stone structure had two floors. On the first, Estrada and Schiller each had a large office. Upstairs were bedrooms for Estrada and Schiller in one wing. The other held half a dozen prison cells the Spanish had constructed, knowing that in all of their activities in South America there were always people to kill—others to incarcerate and torture. A barbed-wire-topped chain-link fence surrounded the property on three sides. On the fourth was the river. Armed soldiers manned the gatehouse at the end of the only access road in front.

It was early morning; the sun was shining. More rain would come later in the day.

Past the gatehouse drove a van carrying four Argentine generals, longtime friends and colleagues of Estrada, who would be in the field directing the attack.

The four assembled around a table in Estrada's office with Schiller and Estrada. The mood of the six was jovial, pleasing Estrada, and matching the bright spring day. For decades, the Argentine military had been maligned and regarded with contempt by one incompetent civilian ruler after another. Well, those days were over. The military would rule again in Argentina. This time they wouldn't have to fight their way in. On the heels of a smashing victory against those illiterate Brazilians, the people would sweep Estrada into power. It would be a great day for the Argentine military. A great day for the Argentine nation.

"We have two items of good news," a beaming Estrada announced with a lit cigar in his hand.

All eyes were looking at him, waiting expectantly.

"First, I personally spoke with General Sanchez in Porte Allegre. He assured me that most of the key Brazilian army commanders in their southern sector are on board. In that region, they despise the federal government. They will order their soldiers not to resist. Sanchez is worried about casualties from our weapons. I promised that we would only fire if fired upon. Is everybody clear with that?"

In unison, all four generals replied, "Yes."

"Excellent. The second bit of good news is that the Americans will not intervene. The decision was made by President Treadwell. That's the last piece that had to fall into place. So now we can finalize our plans."

He paused to puff on his cigar. He had been a happy man since Gina had called last night to tell him about Treadwell's decision. "Now let's talk about logistics."

Estrada picked up a pointer resting on the table. With long purposeful strides, he walked over to a large map of the area taped to the wall. Then he targeted four specific points along the Argentine Brazilian border. He assigned each of them to one of the generals in the room.

"At first light, 600 hours, Wednesday," he said, "four days from now, our planes will bomb the Brazilian air bases and eliminate their air force as a factor. An hour later, each of your units will smash across the border. If Sanchez proves to be wrong, and you encounter resistance on the ground, then I'll call for air support. Regardless, you push your tanks and troops eastward as fast as you can. And you don't stop moving until you've reached the Atlantic Ocean." He paused for a minute. "Now are there any questions?"

One of the generals raised his hand. "You said that the Americans won't intervene."

Estrada nodded.

"But how can you be sure of this?"

"Our secret weapon. Thanks to a friend in Washington I have complete control over Treadwell. He'll do whatever I want."

Washington

B ryce arrived at his office at the law firm at eight o'clock Sunday morning. After spending so much time on the Argentine issue, he needed an hour to read his mail and check e-mails for firm business. At nine, he was scheduled to meet with the other two members of the firm's executive committee.

The law firm's fiscal year ended on December 31st, and it was time to begin thinking about how to divide up the year's profits. This had been an incredible year for the firm. Thanks to Bryce's close relationship with the president, vast numbers of new clients from corporate America as well as giant foreign corporations retained the firm hoping to gain some advantage from the magic of Bryce's name in their legal dealings with the United States government. Those clients were charged "premium billing," which meant adding a hefty amount on top of the normal fee calculated by multiplying the hours lawyers worked by their normal seven or eight hundred dollar hourly rates. Bryce's own rate was $1,500 an hour. That was a perk of having access to the Oval Office. As a result, the firm was awash in money. A local auto dealer who sold Bentleys and Rolls Royces was repeatedly being summoned to the firm's offices to discuss the availability and differences among various models. And as long as Treadwell stayed in the White House, the lawyers at Bryce's firm would party on.

It was no different than what happened in any administration in Washington. One or more law firms always caught the giant wave and, like a champion surfboarder, rode it to financial ecstasy.

Later on that Sunday, the office would be bustling as young lawyers, anxious to make their mark and gain the position of partner at the cash trough by exceeding the target of three thousand billable hours a year, would be hunched over their computers, composing briefs and memoranda. But at eight o'clock, the posh wooden corridors, covered over by oriental carpets, were quiet.

Bryce's secretary was already at her desk, poised to provide help when he needed her. Rarely did Bryce have anything for her on a Sunday that couldn't be done on Monday. Still, she smiled and endured the ridiculous waste of giving up part of the Lord's day in return for the large bonus that went with being the managing partner's number one secretary.

"Morning, Sue," Bryce said, as he passed by her desk without looking at her.

"Morning, Mr. Bryce," she responded. "The firm's financial information that you wanted is on your desk, and I'll get you a cup of coffee."

Once he was inside his office, Bryce turned on his computer. Waiting for it to boot up, he noticed that the voice mail light on his telephone console was red.

Bryce hit the listen button. What he heard was Gina's voice, leaving a message at six fifty that morning. "I had a really good time last night, William. Thank you very much and for the earrings . . . I'm sorry, but I'll have to miss the football game today. I just received a call from my editor. He wants me to go out of town to cover a story for a couple of days. I'll call you when I get back . . . I can't turn him down."

What the hell's going on, Bryce wondered. Her excuse had to be total bullshit.

He thought about her behavior since the trip to Buenos Aires. Everything had changed in their relationship. It wasn't simply that she had been cooler to him. They hadn't made love even once. He remembered the last time she had her period, and he checked the calendar. That was only fifteen days ago.

He dialed Gina's home number, but encountered her answering machine. Then her cell phone. Same result. No surprise. She didn't want to talk to him. Otherwise, she would have called him at home or waited until he had gotten to the office.

Bryce replayed Gina's message again and listened carefully. She sounded hesitant and tentative. She didn't say where she was going. And what's more, what kind of an assignment could her newspaper have given her in the middle of the night that would take her out of Washington. The Argentine-Brazilian dispute wasn't only the lead news story, it was the news for that region. And Washington was critical. From a journalism standpoint, it made no sense for her to leave Washington.

There was only one explanation: *Barry Gorman.* That's why everything had changed since Buenos Aires. She had met Barry Gorman there. He'd bet anything she hadn't been with Rosie that night at all. She had been out with Gorman. His initial judgment at the Alvear had been right. She had made a fool out of him, letting her talk him out of it and buying her earrings.

Thinking about Rosie made him recall the sudden phone call she had received last night after dinner at her apartment on her cell phone. That must have been another phony Rosie story. Gorman must have called and asked her to meet him somewhere today. That would account for her change of plans.

She had not only lied to him, but she was off somewhere shacked up with Gorman. In his mind, he had a picture of the two of them naked in bed, his gorgeous Gina on her back, legs spread, and Gorman on top pounding away. That made his blood boil.

He wasn't willing to give her up, but how could he compete with a good-looking, dashing investment banker loaded with money, who was twenty years younger? He couldn't!

It wasn't merely that he wanted to retain Gina. He had more at stake than the woman. She was the linchpin for the new life he contemplated after Claire's departure.

Bryce wasn't a quitter. He never gave up on anything. Tenacious was one of the adjectives used to describe him in his high school year book. So as he sipped his coffee, he thought of how he could win her back.

If he could dig up some shady things in Gorman's past or some embarrassing aspects of his current life and reveal them to Gina, then he'd be able to win her back.

And it wasn't farfetched. After all, Colonel Schiller had told Bryce that he thought Gorman was a phony. Thus far, Schiller couldn't prove it.

Well, Bryce would expose that fraud, but he'd need help.

About six years ago in his legal practice, Bryce had been representing an American computer company, whose technology was being pilfered by a Chinese firm. To uncover the critical evidence, Bryce had hired Dale Briscoe, a former high-ranking official of the Defense Intelligence Agency, who had a PI firm based in Roslyn, Virginia, close to the Pentagon. Briscoe maintained a lengthy list of former FBI and law enforcement officials around the country whom he drew upon as consultants for spot assignments.

Then two years later, Bryce had hired Briscoe in a stock fraud case to establish that the government's main witness had made a killing trading in the stock himself through concealed third parties. Both times, Briscoe's work had been outstanding.

Bryce picked up his Blackberry and scrolled through the directory until he found Briscoe's home telephone number.

"Dale. It's Edward Bryce. Been a couple years. I hope you remember me."

Briscoe gave a hearty laugh. "How could I forget? You're the man of the hour in Washington. The man everybody wants to hire."

Hearing those words, Bryce was bursting with pride.

"Right now, I need you."

"Your wish is my command."

"Ten this morning. My office."

"I'll be there with bells and whistles. Whatever you need, I'll get it for you."

*   *   *

Though Dale Briscoe had a jovial side in personal matters, when it came to intelligence work, the wiry former Holy Cross basketball player was a hard charger. He never said a job couldn't be done. He loved outrageously short deadlines. He took no prisoners. Those were the qualities that Bryce thought made him perfect for this assignment.

Briscoe once told Bryce, "Show me an intelligence agent without holes in the soles of his shoes, and I'll show you a man who's not working hard enough."

So when Briscoe collapsed his six-foot-four frame into a straight chair across from Bryce's desk, the first thing the lawyer asked was if he could see the soles of Briscoe's shoes. With delight, Briscoe lifted one and then the other. Each of them had holes the size of a quarter.

"Tell me what I can do for you," Briscoe said, in his usual, no-nonsense manner.

Bryce had made a copy of the card Barry Gorman had given him in Buenos Aires and printed a copy of Barry Gorman's bio from the Philoctetes website, including Gorman's photo. He handed both of these to Briscoe. "I want you to find out everything you can about this man. Every transgression he's ever committed all the way back. Anything. Was he punished in grade school for putting chewing gum under the desk? You know what I mean."

Briscoe nodded. "You want to expose those things to some mutual acquaintance, or maybe persuade Gorman to do your bidding."

"All of the above."

The investigator glanced at the documents Bryce had handed him. "What do you know about the Philoctetes Group?"

"Personally, I'd never heard of it until a couple of days ago. It's a private equity firm. Gorman has billions of their money to invest in Argentina."

"Why would he want to do that with the economic mess in Argentina?"

"You always cut to the chase. I tried calling his office in San Francisco, but I got a routine voice mail message. I'm afraid I can't tell you much else about the man."

Bryce was ready to end the meeting. "Let's talk about the deadline and your fee."

Briscoe wanted to probe some more. "Have you ever met the man?"

"Once in Buenos Aires last week. He was staying at the Alvear Palace." Bryce bolted upright in his chair. "That reminds me. I should have told you that Argentina's Director of Military Intelligence, Colonel Schiller, is also suspicious of Gorman, but he couldn't point to anything specific."

"Karl Schiller?"

"Yeah. You know him?"

"We cooperated on a couple of projects involving Venezuela when I was still with the DIA. We got along fine, but he's one tough son of a bitch. I'd hate to be on his shit list."

Briscoe put the documents down on Bryce's desk.

"All right," Briscoe said crisply. "Now, let's talk about deadlines and money."

Bryce said, "I want the information tomorrow. Nine in the morning."

"No way. I'll need forty-eight hours. Even that will be a killer, but for you I'll do it."

Bryce didn't argue. He realized tomorrow was unreasonable and expected some push back.

"The second is easy," Briscoe said. "I want a million dollars."

Bryce whistled. "You've got to be kidding."

"Nope. This is worth a lot to you. Here's the deal. I only get the million dollars if I hit a home run. If I don't, you won't have to pay me a cent. Not even expenses. That's it. Take it or leave it."

Bryce realized Briscoe wasn't bluffing. "What's a home run?" he asked weakly.

"A ball that goes over the fence and out of the park."

"Who'll decide if it's a home run?"

"That's the beauty of this arrangement. Never any question about whether a ball goes over the fence."

When Bryce didn't respond, Briscoe said, "So are you in or out?"

"I'm in."

The two men stood up and shook hands. Brisco never liked written agreements; and that suited Bryce.

"See you Tuesday at nine in the morning," Briscoe said, sounding as if he was convinced he would hit a home run.

Los Angeles

Killing time before Gina's plane arrived, Craig was in a bar at the Los Angeles airport sipping a beer because the only wines they had were cheap California rotgut. Although California produced some excellent wines, this dive didn't have any of them. Above the bar, the television was blasting a football game. It was almost five o'clock, which meant the second quarter for the Rams and Forty-Niners.

His cell phone vibrated in his pocket. He pulled it out and saw Betty was calling.

"Hang on and let me move into a quiet place," he told her.

He plunked ten bucks down next to his glass, left the bar, and found a deserted area in the terminal.

"Where are you?" she asked.

"LAX. I'm waiting for a friend to arrive."

"A foreign reporter from Washington?"

"How'd you guess?"

"C'mon, Craig, I've known you a long time. I even understand how you operate."

"Frightening. Isn't it?"

"Let's just say that you're different than other people."

"Unique is good."

"Sometimes."

He pressed the phone tight against his ear waiting anxiously to learn why she was calling.

"Alright. Now that we've both had our fun, let's get serious. I have the dossiers you wanted."

"Anything useful?"

"Extremely provocative."

He realized she didn't want to say any more over the phone. "I guess we better talk in person."

"Exactly. And you have to see some documents I would prefer not transmitting electronically. How soon can you get back to Washington?"

"My friend and I are supposed to spend a couple of days together out here, and . . ." He paused, took a deep breath and gulped hard before continuing. "It would be extremely useful to have those materials to discuss with her. Any chance you can send one of your people out here with them?"

"That's possible, but I'm afraid you and I have to talk." She paused.

He understood how delicate everything was because of the Bryce's relationship with Treadwell. Just as she was spying on Bryce, he could easily have been using the FBI to eavesdrop on her.

As if having read his mind, she interrupted his musing. "I can't believe that I'm going to fly cross-country on your account."

"Well you already flew to Sardinia. Los Angeles isn't nearly as far."

"Don't push it, wise guy."

"Yes, Madam Director. Sorry about that."

"I can get a plane anytime, and I never sleep, so tell me where and when you want to meet."

"We'll be staying at a little gem of a resort called Rancho Valencia in Rancho Santa Fe, south of LA. North of La Jolla. Tomorrow morning I'll pretend to go jogging. At five-thirty let's meet at the gate house near the entrance to the resort. It's on Rancho Valencia Drive."

"You sure you'll be alone? That your friend won't want to go jogging with you?"

"I'll find a way to leave her back at the hotel."

*　　　*　　　*

Craig had selected the location for his meeting with Gina with care. Rancho Valencia was a relatively isolated resort outside of the tiny town of Rancho Santa Fe. He had learned about it from a Carnegie Mellon fraternity buddy, whose father owned a horse farm for racing thoroughbreds across the road.

The resort property consisted of one-story, two-unit casitas spread out on meticulously landscaped grounds, proving that with enough water the desert can bloom. He had reserved an entire casita so that if she yelled and screamed there would be no one to hear her. But all of that would have to wait until tomorrow morning.

This evening was the last chapter in his courtship or, more precisely, his deception of Gina Galindo. He wasn't being a shit, he told himself, as she bounded off the plane, the picture of youthful enthusiasm, a woman in love, her face glowing with excitement and expectation. Dressed in a bright print blouse and short pink skirt, she raced over and threw herself into his arms.

"So tell me what we're going to do," she said, as they roared south with Craig behind the wheel of a BMW convertible on the 405 toward Orange County.

"Well, tonight we're going to have a great dinner at a restaurant called Mille Fleur in Rancho Santa Fe. Then head to the hotel for whatever."

"Can we go swimming tomorrow?" she said with enthusiasm.

"Of course."

"I brought a bathing suit because it's Southern California and I thought it was hot. Tonight it's freezing."

He laughed. "It's the desert. Always cool at night. Tomorrow should be a fabulous day."

"Great. You'll love the bikini. It doesn't cover too much. The nuns would never have approved."

"But they won't be here," he said, and laughed with her.

"Can we go to some movie studios? I read about this tour at Universal. Oh, and I want to go to Disneyland. Can we do that? Please?"

He didn't want to lie to her any longer. "We'll take it one day at a time. We'll make our plans for tomorrow in the morning. How's that?"

"Great," she repeated. As he drove, he noticed her eyes were closing. That was good. By the time they reached the hotel, three or four hours from now after dinner and wine, jet lag and the time difference would have hit her.

At the restaurant, when they were sipping champagne, she blurted out in a solemn voice, "I have a confession to make."

"Should I get a black cassock and put myself in a little booth?"

"That isn't funny."

She was right. He knew he shouldn't have said it because religion was no laughing matter for her, but he couldn't resist.

"I'm sorry, Gina. That was insensitive on my part."

"You're forgiven."

"Anyhow," he said. "You wanted to tell me something?"

She looked away from him. "Before I met you, I was seeing another man in Washington. An older man. You might hear about it from someone else, but even if you don't, I want you to know."

He decided to play dumb. "You want to tell me who he is?"

"Edward Bryce. The man who headed the American delegation to Argentina. I never really liked him, but it was something I had to do." She sighed deeply. "It's all so complicated."

"You don't have to tell me any more if you don't want to."

"I want you to know that after our date at the tango bar in Buenos Aires, I decided to end the relationship with him."

"What did Bryce say about that?"

"He doesn't know. I haven't told him that in so many words, but I ended it in fact. I mean, that way . . . I might see him again, but nothing intimate. You know what I mean."

He nodded. "I know exactly what you mean. Now our food's coming. Let's enjoy dinner."

Dinner at Mille Fleur was great. But after a glass of champagne and two or three glasses of Nuits St. George, Gina slept all the way to the hotel. And once they entered the room, she said, "Do you mind if we wait to do whatever until tomorrow morning? I'm sorry, but I'm really tired."

"No of course not. I get up early and run in the morning. So don't worry if I'm not here when you wake up. I'll be back for breakfast."

"Run as long as you want. I sleep in the mornings." She gave a short laugh. "As late as possible. So we're perfect together."

She used the bathroom first. By the time he brushed his teeth, she was already sound asleep on one side of the king-sized bed.

As he looked at her, so contented, a smile on her face, her breasts rising and falling with each breath, he thought of that old expression, "You're going to hate me in the morning."

Rancho Santa Fe

"I hope you didn't have any trouble finding this place," Craig told Betty as he climbed into the back of the armor-plated Lincoln Town car and sat next to her.

"None at all. The wonders of GPS. Now tell me where we can go to talk and look at documents. I hate sitting on the road. We might have to explain ourselves to some nosey local cop."

"A college classmate of mine's father owns a racehorse farm five minutes from here. They have a small grandstand. After we spoke, I called yesterday to say I was bringing by a friend to watch the morning workout. I don't expect anybody to be there who will recognize you. Just the trainers. The only newspapers those guys read are the racing ones."

"I brought this along just in case." She pointed to a large, burgundy hat resting on a red file folder in the center of the back seat. "Now give the driver some directions."

Craig guided him through the gray gloom and fog of predawn. By the time Craig identified himself to a trainer and they were settled in the grandstand at the Bender Horse Farm, well out of earshot from the trainers, the sky in the east was starting to brighten.

Two magnificent thoroughbreds were thundering by, while trainers, stopwatch in hand, binoculars up to their eyes, watched intently.

"I assume Gina arrived alright," Betty said.

"She's asleep in the casita."

Betty patted the red folder on her lap. "This is going to be rough for Gina. I mean with what she thinks of her father. You'll have to use a lot of care in what you do with it. How you expose it to her. It could be devastating."

He wondered whether Betty, who had never married or had children, had had issues with her own father. To reassure her, he said, "Don't forget about my years alone with Francesca. I know how complex relationships can be between girls and their fathers. Now tell me what you found."

"I'll give you a summary. Afterwards, you can take the file containing the dossier and archival documents backing up every statement. They're all copies. I kept the originals in Washington."

"Go ahead. I'm listening."

She straightened the hat. "Gina's father, General Miguel Galindo, was one of the worst perpetrators of crimes against the Argentine people during the Dirty War. He approved lists of thousands of people to arrest as enemies of the state. Supposedly, for their left wing political views. He decided which ones should be tortured and which ones should be murdered. He even conducted some interrogations himself. All of them disappeared."

"My God. She idolizes her father. Believes he was a great man. A hero of the Republic."

"That's what I figured."

"How accurate is the information?"

"The documents all came from our archives. Intelligence reports at the time and internal Argentine documents. All authenticated."

She paused to push back her glasses. "You also asked me for information relating to Estrada and the kidnapping of babies. Estrada's name never appears in any of our documents. Perhaps he was too junior at the time. A baby kidnapping operation was run by some of the generals, so Estrada could have been working for one of them. They called it Operation Delta. A sadistic choice of title. Delta, the letter D, is the first letter of the word divide. They kidnapped babies, and divided them from their families. Maybe hundreds. Nobody knows. Again, from supposedly Communist sympathizers. They sold these babies to friends and pocketed the cash. There's nothing in the documents linking Gina's father to Operation Delta."

"Are you certain there's no evidence in the documents of Estrada's involvement in the kidnapping business?"

She shook her head. "I asked the researchers several times. The answer is no. Some other names were mentioned. Do you have reliable evidence of your own that Estrada was involved?"

She was looking at him hopefully. "That could help us with Treadwell to overrule Bryce."

Craig paused to weigh the issue in his mind. An affidavit from Maria about Estrada's involvement wouldn't carry the day with Treadwell because Bryce would blow it out of the water as no real evidence. "What I have at this point isn't enough to do the job. Only fuzzy recollections from twenty years ago, Bryce would contend. Or an effort to destroy an innocent man trying to become president of the country."

Still, he might have another way to use Maria to nail Estrada. "Tell me what happened to Gina's father after the Dirty War ended and civilian rule returned to Argentina."

"Initially, there were no prosecutions, no trials, or any other accounting for the perpetrators of these heinous crimes. Instead, the new civilian government reached a tacit understanding with the military to sweep it all under the rug and move on as if nothing had occurred. So for the next three years after civilian rule was restored in 1983, General Galindo continued doing whatever generals do in peace time—supervising officers and so forth."

"And then?"

"He was walking from a restaurant in a town in Patagonia near an army base to his car when a woman raced up to him. Before anyone had a chance to react, at point blank range, she fired three shots into his chest killing him instantly. It turns out she was the wife of one of the men who disappeared. She blamed him for it. The whole incident was hushed up. The official version was that he had been killed by Communist insurgents. Gina was away at boarding school at the time."

Betty handed him the folder. "It's all in here. I'll alert B. J. Walker at the Embassy in Buenos Aires to give you any help you need. Use the same code if you want to get inside to use a secure phone."

Craig opened up the file and began leafing through the papers. "Where are the documents relating to General Galindo?"

She pointed to them. As she turned to look at horses racing on the track, he began reading the documents. Something in one of them caught his eye. "Holy shit," he said recapturing Betty's attention. His face was as white as a sheet.

His heart went out to Gina. Nobody should have to learn about a parent what he now knew. He hoped to hell he could persuade her to do what he wanted without having her know everything about her father.

*   *   *

Craig jogged back from the Bender horse farm carrying the red folder, in order to work up a sweat and give his jogging alibi some validity. As he approached the casita, he was surprised to see the lights turned on. Hopefully, it just meant that Gina had gotten up early because of the time difference. Not that Schiller's goons had found them. Or Bryce had shown up to get her back.

Regardless, he decided to leave the red folder in a corner of the porch, out of sight. He'd pick it up later, when he could slip it into his suitcase without her watching. Then, on tiptoes, he quietly walked around to the back of the casita to the glass sliding door. He had to peek inside and see what was waiting for him.

Feeling vulnerable without a weapon, he grabbed a rock from the ground, held his breath, and looked through the glass door.

Gina was alone.

What he saw when he slid open the door was Gina dressed in a sheer, pale blue silk nightgown and matching robe.

She shouted, "Surprise. I'm up, and I ordered breakfast from room service." The table was fully set. "I wanted to show you I can be domestic."

He laughed. "Thanks. That was very nice of you."

"I hope you'll like what I ordered."

"I'm sure I will. I'm all sweaty. Just let me jump into the shower then we'll eat."

After he emerged from the shower in a terrycloth robe over a pair of underpants, she used the bathroom. That let him bring in Betty's folder and bury it in clothes in his suitcase.

Gina walked over and kissed him. "Breakfast. Then whatever," she said.

"You look fabulous," he told her as she sat down across from him.

"Thank you. Dinner last night was wonderful."

He looked away from her at the lemon tree outside the window. Tell her already, he chided himself. Waiting won't make it any easier.

"I ordered us a wild mushroom omelet," she continued in her bubbly enthusiasm. "I know a lot of you Americans don't think you should eat eggs, but my great grandma lived to be ninety-nine and she ate two eggs every day of her life. So what do you think of that?"

"I'm happy to try it."

"And if we ever have children, and I know that's a big if, then I intend to make them eggs every day and keep them healthy."

He tore off a piece of toast and poured them both some coffee. He couldn't continue the charade any longer. Her line from last evening seemed like the best opening. "I have a confession to make."

The grim, serious expression on his face knocked the smile off hers. Her hand holding a cup of coffee shook. Some spilled out as she put the cup down. "I'm not going to like this. Am I?"

"No. You won't."

"You're already married?"

"I'm not, although that would be easier to explain."

She sat up ramrod straight and gripped the sides of the chair hard, as if that could save her from the storm that was about to blow through the room and blast her away.

"I intend to put my life into your hands," he said. "Literally. I mean that. But I know I can trust you. And I need your help."

She was puzzled. "I don't understand."

"Before I tell you, just remember one thing. Above all else, I believe you're a wonderful person, and I truly care about you."

"But you don't love me?"

Instinctively, he began to duck the question, but he realized that wasn't fair to her. He had to level with her fully. She was an adult. "No, I don't. And I never told you that I did."

"But I thought . . ."

He watched a few tears appear in her eyes. She quickly wiped them away. This is damn hard, he thought. "This isn't about us," he added.

"Then what is it about?"

"I'm not who you think I am."

She was dumbfounded. "You're not Barry Gorman, an investment banker from San Francisco? You don't have $10 billion to invest in Argentina? It's all one big disgusting lie?"

He didn't like doing it this way, but he had no choice if he had any chance of persuading her to help him. Besides, he owed her an honest explanation.

"That's correct. I am not Barry Gorman."

"Then who are you?"

He took a deep breath. "My name is Craig Page. I used to work for the CIA. For the last year, I raced cars around the world. Recently, the CIA recruited me to help them in Argentina."

"So you just spent time with me and made me fall for you because it was part of your job? To get information."

She had said it calmly, but once her words sunk in, her face was contorted with anger. She rose to her feet.

"That's not right," he said. "Remember what I told you. I care for you a great deal."

She took two steps toward him. Without any warning, she raised her hand and slapped him hard across the face. Then she burst into tears, heavy wracking sobs. She ran over to the sofa and buried herself in the pillows, crying.

He waited several minutes. Then he tried to put an arm around her to comfort her.

"Don't touch me," she cried out. "You're scum. You're the lowest there is."

He would have liked to have asked her what the difference was between what he did and her sleeping with Bryce. Wasn't that part of her job? At least he hadn't slept with her. But that wasn't the point. He had deceived her.

He retreated to the breakfast table and sipped coffee in silence, waiting for her to stop crying. He had to admit she had given him one helluva slap. The whole right side of his face stung.

When the well of tears ran dry, she went into the bathroom, washed her face, and returned wearing one of the hotel's terry cloth bathrobes instead of the sheer lingerie.

She sat on the sofa, now ready to talk. He pulled up a chair, facing her across the wooden coffee table.

"Okay, I understand that you're a spy," she said. "But what possible good could you accomplish by spending time with me. I don't have any government secrets."

He gulped hard. "You are extremely close with General Estrada. We knew that you were obtaining information from Edward Bryce and passing it along to Estrada."

She pulled back in bewilderment. "You make *me* sound like a spy."

"Let's not quibble with semantics. The CIA has been concerned about Estrada's agenda for some time. They sent a man, Ted Dunn, to—"

She raised her hand and cut him off. "But why's any of this a reason for you to spend time with me?"

No sense dodging any longer. He decided he'd better come clean about everything. "On our first date in Washington, I had no intention of sleeping with you. I hoped you'd invite me up to your apartment after dinner so I could install a couple of listening devices. I did that after you fell asleep.

"So you bugged my apartment?"

"And your phone."

"My phone too."

"I'm being honest."

"You're a crumb," she shouted. "I don't use swear words like some girls. So I won't call you those other things. Even though you deserve it."

She shook her head in bewilderment while her face displayed anger. "You listened to all of my conversations with Rosie and Edward. You heard me in bed with him." The dread of it sunk in further. "How could you do that and look at yourself in the mirror? It's disgusting."

"In fact, I didn't listen to anything. A machine made transcripts."

"Oh, that makes it right?"

"I'm not proud of what I did. It was necessary."

She wrinkled up her face. "Necessary for what?"

He was relieved they were finally getting to the issue. "I was brought into this because the CIA had sent another man, Ted Dunn, to Argentina to find out what Estrada's agenda was. When Colonel Schiller and Estrada found out about Dunn, they had him killed along with a young Argentine man, Pascual, who was helping Dunn."

She shot to her feet. "That's ridiculous. Alfredo didn't kill anyone. You're slandering a good man."

He opened his robe to expose his bruised chest. "You think I got this walking into a door?" He stood up next to her. With his robe hanging open, in a high voice, he said, "Some men grabbed me when I was jogging in Jorge Newbery Park. They tied my back against a tree. They were sent by Colonel Schiller. One of them beat me with boxing gloves until I threw up and passed out. You think I'm making that up?"

"No," she said weakly. "But Alfredo didn't order this."

"I agree. He didn't. It was Schiller, but he's Estrada's director of security."

"I never liked him."

"That makes two of us. But in Bariloche, where Dunn was murdered, Estrada and Schiller were both involved. You have to believe me."

"You've given me no reason to."

"Then fly back to Argentina with me. I'll let you talk to Antonia in Bariloche, the sister of the dead boy, Pascual. She'll convince you."

Gina looked puzzled. "Why do you care so much if I believe you or not? I'm just one stupid little girl. You don't love me. Why do you care?"

It was time to jump off the high board. He held his breath and went for it. "Because I want you to help me block Estrada and Schiller and the other generals from taking over the country again. They'll—"

She interrupted him. "So that's why you got me here. To persuade me to help you spy. We were never going to movie studios and Disneyland. It was all one more big lie."

"Please," he said, trying not to convey the exasperation he felt. "If the generals return to power, they'll cause so much suffering all over again. You have to know about the Dirty War. You're a student of history. When you talk to Antonia in Bariloche, you'll hear what happened to her father and mother. One killed, one gang raped by soldiers. Do you want that again?"

She was scowling at him. "There were a few evil people in the military then. I don't deny that. But most, like my father and Alfredo, were trying to fight the Communists who wanted to destroy our country. That's our history. Don't you try to manipulate me with a phony version created in the United States."

She had given him the perfect opening to use the material about her father in Betty's folder, but he couldn't. Not here. Not yet. He shifted topics. "The other reason Estrada has to be stopped is because he's about to launch your country on another military adventure that will end even worse than the Falklands fiasco. We now know much of his agenda. We know that the border incident last week with Brazil was a fabrication."

"It was not."

"Read a book called *Inside the Gestapo* by Jonathan Martin. Schiller's grandfather did precisely the same thing to justify Germany's attack of Poland. You think that's a coincidence?"

"I never heard of that."

"It's confirmed in Nuremberg testimony. That proves Estrada is planning to launch a major attack on Brazil. I presume his motive is to rekindle nationalistic feelings in the country and ride that horse to the presidency."

He took her silence as assent, and he continued.

"If Estrada attacks Brazil, he'll be doing incalculable harm to Argentina. He's dreaming. Delusional might be more accurate. Even if the United States stays out of it initially because of Bryce and his relationship with Treadwell, my country will have to change its position when UN and South American pressure becomes too great. Not only will your boys die again in another senseless war, but nobody will want to have anything to do with Argentina for decades. Your country and its people will be a pariah among nations. It will devastate what's left of your economy." He paused to take a breath. "I spent two days with

Alfredo in London. He was charming. I enjoyed being with him, but he has to be stopped."

She locked eyes with him. "If you know so much, why do you need me?"

He lowered his voice and spoke slowly, making certain she heard each word. "I want you to tell me everything you know about Estrada's plans. Also, I want you to help me obtain additional information from him. Without your help, we can't stop him. It's that simple."

Heavy creases appeared on her forehead. "In other words, you want me to be a traitor and to spy on the man who's been like a father to me?"

"I wouldn't express it that way."

"I won't do it," she said emphatically.

He raised his hand. "At least go with me to Bariloche and listen to this woman, Antonia, about her suffering under the generals and what happened to her brother. How he was killed by Estrada to keep secret the Brazilian attack."

She shook her head vigorously from side to side. "The answer is no. For all I know, this woman will be telling me more lies. She has no proof. She could be lying to me the way you lied to me when you said you were Barry Gorman. Besides, I don't want to go to Bariloche. I want to go home to Buenos Aires where I have friends like Rosie. Not devious liars and cheats like you and Edward Bryce. I want to have a normal life again. I'm sick and tired of all of these schemes and manipulations. Do you understand that?" Her voice was cracking with emotion.

"Please. I beg you to reconsider for the good of your country."

"The answer is no."

Craig was at the end of his rope. He had only one other way of blocking Estrada.

"I'll fly you back to Buenos Aires in a private plane. Today. On one condition."

"What's that?" she asked skeptically.

"I want you to spend one hour in Buenos Aires talking with two women. That's all. You don't have to promise to do a thing afterwards. When the hour is up, someone will take you wherever you want to go."

"I don't need your charity. I can get home myself."

She reached for the phone. After minutes of being on hold with the airline, she slammed down the phone and looked at him suspiciously. "What do these women want?"

"Just to talk to you for one hour."

"Who are the women?" she asked hesitantly.

"One is Nicole," he hesitated for an instant. "The other is Maria."

She took her time thinking about his offer. Finally, she said, "Okay, I'll do it, but only for one hour."

*   *   *

Craig used the American Express card Betty had supplied to arrange a private jet to fly him and Gina to Buenos Aires.

At the San Diego airport, as Craig met with the pilot preparing a flight plan in a room filled with maps of the world, one thought came barreling over the top of a hill and into clear view.

Dummy, he chastised himself. How could he have missed it.

That prick Schiller knew that he had only left Argentina for a little while. In Buenos Aires, Schiller had people following Craig incessantly. Schiller would have people monitoring all of the Argentine airports to pick him up on his return. He had been thinking so much about Gina that he had missed it. If he had Gina with him, how in the world could he ever elude his tail.

As he studied an airport map of the region, trying to decide if there was an airport in Argentina that Schiller might not cover, the answer hit him like a charge of lightening out of the sky.

Fly into Montevideo.

The capital of Uruguay was a couple hours drive from Buenos Aires. Schiller had no jurisdiction there. At the airport, he could rent a car and drive himself. The open border between the two countries would enable them to slip into Argentina.

Not wanting to alarm the edgy and unhappy Gina, he waited until they took off from San Diego to tell her they would be landing in Montevideo.

"All of the slots at the Buenos Aires airports were taken," he told her. "We'd have to wait days to land, and I know that you're anxious to get home."

Hell, he'd already lied to her so much. What difference did one more make?

She didn't question him. In fact, she was still so angry she was hardly speaking to him as the plane winged its way across the United States on a flight plan that called for a refueling stop in Tampa. Claiming she was exhausted, she went into the rear cabin, locked the door, and went to sleep.

Before picking up the phone to call Nicole, he carefully rehearsed in his mind what he would tell her. He had no idea whether Schiller's intelligence services would be able to monitor the conversation. They might be picking up conversations coming from airplanes outside of the country. To be safe, he had to assume that was the case.

"Nicole," he said rapidly, before she had a chance to react. "This is the man who wants to buy your house."

An awkward pause, "Yes," warily.

"I want to see it one more time. Let's meet Tuesday at ten in the morning at the house. I'll be ready to give you an offer."

"I won't budge on the price. If you want it, you'll have to come up to my asking. I have a great deal of property. I'll meet you there. We can discuss it."

"Good. I'm planning to bring along the woman friend we spoke about the last time we were together." He was confident that Nicole would remember their discussion about Gina.

"I understand," Nicole said, tersely.

"She wants to meet Maria. She may want to hire her or at least hear what Maria has to say about what's happened in the past on the property and surrounding areas. I find that history is always significant in a situation like this. After all, you're asking me to put up a great deal of money."

"I'll do my best to have Maria here. I don't think that should be a problem."

"See you then."

He hung up the phone and picked up Betty's red folder. For the next two hours, while Gina slept, he read each and every page that had been copied from United States archival materials. They made grim reading. The crimes perpetrated against the people of Argentina during the Dirty War were horrendous. People disappeared and were never heard from again. Murder, torture of all kinds. Prisoners hung from rods and beaten with clubs that had nails at the end. Women repeatedly raped by guards. Prisoners confined to cages with wild dogs.

It stunned Craig to confront in black and white how a wonderful country could have fallen into such a black hole. And in all of the papers Betty assembled, one man emerged as the worst monster of them all: General Miguel Galindo.

Contained within the documents was another troublesome issue. The United States government knew at the time some of what was happening. Craig couldn't tell how much. The United States certainly wasn't an active participant in the Communist witch hunt in Argentina, but it did not actively intervene to stop the generals.

This time would be different, Craig vowed. He had no idea whether Estrada and his fellow generals would wreak as much misery on their own people again, but he intended to do everything possible, down to his last breath, to block them from coming to power.

He had only one tool at his disposal right now. She was asleep in the back of the plane.

God help him for what he was going to do to this girl.

Washington

Bryce watched Briscoe walk into the office, carrying a thin folder in his hand, with a big smile on his face.

"I prefer electronic transfer," the PI said. "I would be uncomfortable walking around with a million dollar check, but if you insist."

"Hold all my calls," Bryce barked to his secretary and slammed the door. He turned to Briscoe. "What do you have for me?"

"You better sit down for this."

Bryce pointed to a brown leather sofa and chair around a marble top coffee table in one corner of the large office. Briscoe sat on the sofa. Bryce on the chair.

"Cut to the bottom line," Bryce said.

"There is no Barry Gorman."

Bryce's head snapped back. "Then who the hell . . ."

"You have to let me lay it out. Piece by piece."

Bryce was impatient. But Briscoe was entitled to do it his way. "Okay. Go ahead."

"First, I put feelers out to my contacts in the Bay area, and I have plenty. Nobody had heard of Barry Gorman or the Philoctetes Group. Even in the financial community."

"His bio said he went to Stanford. BA and MBA."

"You can't believe everything you read on the Internet. One of my people tapped into the University's computer. No record of Barry Gorman."

"How about the San Francisco phone number for the Philoctetes Group?"

"Here's where it gets real interesting."

Bryce leaned forward on the end of his chair. "Tell me."

"I have a friend who works at AT&T. He told me that calls to the number on the card you gave me for the man claiming to be Barry Gorman were routed back to . . ." He paused for a moment, making Bryce wait. Then he continued, "Were routed back to CIA headquarters."

Bryce shot to his feet. "That fucking Betty Richards," he said angrily.

It had to be Betty herself. No underling would have dared do this. Who the hell did she think she was undercutting his authority on Argentina. Sneaking behind his back. Disobeying Treadwell's orders. He had the president's ear in a way she never would. She'd pay dearly for this.

"You did a good job," Bryce said. "You've earned your money."

Briscoe didn't move. "Wait. I'm not finished yet."

Bryce sat back down.

"I have a good friend at Langley in an important position," Briscoe said. "He hates Ms. Richards and was willing to help me. So I called Schiller, had him dust Barry Gorman's suite at the Alvear for prints, and forward them to me electronically. A couple more taps on the computer keyboard and my friend at Langley had them. Isn't modern technology wonderful."

"And?" Bryce asked anxiously.

"He came up with a match. Craig Page."

"No shit!"

"He must have had extreme plastic surgery."

"We have to be damn certain of this."

"That's what I told my friend. He had their top man look at the prints. Then he explained that the Agency had two sets in their files for Craig Page. One from when he joined the agency out of college. The other from when he became director a year ago. Those match. However, following the second set, when he had the plastic surgery, he must have had skin grafting in an effort to remove his prints. But they partially came back. Enough to make a match with the prints Schiller forwarded from the Alvear. Also, I have confirmatory information."

"What's that?"

"My friend told me that Betty Richards and Craig Page were extremely close when he was with the agency. So it would make sense that she would reach out to him to do this job off the books. My friend also made a good guess about when she recruited him."

"Yeah?"

"A couple weeks ago, she made a sudden trip to Sardinia. Reason for trip was vacation. Betty Richards never takes vacations and Craig Page lived in Italy between CIA stints. So I think it's a lock. Now you have it all. A home run."

Bryce transferred the million dollars electronically to Briscoe's account. When the PI was gone, Bryce picked up the phone and called Schiller.

The colonel listened to Bryce's report about Barry Gorman in silence. At the end, he said, "How certain are you of this conclusion?"

"The fingerprints you forwarded to Briscoe matched those for Craig Page on file at the CIA. There is no Barry Gorman. No $10 billion. Only Craig Page, a CIA agent working for Betty Richards."

"Craig Page," Schiller said. "The former CIA director?"

"Yes. He had plastic surgery. He and Betty Richards were close."

"I thought Barry Gorman was a phony all along. Every time I suggested it to Estrada, he dismissed me. Well, he won't be able to do that now."

"One other thing, you can tell General Estrada this CIA agent has been romancing Gina Galindo and undercutting my efforts to help Argentina."

"Don't worry. I will do that."

Bryce now expected Gina to come crawling back to him. And as for Betty, he would use this information to nail her with Treadwell.

"There is one other thing," Schiller said.

"What's that?"

The colonel coughed and cleared his throat. Bryce guessed he was hesitating about whether to tell Bryce about something. Finally, Schiller said in a soft, conspiratorial tone, "Are you truly a friend of Argentina, Edward?"

"Absolutely. I was the one who persuaded President Treadwell not to intervene if an attack occurs, exactly as General Estrada asked me to do in Buenos Aires."

"Excellent. Then I would like to ask you to be with President Treadwell very early Wednesday morning. That's tomorrow morning. To make certain that Treadwell sticks with his decision. If you know what I mean."

Bryce knew exactly what Schiller was saying. The colonel had given him the time for Argentina's attack, and he had given Schiller the information to destroy Craig Page.

Buenos Aires

As Craig slowed the car to a stop in front of Nicole's house, Gina said, "One hour is all I will give you."

Nicole was standing in the driveway restraining her two dogs. The Dobermans were barking furiously.

Craig reached into the trunk and extracted the black duffel containing Betty's red folder.

Inside the house, Nicole asked them, "Would you like something to eat or drink?"

"Nothing for me," Gina said. "I'd just like to use a bathroom."

Nicole pointed her up the stairs. Once she was gone, Craig said anxiously, "Is Maria here?"

"In the kitchen waiting until I come for her."

"Good."

"I can understand why you didn't want to say anything on the phone. Now that you're here, you want to tell me what this is about?"

"Gina's close to Estrada, and she knows a great deal. She could help us big time, but so far she hasn't been willing to cooperate. I'm hoping she'll change her mind when she hears Maria's story about Benito."

Nicole sighed. "I figured it was something like that. You better let me walk Maria through it. She's terrified. Afraid it will get back to Estrada and he'll kill her and her family."

"We don't have to mention that she works for your father. Or anything else to identify her. Tell her that, and I'll do my best to have Gina reassure her before we begin." It was easy to say. He wasn't sure how he'd deliver.

"One other thing," Nicole said. "When you were in the United States, I found a soldier who told me that the so-called Brazilian attack was all bogus. Schiller put convicts from Argentine jails in Brazilian uniforms, shot them, and placed their bodies next to the observation post. They were photographed with weapons at their sides. Pretty horrible, isn't it?"

"Did you get a written statement from the soldier?"

She shook her head. "He was too frightened for that."

"That's unfortunate," Craig said irritably. "Without it, we don't have a damn thing. Didn't your soldier friend realize what's at stake?"

She shot him a severe look. "Have some sensitivity. These are ordinary people. They're scared to death for themselves and their families. And with good reason. They didn't join the CIA the way you did."

His eyes blinked. "Point well taken. I'm sorry. I guess it's up to Gina to carry us the whole way."

They heard the sound of Gina coming down the stairs. "Showtime," Craig muttered.

Nicole led Gina and Craig into the den—the same room where he and Nicole had drunk grappa after their high-speed car chase. To him, that seemed ages ago. Gina was sitting primly on the sofa in front of the wooden coffee table. Craig and Nicole were straight across from her on each side. An empty chair facing Gina awaited Maria.

"You can get Maria now," he said.

"Aren't you forgetting something, Craig?" Nicole asked.

Gina glanced at him with a bewildered look. "It's strange hearing her call you that. I think of you as Barry Gorman." Then she stared at Nicole and added, "I guess I was the only one who didn't know."

"Except for her," he said, pointing to Nicole. "Everybody in Argentina thinks I'm Barry Gorman."

"Is she a spy too?"

Nicole broke in with vehemence. "I'm a citizen of this wonderful country who cares deeply about Argentina and its people. I'll do whatever it takes to preserve our democracy."

Craig had no doubt that Nicole's words and the way she said them made an impression on Gina.

"I brought you here," he told Gina, in a somber voice, "to listen to a woman who wants to tell you what happened to her the last time the generals ruled. Maria's her name. She's absolutely terrified of talking to you. She wanted to speak from another room or with a mask over her face, but I assured her that you were a religious person, as she is, a teacher of young girls. Someone who would listen to her and think about what she said. And whether you decided to act on it or not, you would never mention this to anyone."

Gina sat up straight, startled by the gravity of his words. "No, of course not."

"Good." He turned to Nicole. "Will you tell Maria that?"

"Absolutely," Nicole said. Then she went into the kitchen.

A few minutes later, she returned, leading by the hand a diminutive woman dressed entirely in black with a long skirt that reached practically to her ankles. Around her neck, she wore a large wooden cross. In her hands, she held rosary beads. Her skin was gray and wrinkled, suggesting someone who rarely was out in the sun. Her hair was mostly gray with occasional strips of deep black that suggested it must have been beautiful a long time ago. On her face was permanently etched the pain that she had suffered. Looking at her brought to mind Nicole's description of Maria when she had told him the story—"a woman in perpetual mourning."

Craig watched Gina as she watched Maria. Without even a word being spoken, he realized that Gina felt compassion for this broken shell of a woman.

Maria was trembling so much that Craig thought she might miss the chair and fall onto the floor as she sat down. Gina didn't need any prompting. "Whatever you tell me will never pass through my lips."

"God bless you," Maria said.

"Will you tell her what happened?" Nicole said.

She began speaking in a halting, tentative voice. "The date was December 5th, 1980. I'll never forget that. A little past nine in the evening. I was at home with my three children. The older two, girls, five and three, were asleep in their beds. I had just finished breastfeeding Benito, my six-month-old boy, and laid him down in his crib. My husband was out at a union meeting.

"The soldiers came then. Four of them altogether in their brown army uniforms. The one in charge, the oldest one, in his thirties, a captain by rank, had a scar above his right eyebrow. The others were barely twenty. Two had been drinking heavily. I could smell it on their breath.

"The captain told one of the others to go into the bedroom and get the baby. I screamed and tried to run after him, but another soldier grabbed me. He told the captain, 'I'm going to take this wench into the bedroom and have a little fun with her. Anybody want to join me?'

"But before he could, the captain said, 'Leave her alone.'

"The young soldier sneered and shouted back, 'What's wrong with you Captain Estrada? You can't feel sorry for these people. They're all enemies of the state.'

"The captain took two steps toward the insolent soldier and slapped him hard in the face. 'We don't have time for your games,' he said. 'You were there with Gimo. You heard him say that we have to take six babies tonight. That means five more.'

"I never saw Benito again."

Gina shot to her feet. "What did you just say?" she shouted at Maria, who was terrified by Gina's reaction.

Maria repeated her words in a quavering voice. "I never saw Benito again."

"No. No. Before that."

"'You were there with Gimo. You heard him say that— '"

Once she heard the words again, Gina gave a bloodcurdling cry. "No . . . no . . . no . . . no . . ." at the top of her lungs. It was the worst sound Craig had ever heard in his life. It was the anguish of a woman whose insides were being ripped out while she remained alive, having it happen before her very eyes.

Then she charged across the room toward Maria.

Craig jumped to his feet, fearful Gina would strike Maria, but she stopped short, raised her hand and pointed an accusing finger. "You lied. Didn't you, old woman. Estrada never said 'Gimo.' Admit it. You lied because he told you to." The finger swung around toward Craig. "The evil scheming American told you what to say. Admit it, old woman."

Nicole and Maria looked puzzled. Craig mouthed the words, "Gimo was her father."

Maria refused to be intimidated. "I have never lied in my entire life. Surely, I would not desecrate the memory of my Benito by lying about what happened to him."

In anger, Gina turned on Craig. "A mistake was made. She's telling us what she thinks she heard. She made a mistake. You're exploiting it for your own purposes."

He crossed the room over to the black duffel, took out Betty's folder, and placed it on the coffee table. "Confirmation is in these documents, but I urge you not to read them."

Gina moved in close to him and pounded her fists against his chest. His skin was tender. The blows hurt, but he didn't flinch. His pain was nothing compared with hers. He hated doing this to her, but there was no other way.

"You bastard," she shouted, through clenched teeth on a face of agony. "How could you do this to me?"

"I'm sorry. Truly I am."

"You're not sorry at all. You're prepared to get what you want regardless of how much it hurts me."

He couldn't argue. Of course, she was right.

She picked up the red folder and said, "I want privacy. Where can I go."

"Please don't read the documents. Accept what Maria told you."

"You're not telling me what to do," she fired back.

Nicole said, "You stay here, Gina. We'll leave."

Nicole led them to the hallway outside, closing the door of the den behind her.

She thanked Maria for coming. Then she had one of the men who took care of her house drive Maria home.

Nicole turned to Craig. "How'd you know her father was called Gimo?"

"The first time you told me the story and you mentioned Gimo, I had no idea he was Gina's father. Then when I was back in Washington, I asked Betty to give me the files on her father. I wasn't looking for anything specific. Just playing a hunch that he wasn't a saint and planning to use that to gain Gina's help. Then when I read the documents, I learned that other officers called him Gimo."

Nicole walked toward the kitchen with Craig trailing behind. "I need a drink," she said.

"It's still morning."

She ignored his words and poured herself some grappa. Craig declined, opting for coffee instead.

As he sipped it, he picked up a copy of the morning issue of *La Nación* to see what statements Estrada was issuing to the press, to try and gauge how soon he would be launching an attack. But he couldn't concentrate on the newspapers. The heart-wrenching sobs, the continual crying coming from Gina through the closed door as she read documents that described her father's crimes, were too much.

* * *

When Schiller called, Estrada was at his headquarters at Iguazu making final arrangements for the battle to be launched the following morning.

"We have to talk," Schiller told Estrada. "It's a matter of extreme importance."

"I'll be back in my office in Buenos Aires at six this afternoon. I think we better wait till then."

With information Schiller had described as sensitive, Estrada was afraid to talk by phone. Though it was his country, not theirs, the CIA might have installed its own listening devices.

"I'll be waiting for you," Schiller said.

* * *

An hour after Gina had closeted herself in the den with the documents, Craig saw her emerge, red-faced with bloodshot eyes and disheveled clothes.

"Bathroom," she muttered, and went upstairs.

He heard water running.

Minutes later, she came down, a small towel in her hand, wiping her damp face. She said crisply to Craig, "Call Nicole. You won. I'll help you."

"Believe me, you're the only one who can stop Estrada. If I had another way, do you think I—"

"That's enough," she said, waving a hand at him for emphasis. "I know that the generals can't come to power again. Tell me what I have to do."

The three of them returned to the den. Gina was drinking water. "My throat's sore," she had said. Both women were looking at Craig. It was his show.

"Let's start with what you know," he said to Gina.

She began in a soft voice. "Alfredo arranged for me to have a job at *La Nación*, and he directed them to send me to Washington. He told me that I was to get close to Edward Bryce. He would tell me from time to time what I was to learn from Bryce or convince him to do."

She gave him a sharp look. "Since you bugged my phone and my bedroom, you know all of that."

He turned his eyes away from her and looked down at the floor.

"This was all part of a grand plan of Alfredo's to take over the government and restore Argentina to a position of grandeur. Periodically, he flew me back from Washington to Buenos Aires to explain what he needed. Usually, I came out to his country house on a weekend for those discussions."

She coughed, clearing her throat, and sipped some water before continuing. "From these discussions, I learned that Alfredo was planning to launch a major attack on Brazil."

"Do you know when?"

She shook her head. "The exact date. No. Just that it will happen soon. And he's going to do it for the diamonds because he says that the new wealth for our country will be the driver to sweep him into power."

Craig remembered her waving her finger at him in the tango joint and singing the song from *Gentlemen Prefer Blondes*: "Tell me about the diamonds."

"A week or so before I met you in Washington, I was staying at Alfredo's country estate. He wanted to talk to me about what I was doing with Bryce and how important it was. Late that night, he had a meeting with Schiller and some of his other generals. I was sleeping upstairs, but the sound of loud voices woke me. My room was near the top of the stairs. So I quietly opened up the door and strained my ears to listen." She looked awkward. "I don't usually do this, but I wanted to know where my work with Bryce fit into his plans."

Craig and Nicole were both at the edge of their chairs as she continued.

"I heard Alfredo say, 'The diamonds in Rio Grande do Sul are ours for the taking. The Brazilian commanders in the area will tell their troops not to resist when we attack. They made that commitment to me at Bariloche. We can slice off the southeast portion of Brazil and make it part of Argentina. When we do that, we'll have control of the diamonds.'"

So that's why they murdered Dunn and Pascual, Craig realized. The diamonds are in Brazil. Not Argentina. Estrada couldn't let anyone find out about the clandestine meeting he'd had with Brazilian military leaders from Porte Allegro. In some ways, it wasn't surprising. That region of Brazil had a history of being fiercely autonomous and resentful of the Central Brazilian government. He remembered reading that Garibaldi fought with the residents of Rio Grande do Sul in a war for independence from Brazil before Garibaldi returned to Italy to help unify it. In addition to a promise of autonomy, Estrada probably offered those Brazilian military leaders a cut of the diamond wealth. "Did Estrada say any more about Bariloche?" he asked.

"Not Alfredo. But Schiller told the generals, 'You must keep this information extremely confidential. The Americans sent an agent to spy on our meeting in Bariloche. Fortunately, we found out and killed him before he obtained any information.' Then someone asked, 'Won't the Americans stop us if we attack first?' and Estrada replied, 'I have plans for dealing with that. We'll fake a small incident and make them seem like the aggressors. We have the president's key advisor in our pocket. It'll work.'"

Bryce should go to jail for life for this, Craig thought. "What about the diamonds? What else was said about them?"

"One of the other generals asked Alfredo if he was certain they were really there in such large quantities."

"How did he respond?"

"Alfredo became angry. He doesn't like to be questioned. He called the man a fool and told him everyone knows this area of Brazil is rich in minerals. Oil and iron ore. All sorts of things. Alfredo said he wanted to find out just how much value there is in the area. So he asked a friend of his, a professor at the University in Buenos Aires, to recommend one of the world's top experts in mineral exploration. The man recommended was a well-known English geologist by the name of Jeremy Barker, an Oxford University professor."

She paused to take a breath. "Well anyhow, Alfredo said that he hired Dr. Barker to spend the month of July this year in the area, doing research and exploratory work that was kept secret by paying bribes to local officials. That was when Dr. Barker made the discovery, but he hasn't told anyone or written any articles.

"Instead, he came to Alfredo and disclosed the information in return for money and a promise to be a consultant on the diamond field development. Alfredo also said that he had Dr. Barker's information checked by an Argentine geologist, whose name I couldn't hear and who was sworn to secrecy. That seemed to satisfy the other generals because someone made a toast, 'First the diamonds. Then the presidential palace, Casa Rosada.' Somebody else shouted, 'To Alfredo Estrada, the next president of Argentina.' Then the meeting broke up, I quietly closed my door so Alfredo wouldn't get suspicious. That's all I know."

"It's plenty," Nicole said, trying to lend encouragement to Gina. "You've been incredibly helpful."

Craig had his head in his hands thinking. "What we need now is hard evidence that the Brazilian attack last week was bogus, and when the large attack will take place. With that, I can go to Washington and turn around Treadwell's decision."

"I'll get the information," Gina said. "Tell me how."

"The only way I can think of would be for you to set a meeting with Alfredo, go in wearing a tiny hidden microphone, and—"

Nicole interrupted. "Don't you dare suggest that. It's too dangerous. If they find out, they'll torture her. All it'll do is get her killed. Find another way."

"There is no other way," he said stubbornly.

"Haven't you done enough to this girl?"

Gina's head was turning back and forth between the two of them, as if she were at a tennis match, while they were discussing her as if she weren't there.

"I'll do it," Gina said.

"No you won't," Nicole fired back.

Gina turned on her. "Don't tell me what I'll do. Everybody else has been manipulating me for the last six months. Now I want to take charge of my own life. I'm doing it, and that's final."

Nicole said to Craig, "C'mon outside. I want to talk to you alone."

"I want to hear this," Gina said stubbornly. "You can say what you want in front of me."

"Okay," Nicole replied. She was glaring at him. "You really are despicable."

"Let her do it. She wants to make up for her father's crimes."

Nicole stared at him hard. "Come on, Craig, you can't expose Gina to this danger. She's suffered enough. Where's your compassion. Leave her alone."

Wide-eyed and with an intensely serious expression on her face, Gina said, "I'm the only one who can do this."

He weighed in his mind Nicole's apprehension. In the end, he said, "Okay, Gina. You can do it. Stay here with Nicole, for a couple of hours. I have to go downtown to see a man about a wire. When I get back, I'll tell you what to do. Then you can call Estrada to arrange a meeting."

Craig's only source for the electronic equipment was the American Embassy. He assumed that Schiller's men were watching all the likely places in case he had snuck back into the country because Argentina, like the United States, was so vast that it had a tough border to control. That meant he couldn't drive into the United States Embassy himself. Nor did he want to risk having an Embassy car come to Nicole's house. That only left one option. Much as he hated riding in a closed trunk, he used his cell phone to call B. J. Walker at the embassy, used Betty's code, and asked B. J. to pick him up at the same meeting place they had used the night of the protests. He planned to drive there and park his rental car. That seemed safe enough.

Washington

Bryce was elated. With what he had given Schiller, he was confident the colonel would kill Craig Page. With his value established to Estrada, he would have fame and fortune in Argentina as well as in the United States. How many other people could have that in two countries? And with the blessing of Estrada, Gina's great benefactor, he was confident she would marry him.

Though Bryce was in love with Gina, he was no fool. Deep down, he had suspected on the visit to Argentina that there was something that didn't ring true about Estrada's story about the Brazilian attack. And Estrada, who had been pressing for all those American arms, was so anxious to have the American commitment of nonintervention.

His call with Schiller had confirmed that Argentina was planning to attack Brazil and do it tomorrow at dawn. Bryce was enough of a lawyer to appreciate that what began as a harmless sexual affair had sucked him into betraying his best friend and his country. But he was in it too deep. His only choice was to put those doubts out of his mind. Everything had progressed too far. All he could do now was strengthen Treadwell's resolve to stand firm on his nonintervention decision, even if a major war was launched by Estrada, contending that he was responding to another Brazilian attack.

When word of the outbreak of hostilities reached Treadwell in the White House early the next morning, if Bryce were asleep in his house in Georgetown, he would have no way of getting the president's ear until after Betty, no doubt relying on what Craig Page told her, convinced Treadwell that Argentina had attacked and convinced the president to change his decision not to intervene. By the time he reached the White House, or even spoke to Treadwell, US war planes would be in the air to help Brazil.

He couldn't let that happen.

He thought about it some more and came up with the perfect solution. It would work because the First Lady was away.

He picked up the phone and called Treadwell. "What do you have on tap for the rest of the day?" he asked.

"Right now, I'm in the Oval Office reviewing Amy's draft for the speech about the deficit that I have to give on Friday in New York before all those financial gurus. Tonight's quiet. Polly's away."

"I've got an idea."

"Shoot."

"How about a change of scenery. Let's go out to my place at Middleburg. We'll have dinner there and stay over."

"I don't know. I do feel like a prisoner. Getting cabin fever in this building. But it's always such a hassle to go out of town overnight. Between Secret Service and the rest of the entourage."

Bryce could tell that Treadwell was on the fence. "Then why not make it fun. We'll take Amy along. Hell, you have the perfect cover. You'll be reworking the speech with her."

"Now you're talking. That sounds great. You want to bring along Gina as well?"

"She's out of town on an assignment for her paper. The three of us will be great."

"Good, I'll call Amy to come over here around seven. We'll take off then. You want to ride in the chopper with us?"

"Naw. I better go down early and get everything ready."

When he hung up the phone, Bryce was very pleased with himself. At dinner, he'd have a chance to lobby Treadwell about Argentina. It didn't matter if Amy was there. She'd never repeat anything. He now had the perfect plan for countering that interfering Betty Richards. What an outrage—sending a spy to Argentina behind the backs of Bryce and the president. In Middleburg, Betty would never have the access to Treadwell that she would at the White House. Tomorrow morning, Bryce would be in complete control of Treadwell.

Buenos Aires

"I assume you want to use a secure phone," B. J. said to Craig once they were inside the Embassy.

"That's part of it. I also need some technical help. I want to fit a woman with a recording device to pick up a conversation in a small meeting. Probably one on one."

B. J. looked uncomfortable. "I hope you don't want simultaneous broadcast outside the building."

"That's precisely what I want. That way I can be in a car or van on the street, making the recording, but ready to go in if she gets into trouble."

B. J. shook his head. "Sorry, we don't have equipment to do that, and I can't get it on short notice."

"Oh for God's sake. What is this?"

B. J. held out his hands. "It's not Washington. That's for sure."

Craig knew it was pointless to argue. "Then what do you have?"

"A microcassette recorder. You can fit it under her blouse. It's extremely high quality. Just tell her to stand reasonably close to the subject. Afterwards, you bring me the cassette. You can listen to it and forward it electronically to Langley."

"It'll have to do," Craig grumbled. He realized he was exposing Gina to greater danger by putting her on her own, but he had no choice. As long as Estrada didn't suspect anything, and he had no basis for doubting Gina, she'd be alright.

While B. J. left to get the recorder, Craig went downstairs to the secure room and placed the call to Betty.

For the next fifteen minutes while she listened in silence, except for a few clarifying questions, he recited in a staccato manner everything that happened at Nicole's house, including what Gina had heard eavesdropping on Estrada about the diamonds and his agreement with the Brazilian Army officers. Also, her willingness to wear a wire for the meeting with Estrada.

At the end, he said, "So if all goes well, by sometime this evening I'll call you and then forward electronically what Estrada said to Gina, which will give you the time of the Argentine attack, as well as convincing evidence that Estrada's acting the aggressor in order to take the diamonds. You'll have an ironclad case to take to the president."

"And if all doesn't go well?"

"I don't even want to think about that."

He couldn't bear to say, "We'll have one dead young woman, and we won't have the evidence."

To Craig's pleasant surprise, Betty said, "I'm not waiting to go to Treadwell. I'll meet with him as soon as I can get on his calendar."

"I don't understand."

"When I think about the report you just gave me, the transcripts you've provided from the bugs in Gina's apartment and on Gina's phone, I am enraged. The absolute hubris of Bryce to use the United States and destroy its credibility in all of Latin America because he wanted to get his rocks off."

"I agree. But I should have the recording from Gina later today."

"Even if you get it, which is uncertain, it would be too much to dump on Treadwell all at once. I have to begin conditioning the president as soon as possible. I'll take those transcripts to the White House. Also, Jonathan Martin's book, *Inside the Gestapo*. I need all the available ammunition. Bryce has been Treadwell's great buddy for more than forty years. This won't go down easy, my telling him that Bryce has been operating as an agent of a foreign government. That he has betrayed Treadwell and the United States. I have to do it in stages. Treadwell knows Gina. If Estrada kills her, that'll make an impression on the president."

*   *   *

Craig took the electronic equipment back to Nicole's house where he explained the plan to Gina and Nicole.

He was looking at Gina. "The microcassette recorder will be positioned with tape against your skin. Under your blouse between the two cups of your bra. In addition to the tape, it will be held in place by skin colored wire that runs around your back."

He turned to Nicole and added, "When we're ready to fit it, you'll do it."

Gina shot him a look. "I'm ready to go. Let me call Estrada's office. His secretary knows me."

"Good. Do it. Use your cell phone."

Craig watched her as she made the call. Despite her show of bravado, he could see her hand shaking ever so slightly. Craig asked Gina to turn up the volume, and he moved close enough to her so he could hear the voices on the other end.

"I have to see Alfredo," Gina said. "It's a private matter that's quite urgent."

When Gina hung up, she reported what the secretary said: "I should come to his office in Defense at seven this evening."

For the next hour, Craig went over, again and again with Gina, the script for her conversation with Estrada and what they needed from it:

the time of the next attack; an admission that last week's incident was a fake; and that the objective of the upcoming attack would be to seize the Brazilian diamond fields.

During the discussion, Nicole remained quiet. It was so out of character for her that Craig realized it was her way of showing her distress over what he was doing with Gina. He didn't care. This was the only way to get the information he needed.

"Try to stay close to Estrada during your discussion with him," he said. "That's essential for us to get a good recording."

"Afterwards, where will I meet you to give you the cassette?"

"Remember El Bodegon, the tango joint we went to after the Alvear dinner?"

"Sure."

"I'll be there from seven on."

"Sometimes Alfredo likes to take me out to dinner."

"If that happens, go into a bathroom, take off the recorder, wire and other stuff, then put it all in your purse to minimize the risk of him seeing anything. Then meet me after your dinner with him."

"I'm sure I'll be at El Bodegon by eleven at the latest."

"I'll stay until midnight."

She didn't ask what would happen if she wasn't there by then. None of them wanted to contemplate that possibility.

*   *   *

Gina had firmly committed to memory Craig's instructions for how she should play the conversation with Estrada. Having those firmly in mind worked wonders to keep her fear under a measure of control as she walked through the glass doors of the somber, gray, stone Ministry of Defense. She was dressed in a long sleeved, dark brown cotton blouse and a beige skirt that ran well below her knees. Under her blouse was the microcassette recorder that Nicole had installed. The skin colored wire running around her back was tight and made indentations in her skin, but that didn't bother her.

Walking up to the reception area in the center of the lobby, she couldn't keep her knees from wobbling, no matter how hard she tried.

The Army officer, alone at the desk, recognized her from previous visits to Estrada. Though he put her through the motions of signing in, no identification was required. No metal detector for a friend of Estrada. He told her she could proceed up to Estrada's office without an escort. Quickly, she crossed the reception area to the bank of elevators.

As she exited the elevator and walked along the dimly lit marble corridor, the clicking of her heels seemed excruciatingly loud. Settle down, she admonished herself. He'll have no reason to suspect a thing unless you give him one.

Passing Colonel Schiller's office, she turned her head ever so slightly and looked into the open doorway. The colonel sat at his desk staring into the corridor. He nodded and gave her a short, sadistic smile.

Inside Estrada's suite, she expected to see one of the generals' secretaries, but their desks were vacant. All of the papers out of sight. He must have let them go home, she decided. Nothing unusual in that, given the hour, though it underscored how very much alone she felt.

Still, she had no doubt she was doing the right thing. It wasn't simply that she had to atone for the sins of her father toward Maria and other innocent people, Estrada had been part of the baby kidnapping operation and God only knows what else. He couldn't be permitted to take over the country.

With what she now knew, it amazed her, walking into Estrada's huge corner office, that he looked perfectly normal and relaxed, with his feet up on his desk, reading a document in a black binder. A lit cigar rested in an ashtray close to his right hand. Convinced he didn't suspect a thing, and how could he, she breathed a large sigh of relief.

He sat upright, pointed to a stiff wooden chair in front of his desk, and she sat down.

"I was surprised that you were back in Argentina," he said. "Intrigued by your message that you had something urgent to tell me."

"I was afraid to use the phone."

"If it's that sensitive, you were wise to come in person. Tell me about it."

His eyes were boring in on her with such intensity that she glanced down at her hands folded in her lap.

Before she had a chance to speak, the telephone rang. Estrada picked it up, listened for a couple of seconds, said, "Yes, I understand," and hung up. He turned back to her.

Ready with the words Craig had given her, Gina began in a firm voice, hoping to sound spontaneous. "Edward Bryce suspects that he was duped by you and Colonel Schiller when he was in Argentina last week. He now believes that the Brazilian attack was bogus—a fabrication by you and Colonel Schiller to make it look like Brazil initiated the action to justify a large Argentine attack in the very near future." She paused for a second to let her words sink in. "As soon as I heard this, I immediately flew home. I thought you should hear it in person"

Estrada looked troubled. "Did Bryce give you any basis for his suspicions?"

"He remembered reading in a history class in school that Colonel Schiller's grandfather used precisely the same tactics for the German army to justify their attack on Poland in 1939."

Estrada puffed on his cigar and blew smoke into the air. "That's preposterous. The notion that we manufactured the attack." Estrada said it in a tone of incredulity.

"But that's what Bryce said."

"What did you tell him?"

"Precisely what you just said. I think I used the word ludicrous, but . . ."

"But what?"

She swallowed hard. Craig had told her this was the key point. "I knew that Bryce was right."

"Really. How did you know that?"

"The last time I stayed at your country house, late at night, you had a meeting with Colonel Schiller and some of the generals. Honestly, I had no intention of eavesdropping, but I woke up to go to the bathroom. I had trouble falling asleep, and I heard certain things."

He locked eyes with her. "What things?"

"That a small Brazilian attack would be fabricated. That it would be followed by a large attack by our army to cut off a portion of Brazil and seize territory with valuable diamond deposits."

Craig had told her that the next words Estrada said would be the most important. In view of her relationship with the general, Craig expected Estrada to confide in her that what she had heard that night in his house was correct. Then it would be an easy matter for her to follow up by asking him when the attack would take place. Once he gave her that information, she would have on the tape everything that Craig needed. She should then drop the subject and move on.

She waited anxiously for Estrada to respond. Instead of saying a word, he rose and walked over to a window across the office. There, he stood looking out into the night as if he were deep in thought. Gina was alarmed. Craig had told her that if Estrada was too far away, the recording device wouldn't pick up what he said. Craig hadn't told her how far was too far. But this was a key point. On the verge of panic, she sprang up and walked toward Estrada. At a distance of ten feet, she stopped, waiting for him to say something—the words that would incriminate him.

Without opening his mouth and without any warning, he wheeled around abruptly, charged toward her, and with both hands ripped open her blouse at the center where it was buttoned. Too stunned to move or speak and paralyzed with fear, she watched in horror as he pulled a small army knife from his pocket, cut the wire, roughly pulled the microrecorder away from the tape fastening it to her skin, and tossed it into a large pitcher of water on a nearby table. The device sank quickly to the bottom where she realized it couldn't record a word.

Estrada picked up the phone and dialed a number. "Yes," he said.

Seconds later, Schiller raced into the room. She cowered against the wall, trying to hold together the two sides of her blouse to cover herself. Schiller sneered at her, picked up the pitcher, and left the room as quickly as he came, shutting the door behind him.

Estrada was now glaring at her. "Your friend, Craig Page, the CIA agent . . ."

In midsentence, he paused, letting the name sink in, making sure she understood that he now knew Barry Gorman, the investment banker, was Craig Page, a CIA agent. Then he continued. "Your friend, Craig Page, must think that we are stupid in Argentina. It's a pity you'll never see him again, or you could explain to him how wrong he was."

"I don't understand."

"Of course, I suspected that he would have you outfitted with a recording device, so Colonel Schiller installed a concealed detector above the door to my office. We set it on mute, but the response when you entered, went right to Colonel Schiller's office. Now, let's have a real conversation, you and I, my young friend."

She held her breath wondering what was coming next.

"For openers," Estrada continued, "tell me whether Craig came back with you, and how the two of you got into the country."

"I flew into Ezeiza. I don't know about him."

Estrada shook his head in disbelief. "We checked all the planes over the last few days, commercial and private. Neither of you was on any manifest. We were watching the airports. Please don't lie to me any longer."

His face was twisted in a horrible mask of anger that provoked an expression of shock and terror on hers.

"Where are you meeting him when you leave here?" Estrada demanded to know.

Unwilling to lie again, she looked down at her feet and remained silent.

"I'm willing to forgive you for everything you've done so far," he said. "I'll consider it an unfortunate error induced by young love."

His words gave her a tiny basis for hope that she might be able to extricate herself from this situation. She watched him, waiting for the other shoe to drop. To hear what he was offering.

"In return," he said, slowly so she didn't miss a word, "I want you to go to your meeting with Craig tonight. Tell him that the device fell off before you got to our meeting. So you discarded it. When we spoke, I explained to you that he was wrong in thinking that last week's attack was bogus or that a large attack would be coming. I will have people following you to make certain you do what I'm asking. Do you understand?"

When she still didn't respond, he grabbed her by both shoulders and shook her violently. "What the hell's wrong with you, girl? Are you crazy?"

It was all too much for her. Totally out of her element, despite her effort at self-control, she began crying.

"At least tell me where and when you're meeting him," Estrada screamed at her. "We'll kill him and let you live."

The implication was that if she didn't tell, she would die. She thought about the documents in the folder Craig had given her at Nicole's and she refused to betray him.

"If your father ever had any idea that you became a traitor to our country . . . Well I hate to think of that. It's good that our hero Miguel Galindo rests in peace."

If Estrada thought evoking her father's name would make her yield, he was mistaken. It had the opposite effect. She recovered her composure and fortified her resolve.

"My father was no hero. I know now what he did. What you did with him. You were a bunch of murderers and kidnappers."

With the back of his hand, Estrada lashed out and smacked the side of her face, knocking her to the ground.

"He's been feeding you lies," Estrada shouted with saliva coming out of his mouth.

The pain on her face was sharp. Still she raised her voice to respond. "I saw documents from the time."

"All American lies."

"Documents generated here. Orders signed by my father."

"I've treated you like my own daughter all these years. In return, you betray me. And you betray his memory. You're both pathetic and contemptible. And do you know what else?"

She looked up at him, fearful of what he planned to do with her.

Estrada continued, "Your American friend has done me a big favor, tipping his hand by sending you. We'll advance the attack. The Americans will never be able to stop us."

He called in Schiller. "Have the pilot fuel up my plane. We're going back to Iguazu. Right now. From the air, we'll notify the generals. We'll launch our attack several hours earlier. Before the Americans have a chance to move their satellites into place."

"I'll notify the pilot right now."

"Good. I had planned to remain in Buenos Aires when we attacked and keep the city under control. With the American CIA so close on our tail, everything could become much more complicated. You and I better stay up there for the next twelve hours."

Schiller nodded his agreement. "What do we do about her?" he said pointing toward Gina. His tone suggested that he wanted to dispose of her as he would a piece of garbage.

"I haven't decided yet," Estrada replied. "For now, we'll take her with us. Put her in one of those cells on the second floor of the castle.

If the American is as hooked on her as she is on him, she could be valuable in a barter."

Middleburg, Virginia

Bryce realized something was wrong as soon as he saw Treadwell.

The presidential party arrived at Bryce's country house at seven thirty in the evening. From the flagstone veranda, Bryce watched the two choppers descend from the dark sky and land on the broad expanse of grassy field covered with leaves in beautiful fall colors.

Bryce saw a weary looking Treadwell climb down the stairs followed by two Secret Service agents. Behind them came Amy, carrying a heavy briefcase, the collar of her fur coat pulled tightly against her neck to brace against the cold. Bryce was struck by how young she looked compared with the president. Then he thought about Gina and put that out of his mind.

From the second helicopter, Dr. Deborah Lee emerged with a military aide and three more Secret Service agents. Roaring up the road and through the gate that marked the entrance to Chesterfield were two more cars loaded with Secret Service. Bryce had arranged plenty of food for the entire crowd. His plan was to set out dinner for the Secret Service in a small guest house in back of the main house. That house was also equipped with a large-screen television set where those members of the security detail who weren't on duty guarding the house could relax at the same time Bryce had dinner in the main house with Treadwell, Amy, and Dr. Lee.

Bryce was bewildered as he watched the president walking along the lawn, brightly lit by floodlights, toward the house. Treadwell should have been smiling. He was beginning an overnight in the country with his mistress, away from the pressure and fishbowl atmosphere of the White House. Instead, what Bryce saw was tension written all over the craggy face of his old friend.

Whatever had happened to upset Treadwell, Bryce was determined to change it. "Dinner in an hour," he announced cheerfully. "Cocktails and local oysters in the study, whenever our distinguished president, Amy, and Dr. Lee can join me."

Treadwell brushed the logistics aside. "You and I have to talk," the president said in a stern voice. "Right now."

When he was alone in the study with Treadwell, the door closed and they each had a Johnny Walker blue label on the rocks, Bryce said, "What happened? Tough day at the office?"

Treadwell walked toward the crackling fire, put his drink down, and turned toward Bryce. "Betty Richards came to see me."

Uh-oh, Bryce thought. Now that he knew she had Craig working for her, he was expecting the worst. Still, as an experienced trial lawyer, he believed in going on the attack to overcome adverse evidence. "What'd the old biddy want?"

"She's had Craig Page in Argentina undercover. Apparently, he had extensive plastic surgery after I fired him as CIA director. He was racing cars in Italy when she recruited him. Craig's learned—"

Bryce cut him off. "That's outrageous. She never told us that she sent Craig down there in all of the meetings we had about the situation in Argentina. It's underhanded, deceitful, and duplicitous. I hope you told her that."

"Actually, I was thinking that initially. But I had to listen to her because she made a powerful case that Estrada totally duped you and our delegation. She said that the Brazilian attack was phony. It was just a show to justify a larger attack that could come at any time—the way the Nazis did in Poland."

"That's ridiculous. It's—"

Treadwell raised his hand. "Hal West corroborated her account. You never brought me the information he learned from the Brazilian military. Even though you told him you would."

All of the color drained from Bryce's face.

"On top of all of that," Treadwell continued, "Betty told me that you've been feeding information to that Argentine girl. What's her name?"

"Gina Galindo."

"Yes, Gina. She's been passing it right back to Estrada. That's what's eating me up inside." His voice was cracking with emotion. "You're my oldest and closest friend. You've made a fool out of me with the Brazilian president. How. . . how . . . how . . ." he stammered, sounding distraught. "How could you have done this? It's outrageous. It's horrible."

Bryce's face grew beet red. "I can't believe Betty made up a story . . ."

Treadwell raised his hand. "Don't you lie to me," he said raising his voice.

"I wasn't lying. I was . . ."

"She gave me transcripts of conversations between you and that girl. In her bedroom and on the phone. They're in the briefcase Amy has. You can read them."

Bryce knew he had been caught red-handed. He slumped down in a chair. Trying to argue that the transcripts were phony was futile and would outrage Treadwell further. He didn't dare do that. Ditto for reminding Treadwell that recording in that manner was illegal.

Bryce thought he saw a way to dig himself out of this mess. "I suspected all along," he said softly, "that Gina was working for Estrada. I was extremely careful in what I told her. Only facts that reflected policies you decided on that would have reached Estrada in any event, such as your decision to sell certain weapons to Argentina."

"You should have told me about all of this," Treadwell protested. "I even had that girl to the White House. Not a good thing to do for an agent of a foreign government, who I'll bet never even registered."

"You're right. I should have," Bryce said, sounding contrite. "I'm sorry for that."

When Treadwell didn't respond, Bryce thought he had won a reprieve. He tried deftly to change the subject. "Personally, I doubt that Betty was right about the Brazilian attack being bogus. If—"

Treadwell cut him off.

"I told Betty, and I want you to understand that the last decision we reached on nonintervention was only applicable if Brazil attacks first. I told her, and I told the presidents of Brazil and Argentina in phone calls, with Betty still in my office, that if Argentina attacks first, we will come to the assistance of Brazil militarily, if that's what they ask. I've told General Forbes to focus satellite surveillance on the area. Also, to move our Air Force planes to nearby locations. I told him to let me know if Argentina attacks first and Brazil wants our help. In that situation, I would be willing to use American planes in support of Brazil."

Bryce realized he could never recover his position of trust with Treadwell. When this was over, the best future for him would be in Argentina where he could live, not only as Gina's husband, but as a key adviser on world affairs to Estrada, who was certain to become president. That thought led him to defend Estrada. "I would like to review the evidence Betty and West relied upon for their conclusion that the Brazilian attack was bogus. It may be that they made an honest mistake in assessing intelligence information. It won't be the first time the CIA has done that."

Treadwell shook his head vigorously from side to side. "We have a long night here together. I intend to weigh carefully what you've just said before I decide what this means for our relationship and your involvement in my presidency. Perhaps, I should turn this over to the attorney general to determine if there's cause for prosecution, or perhaps I should accept your explanation and overlook it. I'll let you know about that in the morning, but . . ."

The veins were protruding on Treadwell's neck. His breath was coming in short spurts. He paused for a second; then he continued. "But regardless, you will be recused from any issues relating to Argentina in any way. Do you understand that?"

Feeling relief that Treadwell, at least for now, was not pursuing a criminal prosecution, Bryce responded in a conciliatory manner. "I do," he said softly.

"That means you will not have anything to do with matters concerning Argentina."

Bryce was tempted to respond, "You don't have to define the word recusal for me. I was near the top of my Harvard Law School class." But he bit his tongue.

"I understand, Mr. President. Now let's get the others for cocktails and dinner."

Once Treadwell, Bryce, Amy, and Dr. Lee filed into the dining room, Bryce's chef, Jean Pierre, took over. Cooking for the president of the United States, he had spared no effort in the preparation. A variety of hot hors d'oeuvres were followed by cold salmon mousse. The main course was roast pheasant, followed by salad and then a flourless chocolate torte in the shape of the White House.

Jean Pierre's efforts were wasted. The group ate in a tense, grim silence, matching the president's mood. Intermittent conversation was strained. Dr. Lee and Amy looked perplexed. Bryce made no effort at levity.

After dinner, Bryce suggested a game of billiards downstairs, hoping that might lighten Treadwell's mood. In response, the president announced, "Amy and I are going upstairs to work on that economic speech." He turned toward Bryce and added, "And don't you call Gina Galindo or anyone else about what we discussed. I don't want you to have anything more to do with the Argentine-Brazilian dispute."

Bryce watched in dismay as Treadwell trudged up the stairs slowly with Amy two steps behind.

Buenos Aires

It was eleven thirty and El Bodegon was filling up. Seated alone in a dark and dingy booth with the single beer he had ordered hours ago, Craig listened to the melancholy tune with despair. It described two lonely people, star-crossed lovers, helpless to deal with powerful forces in the world. The song had been written during the Dirty War and played surreptitiously while it raged.

A flaming redhead in her forties, Craig guessed, with an hourglass figure came over, wanting him to tango with her. She held out a hand and swayed her torso with the rhythm. Craig shook his head, and she drifted away.

He asked the proprietor behind the bar for the umpteenth time whether he had a call for a man named Barry Gorman. The gray-haired man with a thick, bushy beard looked at Craig with a kindly expression and said, "Not yet, but I'm sure she'll call soon."

Back in the booth, he glanced at his cell phone one more time. It was fully charged. There were no messages. He willed it to ring, but it remained as silent as a monument in a cemetery.

Distraught and desperate with worry about Gina, he watched the hands of his watch slowly advance toward midnight. Then he made his move.

Using his cell phone to make calls was risky, but he was at the point where he had to take chances. He called Nicole.

"She never came to El Bodegon," he whispered into the phone. "Did she call you?"

"I haven't heard a word."

"Estrada must have gotten suspicious and arrested her. But how could he?" As he said the words, Craig was racking his brain for answers. His plan had been so good. The script perfect. The only possibility was that Schiller had learned his true identity and told Estrada. Bryce had been suspicious, but Bryce would have railed at Betty if he had found out. All that was irrelevant. What mattered now was that Schiller and Estrada had Gina in their clutches and were doing God only knew what with her.

"You won't want to hear this," Nicole told Craig, "but Estrada could have persuaded her to tell him everything you're doing."

"You can't be serious. You were there when we worked with her. She was determined to get what we wanted."

"She's also young and impressionable. Untrained to do something like this. A genuine patriot. Believes in her country. Estrada was like a father to her. You spent time with him. He's charismatic."

"That's ridiculous." Craig said the words, but they were lacking conviction. "I'm tired of speculating. I intend to get some answers."

"What are you going to do?"

"On the chance that somebody might be listening in, he refused to tell her. "Stick by the phone. I'll call you."

He paid the proprietor generously for using the booth all evening. Then left El Bodegon.

Out on the street, he raised his hand for a cab. In an instant, three of the little black and yellow cars pulled over. Craig took the second one and told the driver to take him to an intersection two blocks from the Ministry of Defense.

When the cab stopped, he climbed out and looked around nervously. No sign of anyone watching him. He took a long circuitous route to cover the two blocks, satisfying himself there was no surveillance.

The dusky, gray, stone building, in need of a cleaning, looked even more dark and gloomy from the outside. Craig remembered the corner location of Estrada's office on the third floor. From the street, there were no lights visible in that suite.

Badly in need of a weapon, he was now sorry he hadn't asked Betty to bring a gun for him when she came out to California.

He opened one of the thick glass double doors and walked inside the dimly lit lobby. A single man was sitting behind the wooden counter—a soldier whom Craig remembered being there the one time he had visited Estrada in the building. The man who had asked for his ID and had been firm but professional in directing him to sign the visitor's log.

With confidence, he strode up to the reception counter.

"I'm Barry Gorman," he said. "I'm sure you remember. I was here about ten days ago to meet General Estrada."

The man nodded mechanically. His face was a blank. Craig couldn't tell if he remembered.

"The general's not here," the soldier said.

That was a start, Craig thought. Now he needed the rest of the information.

"I'm aware of that," he said calmly. "But General Estrada told me that he would leave a note at the desk authorizing you or whoever was on duty to take me up to his office so I could retrieve some important papers I need for a meeting with him tomorrow."

The soldier stared at Craig with a bewildered expression, but remained silent. He'll never take a chance on letting me up, Craig decided.

Peering over the counter, Craig saw that the soldier was seated at a desk with three drawers on each side. "Perhaps someone left the note in one of those drawers," he said pointing.

The soldier began opening the drawers and searching inside. Intent on what he was doing, he never noticed Craig swiftly cut around the desk and swing up behind him.

Craig took one step forward and looped his right arm around the soldier's neck. He pressed his powerful right forearm against the man's throat and yanked back.

As the soldier struggled, Craig kept pressing, choking off the air supply to his body. Gradually, the man's thrashing subsided.

Craig watched the color drain from his face. His body went limp. *Careful*, he cautioned himself. *Careful. Not too much or you'll lose him.*

He released his hold and the soldier tumbled to the floor.

"Shit, I lost him," he moaned aloud, furious at himself.

He leaned over and tried mouth to mouth, pumping air back into the man's lungs. An eyelid fluttered. He was coming back. Barely conscious now, he looked up at Craig with a terrorized expression.

"Listen up," Craig barked, "you tell me what I want to know and you'll live. You fuck with me and you're a dead man."

The soldier blinked his eyes and Craig took this as acquiescence.

"Where did General Estrada go?" he asked.

"Up north," came the response in a hoarse whisper.

"To his headquarters at Iguazu?"

"Yes . . . yes . . ." was the faint reply.

"What about Schiller?"

"He went with Estrada."

"And the girl, Gina?"

The man hesitated. Craig saw that he had a knife in a case at his hip. Craig took it out and held the sharp blade close against the soldier's throat.

"What about the girl?"

"They dragged her with them. She didn't want to go. She was yelling, 'Don't take me.'"

"That bastard, Estrada," Craig shouted.

No point killing the soldier. He had gotten what he wanted. With the knife in one hand, he dragged the man into a coat closet off the lobby. He stripped off the soldier's shirt and cut it into strips that he used along with the man's belt to tie the soldier's hands and feet. Then he picked up a wooden coat hanger and smashed the guard on the head hard enough to knock him out, but not do any real damage.

Craig took the man's pistol holstered at his hip, as well as the knife, and left him in the closet with the door tightly closed.

Back at the reception desk, he picked up the soldier's Uzi, which had been resting on the floor near his feet. He concealed it in an empty shopping bag that had been in the trash bin. Then he walked quickly through the front door.

Out on the street, he stopped and looked in every direction. An eerie silence had settled over the area. No pedestrians. No cars on the road.

He walked two blocks, then ducked behind the corner of a building so he wasn't visible from the street. From there, he called Nicole.

"You once told me you know where Estrada's headquarters is at Iguazu. In an old castle, right?"

"Yeah. Why do you want to know?"

"Because I'm going there right now. That's where Estrada and Schiller are. And they have Gina."

"Are you crazy? Planes don't fly at one in the morning. There won't be anything until seven or eight at the earliest."

Craig wasn't deterred. "You must know somebody who flies private planes for rich people. Call him and tell him I want to go now. Money's no object. With a big payoff, he'll put off sleeping for a few hours."

From behind the building, Craig saw a police car advancing slowly down the street from his left to his right.

"Hold on for a minute," he told Nicole.

The pistol was in his pocket. He gripped it hard. If the car stopped, he'd fire first and ask questions later.

The police car slowed down.

Craig held his breath.

Inexplicably, the police car resumed its normal speed. It must have been a routine patrol.

"I know someone," Nicole said. "Manuel Rodriguez. He owns his own plane. He flies it for lots of company execs."

"Then call him. If he won't do it, find someone else. I'll wait to hear from you."

He hung up and stared at his phone. C'mon, Nicole. Come through for me.

She did. Two minutes later, his phone rang.

"Rodriguez wants twenty K US. He'll take plastic. In an hour he'll be at Aero Parque Jorge Newbery to fly us up there."

"Who's the 'us'?" he said. "I couldn't put you at risk like that."

"Gina will need help, and even someone as brilliant as you won't be able to do it on your own."

Her vehemence reminded him of Elizabeth. He had no chance of telling either of them what to do.

"Okay. Okay. I'll be glad to have you. I'll find a cab and meet you at the airport."

"Tell me where you are. I'll pick you up."

*   *   *

Rodriguez insisted on receiving a verbal authorization from American Express for his payment before letting Craig and Nicole on the plane.

Once he had that, he moved quickly to fuel up and file a flight plan. Minutes later, the three of them took off.

Inside the Learjet, Craig demanded that Rodriguez leave the door to the cockpit open. Notwithstanding Nicole's confidence in the pilot, there was something Craig didn't like about the man. He knew that plenty of danger and risk awaited them in Iguazu, but he wanted to make certain they were able to walk down the stairs of the plane on their arrival.

Iguazu, Argentina

From the castle in Iguazu, Estrada arranged a telephonic hookup with his top generals. "Zero hour is right now," he said. "I want all of our planes in the air immediately. The initial objective is to knock out the entire southern sector of the Brazilian Air Force on the ground before they have a chance to put their planes into the air. Then exactly one hour from now, I want tank and infantry moving east at all locations. Don't stop until you reach the sea. Is that clear?"

In unison came the response. "Yes, sir."

Estrada hung up and turned to Colonel Schiller. "Where's Gina?"

"The girl's in a prison cell upstairs," Schiller said. "I have a soldier guarding her."

On the flight to Iguazu in a military plane, Schiller had urged Estrada to give him an opportunity to interrogate Gina in his own way. This meant various forms of torture with which Estrada was familiar, but Estrada had rejected the colonel's proposal, telling him, "Let's discuss it in Iguazu."

Now Schiller renewed his request. "If you leave me alone with her for just an hour, I promise she'll tell me everything she knows about Craig Page and the Americans."

Estrada glared at the colonel. "Leave her alone."

Schiller pressed him. "The little bitch betrayed you. I intend to tie her down in a bed and have my way with her. Just to loosen her up. After that, I'll interrogate her. If she doesn't talk, I'll insert a stick, wired to pass an electric current into her vagina. That will change her mind."

"And what do you hope to gain?"

"Information about how much Craig Page knows about our plans and who he's working with in Washington. What the Americans are planning to do. Whether Bryce is really with us or playing both sides."

"You think she'll know all this?"

"There's only one way to find out."

Though furious at Gina's betrayal, the normally decisive Estrada was torn about what to do. Schiller had a point. It would be an advantage to find out what Craig Page knew and Gina might have that information. After what she had done she wasn't entitled to mercy.

And yet . . .

Miguel Galindo had been more than a hero, a friend, and a revered commanding officer for Estrada. Miguel had been a surrogate father for Estrada, who had been an orphan. After the death of Gina's mother, Miguel had made Estrada promise that if anything happened to him, Estrada would take care of Gina. Following Miguel's assassination Estrada lumped her together with his own four children. He never treated her differently from any of them.

Estrada couldn't do it. He turned to Schiller. "Leave Gina alone. She's irrelevant. It's too late for the Americans to do anything. By the time they wake up in Washington, all of southeastern Brazil will be in our hands."

When Schiller didn't respond, Estrada added, "If you want to focus your intelligent effort, do it on Craig Page."

Estrada was angry at himself for being deceived by the Barry Gorman cover. After Dunn, he should have been more vigilant. The $10 billion had blinded him. Schiller had warned him that's what was happening, but he chose to disregard Schiller's advice, believing he was able to determine for himself whether Barry Gorman was genuine. It was his own fault that he was in this situation.

"When we get our hands on Craig Page," Estrada said, "we'll deal harshly with him. We'll give him no mercy."

Middleburg, Virginia

Asleep in the master bedroom at the far end of the second floor, Bryce was awakened by the sound of a woman screaming. It was an awful, piercing yell that conveyed a combination of fear and terror. A desperate cry for help.

He shot upright in bed and tried to orient himself. Was he dreaming? The cry was coming from the far end of the corridor, from the guestroom Treadwell and Amy were using. He wasn't dreaming. It was Amy who was screaming.

After glancing at the clock that showed it was 3:12 a.m., he jumped out of bed and ran down the hall in his pajamas. Amy was standing in front of the door to the guestroom, her robe open in front She looked like a wild woman, strands of hair flowing over her face. She held her arms high over her head and shrieked. "Help me. Somebody! Please! God, help me!"

Bryce heard noise on the stairs behind him. He whirled around and saw Dr. Lee, clutching her black doctor's bag, and a military aide racing up from downstairs.

"Quick," Amy cried out. "Come quick. It's the president. He's having an attack."

Dr. Lee followed her into the bedroom with Bryce right behind. There, he saw Treadwell lying on the bed in obvious pain, moaning and gasping for breath. His right hand was in a tight fist against his chest. His skin color was gray, and he was drenched with sweat. Bryce was no doctor, but he was convinced Treadwell was having a heart attack.

Dr. Lee shouted to Amy, "Go into the bathroom. Get me one of his nitroglycerine tablets."

While Amy ran off to retrieve the medicine, Bryce was staring at the celling wondering what all this meant for him.

He tried to focus on what was happening. Dr. Lee placed her ear against Treadwell's mouth, listening for a breath. She then put her fingers on the side of Treadwell's neck, feeling for a pulse.

"He has a pulse, but it's thready," the doctor said to Bryce. "Go get Cummings, a secret service agent. He's had paramedic training. Tell him to bring me the oxygen and defibrillator. Also, tell him to have them rev up one of the choppers."

Northern Argentina

"We can't fly into Iguazu," Rodriguez announced to Craig and Nicole from the cockpit over the plane's PA system.

That brought the two of them racing forward into the cockpit. "Why the hell not?" Craig said.

"War's broken out in the area. It's too dangerous. Besides, my insurance won't cover the plane for loss in a war."

Craig pulled the gun out of his jacket pocket and shoved it against the back of the pilot's head. "This trumps your insurance policy. We're going to Iguazu. The plane's staying on the ground until I locate and bring back another passenger. Then we're returning to Buenos Aires. Now either you fly this plane or I do."

Faced with silence from the pilot, Craig added, "When you think about your options, you better factor in that if I have to fly, when we reach Iguazu, I'll put a bullet in your brain and leave your body to rot in the heat up there. Where I come from, that's what we do to people who don't keep their word."

Rodriguez looked at Nicole with loathing. How could she have set him up with this lunatic? His whole body was trembling with fear. "No. No. I'll fly."

"Good. Now Nicole and I will go back there and sit down. I'll be watching you with the gun in my hand. If you try to call anybody or you take this plane off course, I'll be up here yanking you out of this seat so fast your head will spin."

With that, Craig and Nicole returned to seats in the front of the passenger cabin. Through the open cockpit door he was watching Rodriguez, ready to spring forward as he had threatened. He handed the gun to Nicole. "Keep your eye on your buddy Rodriguez."

Then he pulled out his cell phone and called Betty. There was no time to worry about a secure phone.

"The war has started," he blurted out.

To his astonishment, the CIA director said, "I know it. General Forbes just called me. Our satellite photos establish an attack by Argentina along a broad front. They've destroyed most of Brazil's Air Force on the ground. Their troops and tanks are advancing fast. Opposition is light."

"That's because Estrada made a deal with some of the Brazilian commanders to betray their government." He pounded his fist against the seat. "Shit, that bastard Estrada will succeed."

"Maybe not," Betty said with conviction.

"You're either dreaming, or you know something I don't."

"A lot's happened here. This afternoon I made your case to Treadwell one-on-one. I gave him the Gestapo book and your transcripts."

"And?" Craig held his breath.

"He made it clear to the presidents of both countries that if Argentina attacks and Brazil asks for our assistance, we'll give them air support."

"No shit. He really did that?"

"Treadwell is not a bad guy. He may have been a little blinded by Bryce, but that sometimes happens to all of us with people we like."

"C'mon, Betty, the war's started. What are we going to do?"

"General Forbes has an aircraft carrier offshore. We're ready to move in with planes, helicopters, and the works. Only from the air. No ground troops. General Forbes has told all of this to the president of Brazil. It's up to the Brazilians to call and ask for our help. We won't act until we hear from them."

"Well, they better call soon."

"Where are you?"

"Nicole and I are en route to Iguazu." Now that the war had started and the United States might intervene on the side of Brazil, time was of the essence. Quickly, he explained what happened to Gina. "I have to get her out of Estrada and Schiller's hands before their world turns to crap, or they might just take it out on her."

"Go to it," Betty said and hung up.

He turned to Nicole. "How's our friend Rodriguez doing?"

"From time to time he turns around and glares at me, but otherwise he's sticking with our deal. By the way, I didn't know you could fly a plane."

He laughed softly and whispered in English, "I can't."

She shook her head. "So all Rodriguez had to do was hand you the controls. You'd have no choice but to let him fly us back to Buenos Aires."

"You got it. Ever play poker?"

She handed him back his gun. "Okay, what happens when we land in Iguazu?"

"Change of plans," he said. "Because of that prick Rodriguez, we can't leave him alone with the plane while we go to find Gina or he'll take off and fly out, which will leave the three of us stranded."

Nicole shook her head. "I know where this is headed. That means one of us has to stay at the airport with Rodriguez and the plane. And I drew the short straw."

"Or the long one, however you define it. Now tell me where the castle is and what the surrounding area looks like. I'll have to move fast."

Middleburg, Virginia

"What do you think, Doctor?" Bryce asked.

Dr. Lee glanced up from Treadwell's sweating body at Bryce standing in the doorway to the bedroom. "No question about it. He's had a massive heart attack."

"Will he make it?"

"My guess is it's about fifty-fifty. He'll need an emergency cardiac catherization. I have him stable now, which is all I can do. We can't start with a local hospital. We'll get him in the chopper and take him to Bethesda Naval. I called and alerted them. The cath lab is standing by."

Bryce admired Dr. Lee's cool professional manner in dealing with the crisis. She directed two of the secret service men to place the president on a stretcher. The oxygen hook up and telemetry leads were maintained with great care. They navigated the staircase and took Treadwell out through the front door and across the lawn to the waiting helicopter. The military aide walked two steps behind.

Once Dr. Lee made certain the president was secure and the pilot ready to lift off, Bryce, standing close to the chopper, watched Dr. Lee remove the cell phone from her pocket. He heard the doctor in a steady voice call Don Caldwell, the president's chief of staff, waking him up to state, "I regrettably must report to you that President Treadwell had a serious heart attack at 3:12 a.m. Twenty-three minutes ago. President

Treadwell is unable to discharge the powers and duties of his office. We're about to take off by helicopter to Bethesda Naval."

As Bryce watched the chopper lift off, he realized the significance of Dr. Lee's call. The doctor was complying with strict protocol of the Twenty-fifth Amendment of the Constitution. The process had now been activated to ensure a proper transfer of authority to run the country. Bryce knew that protocol very well. Caldwell would now notify the president pro tempore of the Senate and the Speaker of the House. In a matter of minutes, Vice President Worth would be the acting president.

*   *   *

Twenty minutes later Bryce was standing on the porch of his house, staring into the dark sky. What a disaster. The last thing on his mind was Treadwell. He was thinking about himself. His whole life was about to become unhinged. He was now being tossed around in the middle of a vortex.

Behind him, Bryce heard the phone ringing. That snapped him back to reality. He ran into the living room and picked it up. It was General Forbes, telling Bryce, "I have the Brazilian president and the chief of staff of their armed forces holding on another line. They've been trying unsuccessfully to reach President Treadwell. I've learned from the president's secretary that he's with you."

Bryce hesitated for an instant. He had to find out what was happening so he could decide how to play it. "That's right," he said, "but the president can't come to the phone right now. Tell me what the question is, and I'll take it to him."

"Satellite photos confirm that Argentina has attacked. Brazil wants our air support. The president told me this afternoon that's what he intended to do in this situation. I just want to make sure that's still his decision."

Bryce gripped the phone hard. Running through his mind was the indisputable fact that whether Treadwell lived or died, Bryce was finished as a player in Washington. If Worth became the president, Bryce would be faced with a criminal prosecution because the vice president was so close with Betty. Even if Treadwell made it back to the White

House, a referral to the attorney general of Bryce's conduct was possible. But in Argentina he would have a future with Estrada. And with Gina. Beautiful, sensuous Gina.

It was the moment of truth. The golden ring was there. He either had the guts to seize it, or he didn't.

"Wait a moment," Bryce told General Forbes. "I'll go and ask the president."

Bryce cupped his hand over the mouthpiece of the phone, while he watched the sweep second hand of his Rolex make a full revolution. Then he picked up the phone.

"The president asked me to tell you, 'Do not,' and he emphasized, 'underline the word 'not,' take any action to assist Brazil against Argentina.'"

"But . . ." a stunned Forbes stammered. "I don't understand."

Bryce knew that Forbes was aware of the close relationship between Bryce and the president. He wouldn't dare challenge Bryce.

"Treadwell is the boss," Bryce said.

"I guess so," Forbes replied in abject resignation. "I'll tell the president of Brazil we won't do anything to help them."

"That's what President Treadwell wants," Bryce replied and he hung up.

As he turned away from the phone, Bryce noticed Amy sitting in the middle of the stairs in a bathrobe. She must have been listening to his phone conversation.

Bryce pointed a bony finger in Amy's direction and narrowed his eyes. Through clenched teeth, he told her, "You better forget that you heard anything I said, or . . ." He paused for a minute to make certain he had her attention. "Or I'll go to the *Washington Post* and *New York Times* with the story of your relationship with the president. I'll make sure they drag you through the mud. For the rest of your life, you'll be known as Treadwell's little whore. Your life will be ruined. Now get dressed and get the hell out of my house."

"Screw you," Amy shouted.

She shot him a look of contempt and walked back up the stairs.

Bryce grabbed his cell phone and called American Airlines. "I want the next flight from Washington to Miami and connecting there to Buenos Aires."

As he waited for the ticket agent to come back to him with the information, through the corner of his eye he noticed Amy was staring at him from the top of the stairs.

Northern Argentina

Craig had an incoming call from Betty.

"Where are you?" she asked.

"In the air, about thirty minutes from landing in Iguazu, which is on the Argentine border with Brazil. Hell of a sound and light show from up here. Explosions everywhere off in the east. It looks like Argentina's on the move. In some sectors, the Brazilians must be firing back, but from up here it looks like Argentina's already deep into Brazilian territory."

"Things may be changing soon."

"Why's that?" he asked, now hopeful.

"Treadwell had a heart attack."

"Holy shit!"

"He's at Bethesda Naval for surgery. The doctors are saying it's fifty-fifty on his survival. Vice President Worth is now the acting president. But there's one nasty little wrinkle."

"What's that?"

"Treadwell was spending the night at Bryce's Middleburg house. I received a call from Amy, the president's speechwriter, who was also there. She told me that Treadwell had his heart attack at 3:12 a.m. Dr. Lee, the president's physician, set in motion the Constitutional transfer of power at 3:35 a.m. Worth was acting president a few minutes later. Then, at 3:55 a.m. General Forbes, who was unaware of the president's heart attack, received a call from the Brazilian president asking for our help. He learned from the president's secretary that Treadwell was at Bryce's Middleburg house. That bastard Bryce, purporting to relay a message from the president, told Forbes to reject the Brazilian's request for help."

Craig blew a long, low whistle. "That sounds like a criminal offense to me."

"Absolutely. We're moving up on it right now."

"How about help for Brazil?"

"As soon as I got off the phone with Amy I called Worth. US planes should be in the air momentarily."

"That's a relief," Craig cried.

He was racing against time to get Gina out of Iguazu before Estrada's world collapsed and he turned on her—if she was still alive.

Iguazu

At Iguazu Airport, Craig told Rodriguez to taxi to a deserted spot on the landing field and park. He borrowed a pair of night vision binoculars and a flashlight from the pilot and offered his pistol to Nicole, but she said she had brought her own.

"Good. Stay in the plane and watch Rodriguez," he told her. "Keep your cell on. I'll let you know when I'm coming back with Gina."

In view of the hour, the airport was deserted. Craig set off in the direction of the terminal with the pistol in his pocket and Uzi in his hand.

Off in the distance, he heard loud blasts as the sounds of war filled the night air. In the deserted Hertz lot he selected a Toyota sports car that would give him speed, hotwired it, and blasted through the wooden exit gate from the lot.

Judging from what Nicole had said in the plane, he had about a twenty-five mile drive to the castle that served as Estrada's headquarters. She had told him that the two-story castle stood on a small mound and backed up to the river flowing into the Iguazu Falls. It was set back from the highway, about a quarter of a mile. The gatehouse on the road was manned by armed guards. In both directions from the gatehouse, a high, barbed-wire-topped electrified fence paralleled the highway and encircled the property on all sides except in the back where the river ran. A narrow dirt road ran from the gatehouse to the castle. On both sides there was heavy vegetation, trees, high grass, and bushes—everything you would expect from near rain forest conditions. From the road, which was as close as Nicole had gotten, she hadn't seen much in the way of guards around the castle. Her guess was that with the gatehouse, fence, and river behind the castle, Estrada felt he didn't need much.

As Craig roared along the highway from the airport to the castle he saw very few vehicles. Not surprising, given that the Argentine army was already on the Brazilian side of the border. Civilians must have already fled westward to escape the war in case the Brazilians beat Estrada's forces and moved into Argentina, or they were hunkered down hiding in safe places until the fighting was over.

He turned on the radio to get war news, but all he heard was music. Estrada was freezing the public out—at least for now.

*   *   *

As Craig drove, Estrada cursed. Reports were reaching him of American planes entering the fray. His own air force had until now been in complete command of the skies, but was being challenged. And they were no match for the high-tech American electronics or the crews using them.

Argentina had already lost ten planes, and some of their pilots were flying out of the fighting zone to avoid contact with the Americans. Even worse, the Americans were bombing the advancing Argentine troops.

Estrada was on the phone constantly rallying his forces. "You can handle the Americans as well as the Brazilians," he shouted. "You just have to steel your courage for a tough battle. This doesn't have to end like the Falklands. This time, we can prevail."

*   *   *

A hundred yards from the gatehouse in front of Estrada's headquarters, Craig pulled over to the side of the road in an area of thick vegetation. He opened the hood and trunk, then climbed out and walked around to the front of the car, pretending to examine the engine. Off in the distance where the battle raged, thunderous explosions kept blasting into his ears. The flash of bright lights filled the still dark sky. His guess was that daylight would be breaking in the next hour. He didn't have much time.

He left the hood open and went around to the back of the car where he could look at the gatehouse through the binoculars without being seen. There were two soldiers inside. As he expected, one of them walked out of the gatehouse. Gripping a machine gun tightly, he walked along the road toward Craig's car to find out what was going on.

Craig reached into the trunk and grabbed Rodriguez's flashlight. Then he crossed back to the front of the car. When the sentry was in earshot, Craig began cursing. "Fucking carburetor. That mechanic screwed me over. The new carburetor's no damn good."

Cautiously, the sentry approached.

"You know anything about cars?" Craig called over his shoulder.

"A little bit," the sentry said.

Craig kept his head down, so his face couldn't be clearly seen in the event that his picture had been circulated. He was shining the flashlight into the engine.

"There's the problem," he said to the sentry, while focusing the beam of the flashlight on the carburetor.

When the sentry leaned in to look, Craig pulled his own head and body up. With a single, swift motion he swung his arm and smashed the plastic flashlight into the sentry's skull with such force that the casing cracked along with the man's bones. Before the sentry fell to the ground, Craig grabbed him around the waist and pulled him off to the side of the car where they wouldn't be visible from the road.

In the heavy vegetation Craig stripped off his own clothes, then the sentry's. In seconds, he put on the Argentine army uniform and cap. The man was four inches taller and ten pounds heavier. The clothes were baggy, but didn't look ridiculous. The man's army boots were much too large. Craig would have to cover a lot of ground. He decided to stick with his own shoes.

The sentry's Uzi was similar to the one Craig had taken from the guard at the defense building, so he kept the one he had. He shoved his pistol into a jacket pocket and the knife in another one.

Then he set off on foot down the road toward the gatehouse. At a distance of twenty yards, the other soldier came out and stared at Craig. It was still dark. He was hoping the soldier couldn't tell it wasn't his comrade until Craig was much closer.

"It's nothing," he said in Spanish. "Damn fool's car broke down."

There must have been something about his appearance or the sound of his voice, or perhaps the other soldier had sharp eyes. Without any warning, he went back into the gatehouse. Craig was convinced he was going for his weapon. The last thing Craig wanted right now was a burst of automatic fire that Schiller and Estrada might hear.

He raced across the road and dove into the bushes, grabbing for his knife as he ran. When the soldier came out of the gatehouse with his Uzi in hand, and looked around, he didn't see the imposter. He turned toward the bushes on the same side of the road as the gatehouse and searched.

Craig now had a clear line on the man from behind, but he didn't want to risk the sound of even a single shot from the pistol. So he snuck up behind the soldier, the knife in his right hand. Before the man could react, he looped his left arm around the man's neck and plunged the knife into his chest with precision. He wanted a clean kill so his own uniform wouldn't be bloody. The man's head snapped back, but he had no strength to resist. Craig heard a gurgling noise from his mouth. He pulled the sentry into the bushes and left him there.

From inside the gatehouse he looked at the castle through the binoculars. There were no guards in front of the building. Lights were on in two first floor rooms. On the second floor, he saw three windows with bars. That must be where they're holding Gina, he decided.

Before he moved, he reached for his cell phone and called Betty. "What's happening with the battle?" he asked.

"The tide's turned. Once we came in, Brazilian troops decided to fight. Our planes are blasting away at the Argentine ground forces. They've taken their planes out of the sky. What about you?"

He told her where he was and what he was doing. "We're down to the short strokes now," he said. "If our forces can spare a chopper, tell them to keep it ready. I may need help on the next part. Could get real dicey."

"I'll do my best to get you a chopper."

He hung up and turned toward the castle. Though it would take longer, he rejected the dirt road and ran through the high, heavy grass and bushes. In spots, the ground was soft and muddy. It was slow going. The vegetation gave him good cover. He thought about Ted Dunn. He hoped that Schiller and Estrada didn't have dogs.

Northern Virginia

As he drove to Dulles Airport in the darkness, Bryce was perspiring heavily behind the wheel of his car. He was dressed in a suit and tie, but his starched white shirt was soaked under the arms.

He turned on the car radio to an all-news station and heard: "This is a CBS newsflash: President Treadwell has had a heart attack. He is en route to Bethesda Naval Hospital but we do not have any word about his condition. In the meantime, Vice President Worth has assumed the presidency."

Bryce's whole body shook as the enormity of what he had done struck him. He steadied himself and continued listening to the radio. He didn't hear anything about the war between Argentina and Brazil.

He was worrying needlessly, he told himself. Neither General Forbes nor Betty would be able to piece together what he had done. Even if they did, by that time the battle would be over and he'd be safely in Argentina. Estrada would never grant a United States request to extradite him. Not Edward Bryce, who had provided Estrada with the arms needed to defeat Brazil.

As for Amy, Bryce was convinced she would heed his warning. Speaking up would mean the end of her life as a practical matter. No one would risk seeing their picture on supermarket tabloids and being known as the president's little whore.

No, he was safe. He should stop worrying and act calm.

At Dulles Airport, he parked in the short term lot. It didn't matter. He had no intention of returning to the United States to pick up his car.

Without baggage, check-in was a cinch. At a kiosk, he got a boarding pass for his flight to Miami; then to Buenos Aires. By the time he reached the gate, boarding had begun.

Perfect.

He took his seat on the aisle in the second row of the first class cabin. The man on the window seat was engaged in a tense conversation about a business deal. Bryce would be glad to leave all that business stuff behind.

When a flight attendant asked Bryce if he wanted something to drink, he told her, "Scotch on the rocks." That prompted her to raise her eyebrows. Bryce pointed to the sunrise through the window and said, "It's almost daylight."

She smiled. When she brought the drink, he took a sip, closed his eyes, and leaned back. He felt great. He was safe, getting out of Washington in the nick of time.

He felt a tap on his shoulder. Assuming it was the flight attendant picking up his drink, he said, "It's all yours."

He expected her to say, "Thank you."

Instead, he heard a man's booming voice, "Mr. Bryce, you're under arrest."

With a start, Bryce opened his eyes and shot forward in his seat. He saw two burly Virginia state troopers. One was holding handcuffs. He clamped them on Bryce's wrists.

Iguazu

Once he reached the driveway in front of the castle, Craig stopped running. Dressed in his Argentine army uniform, he calmly walked inside the stone building. As he cut across the entrance foyer toward the highly polished wooden staircase leading to the second floor, he could hear the sound of men's voices. It was Estrada and Schiller. They were having a loud, acrimonious discussion with Estrada doing most of the shouting. Betty was right, Craig decided. Things were not going well for the Argentine army.

Climbing the stairs, Craig walked softly, as a soldier might, his head held high.

At the top of the staircase, he quickly looked in both directions, trying to size up what he was facing. On the right side, halfway down the corridor, he saw a single soldier standing in the dim light in front of a cell. From behind the bars, he heard Gina softly singing a hymn.

As he turned in that direction, the soldier moved forward to cut him off. The man was gripping his gun hard.

"They sent me to relieve you," Craig said.

"That's good," the man said. "Because she's driving me crazy with her singing, but Estrada said 'don't lay a hand on her.' So you can have the job."

The soldier was so anxious to depart that he never bothered to study Craig's face. He reached into his pocket and tossed Craig a set of keys. As he passed Craig on the way to the stairs, Craig suddenly lashed out and plastered one hand over the man's mouth to keep him from screaming. With the other, he punched the man hard in the kidneys. He felt the soldier go limp.

Quickly, he pulled him toward an empty cell with an open door. Once he had the man inside, he laid him down on the floor. He peeled the sheets off the bed and cut them into strips with his knife. He bound the man's hands and feet and tied some material over his mouth. Using the handle of the knife, he hit the soldier hard enough in the head to knock him out, but not kill him. Then he kicked his body under the bed—out of sight.

Before proceeding to Gina's cell, he paused for a minute to look out of one of the windows facing the river in the back of the castle. Daylight was just beginning to break. They were about a mile upstream from the Falls that were on the left. Directly behind the castle was a dock with a sleek white motorboat. On the deck were half a dozen sailors. Estrada's insurance policy, Craig decided. If the battle went badly and escape by land was difficult, Estrada could leave the area by boat. There was a second dock about fifty yards upstream from the motorboat to which two empty pontoon boats were tied.

He was sorely tempted to go downstairs, confront Estrada and Schiller, and kill them both. But he banished that thought. A firefight in the castle would bring the troops on the boat and perhaps others stationed nearby. Besides, it would be up to the Argentine government to deal out its own justice for Estrada and Schiller when this was all over.

On the toes of his feet with the keys in his hand, he walked down the corridor to Gina's cell. He saw her before she spotted him. She was dressed in the same clothes she had been wearing when she had left Nicole's house. She was lying on top of the prison cot looking up at the ceiling, singing a hymn.

Through the bars, he whispered, "Don't make any noise. I've come for you."

Her whole body gave a start as she sat upright on her bed. She opened her mouth to scream with joy, but his words must have sunk in. She didn't say a thing. Instead, she climbed off the bed and ran to the door of the cell.

Craig found the right key on the third try.

"Oh, thank God," she whispered as he unlocked and opened the door.

"Don't thank me until it's over," he whispered back. "Now let's get the hell out of here."

With the Uzi in one hand, he raced toward the staircase. Gina was two steps behind. When they were halfway down the stairs, Gina, in her anxiety to get out of the building, lost her footing on the slick polished wood and fell down. She skidded past him on her back and rear end, landing at the bottom with a thud.

Uh-oh, he thought, Estrada and Schiller will hear us. But he didn't wait to find out. Hoping she hadn't broken anything, he grabbed her by the hand, pulled her up, and continued toward the exit. Fortunately she could still run.

His plan was to follow the same route through the vegetation to the gatehouse and then to his car.

*   *   *

Inside Estrada's office the general was on the phone with one of his commanders who was apologizing because he couldn't halt the retreat of his forces, when he and Schiller heard the thud from the bottom of the stairs. Estrada looked at the colonel with an alarmed expression. Without saying a word, Schiller pulled his gun out of the holster at his waist and ran in the direction of the noise.

Moments later, breathless, Schiller raced back into Estrada's office and began cursing. Estrada hung up on the commander.

"She's gone!" Schiller blurted out.

"Page must have gotten her out."

Estrada picked up the phone and called the gatehouse. He'd stop them before they exited the property.

No answer.

At least one of those men had to be in the gatehouse at all times. So Craig must have taken care of them.

Damn Craig Page!

Estrada had another group of twelve soldiers in a barracks, a quarter of a mile away. He called the commander of the unit on the phone and barked orders. "Get your men down here on the double. Secure the gatehouse. Destroy any cars on the road and search the property inside the fence for intruders. Shoot to kill."

Estrada walked over to an electrical panel on the wall. He threw a switch activating a piercing siren and floodlights in the vicinity of the castle.

He was confident he had closed off Craig Page's escape with Gina.

*   *   *

Once Craig heard the siren and saw the lights, he realized what had happened. "Can you go faster?" he called to Gina. "We have to get through the gate and into our car before they catch us."

"I'm okay. I'll keep up."

Over his shoulder he heard the firing of automatic weapons from the castle. His guess was that soldiers were spraying shots blindly hoping to hit them.

They'd lose a little time, but he swung their route wider to the left, plunging them into denser forest to avoid the reach of the floodlights. Close to the fence they could circle back to the gatehouse. He used the Uzi and his arms to push back the prickly branches, bamboos, and luxuriant palm trees in order to make a path for him and Gina, who was close on his heels.

She called, "Don't worry. I'm keeping up."

As he ran, he glanced at the area where he had parked the car. The sky was light enough to see. It was still there.

Seconds later, he watched in horror as a jeep approached his car. From the front seat, a soldier aimed a grenade launcher and scored a direct hit on the car. There was a loud explosion, with flames shooting high into the air. Estrada was tightening the noose.

The realization that his route of escape had been cut off paralyzed Craig for an instant. He stood frozen to the spot, Gina at his side, her whole body trembling.

There has to be another way out. Think, goddamn it. Think.

Gina was mumbling prayers.

He could call Nicole and order the pilot to come here for them. That was no answer. Schiller would blow up the plane before it even landed.

Think.

The river. A pontoon boat. That was it.

Then he thought about Nicole. He expected Estrada to send troops to the airport to capture anyone who came with him. He had to make sure Nicole got out while there was still time.

He whipped out his cell phone and called her. "I have Gina. You don't have to worry about us. We have another way out. Save yourself. Have Rodriguez fly you home."

"Are you sure you want me to leave?"

"Absolutely. And do it fast. Before they search the airport. Please—I want you to get back safely."

"Thank you," she said softly.

Next, he called Betty. "Send the chopper for us. If we make it, Gina and I will be in a pontoon boat on the river moving upstream from the castle. I'm wearing an Argentine army uniform."

They didn't have any more time to waste. He grabbed Gina's arm and pulled her parallel to the river through even thicker grass and bushes. They trampled wild orchids and begonias. He'd have to make a guess at where the dock was that held the pontoon boats, then cut to the left.

Branches and sharp thorns scratched their faces and bodies. His arms ached from battling bushes and trees. Even in the early morning hours, the heat and humidity were stifling. Sweat poured down his face and mixed with blood from the scratches. He stumbled on a root, but kept running.

He didn't know how badly Gina had been hurt in her fall down the stairs, but he had to hand it to her. She didn't whine or complain, and she kept up the pace.

The pontoon boats.

Their last chance. Their only chance.

From behind him, back at the gatehouse, he heard volleys of gunfire from automatic weapons. The noise terrified macaws, whose screams added an eerie note to their fight for survival.

The soldiers who had blown up his car had entered the property and were pursuing them. He hoped to hell the vegetation was too thick for the jeep. He desperately needed the extra time he would have with the men on foot.

It was almost full daylight now. The soldiers would have no trouble spotting their heads if they stuck up above the bushes. "Keep your body low," he shouted over his shoulder to Gina.

The pontoon boats. Where the hell are the boats?

Here, he decided.

They had to make their cut to the left right now. He turned sharply and increased the pace. Gina was right behind him. The gunfire was growing louder.

They burst through the vegetation into a clearing that ran along the river. Their faces and arms were streaked with blood. Craig wiped the sweat from his eyes to focus on the river.

Fog and mist hung over the water. Straining his eyes to see through it, he spotted the dock only ten yards away on the right.

He heard the shouting of men, the firing of automatic weapons close by, following their route to the river. The soldiers were closing in on them.

He grabbed Gina by the arm and ran toward the dock. When they reached the first pontoon boat, he shouted, "Jump in." He untied the rope securing it to the pier and followed her into the boat.

"The engine better be working," he said as he revved it up. Immediately, it kicked over. "Hold on tight," he shouted to Gina. They roared away from the dock, heading upstream, away from the Falls.

And just in time. Four of the soldiers who had been pursuing them from the gatehouse reached the edge of the river and began firing. The boat was barely outside their range.

They were free from Schiller and Estrada. They had made it.

He looked skyward through the morning mist, expecting to see the chopper any second. But he couldn't see a damn thing.

Frantically, he took one hand from the wheel and called Betty. "We're on the river in a pontoon boat. Where's the fucking helicopter?"

"Should be there any minute," she said. "I just spoke to Forbes. It's a little dicey. They have to fly around the battle zone."

Meanwhile, he had no choice but to keep pushing the boat as hard and fast as it could go—increasing their distance from the castle.

*   *   *

Suddenly Craig heard an ominous sound. Behind them was the roar of a powerful motorboat.

While he steered the pontoon boat, he tossed Gina the binoculars. "Keep your body as low as possible. Tell me what's coming."

He knew the answer before she said it. "A white motorboat. I see Estrada and Schiller on board along with at least six sailors."

"We're fucked," he said. "Where's the goddamn helicopter?"

She responded to his curses with prayers. That can't hurt, he decided. We need all the help we can get.

The pontoon boat was no match in speed for Estrada's craft, which was rapidly closing the gap between them.

At a distance of twenty yards, the motorboat cut its speed and maintained a constant distance.

Through a bullhorn Estrada called out, "We urge you to surrender. No one will get hurt. Turn off your engines. We will come for you."

Craig cut his engine to a very low idle and steered the pontoon boat around to face Estrada's boat, making it appear as if he intended to comply.

At a distance of ten yards, without any warning, Craig let go of the wheel and grabbed the Uzi from the floor of the pontoon. "Hit the deck," he called to Gina. Then he aimed and blasted away. In the hail of gunfire, bullets ripped into Schiller's body.

Craig kept firing shots, striking the captain in the head, who collapsed to the deck. That caused the motorboat to veer wildly. Estrada was out of sight. Craig took down two more sailors. Before the others could get off a decent shot from the spinning and twisting boat, Craig turned up the engine of the pontoon and tore away downstream in the direction of the Falls.

A minute later, one of the other sailors grabbed the wheel and turned the boat around. They resumed the chase, now heading downstream after the pontoon. Glancing quickly over his shoulder, Craig saw Estrada standing tall, an Uzi in his hand.

Craig looked skyward with despair. Where the hell is that damn helicopter? He called to Gina, "Keep your eye on their boat."

Craig couldn't stop now or turn around. He knew Estrada would kill them both. Yet, if they kept going, in a matter of minutes they would be going over the Falls to a certain death.

"What do you see?" he shouted to Gina.

"They're setting up a big weapon," she called back.

He glanced over his shoulder and saw Estrada's crew loading up a mobile grenade launcher. From this distance, there wasn't much chance of missing the pontoon. The blast would blow apart the pontoon and might even cause the engine to explode. Either way, they were doomed.

Better the unknown to a certain death. He shouted to Gina over the roar of the engine: "Out of the boat. Into the water. Now. Roll. Keep your body low."

She looked at him as if he were crazy.

"Into the water," he screamed. "Drop deep under the surface. Once they fire that weapon, we have to avoid flying debris and burning particles."

As the sailor standing next to Estrada took aim with his grenade launcher, Craig shouted, "Now move. Follow me."

Keeping low, he dove into the water, getting clear of the engine of the pontoon. She copied his movements.

He held his breath and dove down under the swiftly moving muddy water. From the tremors in the water, he was certain the grenade smashed into the pontoon, blasting it into hundreds of pieces.

When he came up, he frantically searched for Gina. Her head was bobbing in the fast moving current of the brown, muddy river, slightly downstream and off to one side. She had survived. She was waving her hands wildly. They were both too far in the middle to have any chance of reaching shore with no overhanging branch or anything else to grab hold of.

From Estrada's boat, sailors began shooting at them with rifles and machine guns. He felt as if they were fish in a barrel at an amusement park. "Ping." A bullet hit the water two feet away. Spray from the impact smacked him in the face.

He and Gina had one edge. The river was swollen with spring runoff from a winter of heavy snowfall. The strong and erratic current made it impossible for Estrada's men to get off a good shot.

Then suddenly Estrada's boat stopped moving. The powerful engine reduced to a low din. At first Craig thought the boat had a mechanical problem, and he felt a sudden ray of hope. Then he realized what Estrada was doing. He had no need to pursue or even shoot Craig and Gina. In a few minutes, the water would pull them over the Falls to an almost certain death on the rocks below. Craig thought again of getting to shore, but the river was too wide for that and the current too powerful. In front of them, the thunderous roaring of the water pouring over the Falls was so terrifying that Craig could barely think.

But what could they do?

Now they were finished. He was certain of it.

He could still see Gina's head. He shouted out, hoping she heard him over the roar of the water, "I'm sorry. I did this to you. I'm . . ."

Before he finished the sentence, he heard the sound of a helicopter approaching from behind. Craig twisted around in the water and watched in amazement and joy as an American Blackhawk shot a laser-guided Hellfire missile that blasted into the engine of Estrada's boat, setting off a huge explosion. The sound was deafening. Flaming pieces of debris and body parts flew into the air. Craig covered his face to avoid being struck by sparks or burning material.

"Goodbye General Estrada," he called to the remains of the man who had set all of this in motion. But he had no time to savor the victory. That chopper had only a minute or two to pull them out of the water.

Knowing how close they were to the Falls, Gina was terrified and screaming hysterically. "Help, help!" She was waving her arms frantically.

He watched the chopper drift lower and closer to them. A rope ladder was dropped out of the side door. Through a bullhorn, a Marine shouted, "We're coming for you first, Craig."

"No. No," Craig shouted back. "Get the girl first. Then me."

"It won't work that way. You have to be holding on to the ladder, or we have no chance of picking her up."

Craig knew they were right. He had to do it their way.

The maneuver was one that Craig had done countless times in a CIA training course. But the fast moving current made an always difficult operation even tougher. He reached up to clutch the rope with one hand first. After that, he would grab it with the other.

The swaying rope ladder was directly overhead. He grabbed for it. His hand was on the last rung, but the water pulled him away.

"Shit."

"We're coming back," the Marine called.

They had lost precious seconds. Keep calm, Craig told himself. They'll get you. You'll have time to rescue her.

The ladder was overhead again. This time, he willed his body with all the strength he could muster to thrust his body up out of the water with both hands above his head and his eyes riveted on that last rung.

He had it.

His arms ached. The pain was almost unbearable, but he held on.

Both his hands were tight on the rope. It was cutting into his skin, but he was impervious to the pain.

Now came the hard part. "Let's get the girl," he shouted.

One of the Marines was halfway down on the ladder. Another one was on the second step. Each one reached out a hand to the man below until they had a human chain. Each of them stretched to the limit. The chain only as strong as the weakest link. "Don't try to pull her up," the Marine shouted to Craig. "Get her in your grasp and hold her. We'll go over to shore and drop you both on land."

The Falls were looming closer and closer. Craig's right hand was tight in the clutch of the Marine above. His left was poised for now on the last rung, ready to reach for Gina. From his vantage point, he could see over the top of the awesome, deadly Falls. One pass was all they would have time for. One and no more.

"I'm coming for you," he shouted to Gina. "Stay calm."

With incredible skill, the pilot lowered the chopper so they were right over Gina. Craig took a deep breath and tried to harness his remaining strength. He reached his left arm down, grabbing for Gina's raised right hand, extending his arm, almost numb, to the limit of the shoulder socket.

He made contact with her tiny hand. He willed his body to ignore the searing pain in his right arm and shoulder. "Hold onto me," he screamed.

Frantically, he tried to tighten his grasp to get a firm hold on her hand. But it was moist and slippery. Her body too weak from the ordeal to help him. With every ounce of strength in his body, he tried to get a solid grip.

He felt her slipping away.

God no.

No.

No.

No.

She was gone. Helplessly, he watched her young, beautiful body with so much promise for life cascading head first over the Falls and into the abyss below.

He felt a tugging on his arm. The Marine above was pulling him up. They were closing down the human chain, pulling the men one by one into the helicopter.

Once Craig was inside, the pilot said, "I'm sorry, sir. We did everything we could."

"It's not over yet," Craig said stubbornly. "She might have missed the rocks below and been carried up in the water. People have survived worse. Fly over the area below. We may be able to pick her up there."

"We have a problem doing that," the pilot said, sounding sympathetic. "We're low on fuel. We have enough for one pass over the water below the Falls. Then we have to head back. I can't take a chance on having to put this baby down in what's now become enemy territory."

Craig was ready to argue, but he held back, hopeful they would find and pick her up on the first pass. The rear tail gunner moved up close to Craig. The two of them peered out as the chopper flew over the swirling, foaming water—an implacable foe that had no intention of relinquishing what it had taken.

"Not much chance anyone would make it going over those Falls," the gunner said to Craig.

"She's alive," Craig snapped back. "I know it."

Leaning out of the helicopter, Craig focused hard on the white water below the Falls. They were so low that spray drenched his face. He struggled to see through a dazzling series of rainbows. No matter how hard he looked, Craig didn't see any sign of Gina.

"Make another pass," he called to the pilot. "We can't let her die."

"I'm sorry, sir. We don't have the fuel for that. We're out of here."

Craig stood up. "Then I'll fly the damn chopper myself."

He started toward the front of the helicopter. Before he reached it, the gunner raised his machine gun and smashed the handle against Craig's head. He knew he was blacking out, but that was all he felt.

EPILOGUE

June the Following Year

In Mendoza, at a girls' Catholic school, a young woman, concealing her beauty in a matronly black dress that extended almost to her ankles, with a small gold cross around her neck, her hair braided behind her back and tied with a rubber band, walked into a classroom and stood behind the teacher's desk.

"Tell us about the United States," a twelve year old in the front row with curly brown hair and a bright, shining face asked.

"Our world is here," the teacher replied. "Today, we'll talk about General Jose Martin and our own wonderful history. There is nothing the United States has that we do not."

Her response was met with a collective groan from the students.

"Please, Miss Galindo," another girl said.

"No. I won't change my mind."

The students looked at her with disappointment, but she didn't care. Gina felt more at peace than she had in years. After going over the Falls, she had miraculously avoided hitting a rock. The current had carried her a mile downstream and then into a clump of trees. Unconscious, she was rescued by two fishermen.

Now, she was back home where she belonged.

*　　*　　*

At Linate Airport in Milan, Craig sipped a double espresso in a café while waiting for Luigi's plane from Rome to arrive. Tomorrow they would begin the grueling three day rally race centered in Stresa and looping around Lake Maggiore.

287

As he sipped, he thought about Nicole. When he returned from Iguazu to Buenos Aires, they had one final meeting at her house. She thanked him for saving her country from the horror of Estrada's rule. He told her that he never could have succeeded without her help. She handed him a gift-wrapped bottle of grappa made in Mendoza. "When you drink it, think of Argentina," she said.

"I'll also think about a courageous woman who runs a shoe store."

He pulled from his bag a copy of the *International Herald Tribune,* still in the plastic wrapper it had when it arrived at his apartment in Milan, and glanced at the front page. Under Elizabeth's byline, he read that President Treadwell had suffered another heart attack and died. Vice President Doug Worth had been elevated to the presidency.

Craig leafed aimlessly through the pages until the word Argentina caught his eye. A headline read: "British geologist concedes error about Brazilian diamonds." In the article, the geologist, Dr. Jeremy Barker, admitted that he had reached a faulty conclusion on insufficient evidence. "There are traces of diamonds in the area, but not in sufficient quantities to be commercially viable." He apologized for any damage this may have caused.

About the Author

Allan Topol is the author of nine novels of international intrigue. Two of them, *Spy Dance* and *Enemy of My Enemy*, were national best sellers. His novels have been translated into Japanese, Portuguese, and Hebrew. One was optioned and three are in development for movies.

His most recent novel, *The Russian Endgame*, is the third in a series of Craig Page novels, following the successful *China Gambit* and *Spanish Revenge*.

In addition to his fiction writing, Allan Topol co-authored a two-volume legal treatise entitled *Superfund Law and Procedure*. He wrote a weekly column for Military.com, is a blogger with The Huffington Post, and has published articles in numerous newspapers and periodicals, including the *New York Times*, *Washington Post*, and *Yale Law Journal*.

He is a graduate of Carnegie Institute of Technology, who majored in chemistry, abandoned science, and obtained a law degree from Yale University. As a partner in a major Washington law firm, he practices international environmental law. An avid wine collector and connoisseur, he has traveled extensively researching dramatic locations for his novels.

For more information, visit www.allantopol.com.